I0831368

WOLF ROULETTE

SUPERNATURAL BATTLE: WEREWOLF DENS

KELLY ST. CLARE

Wolf Roulette
by Kelly St. Clare

Edited by Hot Tree Editing
Cover design by Covers by Christian

ABOUT THE AUTHOR

When Kelly is not reading or writing, she is lost in her latest reverie.

Books have always been magical and mysterious to her. One day she decided to unravel this mystery and began writing.

Her works include *The Tainted Accords, Last Battle for Earth, Pirates of Felicity, Supernatural Battle,* and *The Darkest Drae.*

Kelly resides in New Zealand with her ginger-haired husband, a great group of friends, and whatever animals she can add to her horde.

Join her newsletter tribe for sneak peeks, release news, and disjointed musings at kellystclare.com/free-gifts/

WOLF ROULETTE

1

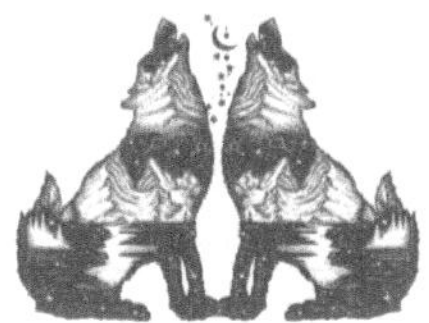

Nose to the ground, we loped through the forest. Fallen tree trunks, tangled vines, and sudden drops made up the rugged south side of Deception Valley.

More to consider.

More to adjust to.

Perfect terrain for a wolf.

Booker loosened her mental hold on our four legs, so I could take control. Our tongue lolled when I didn't miss a beat.

What are we going to do? she thought at me.

I weaved between low branches. *Hmm?*

My innocent tone didn't fool her for a second.

We have a problem. You still consider the tribe your pack.

Rhona exiled me, Booker. I'm not part of the tribe anymore. Even if I wanted them to be my problem, they're not.

She answered after a beat. *Pack is pack, Andie.*

A rock thudded on the ground ahead of us. We lowered to our belly, ears twitching for any sound. A growl erupted from behind, and there was only time to spin toward the menacing sound before a huge brown wolf exploded from the shrubs.

Greyson pinned us to the forest floor and licked our muzzle. *Got you again, beautiful wolf.*

We're still recovering, Booker snarled back.

Lie.

Physically, we'd recovered from Rhona's mistreatment in a day.

Greyson freed us to circle the area and check for enemies. When he returned, the giant wolf lay mostly on top of us again.

Busy day? I asked.

Sascha always seems busy, but never really gets anything done.

I grinned. *Is that right?*

He has something to discuss with you. Shift.

Ignoring Greyson's lack of manners—wolves really didn't possess them—I obeyed. When the *cracks* and *pops* of our shifts faded, I snuck a peek at the naked male beside me.

Yummy.

My scent tangled with Sascha's, but I frowned. The river water part of his smell was churning. "What's wrong?"

Sascha hooked some of my dark auburn hair, letting the strands slide over his finger. "The pack has filed a formal complaint against the tribe."

My eyes narrowed. "About what?"

"A steward attacked our marshal." He met my gaze.

His meaning clicked. My jaw dropped. "You're making a formal complaint against *me.* Daniil attacked Rhona."

"Or was he responding to your aggression?"

Oh, brother. "My *Luther* aggression."

"That makes no difference. You were part of the tribe at the time. Stabattse was called. There are penalties for an attack during that ceremony."

I shook my head. "That's crazy."

Though if the situation were reversed, I'd probably use the same tactic to win penalty points in Grids. And my ex-head team would anticipate the pack's move, even if I hadn't. They'd prepare a counter-negotiation.

I needed to butt out.

Rhona was head steward now.

"Have I hurt your feelings, little bird?" Sascha continued playing with my hair.

Had he? "Not really. I just remembered who I am and who you are."

Told you. Booker's voice rang in my head.

Okay, okay. I still consider the tribe pack and it's a problem.

My sister treated me like shit recently, but the *Ni Tiaki* were so much more than Rhona's actions. I'd met and connected with tonnes of stewards, Wade and Cameron included. Maybe expecting my loyalty to them to dwindle so soon after they exiled me was naïve.

It would take longer.

Sascha stiffened. "Who you were doesn't mean anything, Andie. You're part of this pack."

I *lived* with the pack. There was a difference. "The stewards are my people. That might change eventually, and if it does, I'll let you know. Until then..."

He released my hair and studied me. The corner of his mouth lifted after a brief pause. "You're not the type of person to switch allegiances in a hurry. That was wishful thinking on my behalf. I just want you to feel at home here."

"You know I want that too. I'll try." I rested a hand on his bare chest.

"That's all I ask." He brushed a thumb over my cheek. "Your tribe will come back with a complaint about Daniil's attack on Wade."

That's what I thought too. "You don't have to do that."

"What?"

"Soften the blow. I understand that you intend to win Victratum. I understand your responsibility to the pack." The real issue was the loyalty and responsibility I felt for the *opposing* team. "Hey, maybe until things change, it's best you don't tell me anything to do with pack strategy."

His pine scent muted.

He didn't like my request. I didn't really like it either, but if I was offered crucial pack information, I'd be torn between my bond with Sascha and my oath to the tribe.

Best not to be in that position at all.

"Noted," Sascha said at last. "Let me know if that changes."

The sooner, the better, in my opinion.

I stared at the rustling canopy again. "How's the pack doing after Daniil's death?" The Luthers' marshal had torn himself out of my lethal grip to end his misery.

"They're getting there." Sascha blew out a breath. "Pascal's explanation made things easier for my wolves in some ways and harder in others. For me too. I pity Daniil as much as I'd like to hurt him for what he did."

One guess why.

Sascha and I were still in the midst of our mating call. Like me, he had to wonder what our eventual fate would be. Would we find each other worthy or unworthy?

Perhaps the choice to mate seemed straightforward.

Immortality or death.

Immortality.

Ability to have children or not.

Children.

Yet to meet someone and have such astronomical choices to make, seemingly overnight, *wasn't* a simple thing. Nature preferred to offer stone-cold ultimatums, but reality didn't work that way. Marriage and having kids were decisions people usually made over years or decades. And when a centuries-old game and werewolves were chucked into the mix, things got extra complicated.

I bit my lip. "How are you so sure about me?"

He moved closer.

Don't look at his junk, Andie.

"I had advantages you didn't back then." Sascha smiled. "I watched and listened to your interactions with others and saw you were cunning and kind. The mating call made me *want* you, but when your pain became my pain, and your joy and laughter were mine too, I knew I loved you."

Love.

My heart pounded.

The last time I heard those words, I ditched the guy in minutes. This fear was different though. When Logan said the words, I feared reciprocating his sentiment. With Sascha, I feared how much I already felt.

Admitting this to him always seemed sure to end in disaster—so many barriers had existed between us from the start. But now I was on pack lands with him. For good. That was one major barrier out of the way.

Maybe—*maybe*—I could open up more.

Sascha kissed my eyelids. "I love you, Andie Charise."

I looked at the man before me. What if I just went for it? Took the leap people always talked about.

Here goes. "I'd really like to kiss you."

Sascha brushed his thumb under my eye and studied the tear I hadn't noticed falling. I didn't move when he focused on my face.

"You're crying." Sascha's breath caught as the scent of my fear saturated the air.

He pressed his lips to my palm, then cupped my cheek. "Don't be scared, little bird. Not with me."

"I'm not scared of you." I trailed a finger over the expanse of his naked chest, enjoying his shiver.

"Just of everything else?" His voice was unbearably soft.

Another tear fell. *Yes.* Shrugging a shoulder, I brushed the tear away. Sascha caught my hand again and drew my wet finger into his mouth.

I jerked as warmth pooled low in my stomach.

He rolled to hover above me, and I gazed up at him.

"I've wanted to kiss you for a very, *very* long time." Sascha gripped the curve of my hip.

Tell me about it. The thought of his lips touching mine plagued me night and day. We'd been intimate in other ways—maybe in ways people considered more physical, yet somehow this kiss meant more than all those moments.

When I kiss you because no one else exists for me any longer, I want you to kiss me back just the same.

For better or worse, no one else existed for me anymore. From here on out, I planned to embrace it—fear and all.

Sascha sounded near physical pain. "Just so we're clear, my answer on sex is the same."

Such a hold out. "Agreed."

"You're so fucking beautiful."

I strained upward as he bore down.

Our lips touched.

His weight drove us both to the ground. I moaned into his hot mouth at the soft feel of his full bottom lip.

Firm.

Confident.

Oh my god!

We rolled without breaking apart, and I straddled his lap, clutching his face to mine. Our tongues didn't dance—they moved with a starved hunger that we could never fill.

Air wasn't necessary.

Not when I could feel *this*. His groan vibrated through me.

I needed more.

So much more.

We disconnected for a sliver of a second.

White-hot fire slammed into my chest, catapulting me back. *Ouch.* That shit hadn't happened since the touch meet. I choked as wave after wave of scalding heat slammed into me.

Red blanketed my thoughts.

No.

We didn't want this.

Body shaking, I assumed the crouched position and raised my arms in the Cleopatra-like position. Sascha's furious snarls rocketed across the space.

Our eyes met.

"*Doore koh e baka*," I hissed.

Like a bucket of water poured over my head, the heat broke. I toppled forward onto my hands and knees. *Shit.*

Panting hard, I touched my lips. *That was... incredible.*

Sascha walked to me and ran a hand down my back, taking care to brush over my ticklish spot.

I sat back on my haunches.

His eyes were as rounded as mine.

"That was far better than any dream," he breathed. "I've found a new obsession."

So had I.

I rested a hand against his jaw and leaned in.

We sighed as our lips touched.

This couldn't be real.

"Feels so damn good," he spoke into my mouth.

Good was the understatement of the century. If I'd ever needed an occasion to use the word *wondrous*, this was it.

The scent of our lust rose hard and fast.

Sascha rested his forehead against my breasts. "Fuck."

My shoulders shook. "This will make things harder."

"It already has."

Yeah, something was jabbing me in the ass.

Snorting, I climbed off him.

His want seared across the distance. "Do you need any relief, mate?"

As odd as the concept of sexual relief sounded, the partial heats I'd experienced in the past weren't a joking matter. They were borderline painful in their intensity.

I turned my focus inward. *Huh.* "I'm okay this time."

Sascha's disappointment curled around me.

I'd always reacted after the meets. Minor reactions at first, but they got stronger each time. I felt nothing now. "Is that weird?"

"Our mating gifts have been off-balance from the start. I'm not worried."

I didn't comment on the blatant concern rising from his skin.

Instead, I hugged my knees to my chest. “What does *doore koh e baka* mean?”

“*I find you unworthy.*”

Well, that was freakin’ horrible.

He bent a leg up, regarding me as if his erection wasn’t the elephant in the room. “What did you think it meant?”

A really long no. “Never mind. Is it the Luther language?”

He nodded. “No one really speaks it anymore. Purely ceremonial.”

That was a shame. Something I loved about my tribe was how well our history was preserved. Not that I could speak any of the indigenous language, but the songs and stories crafted from it were beautiful.

Sascha cleared his throat. “We should be able to mind-speak in two-legged form after the kiss meet. Let’s give it a try.”

We could already mind-speak partially shifted or fully shifted. But those restrictions were inconvenient sometimes.

“Come here then.” I crooked my finger.

He latched onto my ankle and dragged me across the mossy grass.

His voice was solemn. “I win.”

My twitching lips ruined the effect of my glare. “I’ve never had to take so many showers in my life.”

Sascha peered intently at me.

“... Are you doing it?”

He leaned closer. “Trying to.”

Mind-speak was easy. The words just needed to be pushed in the other person’s direction.

Join me in the shower? I thought at him.

No reaction.

“Nothing?” That’s all I did in four-legged form.

I inhaled the spike in his concern.

Still, Sascha was right. Our so-called *mating gifts* had never worked properly. They came in at random.

Well, not *exactly* at random.

They arrived whenever I'd accepted Sascha's presence in my life a little more.

So maybe this didn't make sense. We were closer than ever. Or at least, I'd taken a huge step toward him. "Is there anything you're worried about? With us?"

"My feelings remain the same," he answered. "And you, mate?"

"Not that I'm aware of."

He interlaced his fingers with mine. "Then let's put it behind us."

I frowned. "You don't think it has to do with me being on pack lands, do you?"

My wolf was a sigma after all.

Are you okay about this? I asked her.

For me, this is no different to interacting with the tribe. I'd prefer to be alone, of course.

It wasn't Booker either.

Sascha tensed. "You don't like living here?"

That wasn't the problem. "Moving here is the only big change I can think of."

"A lot has happened lately. Moving here is the least of those changes. This is probably nothing, little bird. Yeah?" He wrapped an arm around my shoulders.

I rested my head against his chest. "Yeah."

2

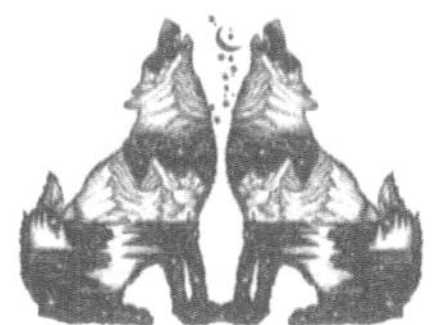

I rolled in Sascha's gigantic bed and encountered coldness instead of his overheated body. I consulted the elastic band sensation under my ribs. He was a couple of buildings over in the pack house.

Sun blared inside the open patio doors, and I took my time stretching.

Last week, waking after dawn would be laughable. But I wasn't head steward anymore, so *fuck it*. Plus, things were kind of awkward with the pack, so sleeping in meant less time in their company.

We could live in the forest, Booker said hopefully.

I padded to the wardrobe. *Good try. Hey, if you're a sigma, does that make me a sigma too?*

You're human. Humans don't have statuses off the media because they're stupid.

I tucked away a grin. *You mean social media?*

She sniffed.

My wolf was vain and haughty and anti-social to the extreme. *I'm so glad you're with me.*

Then listen to my plan. We leave the pack and eat the sister's heart.

Booker liked to refer to Rhona as *the sister* and talk about eating hearts. To my knowledge, we were yet to eat any, but I'd blacked out for the night of the new moon, so...

I grimaced and opened the wardrobe. *I'd love to dress in my own clothes again.*

But then Sascha couldn't see you in his shirts.

And he really enjoyed that.

I shoved his *Den's* suits aside and peered into the back. Stacks of shoes. Man, his wardrobe was super organised. He really didn't want to see what mine normally looked like.

Pushing his suits the other way, I crouched inside the wardrobe.

Boxes.

No clothes though. *Ugh.*

I stopped mid-rise as the scribbled name on the boxes caught my eye.

Andie Charise Booker/Thana

Craning my head, I took in the columns of boxes stacked to the ceiling. Two across. Two deep. Eight high. Thirty-two of them. All of those I could see had my name written on the front. "That's not creepy at all."

Standing on tiptoe, I heaved a box down and worked the lid free.

My brows drew together as I hooked underwear on my forefinger. Lacey and midnight blue. Definitely mine. "You are the biggest, *biggest* creep."

Still, I did need underwear.

So, creepy... but handy.

This had to be Sascha's research from the capture meet. How the hell could my life fill up thirty-two boxes? How about three lines?

Benefactor of crappy childhood.

Receiver of shitty lies.

Poorer than dirt (see above).

I drew out two dresses—one was an elegant crimson cocktail dress, the other a tube dress that, from memory, barely covered my ass.

Both went missing months ago.

Why do you hint at showing your butthole with these dresses instead of just showing it when he does something right? Booker asked.

Just a human thing, I guess.

Why did Sascha pick these dresses in particular? Digging deeper, I located a tee shirt and a mini skirt. *Ha!* Jackpot.

Maybe wearing my own clothes would mean fewer glares from the pack.

What will we do next? my wolf asked.

I set the box aside and dragged another down. *Like, today?*

No. What's the next move?

Sitting back, I sighed. Even when Ragna died, I'd had a house to clean and sell, then came the car and driving to Deception Valley. Becoming a steward, then head steward.

Now...

I'd always coveted the life of people without a care—how they flittered from place to place. When I'd dreamed of that life though, I'd chosen it. The head steward position was *taken* from me. I still carried all the cares of that role but none of the power to do anything.

Entering tribal lands was a big fat no.

Leaving Deception Valley was a bigger fatter no.

I had to stay on pack lands, but the tribe were my people. Then there was what I felt for Sascha.

How did I make a single fucking move? *What would you do?*

Live in the forest and return to mate with Sascha Greyson at intervals.

I laughed despite my aching heart. *You want to use Sascha for his body?*

He has what I need for pups. We can accept the good part without any of the pack leader baggage.

She considered that baggage, not me, but I envied wolves' clarity sometimes, if not their ruthlessness.

I riffled through the contents of box two. Several of the items were discarded capture-meet gifts. Fuzzy pyjamas, pine-scented candle, saxophone reeds, a sudoku book, and a yellow tulip he'd since preserved between two transparent boards.

My heart squeezed. He'd pressed the first flower he gave me. When he was stalking me against my will, but still. *Adorable.*

"What are you doing?

I jumped, inhaling thyme. "Mandy. I'm looking for clothes."

"Are you sure? Because you're really looking through boxes in Sascha's wardrobe."

Busted. I grabbed the Sudoku book and replaced the boxes on top of the column before swiping up my clothes.

Mandy blocked the exit

We were at the same eye level.

I smiled—that always freaked angry people out. "Can I help you?"

"You can leave." She stood aside.

I deposited my finds on the bed.

Mandy smelled all kinds of sour. The thing about Luther senses… it was hard to keep feelings a secret. "For what it's worth, I do wish that we hadn't ended up on opposite sides."

Mandy could have been a friend.

She crossed her arms. "I don't care that you're on the opposite side. You could hardly control that."

"Would you like to tell me why you dislike me then? I have a busy day ahead."

Her gaze shifted to the Sudoku book.

Bad joke?

Mandy balled her hands. "Sascha breaks his back to prove himself to you. He's done so over and over again. What have you ever done to show him *you're* worthy?"

Sascha's patience and support were incredible, but I wasn't about to beat myself up for using logic over my heart. Practical decisions had kept me alive during my childhood. Trusting emotion wasn't an easy thing. "Did Sascha ask you to speak with me?"

"No—"

"So you took it upon yourself?"

Her cheeks tinged pink, but the tattooed blonde drew herself taller. "He deserved someone to speak for him."

No one else had interfered so far. Was this a delta thing or a Mandy thing? I'd only learned a little about the differences between wolf statuses so far. "You decided that person should be you. Why?"

She'd struck me as playful and intelligent in the past. Not inquisitive. She definitely cared about pack losses and took them hard. Did she like to fix other's problems?

Her lip curled. "No one else wants to stick up for him."

I took a stab in the dark. "If the mating call between me and Sascha doesn't work out, it's not your fault. That's just life. Nothing you do will change the outcome."

Her eyes darkened. "He deserves more than someone who only ever hurts him."

Nature had ensured that unless I moved *toward* Sascha, anything else would hurt him—and me—by default.

I dipped my head. "Noted. Anything else?"

"Sascha sent me to tell you that he'd left for his grid runs. The meeting ran over."

Which explained why he wasn't in here shutting her the hell up. "Sure."

After a withering look, Mandy left.

Shaking my head, I grabbed the T-shirt, mini, and underwear, and entered the open-ceiling shower adjourning the bedroom.

Cool water from the stream flowed over my head, and I shivered. Luthers ran hotter than humans, and my showers since first shifting had dropped from hot to lukewarm, but the straight-up cold shower was hard to grow accustomed to.

After washing my hair, I foamed pine-scented natural body wash over my body and rinsed off. I swear Sascha was trying to make me smell like him.

Dressed in my own clothes, I grabbed the Sudoku book and located a pen in a bedside drawer. Breakfast was still on, but after

Mandy's hostility, I opted to traipse to a bench by the stream instead.

I missed my tribe.

The sun rose higher as I worked through several Sudokus in quick succession.

When did I last get time for this? I couldn't remember. It had to be back when I worked *The Dens*.

"Do you mind if I sit?" The wolf looked around thirty to the unknowing eye. My sniffer said otherwise. Like counting rings on a tree stump, I could tell this guy was older than any other Luther I'd scented before.

I swung my legs off the bench. "Of course."

I searched for his scent but didn't find one.

Curious.

"I don't usually have to share my fishing spot." The ancient wolf sat and busied himself with a tackle box and rod.

Make him go away, Booker snapped.

He glanced at me. "You prefer to be alone?"

"Not me." A tinge of decay hung in the air. "Not all the time. My wolf does."

The air cleared.

The man nodded. "Your wolf can leave if she wants. I'm not moving."

Get that? I asked her.

I'll make him move.

We both knew that was bullshit. There was a definite difference in power between this wolf and me. My instincts warned that taking him on would be a huge mistake.

Did Luthers gain power as they aged?

"Your mind is busy, young wolf." He cast off. "You'll scare the fish away."

"Sorry," I said demurely. "I'll think quieter."

He shot me a suspicious look, and I jotted a number on my Sudoku.

"Busy week you've had," he said next.

"Weren't you worried about scaring fish?"

As he grinned, the wolf displayed sharp teeth that my peripherals couldn't fail to notice. "Here I thought you may be interested in what's happening. I've come from a pack meeting."

"Keep it to yourself, old wolf." Who was this guy anyway? Only important Luthers sat in on pack meetings.

His brows climbed. "Old wolf. That might be a first." The Luther twitched the line. "The tribe came out on top of the Stabattse negotiations."

My curiosity sharpened despite myself. "How?"

"Sascha made an official complaint about your attack on our marshal. We knew the tribe would come back with the kidnapping and injury of their steward."

Wade.

"They surprised us with something else." The wolf reeled in his line and cast again with a flick of his wrist. "The new head steward raised the point that you were bitten in Water resulting in the transformation to a werewolf. She considered this fate synonymous with death."

Ouch. Apparently, I was dead to Rhona.

"The loss of head stewardship must have hurt." The wolf changed the bait on his hook.

"Nope. Never wanted it."

"Truth."

That surprised him? Cool. "What was the verdict?"

"Daniil's biting offence occurred outside of Victratum and therefore carried a steeper consequence. The pack earned three penalty points."

Shit. Hefty. Five penalty points resulted in the loss of a grid. I'd use those points to tribe advantage well and truly.

... But the head team would guide Rhona on that. *Jesus,* I had to stop agonising over this stuff.

"You're surprised," he murmured.

I shrugged a shoulder. "Yes and no."

"Well," the wolf cast again, "you may be interested to know the next grid is Sandstone."

I'd assumed it would be.

"We have an airtight strategy."

Seriously, what was this guy's angle? "Better keep it that way then."

"The tribe inspired it actually. Remember the wires your side shot across the quarry to explode wolfbane balloons over us? We'll use the wires in a different way."

My stomach dropped.

The Luthers entered on the ground level. *Crap.* They'd shoot ropes upward to help them climb.

The major problem the Luthers faced in Sandstone was neutralising our high-ground advantage.

They could win with this strategy. And it wasn't something the head team could put together.

Dread filled me. *Fuck!*

The old wolf jerked his line and reeled in earnest. A moderate-sized trout was dragged over the bank, but the wolf unhooked the fish and threw it back. He baited the hook again. "Your human friend is here."

Wade's Jeep was winding between the bungalows. Grabbing my Sudoku, I quickly stood. This guy was freaking me out big time.

"Goodbye, young wolf," he murmured.

"Bye, old wolf."

I hurried toward Wade.

My friend hopped out of the car, only a smidgen stiffer than usual after his ordeal at Daniil's hands.

"I'm so glad you're okay." I hugged him gently.

"Are you kidding? What happened to me was nothing, baby girl. What about you?"

"*You* must be kidding. You were injured and kidnapped because of me and probably spent an entire day wondering if you'd die. I'm just so relieved you're safe."

He turned in a full circle. "As you see, I'm fine. You're not harbouring some sense of misplaced guilt, are you?"

She is, my wolf said for my ears only.

"He took you to get to me." I peered up into my friend's gorgeous grey eyes.

They softened. "The guy was messed up. That had nothing to do with you, so stop being selfish. I'd like my own drama for once. But you know what's humbling? Training to fight Luthers for ten years and having your ass kicked within seconds."

Yeah.

Humans were fragile.

Wade opened the boot and pulled out a huge bag.

I eyed it. "Uh, what's all that?"

"My stuff. Your stuff is in there too."

My mouth dried. "*Why* have you got your stuff?"

"I'm moving off tribal lands in protest of how you were treated."

Fear bolted through me, and I gripped his arm.

His brows shot up.

Shit. "Your entire family is there. You've grown up in that community. You can't do that for me."

"I can and I will. My family will understand."

Sliding my phone free, I rattled off a message, sincerely hoping the pack wasn't watching me.

I need you and Cam on the inside.

He read the text.

They were my last connections with the tribe. Without them, I'd lose touch on what was happening. And if I ever needed to get in touch with the tribe...

I needed Wade to stay put. "I don't think this is a choice you should make rashly."

He played along. "I've had three days to think about it, Andie."

"The gesture is appreciated. Really. I just can't let you do that.

Your mum would be so upset. The tribe means more to you than you think."

"Perhaps you're right." He pinned me with a curious look.

I slid my phone away. "I'm always right. Give it some time. Everything is pretty raw."

He groaned dramatically and chucked his huge bag back in the boot. "I'll do it for you."

"Thank you." I squeezed his hand.

I couldn't lose this last connection to the tribe yet.

When they succeeded, I felt triumph and relief. The thought of them failing seared me with ice-cold horror.

Unless that changed quick, it could be a big fucking problem.

"If you won't let me make a dramatic declaration of friendship, then how about a drink?" Wade leaned into the Jeep and drew out a chiller box. "Figured you'd need one, and I'd like to run an experiment on Luthers and the effects of alcohol."

"I humbly consent to be your test subject."

"Good. Because I want to know what Rhona did to you. *Everything.* You and Cameron are sugar-coating the truth. I don't cope well with falsehoods, Andie."

Understatement.

I held out my hand. "Better give me a few of those then."

3

I wrapped a towel around my body after the second shower of the day. How did Luthers stay clean all the time? That should be the topic of Wade's next study.

"I hoped to catch you so we could run together." Sascha stood in the doorway, clad only in worn jeans. Tangled, dark-brown hair fell just shy of his muscular shoulders. His honey eyes were almost impossible to look away from.

I inhaled his tantalising mix of pine, river water, musk, and sweat. "I didn't know when you'd be back."

I dug through the bags of clothes Wade packed for me.

Sascha's hands gripped my shoulders, and we both relaxed at the contact. For a few breaths, I enjoyed the feeling of rightness.

Then the old wolf's words came tumbling back.

Sascha kissed the back of my shoulder. "Wade visited?"

I shivered. "We tried to get me drunk."

His lips twitched against my skin. "How did it go?"

"Not well."

"It takes a lot of strong alcohol to overwhelm our accelerated healing process. Even then, your wolf won't get drunk. Just you."

Huh, go figure. I gathered my clothes and walked back to the bathroom.

"Why are you changing in there?" he called. "You've never done that before."

I towel-dried and stepped into underwear and then a bra. "No reason."

"I like seeing you naked."

"Believe it or not, I gathered that." Tugging up high-waisted black jeans, I shrugged into a pink midriff jumper.

I dumped my towel in the hamper and returned to find Sascha sitting on the bed with the duchess comb he gave me.

"Will you let me brush your hair?" he asked.

I lowered my gaze. "Not tonight. It's tangled."

Sascha handed over the comb without a word. "Let's test the mind-speak again."

We stared at each other.

Hello? I thought at him.

He smiled after a leaden moment. "Not yet."

"Guess not." I took the comb from him.

Sascha tilted my chin. "Beautiful wolf, is something the matter?"

My cheeks warmed under his intense focus. "A wolf came to me at the stream today."

"*What wolf?*" His hands swept my sides. "What did he do?"

Whoa.

"Uh, not whatever you're thinking."

Sascha closed his eyes and opened them after a long exhale. "I thought your presence here would help me control the mating call, but the presence of other unmated male Luthers is doing the opposite. Forgive me."

I struggled against a grin. "You think someone else will catch my eye?"

His shoulders tensed. "More that you will find a worthier partner."

"Nature doesn't work like that."

Sascha faced me. "You and I both know nature isn't everything."

Didn't I know it.

I sat on the bed beside him. "I'm not sure you understood what I meant when I told you the tribe were still my people."

"You meant that anything you see and hear on pack lands that could help the tribe will be conveyed to them."

I blinked at him. "You..."

He crooked a smile. "Is there anything else?"

"You're giving me permission to pass on pack strategies?" This was not how I envisioned the conversation going.

"I know what I would do if our situations were reversed. You don't need my permission."

Sometimes, I felt like I needed another fifty years on the clock to follow him. "What are you saying?"

"I'm saying that it would be foolish of me to hold you to silence when that would tear you in two."

My chest rose. "Where did you come from, Sascha Greyson?"

"The same place we all do, I'd gather."

I leaned forward to kiss his cheek. "Thank you."

He regarded me with complete seriousness. "I realise this is a huge adjustment, but I'd like for you to give pack life a chance. That's the one thing I ask."

"I will. I want to."

"Good. Then be assured, we're using frequency generators during pack meetings. Until you tell me things have changed, that practice will continue. I know when you give your word, you mean it. So when you give it, I'll hold you to your promises. Between now and then, consider me warned."

He spoke of my promises and change of heart like they were certain things. "It's just a lot to get used to."

"Pack is a foreign concept for your wolf. I understand what you feel more than anyone."

It wasn't my wolf. It wasn't the move to pack lands.

"You know I'm here." He swept my wet hair back over my shoulder. "I'm not going anywhere."

And neither was I.

I placed the comb on the bedside table. "Where should I put my bags?"

"The second wardrobe is empty. There are drawers in there, too, ready for you."

Was I about to unpack my stuff into Sascha's bungalow? *Shit*, I was. "I might do it later."

Sascha stiffened. "What's wrong?"

Dammit. "Well. Uh. Putting stuff in your wardrobe feels a lot like moving in with you."

"You have moved in with me."

Yeah, and I'd just grasped that now. "I guess I did."

His heart thumped faster. "Is this moving too quick?"

Too quick in some ways. Too slow in others.

"No." I gestured at the bags. "I've just never..."

This was a line that I never crossed with past boyfriends. Caring for Ragna was always my reason, but looking back, I saw that was just an excuse to keep my distance.

I'd crossed more lines with Sascha than anyone else.

This shouldn't feel so strange.

It *wasn't* strange.

"I'd prefer you stay in my bungalow." His eyes darkened.

And I could guess why.

The thought of me jumping in bed with another male Luther was laughable, but the mating call must whisper all kinds of things in Sascha's ear.

I rested a hand on his arm. "I want to stay in here with you."

He released a pent-up breath. "Thank fuck."

"That bad, huh?"

"You have no idea." He growled and then leaned forward to kiss me.

My toes curled against the wooden floor as warmth seeped through every part of me. "Mmm, that won't ever get old."

"Agreed, mate," Sascha whispered. "Now let's go to dinner. I'm starving."

This girl needed a moment to collect herself. "I'll be right behind you."

I listened as he left the bungalow and entered the pack house.

My phone buzzed.

Wade.

I've waited five hours.
Why the hell do I need to stay put?

The wait would have killed him, but I didn't want to message him until I spoke to Sascha.

What do you think? I asked Booker.

You want to tell the tribe, so do it. It's not your problem that Sascha Greyson has a rebellious pack member.

Rebellious wasn't how I'd describe the old fisherwolf. He was testing my loyalty. The Luther literally reeled in a fish with bait and threw it back in the water. His information was a poorly concealed trap.

If I keep my mouth shut, I betray the tribe. If I tell the tribe, I betray Sascha. I groaned.

If you betray your pack, then you betray Sascha too, she replied.

... Could you dumb that down for me?

There's a reason you didn't react with a partial heat after the kiss meet. There's a reason neither of you received the next mating gift.

I stilled. *Why?*

You know why, she said softly. *If you cannot give Sascha Greyson all of you, then neither of you will be happy. You're only giving him part of you, even now.*

I wasn't great at hearing these things, but my wolf was nearly always right on such matters when she chose to chime in. I'd barely glanced at Sascha tonight until he confronted me about my mood. The distance I'd subconsciously erected between us had everything to do with what the old wolf told me about the pack's Sandstone strategy and everything to do with my failure to pass the news on to the tribe. *What should I do?*

If the answer were obvious, we'd be on that path already. But you know what to do right now. Trust your gut.

Taking a deep breath, I texted Wade back.

I know the pack's plans for Sandstone.
It's bad.
I need you to tell Rhona immediately.

He texted back.

You want me to help her?!
You must be out of your fantastic mind.

Felt like it.

Please. This is for the tribe.
It's important.

Not waiting for a reply, I sent through the details of their strategy and added my theory after.

Three dots appeared.

On it, baby girl.

Tension drained from my shoulders.

This shit was one twisted, hellish mess.

Sliding my phone in my back pocket, I walked out of the bungalow.

The lawn and stairs outside the pack house were filled with pack members making the most of the warm summer evening. While Luthers came and went for breakfast and lunch, they all made an effort to gather for the last meal of the day.

Which was awesome for me.

I ignored the hundreds of curious eyes and the hundreds more hostile eyes and entered the huge bungalow.

My nose twitched at the scent of gravy and potatoes.

Hot damn.

I hurried to load a plate with vegetables and chicken. Dousing the food with rich gravy, I scanned the pack members sitting on the floor and eating.

The bungalow was always divided down the middle with females on one side and males on the other. The only place that didn't obey that rule was the leaders' table. On it sat Sascha and his five status representatives, Hairy, Leroy, Mandy, Grim, and Lisa.

I'd sat at that table every night since arriving. An empty chair waited there for me.

But to my eyes and ears, the hostility against me had grown in the last few days, not diminished. Therefore, I was doing something wrong, and I'd promised to give pack life a real shot.

Scanning the females again, I puzzled over their seating arrangement. They were in clusters but moved in a weird shimmer.

So did the male side.

Like a mass wave at a sports game, those towards the exit would only eat when those closer to the leader table had eaten before them. I focused on the women closest to Sascha's table. Almost as one, they took a bite. Then the group down from them did the same. This repeated all the way to the door and to those groups I could see just outside.

Why did they do that?

It sorted out where I was sitting at least. I wasn't waiting to eat for anyone.

I sat cross-legged on the ground just in front of the first cluster and dipped a roasted potato in the gravy.

"What are you doing?" a pretty brunette asked.

"I'm about to cover this potato in as much gravy as possible. Then, I will eat it." I followed the explanation with a practical demonstration.

Her blue eyes slitted. "You can't eat here."

I swallowed. "I beg to differ. I just did."

"This is where alpha females sit."

Sascha's mother was here, but she didn't interfere.

"I'm a sigma female," I replied. "Why do you think your rules mean anything to me?"

"A sigma in a pack has to obey pack rules."

I covered another potato with gravy. Should have poured more on. "Where do your pack rules suggest a female sigma sit?"

"Wherever you can hold a position," she answered, a slight sneer in her tone.

"I'm holding this one just fine." I shoved the second potato in my mouth and selected some broccoli. *Gross*, but green stuff was supposedly good. Did copious amounts of gravy cancel that out?

I watched the other women. Around half of those between me and the door were eating after I did. The others seemed to be holding off in support of Miss Rules here.

The brunette leaned forward to meet my gaze. "I'm telling you that you can't sit here."

I held her gaze. "I'm telling you that these potatoes are really good, and I'm not waiting to eat them in whatever queue system your pack has going on. If you'd like me to *not* sit here, then I suggest you attempt to move me."

I felt a very slight pressure on my mind.

Huh, fancy that.

A strong wolf could force their way into the minds of a weaker wolf. Sascha had such power as pack leader, and I'd accidentally done it to Daniil to locate Wade.

What I felt now was a much weaker version of that.

My smile widened. "Are you trying to move me with your mind?"

Her eyes flashed and the pressure in my head mounted.

Feeling blindly, I located another potato on my plate and brought it to my mouth without breaking our stare. A bead of sweat broke out on the woman's forehead.

"How long does this go for?" I asked after swallowing.

Sascha's mother answered. "Until one of you backs down."

Oh, brother. "For the record, I just wanted to eat potatoes and gravy."

Can I get a hand? I asked my slumbering wolf.

She yawned. *What?*

It's a status battle thing. Thought you might like to partake.

Booker was awake in an instant. Establishing hierarchy ranked just below eating hearts.

We'd only used this mental attack thing in the midst of a fight before, so I followed Booker's lead to locate the power deep in our chest. It usually sat there unnoticed, but from the mind battle with Daniil, I knew this energy could drain away.

That must be why the woman was slowly ramping up her attack. She didn't want to overcommit.

Let's just use a little bit of what we used on Daniil.

Got it, my wolf said gleefully.

I felt the energy rising through my chest and throat. It built in my mind, and I felt the rushing moment Booker unleashed it on the woman.

The pretty brunette thumped to the ground.

My jaw dropped as the muted conversation in the room seized.

"How much did you use on her?" An angry blonde leaned over the unconscious brunette.

Yikes. "Just a bit."

The blonde picked up the brunette and left the room, accompanied by a few other women.

Look at us making friends, I told my wolf.

She didn't answer, fast asleep again. I seriously envied her sometimes.

Sascha's mother smiled at me. "Kara's fine. She'll wake in no time. You just overwhelmed her mind." She raised her voice. "While we're on the subject, would anyone else like to challenge Andie for assuming the top position?"

Just in case, I shoved a baby carrot and potato in my mouth.

No one from the nearest group seemed overly keen, and conversation resumed after several tense minutes.

I chewed on a slice of chicken and watched the wave as the females ate after me. Some still refused to eat.

Guess they'd go hungry. No skin off my fangs.

Sascha's mother moved closer. "I'm Evelyn. You may not remember me."

"I remember. You were knitting."

His mother was definitely one of the older wolves I'd smelt, but I didn't feel any danger in her company.

Sascha's mother smelled like pine—just like her son. I'd noticed that Wade's mother smelled like salted caramel too. Children seemed to inherit their mother's scent as their primary smell.

"Are you recovered from your battle with Daniil?" she asked.

"There were wounds on my torso and legs, but they've healed." The fight with Daniil was the easiest part of that night to process.

"I'd like to bring an issue to the pack leader," a woman called from halfway down the bungalow.

She was small with a pointed face and large brown eyes.

"Delta," another alpha muttered under her breath.

"Rosalie, I will hear you," Sascha replied from the head table.

The occupants of the pack house fell silent.

Crap, this was probably about me. I shoved the three remaining potatoes in my mouth.

Evelyn rested her hand on my thigh. "Best not to eat when Sascha isn't, dear."

Hell would freeze over first.

Rosalie drew herself tall. "Your potential mate has joined our midst. She sleeps in our territory and uses our water and supplies. She eats our food. By our pack law, everyone on our territory must contribute."

Luthers darted looks at me, and I paused in chewing, cheeks filled with potato.

Sascha leaned back in his antler throne. "I had thought to give Andie time to recover from her ordeal."

"From her own lips, we've heard that she is healed."

Sascha remained impassive. "There are wounds other than the physical. You saw what was done to her."

Ugh. I resumed chewing.

"Are there other pack members who support this claim?" he asked.

Swallowing, I counted the hands.

A lot of hands.

The thought of me freeloading was the most hilarious thing to happen in a long time. *Me,* who'd made sure the bills were paid as best as possible since age eleven and who'd cared for her sick fake-mother, taken on her debt, and then somehow ended up caring for more than a thousand tribe members.

I snorted and slapped a hand over my mouth.

"Andie?" Sascha said. "Do you have something to add?"

"No. Nope." My voice was strangled. "Sorry. Continue."

He focused on Rosalie again. "What do you propose?"

"That she pays her way. She could help in Clay or Water."

I wouldn't mind that actually. The tribe knew precious little about pack operations in those grids.

"The Dens," Hairy interjected. "She can play music again. Profits increased by over 2 percent while she was with us."

Wade brought my saxophone with my other stuff, and I'd wasted no time sneaking the instrument back into the Jeep when he wasn't looking. "I won't play music."

Hundreds of eyes found me again, including Sascha's.

Hairy cast me a confused look.

I'd never touch that saxophone again. "Is there a different job at The Dens?"

Mandy spoke, "How about the casino side of things? You could work a table."

Sascha's growl unfurled like a whip. "You know she won't do that."

Yeah, that bothered me once. But who the hell cared anymore? Life was already as fucked up as it could get. What was one sliver more?

I smirked. "The casino? Sure, why not."

"Andie." Sascha began.

I stood, empty plate in hand. "I'm not sure how it works here, but I'll need to be paid money."

Rosalie crossed her arms. "That's not how it works in a pack."

"I have the rest of my gambling mother's debt to pay off, so the pack will need to make an exception. *Or,* I can find other employment and pay a set fee to the pack for living on this territory and eating your food. I'm fine with either."

Finding other employment could prove difficult though. The tribe owned most of the other companies, barring a few family-run businesses in town that didn't hire outside help. The supermarket and bank would be the best bets.

Murmurs broke out.

I'd wager that Sascha didn't want me off his territory.

He also needed to keep his pack happy.

"We have communal pack funds that each Luther has access to," he eventually said. "Instead of this, we'll transfer the personal share of what you earn to your account. Are you certain that you wish to work in the casino? We can find different work."

I lifted a shoulder. "The casino is fine. When do I start?"

4

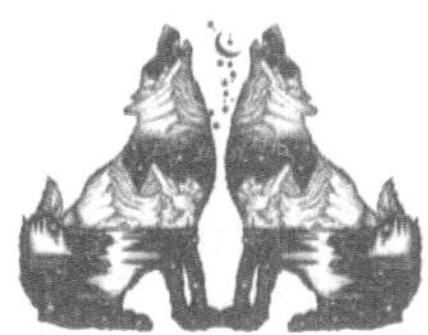

"One pays thirty-five, two pays seventeen, three pays eleven, four pays eight, and twelve pays two," I recited to Leroy, gazing at the roulette table.

The Dens wouldn't open for business until tomorrow night, but my training started three days ago.

Leroy placed a blue chip at the junction of zero, one, and the first twelve box. "If I put this here?"

"Five pays six."

"Good."

I'd always forced my mind away from gambling of any kind, but I doubt anyone could grow up without seeing a roulette table. Consider me surprised that this seemingly random assortment on red and black, odd and even numbers could make sense, but it was starting to.

Leroy picked up his blue counters. "Let's go through the outside bets. What's this?"

He placed a chip on the red diamond.

"Red or black bet. Pays one for one."

The Luther moved the chip to *even.*

"Even or odd bet. Also one for one."

We moved through Dozens, Columns, then High and Low.

Leroy smiled. "You're a maths brain. Ideal, or this wouldn't have worked out. Roulette is one of the harder tables to calculate payouts."

I twisted the roulette wheel absently. "Throwing me in the deep end?"

"Everyone has their preferred table."

I inhaled the slight decay of his oak scent. "Uh-huh. Is this the one no one wanted?"

The alpha grimaced. "It was Daniil's spot."

"I see."

"If there was another table, it would be yours. But game training takes time. It didn't make sense to pull others away from what they have experience with."

I arched a brow. "Really, it's fine."

He shot me a quick smile and moved through the inside bets, sometimes placing multiple chips down. Even if some of the names eluded me, the trick to using the centre column to make calculations proved handy.

"There's one other bet you may see from time to time." He placed counters in a weaving line across the roulette table. "This is a snake bet. The waving shape of the line is the clue. This pays at two to one."

How did that work in with my centre column though? I counted the blue chips. There were twelve of them. My frown eased. *Twelve pays two.*

Alright, I could do this. Calculating the various payouts with actual bet amounts would be another challenge, but with practice, I'd be fine.

"Got it," I said.

"Let's grab a drink before I leave for Sandstone."

The first grid match since the Stabattse was tonight. I'd felt sick with nerves all day. Somehow, they were *worse* than when I was head steward.

As soon as Rhona unleashed a counter strategy for the pack's ropes, Sascha would know what I'd done. Did he really mean what he said a few days ago about understanding my position?

Yet the thought of the tribe losing tonight was horrible.

"Cider?" Leroy asked.

"Pear, please."

He slid it across the bar, and I twisted off the top.

"Right, so job details. There are two shifts. Midday until seven. And seven until two. You'll be seven until two because Sascha wants you here when he is." He winked and took a sip of his beer.

Leroy had the player persona going on, but his level-headedness was unexpected for an alpha—the hot-headed brunette woman from dinner was the prime example of what I expected of their status.

"You'll get two sets of the work uniform. The outfit is on the shorter side, but I swear our female pack members designed them. The temperature in the casino can get uncomfortable for our kind."

I crooked a smile. "I'm Thong Girl. Simple things like lack of clothing in public places doesn't scare me."

"Of course. My apologies, Thong Girl. Now, while training with a mentor, you'll begin at seventeen dollars an hour."

Seventeen dollars multiplied by twenty-one hours, minus tax. *Right.* Not great. I'd earned more playing saxophone. "What about when I'm working without a mentor?"

"Twenty. During quarterly reviews, your table management will be assessed. Any pay rises will be decided then with a cap of twenty-five dollars per hour."

"Sascha didn't say how much the payment to the pack would be."

Leroy pressed his lips together. "The pack decided that one hundred and fifty dollars a week would suffice."

On the head steward salary, I could have paid off the remaining five-thousand-dollars of Ragna's debt within two months. It would take over a year to be rid of the debt at seventeen bucks an hour. Slightly less with a pay rise.

"Is there a problem with one hundred and fifty?" I asked.

"Sascha believes it's too steep and that some pack members are penalising you for your past."

I'd say that was plausible. "And for Daniil's death? He must have family."

"Parents. Two siblings. Most can admit you were protecting yourself. There's no denying he was much loved, but after hearing your marshal's explanation, most who mourn him feel just as much confusion as they feel grief."

"Grief is hard enough without betrayal creeping in."

"Your mother?"

"And Herc. But mainly Ragna, yes."

Leroy set his beer down. "As back room manager and Sascha's lead alpha, I need to ask. Will your mother's gambling past be an issue?"

"It won't be an issue." My voice was firm.

He toyed with his bottle. "It just seems cruel to put you in the casino. I'm sure Mandy didn't mean to suggest—"

"Mandy absolutely meant to challenge me."

"It's not her job to challenge you." Leroy growled low. "It's her duty to obey Sascha's orders and give sound advice when asked."

I sipped the over-sweet cider. "That sounds a lot like something an alpha might say."

"An alpha who knows his weakness, yes."

"So what? You give over control to Sascha to remove your alpha inclination to *take* control?"

He smirked "You're observant. I'll give you that. I saw the way you figured out the eating hierarchy."

I found the varying statuses fascinating. Every wolf had a different personality, but statuses displayed consistent strengths and weaknesses. Nothing shook Grim the gamma, but he contributed least in meetings between the pack and tribe. Mandy the delta came across as mostly easy-going but had a failure complex or possibly a massive, ambitious streak. Hairy the beta was level-headed and empathetic, but that made him want to please everyone and he could overthink things. Leroy's smiles came easy, but I bet he struggled with the control aspect of alpha status a lot.

"Not sure I made many friends that night," I murmured.

He finished his beer and disposed of the empty. "You'd be surprised how many Luthers respect power traditions. Some take issue because of what you were, but the rest saw you assert dominance over one of the strongest female wolves in our pack. Easily. That holds sway with them. Sascha is very proud."

I'd caught that.

By refusing to eat after others, I'd taken a step toward the pack. I wanted to take more steps. Without delay.

Leroy swept away my empty. "I'll meet you late tomorrow morning for the last training modules. Sorry about the rush on this. We usually spread training over a couple of weeks."

The quicker I started work, the better. I wanted a distraction so badly.

Leroy consulted his watch. "Shit, I need to get going. The run to Sandstone takes a while."

"I bet." Bile surged up my throat as I followed him to the door.

He glanced at me after locking up. "Will it be strange not to be there?"

Strange? No. Unbearable? Yes.

The only thing worse would be to watch from the sidelines.

"It's… an adjustment." I borrowed Sascha's word.

The tribe would be okay.

Rhona had this in the bag.

"Andie?"

I jolted at the soft voice.

"Sorry," a petite Luther said. "I'm interrupting your thoughts."

I faintly recognised her. It was the pup's mother. "Not at all."

I'd just finished speaking with Margaret Frey. She was too old to battle in the grid, and since my Luther secret came to light, I'd wanted to fill in the Frey's on Murphy's real fate. The only part I amended was Pascal's involvement in his death. She was blackmailed into silence, and it wasn't fair to lay blame at her door for Herc's actions.

"How's Axel?" I asked the woman.

Three times a day, a frantic search started for the pup. He was mischief.

As if hearing his name, Axel bounded from the grass and leaped onto the bench next to me.

"Hello, healthy boy," I cooed. "Aren't you *big* now?"

He jumped to lick my face.

"Axel," his mother scolded.

I scooped him up. He'd really grown. Pretty soon, he'd be too big to hold like this.

His mother smiled apologetically. "I'm Jemma. Mum of Axel. Mate of Credence."

Credence. Didn't ring a bell. "Nice to meet you. I'm Andie."

The woman grinned. "So I've heard. I won't trouble you long. While you and Leroy were gone, your friend dropped this off."

Peeking over the bench, I stared at the saxophone case in her hand.

For fuck's sake.

She blanched. "It's yours, isn't it? He said you forgot it."

I released Axel and took the saxophone. "It's mine."

Her nostrils flared. "I can put it somewhere else if you like?"

"It's fine. I've just gone off music. Thanks for bringing it."

Axel placed a paw on the case and whined.

"There's an instrument inside, little pup," I said.

He growled.

My brows shot up. "I mean *big* pup."

That earned me a tail wag.

Paw on the case, he whined again.

Jemma patted his ear. "If you want to open the case, Axel, you know what to do. You'll need human hands."

Axel ran off without another word.

Jemma gazed after him.

"He doesn't like two-legged form?" I asked.

She sat. "It's not unusual for babies to shift and remain as wolves for a time. It's an instinctual survival thing. Usually, they shift back and remain in two-legged form until the start of puberty when they go through their first official shift. Axel has been a wolf for nearly two years."

"Is that dangerous for him?"

"There's a lure to the power of wolf form that must be balanced by our human mind. Sometimes, Luthers fall prey to their wolves and turn feral. They remain in their four-legged form forever."

Axel was the only pup in the pack. There must be huge pressure on her *and* him. "Then we can only continue to give him prompts and wait for him to do the rest."

She released a breath. "I hope it's enough."

What a massive burden to carry. Smelling that she was near tears, I changed the subject. "Mothers don't fight in the grid, I gather?"

"Mums with dependent pups stay back, and some of the older, unmated wolves too. Just over fifty remain behind right now."

This place was so quiet when most of the pack was gone. I liked the noise. It reminded me of the manor's bustle.

A male wolf's howl shattered the calm—*Greyson.* Even in this form, I almost partially shifted to answer him.

What does that howl mean? I asked Booker.

Victory, she answered.

Jemma glanced my way. "We won."

My heart sank. How the *hell* did that happen?

She hesitated. "It must be hard to stay here when everyone you care about is on the other side."

Not everyone I cared about, but most of them. "It is."

I caught sight of Axel watching us from the grass. Setting the saxophone case on the ground, I flicked the catches back and opened the lid.

My mouth dried.

I hadn't looked inside this case since Herc died. I'd last played when we scattered Ragna's ashes at the red oak in her meadow.

How did the instrument look the same? Gleaming brass and the same shape. I bet it even felt the same.

How, when I'd changed so much?

Aware of Jemma's attention, I focused on the pounding approach of the seven hundred grid Luthers, my eyes on Axel's wiggling approach.

He wormed closer on his belly while we pretended not to notice.

Bounding up at last, he peered into the case, cocking an ear.

"This makes music," I told him. "Do you know what music is?"

"Like The Wiggles," Jemma said.

Werewolf pups watched *The Wiggles. Okay.*

The pup stared at the saxophone and rested a paw on top of the bell.

I scratched his back. "You need fingers like mine to play it."

He pushed the case toward me with his nose.

My chest tightened. "Oh. Not right now. I—"

"Andie is tired, Axel. Maybe you can ask her to play another time."

She heaved him up. "Goodnight, Andie. Sleep well."

Wolves raced from the forest, sprinting between the bungalows. They poured onto pack lands, yipping and snapping at each other's feet in play.

The tribe lost Sandstone. Unless the fisherwolf played me, I couldn't see how they fucked it up. The counter-strategy wasn't complicated.

I texted Wade.

What happened?

A huge brown wolf padded to my side.

I regarded Greyson. "Congratulations. That's three grids."

Not only that, Sandstone was one of the harder grids for the pack to win. This wasn't good for the tribe. It wasn't good for Rhona either. I understood more than anyone the amount of pressure on her as the new head steward.

Greyson sat and rested his chin on my head.

Did he know I'd passed on pack strategy? His scent was pure happiness and pride. Sascha either didn't care because they'd still won or Rhona disregarded my tip entirely.

"You're dribbling in my hair." I shoved him away, keeping my tone light-hearteded. "Go celebrate with your pack."

After licking my cheek, he trotted away.

I consulted my buzzing phone.

Your sister is an idiot.

That told me everything I needed to know.

He messaged again.

I thought she had a secret counter operation.
Nope.
Total landslide.
I'm telling everyone she knew about their plan and did nothing.

I snapped upright, typing back.

Please don't!
You're angry at her. I am too.
The tribe doesn't need more turmoil.

Rhona's pride got in the way of accepting my help. Though if she'd decided my transformation to a Luther was akin to me dying, then no wonder. It was foolish to tell her so directly.

I'd need to be smarter in the future.

Much smarter.

The Luthers' celebration soared as more pack members

returned from the grid, and my devastation swelled in tandem with their joy.

I was aware what this win meant to them.

To Sascha.

Even so, I couldn't sit here and be happy while knowing what the tribe currently felt.

Booker. Want to get out of here?

If there's one thing my anti-social companion could be depended on, it was leaving others behind.

Thought you'd never ask.

5

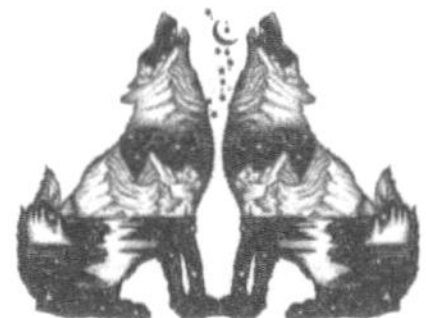

I dabbed shimmer on my lids over the rose-gold shadow. Gathering my hair in a high pony, I pulled some tendrils free to frame my face.

The uniform was laid out on Sascha's bed.

If Leroy hadn't specified that women designed this, I'd assume male alphas absolutely had a hand in it.

The tight, short jumpsuit was made of satin. While the top half plunged at the back, the front was high and collared. I wiggled into the thing, working the suit over my hips.

Yikes. Would this zip up?

"Need a hand?" Sascha entered the room.

I swear he listened for sounds of me changing and *happened* to appear.

I eyed the biggest obstacle to success. My boobs. "Yes, please."

He crossed the room at Luther speed, hands reaching for the zipper situated low on my stomach. Christmas had come for Sascha Greyson.

I sucked in as he drew the zipper up over my belly button and waist.

The zipper stopped beneath my boobs.

"Hold on." I held the ends of the jumpsuit over my breasts.

Air lodged in his throat. "*Cleavage*."

"The zipper, Sascha." I tucked away my grin.

Blinking several times, the Luther drew the zipper up to the base of my neck. His hand lingered there, the other curling around my waist.

"Suddenly, I'm looking forward to work tonight," he murmured.

I tugged the suit down. "I feel like my butt is half out."

He circled behind me and swore. "There wasn't a bigger size?"

"I don't know. Leroy gave it to me."

"Never let an alpha pick out your clothes—*either* gender." Sascha grabbed the red tie and clipped it into place, folding my collar down over the top. "Each time I think you couldn't be sexier, you prove me wrong."

I broke our burning stare. "Don't you smoulder at me. I'll be late."

He hooked my waist and drew me back against his body. I shivered as he moved his mouth to my ear. "Guess what. I'm the boss. You can be five minutes late. Plus, I'm taking you there."

Oh... "I thought I could just drive."

"Nonsense. I'm going. You're going. We might as well share a car, and I don't fit so well in yours."

Had I ever seen Sascha in a car? "What do you drive?"

My continued axe-swinging lumberjack fantasy associated Sascha with a rundown pickup truck.

"Just an old pickup truck," he answered.

Knew it.

He changed into a crisp, black suit, and I grabbed my purse.

We walked outside to a faded blue truck. The leather seats were torn. Only the driver seat was spared from the layer of dust coating the dash and passenger seat.

"Shoot. Hold on." He reached into the back and spread a blanket over the passenger seat.

"Thanks." I hoisted myself inside. "Sascha, I can feel you looking at my ass."

"Forgive me, mate."

I grinned. He was so full of shit.

We rumbled out of pack lands and drove along the south side river road.

"I've been meaning to ask how you are after the Sandstone turnover," he said.

I rubbed my arm. "I mean, one of us has to lose."

The thought made me frown as obvious as it was.

One of us *would* lose.

"You shifted and left." He glanced my way. "Was our reaction too much?"

"The pack deserves happiness too. I know that."

"I'm just aware this is a difficult adjustment."

Adjustment. There was that word again.

I nodded. "Being on pack lands while the tribe played Grids was harder than expected. Harder still because they lost."

My answer saddened him.

"Is there anything else worrying you? You've seemed distant today."

"Just stressed about my stewards and how they're coping." I focused out of the window.

"Of course. It would be unreasonable to expect otherwise. Thank you for trying with the pack regardless."

Me doing so overjoyed and relieved him big time. "I won't stop trying. But I'm starting to wonder if I'll settle in as things are."

"Give it more time," he said low.

I inhaled his sharp spike of desperation and my chest tightened. "I will, Sascha. Just thinking aloud. Don't worry about it."

His borderline panic didn't abate, and I shut my mouth for the rest of the drive.

We crossed the bridge into town.

Main Street was packed with people decked in their gambling finery. Jewels flashed and laughter rang out. Sascha drove up the hill, turning in behind *The Dens*.

He parked and killed the engine.

We sat in the dark.

I grabbed the handle. "See you later."

"Please don't feel so sad and alone, beautiful wolf. We'll figure this out."

I opened my mouth to answer but my words scuttled off into the night. I closed the door without replying and entered the back door of the club.

The Dens had a hypnotic, erotic vibe that pulled patrons from hours away. The deep thrum of the deejay's music worked its way into me, loosening some of the darkness gripping me.

"Seen Leroy?" I asked Grim.

He jerked his head. "Back room."

I found the alpha working the exchange counters. "Who am I tagging today?"

"Andie, hey," he said. "Lisa's holding down the roulette fort. She'll mentor you." He dug around under the desk and passed me a trainee badge.

"Anything in particular you want me to do?" I pinned the badge to my jumpsuit.

"Watch Lisa work. We'll catch up later to see where you're at. I'd like you to spend time working the table under her supervision either tomorrow or Saturday."

The hairs on the back of my neck rose and the elastic sensation under my ribs confirmed Sascha was somewhere behind me. "Sure."

Without looking back, I entered the casino.

Money-green felt coated every playing surface in the huge space. Bright neon lights flashed from the slot machines. An excited bustle filled the air, punctuated with groaning exclamations as someone lost.

I'd hated these places for as long as my memory stretched back. Shoving away unwelcome thoughts of Ragna, I weaved between the drinking patrons towards the roulette table.

Four people already played.

Lisa greeted me as I took up position behind her. She set the roulette wheel moving anti-clockwise and spun the ball clockwise around the top edge.

I checked out the four non-value chips laid out above the wheel. Brown, blue, grey, and burgundy were in play. Lisa had set the denomination on top of each of the four chips to help her remember each person's bet. Burgundy was playing at twenty dollars a pop. Rich guy.

The ball landed on 29.

Lisa cleared the losing bets of grey and brown. The older woman with blue had placed a red or black bet and won.

One for One?

Lisa pushed her another blue chip.

Correct.

Burgundy had laid three split bets. One bordered 29.

A bet on two squares paid seventeen times the bet. Burgundy's chips were worth twenty dollars.

Three hundred and forty. Even losing two chips, that was a good haul.

Lisa counted his payout and I watched to confirm my answer was right.

Another woman approached the table. "May I join?"

"Of course, ma'am," the omega replied.

The woman slid over twenty blue casino chips. "Ten-dollar bets, please."

Lisa slid over twenty pink non-value chips in return.

The others were placing their next bets and the woman hurried to do the same.

The woman on grey won a straight-up bet a few rounds later, and I smiled as the table congratulated her.

"Well done, ma'am." Lisa paid out her chips.

I checked my answer again.

Yep, one hundred and seventy-five.

This was a memory game, really. Lisa was faster at calculating the payout because she knew the patterns. Most bets would be the same amounts—one, five, ten, or twenty dollars. With practice, I'd memorise the common payouts and not have to think so hard.

The game continued, and I listened to how Lisa interacted with the patrons. Other Luthers circulated the room, taking drink orders from the gambling patron. The volume increased steadily, and the dealer at a high-roller blackjack table cut off a drunk patron.

"Full table, sorry," Lisa said to a suited man who'd doused himself in far too much cologne.

Lisa murmured over her shoulder. "If you forget which bet belongs to who, check the piles in front of them."

Ah, that made complete sense.

I studied the omega. Out of Sascha's head team, I'd had the least interaction with Lisa. Omegas seemed the timidest of the different wolf statuses. Peaceful but anxious.

The Luther fidgeted, shooting me a quick look.

She didn't like me watching her?

Leroy, Hairy, or Mandy would have confronted me about something they didn't like. Grim wouldn't care. But Lisa didn't do anything.

I wondered where omegas sat in the pack house for dinner. After me came female alphas, then betas and deltas. Who came after that? Gammas or omegas?

No one won the next round.

"I feel ready to have a go," I told Lisa quietly.

She collected the lost bets. "Leroy said you'd watch tonight."

Yeah, but I felt ready. "I have the hang of it."

"Maybe tomorrow night."

Her cherry blossom scent firmed.

Interesting. She really wasn't going to let me.

Leroy tapped me on the shoulder. "Break time."

"You can't take her away," Burgundy called. "She's my lucky charm."

"She'll be right back," the alpha said smoothly.

Lie.

Cool air washed over me as we exited into the exchange area. "It's *so* much nicer in here."

"Do the uniforms make sense now?"

Did they ever.

Leroy guided me to the bar. "How are you doing?"

"Everything makes sense. I asked Lisa for a turn, but she said I had to wait until tomorrow."

The alpha grinned. "I told her you were just watching tonight. Omegas won't disobey an order—they're incredibly stubborn."

Stubbornness, huh. Did not see that coming. She was otherwise so unconfrontational.

Mandy slid Leroy a beer, ignoring me.

"*Mandy,*" he snapped.

I rested a hand on his forearm. "It's okay. I'm not thirsty."

He growled after the delta. "She's crossing the line."

"If it bothers me, I'll sort things out myself."

He shoved away his beer.

Knew there had to be a bit of alpha hot-headedness in him somewhere. "The night goes fast."

It was already eleven.

"Pretty quick." He glowered at Mandy one last time before facing me. "Listen, there's another module we didn't tackle this morning. It's easiest to gain some on-floor experience before we go through it, and—well—I didn't want to—"

"Leroy. Spit it out."

"We train our dealers in how to notice patrons who may have a problem with gambling. It's only 1 to 2 percent of those who come here, but you'll come across it from time to time."

They did? Was that normal for Casinos? "You want me to go through the module now?"

"The last hour of your shift would be better. Things quieten down after one."

"I probably have a diploma in picking up gambling behaviour." My joke fell short.

Leroy fell quiet.

My voice softened. "Though I didn't notice in the end."

This was a conversation Hairy could navigate with ease, but emotions were *not* an alpha's strong suit.

Kudos to the guy—he patted me on the back. "I've heard that people with addictions are excellent at hiding their behaviour to family and friends. In a casino, it's easier to notice."

True.

His discomfort mounted.

"Would you like me to go back to the roulette table?" I scented his relief as I switched the conversation away from icky feelings.

"Spend until midnight at the chip exchange counter to get some interaction with patrons. If you could return to the roulette table for an hour after that, then watch the last training module in my office." He swallowed. "Would you like me in there with you?"

I lowered my lashes. "It would be nice to have a shoulder to cry on."

His eyes widened.

Laughter burst from my lips. "I'll be fine, Leroy. Don't worry."

The Luther rubbed the back of his head. "I can tell it's hard for you."

"I can handle it. Just don't get too close, you'll catch emotions."

He snorted. "Alright, stop picking on the alpha."

Chuckling, I left him and walked through the bar. The deep bass called to me, and my skin prickled.

Glancing across the dance floor, honey eyes met mine briefly before dragging over my body.

I should speak with him.

But what if every conversation just ended in one more wall between us? I had no idea what to do to fix my conflicting loyalties, and *worse* was that I feared testing out new ground in case it drove Sascha and me apart.

Heat climbed into my cheeks at his continued perusal. He wanted to give me space. He also desperately wanted me to go to him. Flustered, I hurried in the opposite direction toward the casino. My shoulders relaxed as I entered the chip exchange area.

An *extra* shy male omega showed me the ropes there, and the hour rushed by as I congratulated and commiserated patrons exchanging casino chips for cash or, more often, more cash for extra chips. Some needed a lecture about the effects of gambling in my opinion, but that might get me fired on day one.

I returned to Lisa and the roulette table for the last hour. She didn't hand over the reins, and with my new knowledge, I didn't press her for a turn.

The number of patrons at our station dwindled from seven to five. Then to two.

"Isn't your brain sore?" I asked when the last had left. Mine was.

"Leroy covered while I had a break, but it's a lot when you're not used to it. I prefer security work."

Couldn't blame her. "I'm meant to watch more training videos now."

"No problem. I'll see you tomorrow."

I re-entered the bar and crossed to Grim, who opened the staff door without a word.

The gamma appeared bored beyond words.

"Grim? What do you think about all night?"

He looked at me. "Food."

Grinning, I entered the hall and immediately scented Sascha in his office.

I pushed open the door to Leroy's office and found the module locked and loaded on the computer monitor.

Brr. It was cold in here. *Remind me to bring a jacket to my next shift.*

Chafing at my arms, I started the video. The presenter had an '80s perm. I loved old-school educational videos.

"Casinos have a duty of care to ensure they prevent and respond to concerning behaviour from patrons who may demonstrate an unhealthy relationship with gambling."

I was weirdly wired from the music, patron noise, and the intense concentration of calculating payouts, but 1:00 a.m. was not the right time of night to learn stuff.

"The exchange counter is a crucial screening area. Failed transactions are an early warning sign that a person is spending more than they can afford."

Shivering on the desk chair, I hugged my knees to my chest.

The door opened and Sascha strode in with his suit jacket in hand.

His shirt sleeves were rolled up, collar opened.

I accepted the token, mumbling, "Thanks."

Standing, I shrugged the massive jacket on and fastened the three buttons at the front.

He leaned over to pause the module. "Andie, I need to hold you."

"Of course." I wrapped my arms around his firm torso, resting my head on his chest.

Sascha squeezed me close, resting his head atop mine. He stroked my back, and I wriggled as his fingers brushed the ticklish spot on my lower back.

The tension gradually drained out of both of us.

I gazed up. "Better?"

"Better is relative."

The mood altered, and he growled low. Sascha captured my lips, forcing my head back. Hoisting me onto the desk, he guided me flat and ran his hands up my thighs before spreading them.

Fire flushed my body, and I reached for his shirt. He let me unfasten the buttons and then resumed our kiss.

I moaned into his mouth, melding my softer lips to his.

He worked my clip-on tie free and tossed it away, then dragged down the zipper of my jumpsuit. My boobs sprung free.

"*Fuck.*"

I let him look his fill. "Been waiting for that?"

"You could say that." Sascha closed over my nipple, and a pleading noise I couldn't recall ever making fell from my lips. I gripped his head with both hands, urging him on. He obliged, and the throbbing between my thighs mounted.

Bursting upward, I forced his mouth to mine again.

Nothing felt like this.

"I want you," I panted.

Picking me up without warning, he pressed me face-first against the wall and clamped his arm across my waist, pinning both arms. His other hand disappeared down the front of my splayed jumpsuit.

He circled my clit.

My head thumped back against his shoulder. "Oh—"

"You like that, beautiful wolf?" he whispered harshly in my hair. "Want more?"

I couldn't touch him, but I could only move my hips slightly. "*Yes.*"

"Tell me what you want?"

The music was loud, but Grim would definitely hear outside the staff room door. I didn't answer.

Sascha paused.

"Don't stop." Gravel entered my voice.

"Tell me then."

"I want your hand on me."

"Here?"

My legs nearly gave way as he pressed again.

He circled once. "Like this?"

"*Please.*"

"What about the other direction?" Sascha reversed his circle and my legs *did* give out. There was a smile in his voice as he held me up. "We have our answer."

His fingers circled faster than humanly possible. It was too much for my mind to process. The jolting waves of pleasure stole away my reason. I writhed against his hand, undone.

He released my arms. I was beyond the point of using them, but my legs shook without his support. Sascha peeled away the jumpsuit from my shoulder and kissed my bared shoulder. His fingers were my only concern. The Luther didn't skip a beat as he rested his teeth against my shoulder.

"Sascha," I choked as my vision went white.

He guided me down to the ground.

Fuck.

Jolts of electricity ran through me and I rested my forehead against the wall as my limbs shook from the aftermath.

Double fuck.

My vision returned and I became aware of the coldness at my back. Forcing my arms to work, I pushed away from the wall and glanced over my shoulder.

Sascha was turned away, shoulders heaving.

"What's wrong?" I blinked through the hot languidness that had settled in my body.

He shook his head, fist pressed against his mouth.

Recalling the last moments before my orgasm, I reached up to my shoulder, craning to see the skin. *Unbroken*. "Did you nearly bite me?" *Shit.* I'd even felt him preparing to do so. "You didn't do it."

He whirled, fangs extended, and eyes pitch-black.

Yikes. I tugged the jumpsuit into place, drawing the zipper up as far it would go without aid. "Is that better?"

Sascha really wasn't home.

I managed to stand—*thanks, legs*. "Something held you back just now. What was it?" Maybe focusing on that would help to regain control.

The time didn't seem right for another meet so soon after the last.

He rested both hands on the desk. "Greyson doesn't want to bite you in two-legged form."

"Okay, and you?"

"When the meets are over, you'll make your choice."

My mouth dried. I stared at him. "I see. And you expect me to turn you down?"

The moment extended.

He closed his eyes. "Will you?"

"I—" Sascha Greyson was everything to me. But making a choice wasn't that easy. We had to get there first. With things as they were, I couldn't see that happening anytime soon.

Or ever.

My mouth dried. *Oh my god.*

That's it, Booker whispered.

That was why I felt so adrift on pack lands though Sascha and I were closer than ever.

I couldn't see a future where we were together and happy.

6

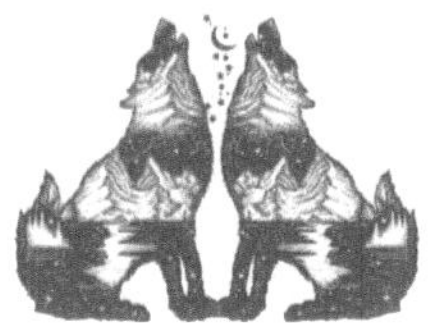

I parked Ella F, more than ready for bed.

Lisa let me run the roulette table for most of tonight. I was confident to continue alone next week.

I shut my car door quietly, aware of the hundreds of slumbering Luthers. In heels, I wobbled over the packed dirt toward Sascha's bungalow.

He was working late—or so he said—so we'd driven separately today.

Light streamed from a bungalow ahead. A smiling woman stepped out, and I stopped short as a second smiling woman joined her, delivering a sweet kiss.

Oh, shit!

"Cam?" I called out.

Both of the women jumped.

Well, this explained rather a lot.

I approached the pair. "Hey."

Cam was always in the pale camp, but she was *really* pale now. "I'm sleeping with a Luther. It's okay."

Did she rehearse that?

I slanted a glance at her companion. I vaguely recalled the wolf's face. Emily, perhaps?

"Just okay?" I asked my friend in confiding tones.

Cam stared at me for a beat. "Good enough to come back?"

"Is that a question or a statement?"

"... Statement."

"Might as well keep it going then. Night." Winking, I wobbled onward to Sascha's abode.

I shoved inside and kicked off my heels. *Sweet bliss.*

Bed. Me.

Soon.

Shower. Smelly.

Knock, knock.

I hobbled back to the front door.

Cam lurked on the other side.

"Done already?" I joked.

She flashed a small smile. "Look, I wanted to thank you."

There was so much wrong in that. "You aren't hurting anyone, Cam. I assume Emily isn't hurting anyone. You being together doesn't hurt anyone. Don't thank me for taking your relationship well. Anyone who takes it otherwise is a small-minded bitchhole."

She tucked away a tremulous smile. "I know. It's just... the tribe."

I understood the social pressures better than most. "You've worried about this for a long time, huh?"

"A while. I'm sorry for not telling you sooner."

Secrets were odd things. They got harder to divulge as the days rolled over. "I'm just glad to know everything is okay. We were worried about you."

She hesitated. "Do you think I should tell Wade?"

"Up to you. If it makes you feel better—I'm a werewolf, and Wade tried to get me drunk the other day. I don't think he's a small-minded bitchhole."

Cameron laughed.

I grimaced. "He doesn't like being out of the know though. Fair warning. At worst, he'll want a King Wade Day."

Cam tilted her head. "Hey, is that why you threw him a King Wade Day? He found out you were a werewolf?"

"Yep."

She grinned in the dark, then frowned. "What's it like to be a Luther?"

"Like feeling more alive and more in tune with people and the land."

She hummed.

I gave in to a question that had plagued me since the Stabattse. "What's everyone saying about me, Cam?"

"Rhona or the tribe?"

"Both."

Cam grimaced. "Rhona is pretty worked up."

"Tell me. I can handle it."

"It's not a matter of you handling it. It's a matter of what a person shouldn't have to handle."

That was a quaint thought. "If you don't tell me, I'll wonder what they're saying. Truly, you won't break me."

"Nothing could break you," she said fiercely.

Is that what she believed? I was held together with sticky tape.

Cameron blew out a breath. "Rhona considers you as dead. The moment you became a Luther, you were gone."

Nothing the fisherwolf hadn't already told me. "Alright. And the tribe?"

"If I had to guess, people don't know what to feel. Obviously, no one expected you to shift into a werewolf. There's shock and anger —an undercurrent of pity. Most knew you, and when you consider someone to be like you, it becomes hard to see them as an enemy. Take it from a lesbian living in a small town."

That news surprised me a lot.

I'd expected the tribe to make piñatas of my face and fill them with fun-sized bottles of wolfsbane.

"Don't get me wrong," she continued. "The people who were

anti-you before are *really* anti-you now, but don't assume everyone hates you. You were bitten against your will. That means something to most stewards."

Tears sparked in my eyes. "Thanks, Cam."

"Don't thank me for taking it well," she quipped.

"Are you throwing my wisdom in my face?"

"Yes."

I jerked my head. "Get out of here. You need a shower."

She bounded forward and hugged me.

"And now I smell like what you two did. So *I'm* going to take a shower."

Did you get that? I asked Booker.

Yep.

The tribe wasn't set against me.

Does that change things? she asked.

I didn't know yet.

But it might.

I was dragged sideways along the warm mattress and tucked against a firm chest.

Peace settled over me once more, accompanied by a slow fire building low in my stomach. I pressed my ass against the presence behind me.

A hand clamped down on my hip, arresting my movement.

I growled in warning.

The fire built. I twisted, winding my hands around Sascha's neck to better inhale his delicious scent.

He swore and rolled onto his back.

I crawled on top of him and collapsed in a heap. He was so toasty. Felt good. Stretching so the length of my body aligned with his, I circled my hips.

That felt even better.

Sascha hardened against my stomach.

"Use a condom," I mumbled.

"*What?*"

I jerked awake, lifting my head.

We looked at each other.

Sascha frowned. "Who were you thinking about?"

My cheeks coloured. I'd been telling *him* to use a condom. That was almost worse than whatever possessive conclusion he'd come to.

He held me in place and his erection pressed on my core. I bit back a groan.

I avoided his gaze. "I thought you were you."

"You did?"

I fidgeted, and we both stiffened.

His hands swept my sides. "Tell me what you need, beautiful wolf."

My flush deepened. I wasn't doing anything surrounded by pack members. "I need to eat."

Dislodging his hold, I crossed to my bags, still scattered over the floor, and selected some jean shorts and a mustard off-the-shoulder blouse that cost me two dollars at a second-hand store. Seriously, people chucked away the best stuff.

"Does the pack's proximity bother you?"

"It doesn't bother you?"

"Everything leading up to and including sex is natural. We don't actively listen to each other's lives, but if someone did, they wouldn't think anything of us pleasing each other."

His mum might be listening.

That weirded me out.

I escaped to the bathroom and brushed my teeth and hair. That would do.

"I thought we could spend time together today." Sascha threw off the top blanket.

I blinked at his naked body. He usually wore sweats to bed.

No wonder sleep Andie got a little wild this morning.

Warn a girl.

His stomach tensed with his movement as he walked toward me.

Oh, boy.

Ducking his head, he laid a gentle kiss on my lips. "You look beautiful this morning, mate."

My heart skipped a beat with his. "Thanks, handsome. I'll see you at breakfast?"

"Sure. About later. I have a meeting. But we can catch up after? There are some beautiful spots in our territory I'd like to show you."

That sounded a lot like a date. We'd never really done that. "Uh. Sure, okay."

He arched a brow.

You are not blushing, Andie.

Yes, you are, Booker stated, snickering after.

I hurried away from an amused Sascha to the pack house. The scent of eggs and bacon wafted out accompanied by the cheerful conversation and laughter of pack members. Things were always busier on Sundays with no one at work.

Get bacon in our mouth, Booker demanded.

I'm going. I'm going.

The sight of a teen girl sneaking around the bungalow stopped me short. Curious, I changed directions and snuck after her, peeking around the corner.

She lingered at the back door to the kitchen, clearly listening to the movement inside. Bacon grease shone on her fingers, and I smirked.

The guts wanted more food.

I scanned the surroundings and clicked my tongue.

The teen whirled, and I beckoned her.

Scowling, she approached.

I lowered my voice to a level human ears wouldn't hear. Luthers wouldn't catch the words over the sounds in the kitchen. "You want seconds?"

"What's it to you?"

"Nothing to me. If you want to pull it off without being caught, you could consider that there's no cover between here and the forest. Where are you planning to run after? And how will you explain your scent in the kitchen?"

The girl planted her hands on her hips. "I don't have to do what you say. You're from that tribe."

Not my number one fan. Or her parents weren't. "I haven't told you to do anything. They're just things to consider if you really want the food."

Should I teach kids how to steal stuff...?

Oh, well. "There's one thing that eliminates your scent for a few minutes."

Her eyes shone. "Water."

"I wonder if hiding in plain sight could be helpful too." I tilted my head to the front of the pack house.

She smirked.

I winked at the teen. "Have a good morning."

Sascha intercepted me at the bottom of the stairs. Humming to himself, he took my hand as if it were the most natural thing in the world.

Was he really so unconcerned?

Did he not look ahead and see us torn apart no matter who won Grids?

I shook off my worry, determined not to ruin the day. Instead, I observed the pack members outside the bungalow. Those farthest from the top table lounged around, enjoying the sun like they could stay there all day. Those Luthers just inside the door darted nervous looks at Sascha and I as we passed.

I had the order.

Alphas, betas, deltas, omegas, and gammas. No way would I have put Grim below Lisa in the pecking order. Just because he was bigger.

"Will you sit with the females today or with me?" Sascha paused by the alpha women.

"Women," I answered.

He brushed a kiss on the back of my hand and left me to my devices. Eyes were on us.

Ugh.

I loaded a plate and sat in my normal spot at the front. Evelyn smiled, but the other alphas ignored me, and I returned the favour.

"Axel!"

The muddy pup raced through the entrance, chased by a frazzled Jemma.

The pup stopped right in front of me.

"Are you being good for your mother?" I said sternly.

He whined.

That was a whopping no.

"She loves you very much. We should try to make our mothers happy if we can."

The pup rested a filthy paw on my knee and cocked his head.

Jemma panted. "Sorry, Andie. He's been at the stream."

"That's okay. What are you trying to tell me, Axel?"

The pup shimmied back and sank to his belly, worming closer where he bounded up and rested a paw on my knee again, whining.

"You want to see the saxophone?"

He barked.

"I can show it to you, but you'll need to wait very patiently while I finish breakfast. Can you do that, big pup?"

Axel planted his dirty butt on the ground and puffed his chest out.

I pressed my lips together and looked up at Jemma. "I can watch him for a while if you like."

She hesitated. "Are you sure?"

I'd noticed that the women in the pack worked together, helping each other with daily tasks and looking out for the younger members. This was one more step toward *adjustment*. "Absolutely. I'll keep him safe."

Jemma curtsied. "I have no fears on that count. Please bring him back if he's too much trouble."

The pup hadn't budged an inch.

"I'm sure we'll be fine."

I raised a piece of bacon to my mouth, watching as Axel's blue eyes followed the action. Considering his gut rested on the floor, I assumed the pup had eaten well.

Making quick work of my food, I fed the little Luther my last piece of bacon. He was just too cute to resist. "Alright. Let's go."

The pup fell into step behind me, and I couldn't blame the other pack members for watching him pass. I was already half-obsessed with Axel too.

I grabbed my saxophone from the bungalow, and we walked to the bench by the stream.

Opening the case, I let the pup study the instrument.

He looked at me expectantly.

"What? This is the saxophone."

I inhaled his sunshine scent. It was muted. The pup was disappointed. Shoving back my misgivings, I rested my hands on the saxophone and freed it from the case. "I'll show you the parts. This is the bell."

The brass was cold.

I worked around the instrument, showing Axel how the keys moved and explaining how it made a sound.

Shuffling forward, he sniffed the brass.

"Do you like music?" I placed the saxophone in the case.

He nodded.

"What music?"

Axel refused to shift back to two-legged form. To me, it made sense to frustrate him. There were things a Luther simply couldn't do as a wolf. One of them, barring mated couples, was talking to anyone with two legs.

The pup stared at me.

I frowned. "I wish I could hear you. Your mother said that you like The Wiggles. Which song is your favourite?"

He stared again.

"Sorry. I can't understand you." I gestured to the instrument. "Is that all you wanted to see?"

When the pup didn't answer, I shut the lid.

He whined.

"I'm not sure what you're saying. Could you tell me another way?"

Axel rested a paw on the case.

"You want to see the instrument again?"

A shake of the head.

"Then let's put this away and play a game. How about that?"

A deep voice interrupted us. "May I sit?"

I looked up into familiar brown eyes. The old fisherwolf.

I moved the saxophone case off the bench.

"Go play, pup. Stay in sight." The order in the man's voice was obvious.

Axel wasted no time waddling off into the long grass.

I kept half an ear out. He was the master of disappearing acts... though I somehow expected that he wouldn't dare disobey this man.

"How are you, young wolf?"

"Shouldn't you be at the pack meeting?"

He opened his tackle box and selected a hook. "Old wolves sometimes get bored of such things."

No scent today either. "Why don't you have a smell?"

"Old wolves get bored of that too."

Luther power must become stronger over time. Either that or their understanding of their power deepened.

"Always such a busy mind," he murmured.

Axel launched after a butterfly.

"I'm used to having a lot to think about," I murmured.

"Indeed. Even now?"

"Always such a busy mind," I repeated his words.

This directionless feeling made matters worse. Existing like this felt increasingly wrong.

Which was terrifying.

The wolf cast his line. "They've decided on Timber."

"You can hear through the frequency generators?" I raised my voice. "Axel. Closer, please."

The pup paused on the edge of the stream before trotting back in our direction.

"Your sister is overly fond of violent measures," the fisherwolf said.

"She harbours a lot of hate."

"That's not harbouring. That's sending her hate out to wage war."

He didn't know her.

If the right person could reach Rhona, she could come back from all this. I'd thought that person was me, but I fucked it all up.

"Never let it be said that you aren't loyal." The man smiled to himself. "She drugged and humiliated you. What on earth could hold you to such a person?"

Rhona was a version of myself. She represented what I could become if I let grief and anger consume me.

If she could recover, then so could I.

"Old wolves have a lot to say on Sunday mornings." I picked up the saxophone case.

He twitched the line. "Not at all. I was simply going to remark that your sister's violent approach is dangerous for the tribe. She unleashed a smaller version of her father's trick in Sandstone."

"A landslide?"

He dipped his head. "We'd prepared for it. And of course, we used the strategy I informed you about."

Rhona would have an equally violent plan in store for Timber. The risk of losing points to serious injury was huge. She couldn't win that way, and who in their right mind would *want* to win that way?

But the head team knew that risk just as well as me. They'd advise her.

I could definitely stay out of this one.

The less I involved myself, the better Sascha and I would be.

"The pack strategy for Timber is inspired." The fisherwolf recast.

"Axel," I called again. The pup paused at the stream's edge again and doubled back.

Little stinker.

The old man didn't stop talking. "We've never considered using the trees, but why not? It's not as if the tribe has the strength and agility to move between them as we do. I believe you were the muse for the strategy."

I leaned down to pat Axel. "Sascha crept up on me one day. I leaped into the tree."

The tribe had nothing against that kind of strategy. All our ground traps would be void. With the Luthers' stealth, we'd be easy pickings.

The head team wouldn't see it coming.

Fuck.

"It's time to find your mother," I said to the pup. "I have a date."

He cast me a baleful look.

"We can play again soon. I promise."

The pup rested a paw on the saxophone.

"If I hear that you're being good for your mother, we can look at the instrument another time."

Axel yipped.

I hummed. "I can't understand you, big pup. Could you tell me another way?"

He flopped to the ground, huffing.

The old man didn't shift his attention from the stream. "Goodbye, young wolf."

I had to find out who this guy was ASAP. He was actively trying to screw things up for the pack via me—and that pissed me off. "Bye, old wolf."

After dropping off Axel to a grateful Jemma, I ambled between the bungalows turning over the fisherwolf's information.

Using the trees would shift the game in Timber from an even match to a total landslide.

Why does that wolf keep coming back? I asked Booker.

Who cares? Just use the information.

I don't like pack members disrespecting Sascha like that.

Then tell Sascha.

If I told Sascha, they'd prepare for counterattacks from the stewards.

No one was around.

Sighing, I drew out my phone.

Wade.
I have more info.

Three dots appeared.

She ignored your last tip, baby girl.
This will just get you hurt.
And what about Sascha?

I swallowed back guilt. He'd hit the nail on the head. No matter that Sascha had accepted my position and priorities, I couldn't deny what felt right and wrong.

Every move feels like the wrong one, I told my wolf.

Something has to be done. The distance between you and Sascha is growing, not lessening.

Exactly. *I don't understand why though.*

You do.

Well, I had an inkling now. *I thought moving to pack lands gave us a future, but the game ending ensures we won't.*

You want a future with him.

I did. So fucking much. *That's why I'm trying.*

I'd taken measures to become closer to the pack, but nothing diminished the loyalty I felt for the tribe. I'd expected to feel more allegiance to the pack as time went on, but if anything, I felt more torn.

I didn't want either side to lose.

The only solution I could think of is that the game would go on and on endlessly.

Booker was a separate entity within me. Her feelings didn't get in the way of what I couldn't always admit to myself. Several times in the past, she'd forced me to confront hard realisations. *Tell me what I need to hear, please.*

One other scenario ends with happiness for you and Sascha.

A lump rose in my throat. *That's impossible.*

She didn't disagree.

For good reason.

Steeling myself, I texted Wade.

We need to go through Pascal this time.
Here's what you need to tell her.

7

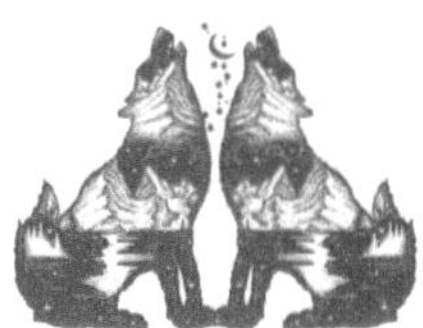

I gestured at my jean cut-offs and white throwover that covered my navy bikini. "I didn't know what to wear."

Sascha was in his token jeans and white T-shirt. "You look incredible."

Two women walking by grinned at each other.

My cheeks flamed. "Alright."

He brushed back a strand of hair that had fallen loose from my ponytail. "Are you blushing?

I glared at him. "Where are we going?"

Flashing a grin, he opened the door of his blue pickup truck. "Hop in, spitfire."

I'd show him spitfire. Batting away his hand and ignoring his deep chuckle, I climbed into the vehicle.

We left pack lands, but instead of turning toward the town at the entrance to pack lands, Sascha turned left. I'd only been down here to play in Clay.

"I've wanted to get away with you for a while." One hand on the wheel, he rested his other arm on the frame of the windowsill.

I shrugged. "Leader life."

"It is. To be clear though. I'll always make time for you."

I tried not to fidget. "Don't worry. I know what it's like."

He directed us around a bend and slowed where the road changed from tar-seal to dirt. "You are my main priority."

It was hard for someone who'd never been anyone's main priority to suddenly become one. Even though I believed him, my natural inclination was to get feisty or make a joke.

Battling with those urges, I settled for silence.

Sascha took my hand, and the tension drained from me.

I wanted to tear down everything between us so badly. Dredging up my courage, I said, "It's a strange concept for me."

"I know, little bird."

Tears stung my eyes.

I wound down the window, letting the warm summer air calm me.

Sascha let go of my hand to navigate the switchbacks. "You're winning over the pack females."

Am I? "Cool."

He shot me an amused look. "It's a compliment. As my mate, you would assume leadership over the females in our pack. They've seen you interact with Axel and Jemma, and I heard them talking about your acceptance of Emily and Cameron. Sometimes, top females have trouble maintaining dominance and inspiring confidence, but you've taken to it as I always knew you would. Your past as head steward may have generated some bad will initially, but really, every member of my pack knows you have what it takes to lead."

I suppose it might have helped to convince them—even with how my stint as head steward ended. "So the males and females are separate entities within the pack?"

He nodded. "As pack leader, my order is final, barring a situation where the females lose faith in my ability to protect and provide. As top female, your advice and opinion will always hold powerful sway with me and with the entire pack."

Hmm.

"What?" Sascha asked.

“Trying to remember if any of my romantic fantasies ever involved being called a top female.”

He laughed and lifted a shoulder. “Some of our terms must seem nonprogressive.”

I glanced down over the valley and my stomach swooped at the drop. “You’re not human. Why would your culture be the same as ours? I’ve never seen any male Luther disrespect a female Luther. The pack seems to acknowledge that there are different kinds of strength, and that one isn’t better than the other.”

Sascha hummed. “I guess so.”

“Where are we going?”

“Not telling.”

I groaned.

He grinned. “You’re not good with surprises.”

“That’s because they’re mostly bad.”

“In your experience?”

I released my belt and scooted into the middle seat, buckling up again. There, I rested my head on his shoulder, feeling the immediate warmth of our connection that made talking so much easier. “People used to kick down the doors for money. Mum went through a phase of borrowing from loan sharks. They weren’t nice.”

Sascha tensed. “How old were you?”

“From nine. It stopped at twelve when I convinced Mum to go to rehab.” We’d sold her car and some furniture to afford it. “I’d sometimes come home to find Mum gone. She’d return days later after emptying the bank accounts.”

His pine scent ignited with anger.

“It was all worth it when she was my mother,” I admitted.

“She’s your mother if you decide she’s your mother.” Sascha turned down a tiny dirt road that led away from the plummeting cliffs.

I sighed. “If she could laugh with me sometimes after Murphy’s death, why couldn’t she tell me the truth?”

“People who hurt that much sometimes want to hurt themselves more.”

"I think that's why she gambled."

"Then it's not unreasonable to think she might have made herself feel worse in other ways. Like not treating you in a way you deserved. Or maybe she believed lying was the best way to protect you."

He pulled over on the side of the small road.

I looked at him. "Guess I'll never know."

Herc's death was shit, and I still held regret over my part in the events of that night, but I'd dealt with his passing for the most part.

"Is this why you won't play music anymore?" He took my hand again.

My voice was hoarse. "Yes."

"One day, you'll play again, and I look forward to that moment. Besides your voice, there's no sound more beautiful than your music." He whispered a kiss on my lips. "I'm not sure how I get anything done when you're around."

I frowned. "Hey, Sascha?"

"Mmm?" He kissed up my neck.

I lost my train of thought. He rested his forehead against my chest sometime after.

"I'm here to show her our territory," Sascha muttered.

My shoulders shook. "Who are you trying to convince?"

He groaned. "Myself. What were you saying?"

Uh... "I was going to ask what you'd do if the pack won Grids."

As soon as the words were out, I half regretted them. The lighter mood we'd managed to grip onto disappeared.

Sascha regarded me. "We'd gain the businesses and the entire Deception Valley territory. My pack would have a permanent home. I'd enjoy not having the threat of death lingering over our heads. I'd have more time to spend with you. Greyson struggles with the demands of pack life, and he'd enjoy more time to ourselves."

In Sascha's mind, I was with him if the pack won.

In that future, did I feel like this? Were we constantly trying to re-establish a strong connection with each other?

"What would happen to the tribe if the pack won?" I asked before I could wuss out.

He took longer to answer. "Our peoples have attempted peace many times, Andie. It has never worked. The stewards will be devastated to leave their ancestors and burial grounds behind, but they *can* leave, and so I believe they must if my people are to finally live without violence and hate."

That's what I'd expected.

The thought of the stewards being torn from their valley was horrifying. To imagine watching their desolation as they drove away filled me with dread.

I wasn't sure I could watch that happen.

Sascha clearly believed I'd stay behind.

And maybe I would if the pack won.

But who would I be? And what would I become in time?

Because time sure as fuck wasn't helping me now.

"You don't like my answer." Sascha's tone belied the sudden horror he felt too.

Could he smell my complete adversity to what he'd outlined?

There was something I had to know. Something that could change everything. "Would you ever consider another ending?"

Sascha's impassive mask swept into place. "My pack are beyond accepting another ending. Fifty years ago, they agreed that only the victor would remain in the valley after Victratum. They are willing to *die* if they lose rather than go on in this way. Good or bad, they want it done."

There wasn't a hint of hesitation in his answer.

And no wriggle room.

Hopelessness filled me completely—a mere hint of what lay ahead.

I couldn't be what Sascha wanted me to be.

Forcing back the crushing sorrow, I broke the tense quiet. "Do we walk from here?"

"Andie—"

"No. It's good for me to know that now. It's..." Shaking my head,

I shuffled back to the passenger side and opened the door. Pausing outside, I released a shaking breath as quietly as possible.

Sascha hadn't budged and I could smell his anguish.

Why did we keep doing this to each other? And when would it stop?

What happens now? Booker asked softly, likely sensing I was on the verge of tears.

My throat tightened.

Something had to change. And fast.

Or Sascha and I were on a one-way ride to destruction.

I paced in the bungalow, checking the time on my phone. The Tuesday tribe gathering was almost over.

My phone buzzed and I scrambled to read the message from Wade.

Rhona has taken measures against their plan.
Telling Pascal worked.

Thank fuck for that.

And also, *shit.*

I had just over twenty-four hours until Sascha realised I'd passed on pack information. This moment was always inevitable, perhaps. But Booker had told me to trust my instincts, and after the tense talk with Sascha earlier today, my instincts burned stronger than ever.

No matter who won, Sascha and I lost.

That wasn't something I could accept.

I slipped my phone away and walked to dinner.

He wasn't in the pack house, and it felt horrible to feel so damn *relieved* about that. But I was. I'd spent the afternoon scenting his anguish. He'd spent the afternoon scenting mine.

We didn't touch once.

More distance. More walls.

It was just easier when I couldn't smell his hurt and pain.

I grabbed some marinade-slathered ribs, adding pulled pork and a steak. Wrinkling my nose, I heaped on carrots and broccoli.

Put the ribs in our mouth, my wolf said.

I sat and obeyed.

"Where's Sascha?" Evelyn asked.

"Unsure," I replied. "At work still?"

She frowned. "He's usually back for dinner."

My reaction to his answer had thrown him. I didn't know exactly what he'd realised in that moment, but maybe similar thoughts to mine were circulating his mind right now.

Perhaps he'd seen that our future may not be quite as he'd envisioned.

Or at all.

I consulted the elastic pull under my ribs. "He's moving fast. He must have shifted and gone for a run."

And if I shifted after dinner, our paths wouldn't cross until bedtime.

"Mandy sure doesn't like you." Another of the alpha women jerked her head to the top table. The woman wore her jet-black hair in a pixie cut.

A quick glance confirmed that Mandy was glaring daggers at me. "I thought that was respect and friendship."

At her snort, the brunette I'd knocked out and the blonde who'd carried her away fixed hard gazes on the woman.

The woman with the pixie cut rolled her eyes. "Kara, get over it. She won the challenge fair and square. If you have another issue, take it up with Andie. Don't expect me to fall in line. You know we're an even match."

"Do you still have a problem with me, Kara?" I asked. When she lowered her gaze, I looked at the blonde. "What about you, Bailey?"

She jerked at my use of her name.

Yes, I use my ears.

"No problem," Bailey grunted.

"Great to hear. Now, Mandy does have an issue with me. She believes that I'm unworthy of Sascha. She's taken it upon herself to be his champion."

The alpha women looked at Mandy, who, judging by her sour scent, certainly heard my words.

Evelyn growled low. "Mandy would do well to remember that it's up to my son to prove his worth, not the other way around."

Her voice was sharp, and the sour edge to Mandy's scent ran to hide.

I gnawed at another rib. "Surely it's up to both people to prove themselves. Both mates stand to lose the same if one says no."

Evelyn smiled. "Logically, yes. Yet it is always the case that males worry incessantly about proving themselves worthier than any other partner the woman could choose. Nature drives them near madness with the urge, and that occurrence transcends mere logic, don't you think? Which is why most wolves use nature's wisdom as their guide in such things. For us, it is the male's task to ensure the positive result of the mating call."

My experience of nature's wisdom to date told me it could go fuck itself.

A commotion at the door stole our attention.

At Axel's growl, I rose to my feet. The pup was dragging something across the rugged floor with all his might.

Oh my god.

I bit back laughter and sat again.

"What's he got?" Bailey asked.

A weakness for curiosity. "My saxophone."

He stopped for three breaks before reaching me. He flopped over the case, panting hard.

"Axel," I said solemnly. "That doesn't belong to you."

Did he drag it from the bungalow? Lifting up the case, I studied the underside. Caked in dirt.

Yes.

Yes, he did.

"Why did you bring it here?" I asked.

The pup whined.

"I can't understand you. Could you tell me another way?"

He growled.

"Axel, I can smell that you're frustrated, but don't growl at me. Just try another way."

The pup placed a paw on the case, and I obliged by opening it. I wish the other Luthers would start talking again.

He placed a paw on the mouthpiece.

I'd prefer that he use actual words, but he *had* figured another way to convey his meaning.

I relented. "You'd like me to play?"

Axel wagged his tail.

I exhaled. "That's not easy for me to do, big pup."

He cocked an ear.

Cool. Looked like I was about to spill my guts to the pack. *Oh, well.* I couldn't feel any worse after the failed date with Sascha.

"I used to play for my mother because she loved the sound," I told the pup. "Then I found out she wasn't my mother. I don't know who to play for anymore, and I'm scared that playing will never feel the same again."

An edited version for a toddler. Even looking at the brass instrument was a punch to the gut. Once, music offered me an escape.

Now, I was a daughter who wanted a mother.

Axel licked my leg. He felt terrible on my behalf.

"Thank you."

The others weren't concealing their eavesdropping one bit.

The pup nudged the instrument toward me.

A denial halted on the tip of my tongue, but I swallowed it back. "That's a very hard thing you're asking me to do, Axel. Do you understand how scared I am?"

My heart squeezed as he took a moment before nodding again.

With trembling fingers, I freed the instrument. "Sometimes, we must do frightening things even when we don't wish to. I'll play for you because I want you to know that some hard things are worth doing."

Grabbing a reed, I shoved it in my mouth, my every movement observed by the nervous pup.

Fixing the reed in place, I settled my fingers on the keys.

I'd avoided playing for so long.

I didn't want to do this. But on this occasion, I had a reason to play.

Taking a breath, I drew in my mouth around the mouthpiece, and the first notes of "Gravity" by John Mayer soared from the bell.

Years of practice made me loosen my throat to create a richer sound. I moved into the piece like it was the first time I'd ever played.

In some ways, it was.

Instead of going to my forest, I focused on the pup before me.

I moved into the guitar solo, which transcribed so well to saxophone, and added some extra embellishments. Nothing too much. This song was beautiful in its simplicity.

Building in a slow crescendo so reminiscent of John Mayer's soft rock blues. Softening for the final bars, I stuck to a simple harmony of the melody, repeating it until I drew the song to a close.

Lowering the saxophone, I smiled. "Thank you for helping me, Axel."

He wasn't as exuberant as I'd expected.

The pup whined and sank to the ground. My eyes widened at a loud *crack.*

I covered my mouth.

Pop.

He was shifting.

Murmurs broke out.

"*Quiet,*" I said sharply. "Let him concentrate."

To my surprise, they obeyed.

Crack. Pop.

Heart in my mouth, I took in the naked, dark-haired boy sitting beside me.

He pointed at the instrument. “Me?”

My chest filled. “Of course, brave boy.”

I helped him grip the instrument. “Kara, please bring Jemma and Credence here without delay.” I moved Axel’s chubby fingers. “Try it like this.”

Glancing up on autopilot, I met Sascha’s honey eyes across the room. My lips lifted in an automatic smile.

Sascha’s face hardened, and he left the bungalow as suddenly as he’d arrived.

Our afternoon rushed back to me. Right. For a second there, I’d forgotten. But surely Axel’s shift made Sascha as ecstatic as everyone else.

Evelyn was watching me. “Is everything okay?”

I adjusted the saxophone in the boy’s eager hands. “I’m not sure why he left like that.”

She lowered her gaze to the happy and wriggling toddler on my lap. “I’d say it has rather a lot to do with the image you’re presenting, dear. Sometimes, when people are hurting, they decide to hurt themselves a little more.”

8

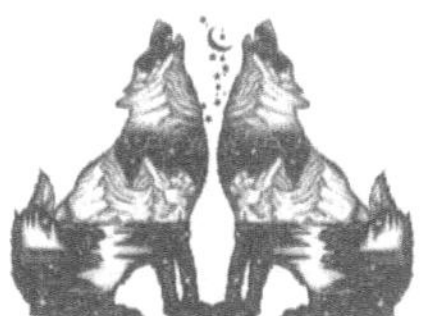

I guided Ella F into the parking spot outside Sascha's bungalow.

Just after 6:00 a.m.

The pack either won or lost in Timber last night. If they'd won, four grids were in their possession and the tribe was on the cusp of exile. If they'd lost, Sascha knew I'd given information to Rhona.

Neither was a result I wanted to face.

Sascha was inside. I had to go inside, too, but after our last conversation, that didn't seem simple.

The bungalow door swung open.

Sascha stood there, fully dressed.

I got out of the car. "I couldn't stick around last night."

"So I assumed."

His calm tone didn't mesh with his bitter scent. Did the pack lose? My hope surged even as my stomach twisted.

Sascha gestured inside, and I took the hint.

Sitting on the bed, I steeled myself. "What happened?"

He walked past to the wicker furniture. "We turned over another grid."

The pack *won* Timber. Sickening fear coursed through me.

"No congratulations?"

I struggled to speak through my reaction. "Did you expect it?"

The tribe only had Iron left.

Dammit, Rhona. She'd ignored my advice again.

"No. But you can tell me how you figured out our strategy to pass on to the Ni Tiaki. We should have steamrolled them, but barely scraped the win."

He knew.

My stomach dropped. "The information was freely offered to me by a pack member. You were well aware of what I'd do with anything that came my way."

A growl entered his voice. "Who gave you the information?"

"A man who smells old and likes to fish."

"No name?" he asked sarcastically.

"I imagine he kept it to himself on purpose."

Sascha drew a hand over his face. "My mate betrayed my pack."

"Why is this a surprise to you? I made it clear where my allegiance was. You said that you understood. I wasn't about to cast the information aside when the wolf forced it down my throat."

He shoved the wicker chair back, rounding on me. "That's when I thought all you needed was time to become part of this pack!"

My breath came fast.

"That's not the case, is it, Andie?" he asked softly. "Time isn't changing a thing."

"I hoped it would," I answered when my tongue unlocked. "But—"

"What about the kissing meet? Did that mean anything to you?"

My chest rose. "You *know* that meant something."

"Then why?" Emotion choked him "If this means something, tell me why it can't continue."

A lump cloyed my throat. I raised my hands. "You're misunderstanding. Just because I'm loyal to the tribe, doesn't mean my feelings for you are less or that they'll diminish."

He closed the gap to grip my upper arms.

I peered into his face and encountered stone-cold fury.

Sascha breathed. "I want to be patient and strong, but I need a sign. What do you feel for me, beautiful wolf? Because I love you."

The words jammed in my throat.

"What do you feel?" he snarled.

I closed my eyes. "Please don't ask me that." *Not yet.*

They weren't words to say when we both felt like this.

"*Tell me.*"

"Son." Evelyn walked into the room.

Sascha didn't break from his intense focus.

She walked farther into the room. "As second-ranking female in this pack, I'm stepping in. Each of you will judge the other's worth after the seventh meet. Not before. If you've already divulged your feelings, Sascha, then that was your choice. She doesn't need to reciprocate, and you have no right to demand answers of her."

The tension drained from my body in tandem with the tumultuous edge to his fierce eyes.

His hands fell away as I stepped back.

Evelyn beckoned to me. "Come away now, dear."

I took her offered hand, glancing back at his silent form. "I'm sorry, Sascha."

Evelyn guided me from the bungalow, saying nothing as I wiped my eyes.

What should I say to her? *Thank you* seemed tactless. Sascha was her son. She'd only intervened as the second-ranking female.

"Why did you do that?" I croaked.

"It's our way. Females stick together. Males stick together. The two halves balance each other."

I inhaled her anxiety. There was more she wanted to say. I studied the white of her lips from where she pressed them together.

Her son's immortality was in my hands.

I lowered my voice. "Don't worry, Evelyn. Sascha is afraid. I know that."

He believed he was losing me, but nothing could be further from the truth. All of my problems were *because* my feelings for him were undeniable.

We approached another bungalow, and Evelyn opened the door. "You can stay here for now."

At Sascha's parents' house?

"Would you prefer to sleep in your car again?" she asked after inhaling. "You're still forbidden from tribal lands."

I hadn't slept overnight, but I wasn't eager for a repeat. "Thanks."

"What's she doing here?" a familiar voice asked.

Fisherwolf sat in an armchair in the sitting room.

Mothershitter. Sascha's dad—should've seen that coming from a mile away.

"*She* was invited to stay here," I replied. "But she's leaving."

"I didn't force you to give pack information to the Ni Tiaki." The fisherwolf said the tribe's name like a curse word.

"No. You did give me information behind your son's back."

"He couldn't test you himself."

"Because he'd already acknowledged I'd fail it. You could have lost the game for the pack tonight. I hope conducting your little test helps you sleep at night."

The old wolf spat, "Once a Ni Tiaki, always a Ni Tiaki. Your kind are poison and a plague."

His scent burst out. I breathed in the river water smell that Sascha also possessed. No wonder fisherwolf tucked it away. I would have connected the dots immediately.

My lips curved. "So you're just another interfering pack member. Not a delta, are you?"

"I'm an alpha who led this pack for two and a half centuries."

"Really well from what I heard."

His brown eyes glittered.

I rubbed my forehead and looked at Evelyn. "I'm going to head out and—"

"You'll do exactly what I tell you," she replied.

Amusement curled in the air.

The female Luther rounded on her mate, snapping, "So will you, Alexei. Do not push me on this."

That wiped his smile away. I didn't dare smirk in triumph.

She patted my arm. "Come with me, dear. There's a spare bedroom that you are *absolutely* welcome to."

What would I do there? Sit and stare at the wall? "I'll take you up on the offer, but I'm heading out for a run first."

I couldn't be within four walls.

Her expression softened. "You know where we are."

Alexei scowled as I left the bungalow.

Most Luthers were already awake and gathering at the pack house. *Ugh,* there was no way they missed the shouting match earlier. Sascha was in there simmering in fury.

I inhaled the pack's upset and anxiety.

Their discomfort didn't sit right with me. I wanted them to be happy. And that wasn't just to do with my bond with Sascha anymore.

I didn't want another showdown with Sascha. We both needed to cool off before sitting down to properly talk.

"*Psst.*"

It was the teen girl I gave stealing advice to.

She ran from the cover of the pack house and held out a bacon sandwich. "Here."

Uhm. That hit me directly in the feels. "Thank you...?"

"Essie." She cast a furtive look at the building and winked, running off.

I bit into the sandwich and continued walking. A soft shout stopped me. Jemma hurried down the bungalow steps, doing her best not to slosh the contents of a mug.

"Andie. Kara said you like Earl Grey in the morning?"

She passed over the steaming mug, and I stared at the tea. "Thanks."

Axel's mother patted my shoulder and returned to the pack house.

What was happening?

Sitting under a tree, I polished off the bacon sandwich and sipped at the Earl Grey tea.

Booker, I have no idea what to do. I blew out a breath.

In the conversation with Sascha, I'd broached my single idea. That attempt resulted in this gigantic mess. I was afraid to push the concept of a compromise with the tribe in case things deteriorated further between us.

You could approach the tribe, she said.

Rhona declared me dead.

She's just one person.

The leader.

One who has lost twice. The tribe hang on by one grid.

True. If there was ever a time to negotiate an end to my exile, it was now. I'd tossed the idea around when I first realised the outcome of Grids had to change, but... *I can't do that to Rhona.*

She did it to you.

And I didn't believe in throwing a punch just because someone punched me.

Bailey and Lisa approached with Rosalie—the woman who'd protested about my lack of pack contribution.

"Some of us are heading out for a swim before our Dens shift. Want to join?"

Something was afoot. "Okay, why is everyone being so nice today?"

Bailey smirked. "You want us to be mean?"

Well. No. "It doesn't make sense."

No one on pack lands missed the throwdown between Sascha and me *or* between me and Alexei. Which meant they knew I'd blurted pack strategy to the tribe and that I'd failed to reassure Sascha.

Rosalie shrugged a shoulder. "You've proven yourself."

When?

"Axel," Lisa whispered. "Amongst other things."

Oh... Were all female Luthers on the same page? I wouldn't hold my breath about Mandy, but everyone else?

A ferocious protectiveness surged in me unlike anything I'd experienced. The force was so strong it robbed me of speech.

Lisa inhaled. "Humans. A van of them."

"What?" I stood, dusting my jeans off.

Bailey shot me a look. "You know these guys?"

I focused on the approaching vehicle. "It's a tribe vehicle."

Stanley was driving.

"What's the head team doing here?" Lisa edged closer to me.

I rested a hand on her shoulder. "I have no idea, but they're not here to hurt anyone." They smelled nervous, if anything. "I assume they're here to speak with me, so I'll skip the swim today—but thanks for the invite. I appreciate it."

The pack females had made me feel so much better with their small acts of kindness. They'd decided to treat me as one of their own. That blew my mind.

Bailey's shoulders tensed. "You're sure you don't need us here?"

"I'm sure."

I strode into the middle of the road and the van rolled to a stop. The head team looked at me.

Pascal opened the passenger door, rousing the others to do the same.

I scanned the occupants for Rhona. She was absent.

The others lined up before me.

"To what do I owe the honour?" I asked.

Pascal broke their terse silence. "Andie. We've tried to call you. Wade too."

"My phone has been off since last night. Has something happened to Rhona? Is she alright?"

Roderick hesitated. "We believe so.'

"What do you mean?"

Stanley's jaw clenched tight. "She and Foley disappeared after Victratum last night. Foley called Billy. They're in Bluff City."

She did *what*?

"What happened?" I pressed.

Rhona wouldn't leave the tribe like that.

"She disappeared after the grid. Foley said she isn't coming back," Trixie said heavily.

"That's impossible." I shook my head. "She wouldn't do that."

Pascal stepped closer. "The Ni Tiaki can't wait for her to come back. She could be gone days, weeks, or years. We came today to ask that you return to the tribe and lead us once more."

Holy shit, Booker muttered.

This was the second impossible thing to happen today.

This was *more* impossible than the pack females accepting me.

"You're kidding me." I met the gaze of each in turn. "You've lost your damn minds."

At the back, Nathan silently agreed with me.

I recovered some brainpower. "The tribe will never accept me back."

"The head team called a tribe vote this morning." Pascal raised her ever-present tablet. "Before the vote, your recent actions were brought to everyone's attention."

I waved a hand. "You can speak openly. The pack is aware of what I've told you."

Her eyes widened, but she passed over the tablet. "Here are the results of that vote."

A huge 79 percent were in favour of my return.

No fucking way.

This can't be true, I said to Booker.

The sister's supporters weren't numerous, she answered.

But... "They know what I am now and what happened with Herc. They know what's happening with Sascha too." I didn't believe these results whatsoever.

"You should know," Pascal grimaced, "that in order to elect a leader outside of the Thana family, we would need to renegotiate the contractual terms of Victratum with the pack."

Ah. That made far more sense. "Is the pack obliged to renegotiate terms?"

"No."

The results of the vote reflected the tribe's desire to win. That was stronger than their hate for me apparently.

If Sascha refused to renegotiate the game contract, and I refused the mantle of head stewardship, the pack could *win*.

Grids could end in days.

I had to speak with Sascha. We *had* to figure this out.

Until then, I'd keep our options open. "The stewards won't benefit from a leader they neither trust nor like."

Stanley cut me off. "Your track record speaks for itself."

"You'd like me to resume head stewardship like nothing happened?"

Roderick answered, "What we heard that day was a shock. To top off the mating call and the details of Herc's death, you transformed into a wolf. Even those of us who'd spent ample time in your company were speechless for days. Don't assume that stewards hate you for what happened or what you are. Personally, I feel like I let you down."

I folded my arms. "Why?"

"You were thrown into this game, something you barely knew, at twenty-one. If you didn't come to us about Herc and the rest, it's because you didn't trust us to support and guide you. For that, I believe the head team and tribe have a lot to answer for. We could have used what happened to our advantage far earlier if you'd felt safe to approach us."

I released a pent-up breath. "I screwed up too. I let fear get the better of me and handled things badly."

He crooked a smile. "Is there a good way to handle what you went through?"

Perhaps not, but if a re-do was possible, I'd change a few things.

"What do you say?" Pascal took her tablet back.

My heart hammered at the possibilities, but I had to stall for now.

I mean, what if I did say yes? The pack took me in when the tribe cast me aside—or at least did nothing to stop Rhona. They'd been shocked and confused, yes, but I was left alone and hurting during that time.

Sascha was there when they weren't.

He'd always been there for me.

This is our chance, I hushed to my wolf.

This was how the pack and tribe could have a future and how Sascha and I could have a happy future too. For the first time in weeks, I burned with conviction.

We had a direction.

I had a goal.

I saw the move Sascha and I had to make to end Victratum for good. Allowing the pack to believe I'd abandoned them wouldn't be easy, but to protect them and secure their place in the valley alongside the tribe, I'd do it one hundred times over.

Sascha's scent rose over the other listening pack members. His four scents had congealed. He'd put himself on the line for me time and again, and our argument had pushed him to the limit. It was my turn to put myself on the line for the life we could share.

First on the agenda—buy some time.

Then I had to re-open the uncomfortable conversation with Sascha. We could work together and finish this.

I regarded the head team. "I have conditions that you'll need to meet. One of them is that if my sister returns to Deception Valley, she won't return to head stewardship. Her actions have proved to me that she is not the best leader for the Ni Tiaki."

Finally, Booker muttered.

"We wholeheartedly agree," Trixie muttered under her breath.

"Another condition," I watched them closely, "is that full allowance is made for my Luther nature."

"What allowances?" Nathan piped up. "The tribe won't like that."

"They'll like it less when I die from failing to shift as I nearly have in the past. That's non-negotiable. I won't conceal who I am for the tribe's comfort."

Stanley pursed his lips. "You're underestimating the resistance you'll face in that quarter."

"Then I can't return. I recommend you return to tribe lands and hold another vote on the issue beforehand." That vote could bite me in the ass, but the tribe were backed into a corner well and truly.

Pascal's lips curved. "Perhaps seeing Andie as a wolf will have the opposite effect to what we expect. Perhaps it will improve relations between the pack and our tribe."

The others didn't seem convinced.

"Those in favour?" Nathan asked.

Everyone lifted their hands.

Roderick lowered his. "Anything else?"

Just one more condition. "There will be an end to extreme violence against Luthers. I don't stand for it, and neither will the tribe under my leadership. I'll step down at any sign of foul play. Without notice."

The head team started to raise their arms.

"No need to vote. That was me telling you," I informed them.

Trixie's breath caught. "Is that a yes?"

Sascha moved for the first time since the head team arrived. I hoped he wasn't about to destroy my groundwork.

Mind-speak in two-legged form would be super convenient right about now.

Glancing over my shoulder, I watched as he stormed from the pack house toward the forest. My ears picked up the *cracks* and *pops* of his shift. The elastic sensation under my ribs tightened painfully as he sprinted away at full speed.

"Get back to me with the vote outcome. Pending a favourable result, I'm happy to talk more."

Greyson's mournful howl echoed to me from deep in the trees.

9

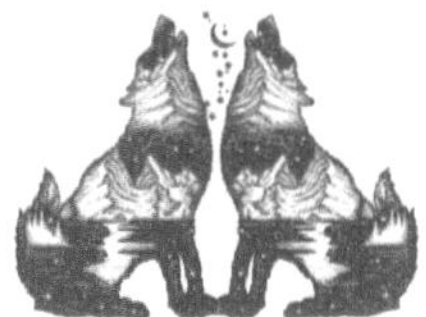

I watched the first rays of light stream in. Sascha's bed lay cold and empty at my back, the blanket smooth, aside from the wrinkles where I'd caught a few hours of fitful sleep.

He hadn't returned.

In the early hours this morning, I'd shifted to speak to him.

He'd slammed the door on that.

I tried running to him afterward, but he was so far away—right on the eastern outskirts of the valley.

Our connection had never felt so tight.

Opening my phone, I stared at the screenshot from Pascal that I received halfway during my *Dens* shift last night.

The tribe voted in favour of my second condition. Well, 64 percent anyway.

I was officially head steward again—or could be.

He's not coming back, Booker growled.

She was majorly pissed.

I was just devastated.

This was a huge misunderstanding, but there wasn't time for Sascha to pull this move. The possibility of Rhona returning from

Bluff City had occurred to me after the head team left. Refusing the position to allow the pack to win wasn't an infallible plan.

The head steward offer could disappear before Grids next week.

It could disappear in mere hours.

Booker. I think we need to do this the hard way. Tears trekked over my cheeks.

We sure do.

I sniffed. *You're in? But you hate human politics.*

For you and reproduction, I'll partake.

I wiped my face. *Thanks, girl.*

Let's go eat some hearts.

I chose to interpret that metaphorically. Dragging out the moment, I peered around the bungalow for anything I might have missed, then started lugging my bags out to Ella F.

One day, I'd unpack them in Sascha's wardrobe.

That was my goal now.

Ironically, to achieve that, I had to take a huge step away from him.

I grabbed my phone and keys and walked to the pack house. Members of the pack roused an hour ago, and the bungalow was steadily filling. Their discomfort had ramped overnight with Sascha's absence—and no doubt wondering what my decision would be.

I ignored the male Luthers, my attention on the females.

Nodding at a sombre Evelyn, I faced the half of the pack who'd somehow accepted me in the short time I'd been here.

I'd accepted them too.

"Your attention, please," I said softly.

The males shut up, too—whoever decided that men didn't like to gossip were absolutely wrong.

My gaze wandered over Jemma and Axel—still in his boy form, then to my bacon-sandwich thief, Essie.

Rosalie, Bailey, Kara.

Emily.

They'd think I was letting them down, and their opinions meant something to me. I wanted them to look up to me.

"During my absence, I want to make it clear that Evelyn is in charge. Is anyone opposed?" I asked them.

Kara tilted her chin. "Your absence?"

In answer, I unleashed the uncertainty and hope and determination filling my every thought for them to scent out. I wasn't joking when I told Booker this was the hard way. "If there are any issues, you're all welcome to reach out at any time. I'll leave my phone number with Evelyn to distribute."

There was more I wanted to say.

Promises I wanted to make.

I nodded at them and walked back to the entrance.

A huge form blocked my path.

"What do you want, old wolf?" I growled.

Gasps rang out.

"If your game is what I assume, then it's a very dangerous one," Alexei said low.

I'd never seen him in here before. Though with hundreds of Luthers around at all times, and the ability to conceal his scent, hiding in plain sight wouldn't be hard. "You're good at making assumptions, Alexei. I won't take them from you. I hope your other fish are in a biting mood today."

Stepping around him, I continued on.

"Young wolves should listen to the wisdom of their elders," he called at my back.

Not when those elders were in denial of their failures. The one thing I'd said to Alexei that truly affected him was my criticism of his success as pack leader. He'd wrapped himself in haunting memories and was marinating in regret and self-loathing.

I left the pack house.

Shoving my keys into Ella F, I stopped to feel for Sascha one last time.

Please come back.

I tugged on the bond and waited with bated breath, but he didn't budge. If he heard my silent call, he didn't respond.

Drawing out my phone, I typed.

Sascha, we can win this together.
I'm not leaving you. I'm trying to make this work.
Call me as soon as possible.
Your Andie

Pocketing the phone, I looked up to find Mandy watching me from the pack house.

She crossed her arms. "Run along, traitor."

"My offer extends to you, too, Mandy." The delta only hurt this much because she cared about Sascha and the pack. "If you need me, I'm a call away."

She scoffed, and I didn't stick around for her caustic response.

I left pack lands.

And left part of myself behind in the doing.

Ugly guilt and sadness churned deep inside, but as I made the drive to the manor, resolve swept those hesitations into the dustbin where they belonged. Slight nerves were overshadowed by an undeniable, endless determination.

Perhaps I lost respect for the game when Rhona used violence against the pack in Clay. But *Sascha* was worth fighting for. I'd play Victratum for him.

I stopped at the manor gates and was greeted by a beaming Cameron.

She leaned through the open window to hug me. "I'm so glad you're back. Welcome home." Cam stepped back and gave the red button a hearty slap. "Get the hell in there and head steward the shit out of us."

I obeyed.

The last time I was here, Wade was missing, and everything exploded in my face.

You did it, Booker said.

I killed the engine. *We did it. And there's far more to do before we can celebrate.*

The head team lined up on the manor stairs. Leaving my stuff for now, I climbed to meet them.

"Welcome back, Head Steward." Roderick bowed slightly.

I nodded. "Thank you."

A few of the regular manor staff had gathered too. I stopped at the top of the steps and faced everyone. "I'm calling an immediate meeting so I can get up to speed on tribe affairs. Pascal, please get in touch with Wade so he can join us."

"Join?" Nathan said.

"Yes. Wade has proved himself to me time and again, and he will be by my side if he chooses it."

The head team filed inside, and I nodded at the trainer, Gerry, Tip-toe Eleanor, *Ha!* Heather, and tree-hugger Jessi, who stood with around ten other stewards from the kitchens and grounds. "Thank you all for being here."

Gerry extended a hand. "I didn't give you a chance when I heard the rumours. Rhona had no right to treat you that way. I'm sorry, Andie."

I couldn't recall the trainer ever stringing so many words together. "Thank you for the chance now."

"Eleanor, is my usual room empty?"

She hesitated. "Yes, but there's some damage."

Let me guess. "Then Herc's old room will do."

I entered the manor.

It was time to eat some hearts.

I stopped at my office to check the contents of the desk. The surface was a mess of doodles and notes scribbled. After an attempt to decipher Rhona's musings, I swept the whole lot into the trash basket. The office was a mess, but the relevant information was in the drawers.

"Wade was called?" I asked, entering the meeting room.

The head team took their seats.

"He's on his way," Pascal replied.

Good. I took my seat. "Any word from Rhona?"

Nathan clenched his jaw. "From Foley. She's refusing to return."

If she stayed away until next Wednesday, I could still help the pack win Grids. "Did Foley say why?"

"Nothing. Just that she's partying in Bluff City and we need to move on without her."

Partying in a city owned by vampires. I couldn't do anything to help her if she was harmed.

Well, I did have one contact there. Maybe it was time to place a call.

"Is there anything else before we get started?" Stanley prompted.

"Yes." I peered across the table. "This new nose tells me many things. You don't like me, Nathan."

His colour deepened.

Whatever. I'd learned my lesson on confronting these things early on. "I'll tell you what I told Valerie. If I ever detect that your opinion is affecting your job, you'll be dropped from the head team without warning. We don't need to be friends to get the job done, and I can empathise with how you feel about my part in Herc's death, but I need the support of every person in this room. If you can't do that, you'll be reassigned."

I listened to his thumping heart as anger rose to the surface.

He tempered it. "I believe my best friend's death could have been avoided. I'm frustrated and upset about that, but I voted for you to return all the same. Herc may have misjudged you in some ways, but he didn't misjudge your ability to lead. I don't like you, but you won't encounter any opposition from me. Not in this room, and not behind closed doors. You're the best leader for this tribe, and the tribe is my life."

Truth. "Then we'll continue."

The door opened, and Wade entered, dressed in a three-piece suit.

"I have arrived." He took the empty seat on my right that Rhona once occupied.

I smiled at him. "That you have. Welcome to the head team." I addressed the others, "Not only is Wade on a first-name basis with the entire tribe, his advice has guided me on many occasions. This team is made up of the most discerning minds the Ni Tiaki has to offer, and that's exactly why, despite his youth, Wade is with us now. In time, I'd like to give him more responsibility with the stewards. Until that time, let's show him how we work."

The head team greeted him with varying levels of enthusiasm.

They'd see.

"Now." I leaned forward. "Please bring me up to speed."

Pascal cleared her throat. "After Rhona cast you out, things here were unsettled. Many disagreed with the violence of what she proposed."

I sat back. "When Sandstone was lost?"

"It got worse. Rhona... It became apparent to the head team that her choices had far less to do with helping the tribe than gratifying her personal issues. Tribe dissent grew vocal, fronted by a steward called Jessi Angel."

She was big on peace. That didn't surprise me.

Stanley took over. "Pascal brought your Timber tip to Rhona, saying she'd spoken to a supplier who'd mistakenly told her the contents of another order from Deception Valley. One for a huge amount of climbing materials."

I'd wondered how she convinced Rhona about that. "Smart."

"We thought up a counter-strategy, but as you know, we lost that grid too."

"What's the current feeling?"

Wade answered, "The stewards were more hostile than we'd seen them since Herc's death, but no one expected Rhona to leave. When they heard the news... you can imagine how betrayed they felt. Three groups have formed. One is peaceful and led by our tree-hugging friend. Another pities you but believes you should be held accountable for what happened to Herc. The third hate your guts. The vast majority of the tribe are undecided."

Okay. "How evenly do you believe the groups are split?"

"The middle group is the largest."

I tapped a finger on the table. "I can't work with the hate group, but I can drown them out with enough numbers." *And a few threats.*

"If I can make a suggestion?" Trixie said. "None of the tribe have heard your side. An explanation could go a long way."

I'd had the same thought at 5:00 a.m. when it became clear Sascha wouldn't return. "Please call a gathering for tomorrow night. The tribe deserves an explanation, and I deserve the chance to tell them what really happened." I exhaled. "Moving on. We know the pack will pick Iron next. This is the closest the pack has ever been to winning. Sascha will throw everything he has at us. Every resource he can spare. Every weapon."

Before I could lose to the pack, I had to negotiate a truce with Sascha.

Until we spoke, I had to assume losing to the pack wasn't an option.

Victratum had existed for more than two centuries.

But I had to win it.

10

I clicked Send.

And waited.

Sascha hadn't replied to my last message, which truly surprised me. I'd thought he'd come to the table once he understood the method behind my madness.

"Come on," I muttered.

I read over my carefully constructed text again.

We need to talk.
I'm doing this for us, I swear.
Just give me the chance to explain how this will fix everything.

I waited for the message to show the usual delivered status. It didn't.

Huh. Reception was fine.

I typed another text.

I wanted you to hear it from me.
The tribe asked me to resume head stewardship, and I accepted.
As head steward, I want you to know that you're always welcome here.

Come home, Rhona.
Love, Andie.

I really did want her back and safe, but if she knew the head steward job was taken, she may extend her Bluff City visit by a few days too—which could make all the difference.

Clicking Send, I watched the space under the message.

Delivered.

I checked my message to Sascha again, but the delivery status still hadn't changed. His phone battery must be dead.

Exhaling, I drew out my laptop and logged into the student portal. One good thing about two weeks on pack lands? I'd sent off my previous assignment and completed another. I only had one more for the semester. If I could scrap a pass on that, this degree would be over.

Adding a bibliography to the end of the current assignment, I submitted it for better or worse. Then I settled in to watch a lecture on the strategic management of human resources. How fitting. In an hour, I'd address the tribe.

Three months ago, I'd been so nervous they wouldn't accept me. Now, I just wanted to know if they'd accept me so I could get on with the job.

The lecture ended, and I shoved my laptop and half-ass notes in my bag.

Grr, the delivery status still hadn't changed. Sascha would have plugged his phone by now—too many people relied on communication with him throughout the day.

I resent the message.

No change.

Bracing myself, I dialled his number. My insides flipped, and I shoved back from the desk to pace by the window.

"Sascha Greyson—"

I smiled widely. "Thanks for picking up."

"—Leave a message."

Beep.

I hung up. "Fuck."

Maybe his phone really was dead. Was I freaking out over nothing?

Dialling Wade, I listened to the ring tone.

"Baby girl?"

"Hey. Could you block my number for ten minutes?"

"Thought you'd never ask." He ended the call.

I waited a minute and then texted.

I'm very attracted to you.

There was no way Wade could resist answering that.

I studied my phone.

The *delivered* notification didn't appear beneath the message.

My jaw dropped. "He didn't."

I dialled Wade again. The call went straight to voicemail.

He did.

Sascha blocked my number.

"What the fuck?" I whispered. It wasn't anything I hadn't done to him in the past, but this wasn't his style. *Jesus.* He must be hurting bad.

More to the point, if he refused to speak with me, this really complicated my plans for Grids.

We have a plan B, Booker said.

Yeah. I know. I had to forge on. The moment Sascha and Greyson cooperated, I could abandon the far more complicated back-up plan.

Speaking of...

I listened to the first sounds of the crowd gathering outside, then checked my phone display. Still time for another call.

Opening the importer details folder, I scanned the list of names, stopping at L.

I plugged in the number and listened to the phone ring.

"Good evening, this is Mrs Le Spyre's phone. You're speaking with Evie."

"Evie, hey. This is Andie Thana, CEO of Deception Valley Exports. I was hoping to speak with Basilia."

"Mrs Le Spyre is out for the evening," the cheerful young woman said. "If you'd like to leave a message, I'll make sure that reaches her when she's back in the office."

Drat. "Okay, please tell her that I'm ready for the chat she offered."

The young woman paused. "Can I get your number, please?"

I recited my details and ended the phone call.

Knock, knock.

Eleanor poked her head in. "Andie. Everyone is here."

I slid my phone away. "Thank you."

Showtime.

Walking out of the manor, I inhaled the mix of curiosity, sympathy, and anger rising from the stewards. I greeted them on my way to the stage.

Nodding at the head team who formed part of the front row, I exchanged a look with Wade, then walked up the steps to the microphone.

I gazed out at the *Ni Tiaki*. "I haven't called this special gathering to celebrate my return. I've called this gathering because I, along with the head team, believe that you deserve to hear an accurate retelling of the events in my life that led to me becoming a Luther. My personal life is my own, but where it affects this tribe, I will be transparent."

Their combined scents cloyed, and I couldn't help wondering if humans subconsciously reacted to other scents though they didn't have the sensitivity of smell to identify them.

"I will tell you about my interactions with Sascha Greyson. I will tell you how Herc came to die. I'll tell you everything I've learned about Herc, about the woman I believed to be my mother, and about the man she loved, Murphy." My gaze landed on the Freys who occupied a section of the front row. They'd given me permission to share Murphy's past with the tribe tonight.

The stewards whispered.

Yep, they'd hear far more than they'd bargained for.

"First." I gripped the mic. "The Thana family has let this tribe down recently. Both myself and Rhona. With my heightened senses, I can smell that some of you don't know what to feel and that some pity what I've become. I can smell those of you who are angry and those of you who hate me." I let my eyes linger on a few.

The whispers swelled.

They didn't like that. No wonder. When Sascha mentioned cataloguing my scents, I'd shied away too. Realising we were open books was an uncomfortable feeling—but I'd meant what I said about refusing to conceal my nature.

I continued. "I mention my senses because, for a long time, we've guessed and theorised many things about the pack. Perhaps you voted me back in because you need me, but I will use my new knowledge of Luthers to help the tribe win Victratum."

A slight hope tinged the air.

I freed the microphone. "In saying that, you need to understand there are things I must do as a Luther. You'll often see me in wolf form. I'm the only red wolf in this area, and that's how you'll know it's me. You may hear me howl sometimes. You may see my fangs and claws or a change in the colour of my eyes. Sometimes, my voice sounds rough and uneven. While these changes scared me greatly at first, the abilities I've gained have only strengthened my connection to this beautiful land." I scanned the silent mass of stewards. "Seeing a wolf can be a confronting thing. Many of you fear or revile what I am. To be absolutely clear, that's your opinion to hold in silence. Any open sign of it will result in me relinquishing the title of Head Steward and walking away. Your acceptance of my new nature is an *absolute* condition of my presence here. So to the forty-three stewards here who'd like nothing better than to see me hang, realign your priorities and place the wellbeing of this tribe where it should be—at the top. That's not a suggestion."

At the start, the stewards didn't know what to think. Now they *really* didn't know what to think.

"Now, I'd like to take you back to the week after Ragna died. To the moment I uncovered her first lie, which led me here to where it all began."

I walked to the training pavilion beside Wade.

Dawn trainings were an important social gathering that I'd neglected during my first stint as head steward. Gerry was on board with me again, and Rhona wasn't here, but if my haters saw this as a rallying ground, I needed to stomp out their efforts without delay.

"How do you think the talk went?" I asked.

Wade hummed. "You gave everyone a lot to think about. Like, a *lot*. They'll need time. It may be worth keeping your door open for a few weeks. Put out a question box like teachers used in puberty class." He pitched his voice high. "*How do I use tampons?*"

Grinning, I shook my head. "Good idea. You're in charge. Set things up and send a message through our text service about it."

"Cool. But do you know what I've been really, really super patient about?"

"Saving a house deposit?"

"What? No. Waiting to ask about you and Sascha! What the hell is happening? You're here. The whole feeding us information while on pack lands too. He must have lost his shit. *You're here*."

"You said that one already."

"Tell me everything."

"I'll schedule time. How's next week?"

"You wouldn't dare."

I laughed. "Where do you want me to start?"

"Well, what was the dynamic on pack lands?" He knew some stuff from texts we'd exchanged.

"So, I don't even know when this came on, but I feel responsible for the women and children in the pack now."

His eyes rounded. "For real? Then why come back?"

“I realised that only one solution results in happiness for the tribe, pack, and me and Sascha.”

“Oh, shit. What solution? Because there’s only one way the tribe will accept.”

Tell me about it. “Both sides need to enter a truce. I haven’t figured out the specifics.”

Plan B was harder for a reason.

Wade didn’t answer.

I lifted a shoulder. “Sascha accepted that I couldn’t choose between the tribe and us, but then—”

“Hold the fuck on. I’m processing the massive bomb you dropped.”

Oh. I waited.

He nodded a few times. “Cool, got it. Carry on.”

“I told Sascha early on that I’d help the tribe no matter what. He told me anything else would have surprised him and seemed super accepting. Except when he found out I’d actually done it...”

Wade sucked in a breath. “His muscles leaped in protest.”

“What?”

“That man is damn attractive.”

I sighed. “Agreed.”

And I missed him.

We lingered outside the pavilion, well apart from the others. “After that, Sascha put up a thousand walls. I didn’t know what to do. Then Rhona ran off. The tribe wanted me back. Sascha shifted and didn’t return before I left. I’ve tried calling and texting, but he’s blocked my number.”

“He did *what*?”

I lowered my voice. “I get that he needs time. But I need him to work with me. Like, *right now*.”

“Dang, baby girl. That’s intense. What next?”

“If he won’t come to the table for a truce before next Wednesday, I can’t purposely lose to the pack.”

Wade held up a finger.

I waited again.

He took longer to nod this time. "Continue."

"In that case, I'll need to win the game to have more control over the end result. Before then, I need to figure out a way to pull the pack and tribe together for good."

Wade blew out a breath. "Fuck me. Is that all?"

"Pretty much." I had a few ideas on the cards, but that was the extent of my current dilemma.

He darted a look at me. "And you're doing all this for Sascha?"

"For everyone."

"But mostly for Sascha."

"You're gonna make me say it?"

"Speak the hard words, bitchhole."

"I'm doing this for Sascha."

Wade's lips curved. "I'm so on board. Maybe I should care more about the centuries-old fight, but you've inspired me to stretch my horizons. What's the first step in Mission Get Dick?"

I grimaced. "Let's change the name for starters, and secondly... what do you know about the Deception Valley Council?"

"Mum's on the council."

"No shit?"

"Yep. There are five members from the tribe on it, and four representatives from the blissfully ignorant public. Obviously, if we really want a certain outcome, the tribe has the majority vote. The council manages the wellbeing of the region—roads and stuff. They have plans."

I arched a brow. "That you clearly pay attention to."

"Pretty sure they submit a report to you every so often. I pretend to listen to Mum talk about it sometimes."

I needed to get my hands on the latest report. "Do you know when the council meets?"

"Every six weeks... maybe? Don't ask me when the next one is."

Gerry's shrill whistle made me jump.

Stewards piled into the pavilions, and we walked up the steps of the closest one to stand at the front.

"Will your mum be okay with me calling her?"

Wade glared at the hoops and cones set out. "You mean because you turn into a werewolf?"

The stewards behind us quietened.

His mum was on my side before, but so much had changed. "Yep."

"Anyone who doesn't trust you because of what you can do now is a fucking idiot," he answered.

Gerry blew his whistle again.

"That's really not nice." I rubbed my throbbing, sensitive ears.

"*Look at her standing there like she's one of us.*"

I smiled.

My first volunteer.

Gerry outlined the training session and instructed us to get into pairs.

Wade turned to me, but I shook my head. "I'm partnering up with my friend over in the back corner."

He followed the jerk of my head and whistled. "Good luck. His name's Bob."

Bob the knob.

Weaving between stewards, I approached a large man somewhere in his forties. Like most of the tribe, he was toned and in great shape.

I tapped him on the shoulder.

His polite smile dropped to an intense scowl when he identified me.

"You're with me." Glancing at his hostile partner, I pointed to Wade at the front. "And you're with him."

My tone didn't exactly leave room for discussion.

When his friend left, I touched the tip of my finger to my earlobe. "Do you know what these ears allow me to do, Bob?"

He didn't drop his scowl.

"They allow me to hear very, very well. I can hear sounds from two kilometres away. So your little comment before, the one where you said *Look at her standing there like she's one of us...* you may as well have spoken in my ear."

We'd attracted the attention of the nearest stewards.

"*Bob*," one hissed. "Shut your damn mouth. You heard her last night."

I arched a brow. "Sounds like those comments may not make you too popular around these parts."

His expression said it all—*Fuck you.*

Ignoring him for now, I obeyed Gerry's shouts and worked through the warm-up.

Jesus, good thing I was a Luther, so I didn't look like a sloppy couch potato.

One thing Rhona always had going for her is that she looked the part of werewolf slayer. I'd skipped the years of dedication, but my muscles remained toned and strong without effort. I was more physically capable than any person in here without trying.

Win.

"Sparring in pairs," Gerry boomed.

I faced Bob.

We circled each other.

"You've got a lot of hate for Luthers," I murmured, watching his legs.

"They're animals."

"Humans are animals too."

He gritted his teeth. "We're here to spar, *Head Steward.*"

The guy sure made *Head Steward* sound like *Motherfucker*.

"Do normal wolves bother you?" I pressed.

"No," he ground out.

Truth. I fucking loved my nose. "Is it that Luthers have the abilities of a wolf on steroids *and* a human brain to use them with?"

Yes.

A definite yes.

I dropped my voice. "What if the werewolves decided to attack us? Even though we're training to fight them, we don't know if what we're doing will work. Would we even stand a chance?"

Fear saturated his anger, but he didn't show it. "You'll probably invite them in."

I met his flinted gaze. "You don't really think I'd do that. You know my stance on extreme violence. You're scared of what I am, Bob, as any animal is scared of their predator. But I'm here and ready to spar with you. Want to know how you'd stack up against a Luther? I'm attending dawn sessions from now on, so our tribe is more prepared in the future. You don't have to like me, but you'd be stupid not to take advantage of what I can offer."

The last part intrigued him.

Something other than fear and hate at last.

I crouched and swept my leg in a circle, dropping him like a sack of shit.

That felt pretty good.

I stepped back. "Don't give a Luther time to see you move. Attack immediately. You place more weight on your left than your right. I picked it up while we circled."

The red-faced Bob clambered up.

He distributed his weight evenly though.

"Attack and don't hold back. I heal fast."

He lunged, drawing back his fist. I avoided the first hit. The second connected with my torso, and I absorbed the impact. Sidestepping, I circled behind. He spun in a comical circle to follow and froze at the sight of my fist a hair's breadth from his face.

"Female Luthers are fast and agile. We're still stronger than you, particularly in wolf form, but your best bet is to corner us in a tight space to fight us. If you're facing a male Luther, open space is best. They're slower to turn and change direction and will use their far greater strength against you. That's why a steward needs to be quick on his feet *and* strong."

Bob nodded. "We should train somewhere more like where we'll really face Luthers then."

He thought I was handing him a guidebook on how to best take down a werewolf. The reality was that without weapons, the odds of a steward taking a Luther down were next to none.

Bob didn't need to know that.

Because without him realising, he was now working with a Luther.

I straightened. "That's an idea. I'll take it to Gerry."

Gerry's damn whistle blasted through the air, and I winced. "That is a hellish sound first thing in the morning."

Walking to Bob, I clasped his shoulder. "Look, no more of the snide comments. I'm a person. That shit hurts, especially when it's from people I'm doing my best to help."

Red tinged his jaw.

I scented his slight shame. "I'll see you tomorrow for sparring. If you're lucky, I'll get my claws out."

Such a treat.

Wade's sparring buddy sent me a scathing look when I joined them. The guy marched back to Bob without delay.

People had no idea how stupid they looked sometimes.

"How did that go?" Wade puffed as he jogged between cones.

I followed, enjoying the light strain in my muscles. "Well. Considering."

"So, look. There's this thing." His salted caramel scent took on an extra sweet edge.

"What do you want?"

"I'm a really good friend to you. I make sure to be a good friend because you're in a great position and have the power to grant me access to things I want."

My lips twitched. "Here I thought we were friends because of our mutual unattraction."

"How can your personality be so good, but the packaging so bad? It's like individually wrapping biodegradable coffee cups in unrecyclable plastic—just makes no sense."

I laughed. "Thanks. What do you want? Spit it out."

Wade yanked me behind a stack of dummies that I'd probably violated once or twice.

"Here's the thing. You mentioned the council. Well, there's this thing I've really, *really* wanted to do for the longest time. Stupid

Judy usually organises it, but you have no idea how dry and boring it is. The potential is huge, and it's not being achieved. You know?"

"I have no idea what you're talking about."

"The Annual Deception Valley Ball," he rushed.

Someone mentioned that a while back.

Wade took my hands. "Everyone comes—the pack too. This ball could be so much more, but—"

"Judy is stupid? Look, if Judy has organised it for years, she won't appreciate me tearing the job away."

Wade checked Gerry's back was turned. "If I can convince her?"

The pack came to this thing?

Part of plan B included desensitising the tribe to Luther presence. This ball could help my agenda. Plus, denying earnest Wade anything was impossible.

"If Judy is okay with giving up the reins, then you can do it."

"Yes!" Wade swept me into a hug. "You won't regret—"

A whistle blew from less than a metre away, leaving my ears ringing.

Gerry glowered at us. "Burpies. Fifty."

Ha! That was nothing.

He narrowed his eyes at my smile. "Three hundred for you."

I groaned. *Mothershitter.*

11

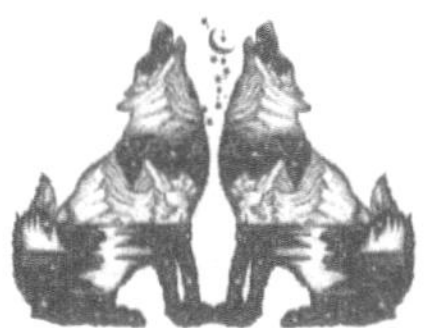

I called again.

"Sascha Greyson. Leave a message." *Beep.*

For at least the tenth time, I texted.

Help me understand what's going through your head.
I want a life with you, Sascha.

At least Victratum meant that Sascha and I were thrown together all the time. Tomorrow, he'd come to the manor to announce the pack's grid choice.

That felt so far away.

My phone rang.

Fumbling to answer, my heart sank when I saw the caller wasn't Sascha.

Private number.

"Hello, this is Andie," I answered.

"Don't sound so disappointed." The woman laughed.

My eyes widened. "Basilia?"

"The one and only.

"How are you?"

“Full of my mate’s blood and curious after your message. I hoped to hear from you again.”

I pulled a face. Blood? *Gross.* “I’ve had more time to wrap my head around supernatural beings. Your offer to talk stuck in my mind.”

Her footsteps were soft in the background. “It’s not easy to think you’re at the top of the food chain one day and then realise you’re nowhere near the top.”

There was that.

I closed my eyes. “I’ve been meaning to call, specifically, because I’m in the middle of a mating call. You mentioned that you were mated last time we spoke.”

Pascal was the only other person I’d spoken to about what was happening with Sascha, but she was so much older than me. I wanted to speak to someone my age.

“Shit, for reals? Is that what werewolves call it?”

“Yep. It’s intense.”

She blew out a breath, flopping down on what sounded like a couch or bed. “How intense? Vissimo drink from each other seven times, and there’s a three-day thrall after each blood exchange where they have big sex.”

“There are seven meets in ours too. The mating call follows a Luther’s senses to begin with. The pair scent each other, then meet each other’s eyes—”

“*Uhm,* romantic. That reminds me of a *Truth Ranges* episode.”

“You really like that show, huh?”

“Understatement. What else?”

I leaned back in the office chair. “They touch each other, then there’s a stalking thing called the capture meet. The last three are the kissing meet, then biting. Sex to finish. Each meet is followed by a heat that the woman can deny if she wants to. I don’t know much about how long it goes for.”

“Kinky. Probably a week.”

I snorted.

“You’ve denied the heat each time then?” she asked.

"At first. Now Sascha doesn't want us to have sex."

"Massive red flag. Get out of there, girl."

"He says I use sex as a weapon."

"And what's he doing with it? Hey, this wouldn't be Sascha Alarick Greyson, *the* pack leader?"

My brows climbed. "You've done your research."

"You took ages to call, so I did some digging. Rich people aren't good at waiting."

"I wouldn't know. I'm Poor with a capital P."

"Ah, that's probably why I like you." She held the phone away and shouted. "Tommy, she's poor like you."

"*Must be cool then*" came the feminine reply.

Was that a rule? "Friend of yours?"

"The best."

"They're important. Does she know you're Vissimo?"

Basilia sighed. "Yeah. It was rocky for a while, but I'm glad for it now. Will you become a werewolf with the mating call, or do you have a choice?"

I hadn't mentioned that yet? "I transformed into a Luther not long ago."

She was silent. "Well that puts a dampener on my plans to invite you to Bluff City to meet face to face."

I stilled.

Did she know I couldn't leave the valley?

"I'll need you to invite me out there," Basilia stated after a beat. "Vissimo are super anal about their territory. Julius will throw a tantrum about a werewolf on his turf."

"Who's Julius?"

"The king. My father-in-law."

My mouth bobbed. The *king*? "Does he rule the whole city?"

"Yeah. Our territory stops before Frankton Gorge."

From what I'd gathered, Frankton Gorge didn't belong to any supernatural race. "I had no idea you were part of the royal vampire family."

"I know, right. Billionaire and princess—so cliché. I'm mated to the king's eldest son, Kyros. He's super hot. And he'd be super angry if I entered werewolf territory without him... When he's angry, we have great make-up sex. Yes. *Yes*, this is a great idea. When do you want me there?"

Had I agreed to invite her?

Well, not only did I want to meet Basilia Le Spyre, but her connections could open other avenues I hadn't considered when first returning her call.

"Is next weekend too soon?" I asked.

"Tommy," she hollered. "Want to go for a road trip next weekend?"

"*Hells yeah!*"

"Tommy said hells yeah. We're in."

"The drive here is five hours—fair warning. But please don't worry about coming into werewolf territory. I'm head steward of the Ni Tiaki tribe who govern this land. I grant you formal protection from the moment you enter Deception Valley until you leave again. You won't be harmed by any pack or tribe member."

"Wait, so Sascha-No-Sex is the werewolf leader. What's this about a tribe?"

I sighed. "We're on opposite sides. Our people don't get on. At all."

Her tone sobered. "I see."

"Yeah. I'll give you a rundown over a lemon and raspberry gin cocktail next week?"

"Make it a strawberry mojito."

I laughed. "Deal."

"Good. I'll be there. Now, go get your growly man, wolf girl!"

She hung up, and I took a moment to process the whirlwind that was Basilia Le Spyre. Only a fool would take her eccentricity to mean she was stupid. It covered a sharp intellect.

Maybe I *should* go get my growly man.

I checked the time.

The Dens would be in full swing.

The last council report lay sealed on my desk and had comprised my Saturday night plans.

I glanced at my outfit. I'd partnered a square-neck black bandeau with tartan slacks. A black blazer toned the ensemble down to something bordering professional.

"Fuck it." I had to see Sascha now, especially with this new potential development.

Grabbing my car keys, I briefly stopped at my second-floor room to ditch the blazer and switch my white sneakers for red heels.

Jumping in Ella F, I selected an appropriate pump-up song. "Good as Hell" by Lizzo playing, I gunned the engine and drove toward town.

Ugh, Saturdays were hell for out-of-town traffic. I parked out near the petrol station and trekked toward the casino.

He was inside. I could feel him.

He'd feel me coming too.

Sascha was gonna listen to me tonight. Or else.

Striding to the front of the queue, I squared my shoulders.

Hairy turned towards me and his smile dropped. I waited as he finished stamping the hands of an elderly couple.

"Hairy, I need in."

The beta lowered his gaze, "Can't do that."

My eyes narrowed. "Why?"

"Sascha's orders."

My gut lurched. *Really?* He didn't want to see me that much?

Ouch.

Hairy flushed, and I grabbed his arm. "He's not returning my calls and texts. We have things to get done. I have to speak to him."

The beta pressed his lips together. I could smell his uncertainty.

"Sorry, Andie. I can't help you. It's not my decision to make."

Patrons called out behind me.

I rubbed my forehead. "Look, could you at least tell him to unblock my number if he doesn't want to meet outside of Victratum duties? This is serious."

Hairy frowned. “He really blocked your number? That doesn’t seem like Sascha.”

I crossed my arms.

He sighed. “I’ll pass it on. Listen, I’ve got to get these people inside.”

I swallowed. “Sure.”

“I really am sorry.”

So was I. I’d apparently pushed Sascha way too far. “Not your fault. Night, Hairy.”

“Night, gorgeous.”

My top wasn’t right.

“I’ve never seen someone change clothes so many times,” Wade whined from my bed.

Herc’s former room was the biggest in the manor. Traditionally, these quarters always belonged to the head steward. With a fresh duvet cover and my stuff filling the drawers, the room now felt like mine.

“Sascha wouldn’t let me into The Dens last night. He doesn’t want to see me, and we’re running out of time. I’m not above using my body to get back in his good books.”

“Then go with the red, puff-sleeve number. White jeans. Gives off a *ruin the innocent girl* vibe.”

Was I going for that? “It’s not too much for a grid announcement?” I stripped out of my sole black dress that was *definitely* too much for a meeting.

Wade rolled onto his back. “It toes the line, but you’re stylish. No one will think twice about it.”

I pulled on the white jeans and red top. The sleeves were slightly puffed, and the scoop neck was held by a drawstring in the middle. I drew the ends tighter and looped the ends into a bow.

“Before you take another hour to decide on your hair, leave it.”

Hands already raised, I paused. “Half up, half down. You sure?”

"Never more certain."

"You, sir, are being sarcastic." I lowered my arms though. "What happened with Judy by the way?"

"Thought you'd never ask. You're speaking to the new Deception Ball organiser." He scrunched his face. "Coordinator? Planner... *Designer*. You're speaking with the new Deception Ball *Designer*."

"Such an honour." I curtsied. "Speak with Stanley about budget, please."

"It'll be epic. Elton John epic."

I smiled at the glee in his voice. "I believe you. Let me know if you want to bounce ideas."

"Don't worry. I've got this. And assuming you can't go with Sascha, want to be my date?"

I sat on his lap and interlaced my hands behind his neck. "I'd love to."

He lifted me, walking us to the door. "You'll need to coordinate your outfit to mine."

"Of course."

"Good. Then let's get to the meeting." Wade carried me out into the hall and down the stairs.

"When does this ball go down anyway?"

"Just under a month. Judy had already started planning, but I'm scrapping everything. Seriously. No taste."

"Was she okay with handing things over?"

His salted caramel scent muted.

I narrowed my eyes. "Wade? What did you do to Judy?"

He kicked open the meeting room door. The startled head team members stared at us.

"We've arrived," Wade sang.

They didn't answer.

The Luthers were only revealed when we fully entered the room.

Shit.

"Ah. Esteemed guests." Wade dumped me unceremoniously in

my chair, plonking down beside me.

Blood poured in my face. We must be late. "I apologise for our tardiness and extend my welcome to the pack members."

I peeked at Sascha.

A painful yearning slammed into me. For weeks, there were no barriers to touching him. To be so close and unable to feel the soothing bliss we felt in each other's arms was torture.

My hands trembled.

Sascha's eyes hardened. "Thank you, Head Steward."

Aware of the mounting tension, I broke our contact to study his team. Lisa appeared on the edge of a nervous breakdown. Grim was, as ever, disinterested in proceedings. Hairy was attentive while Leroy mimicked his leader's posture.

Mandy didn't meet my gaze.

I'd never seen her cowed before.

Weird.

"What's the pack's grid choice this week?" I forced myself to look at Sascha again.

His face hadn't softened.

The outfit was a failure. Should've gone with sexy badass.

Gravel entered his voice. "The pack chooses Iron."

Which surprised no one. "We'll see you there…" I trailed off as the Luthers scraped back their chairs.

They filed for the exit.

"Sascha," I called. "Will you grant me a private word? Perhaps my head team can escort your wolves around the manor."

He met my gaze for a leaden moment. I inhaled his want and need, an exact rival for mine. He wanted to close the gap and touch me. He wanted *me,* but his four scents were brittle and drawn in a way I'd never experienced.

"I think not, Head Steward," he said softly.

Turning, he strode after his wolves.

We need to talk, I thought at him.

Sascha froze in the doorway.

Oh my god, did he just hear me? I inhaled his shock.

He *did*.

"Are you certain?" I asked aloud.

Sascha didn't look back again. "... Yes."

He left.

I curled my hands into fists. *Dammit.* What was I missing here? Sascha didn't have this kind of hate inside him, not for anyone—let alone me. There had to be another reason he was keeping his distance.

Wade's not so gentle nudge roused me.

The head team was watching.

Crap.

Trixie walked to the window. A minute later, she announced, "They're gone."

"It's fair to say things there are extra hostile," Stanley remarked.

That was one way to put it. "I'm not in their good books. I'd hoped to smooth things over today."

"Why?" Nathan said.

"Because hostile Luthers aren't ideal for the tribe." I stood. "And because I'm still in the middle of the mating call with Sascha. Certain things are necessary."

Nathan stiffened. "When does it end?"

"We have two more meets. I can't do them alone."

Wade grinned.

"What happens if you don't complete the meets?" Roderick asked.

"Our discomfort grows progressively worse until one of us cracks. I guess."

They were quiet.

Trixie broke it. "What does it feel like to be apart during the call?"

At this point? I opened my mouth.

Pascal cut in. "Like not touching them is the worst fate imaginable. That touching them will make everything in the world right again."

Her words rang in the meeting room.

The head team and Wade gaped at her.

They had no knowledge about what happened with Daniil.

Pascal grabbed her tablet. "Tomorrow at 8:00 a.m., is it, Andie?"

I smoothed my expression as attention swung to me. "It is. See you there."

The straight-backed marshal gripped my shoulder. "You look lovely today by the way."

A lump rose in my throat. "Thanks."

Reeking of grief, she smiled and strode out.

12

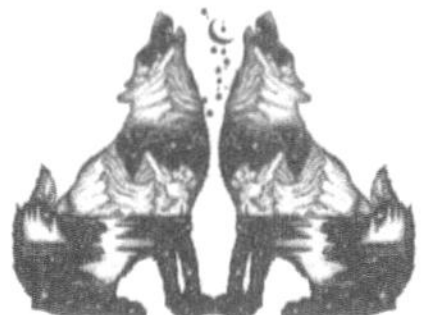

On the muddy beach, I studied the red lake of Iron.

Sascha didn't get in touch after Sunday. As a result, everything depended on the tribe winning tonight.

If the pack won, it was over. And then what? Bile rose in my throat. Remaining behind as my stewards ventured into the big wide, uncertain and afraid, was nearly as horrible as the thought of bitterness creeping over Sascha and me in time.

Which miserable fate would I choose?

We must remain calm, Booker urged.

I steadied my inhales and exhales.

That's it, she said.

"Andie?" Cameron touched my shoulder. "Five minutes to go."

That was my cue. I found a decent-sized boulder and jumped on top.

A sea of nervous faces watched me. The stewards were dressed in thin black wetsuits.

I had to believe in the win or no one else would.

We were ready for this. Iron was our strength.

I pitched my voice higher. "Ni Tiaki, if we lose Iron tonight, we're done. Tomorrow, the pack will take over the guardianship of this valley, and we will begin the process of vacating the homes and land we have loved alongside our ancestors for centuries. We'll forfeit the burial sites of those who are no longer breathing. This is our last chance."

I could feel Sascha close by. Luthers surrounded us.

They were listening.

Good. I wanted them to hear this. "In two hours, this tribe could hang at the mercy of those we've attempted to exile for over two centuries. After this war between us, do you expect them to show mercy?"

I inhaled their fear. "You should be afraid. This is the first time in our history that four grids have been in the pack's possession. Victratum has very real consequences that our ancestors didn't live to experience. But *we* might. We could lose in two hours."

Their fear and uncertainty swelled.

"Remember what you feel now," I told them. "Remember that fear and uncertainty in the future. But *today,* use it to fuel you. Enter Iron and leave nothing behind. By your efforts, we can win, but only if we enter as people desperate not to be ripped from their homes. Because the people we face are desperate not to be ripped from their home, too, and they're so very close to success."

I raised a fist as I'd done in the past. "This grid will not slip away from us."

They murmured it in response.

"This grid will not slip away from us," I shouted.

They shouted the chant back, and the sound echoed through the Iron quarry.

Boom.

I hadn't heard the cannon in weeks.

Fuck, this was it.

Stewards streamed past in their units, working with a precision that bordered on frightening. They slipped into the water to swim to their stations.

Don't you dare join them, Booker growled.

I won't. My trip over the falls with Wade and Cam showed me how easily submersion in water could panic wolves. Not so much of a big deal when the wolf expected it, but without preparation...

I followed Pascal up to the observation deck, and we watched the tribe work in terse silence.

Sascha would throw everything they had at this grid tonight. In an ideal world, they'd overcommit financially, and the tribe would still win, which would weaken the pack in future grids.

As for our strategy, I'd approved three new strategies.

Time dragged cruelly as I agonised over exactly when to make each move.

I had to nail this.

"Five minutes, Head Steward." Pascal was furiously tapping on her tablet—as always. Who knew what she was doing on there? Probably playing Candy Crush.

I spoke into my walkie. "Big Red. Get in position. Over."

Four versions of "Roger that," chimed through. The team leaders confirmed completion of my order three minutes later.

The second *boom* rent the air and my heart took off in a full gallop.

Luthers entered the grid from the beach we'd left, and my eyes tracked Sascha's movements through the red water.

We couldn't shoot the pack there at the risk of losing points for serious injury or death. We had to wait until they climbed to the first level. From there, we'd always relied on the steep ascension to the top level to win the grid.

Not this time.

The first pack members reached the cliffs, and I grinned as Leroy attempted to climb. He slipped and disappeared under the water's surface. Luthers queued at the edges of the lake, waiting for those ahead of them to exit the water.

Hard to climb with environmentally friendly surface lubricant coated over the iron ore cliffs. We only had time to cover the areas where pack tended to ascend.

But it was working.

Hairy punched his claws into the cliff.

My grin widened as he slid downward.

There was a reason the pack used their hands to climb in this grid. Iron ore was soft. Our claws were too sharp and cut through the substance.

Sascha howled.

What's that mean? I quickly asked.

They're going up another way, Booker replied. *That's all I can get.*

I clicked on my walkie. "Big Red. Prepare for Operation Open Day. Over."

Grappling hooks exploded from a series of large guns. The hooks hurtled upward and embedded into the ore.

I studied the long ropes extending between the higher tiers and lake.

The hooks wouldn't hold as well as in Sandstone, but the ropes would help the pack climb faster. Luckily, it was a move the head team anticipated.

Wolves grabbed onto the ropes and pulled themselves up. When the first Luthers cleared the first tier, my stewards opened fire. More pack members took to the ropes as others slowly ascended up the cliffs using their claws.

I waited a while longer before delivering another order. "Initiate Operation Open Day."

Red balloons filled with wolfsbane rocketed down the ropes. Luthers at the front saw them coming and dropped onto the first two levels.

Wolfsbane exploded on those behind.

Ouch. That shit stung.

I didn't wait for Luthers to start up the ropes again. "Big Red. Initiate phase two. Over."

One by one, the ropes were cut. There were pack members on the first two levels now, but that was inevitable.

I scanned the lake. "Damn."

They'd discovered a section of cliff not covered in the lubricant.

Sascha howled.

Spread out and search, Booker translated.

I brought my walkie to my mouth. “Big Red. Prepare Operation Wet T-shirt. Over.”

The pack spread out to search for better routes. I gripped the barrier of the observation tower.

You knew they'd figure it out, Booker said.

Soon, Luthers ascended the cliff faces with ease. My gaze shot to the wet T-shirt stewards hidden behind mounds of iron ore that we asked quarry workers to form yesterday.

I licked my dry lips. “Big Red. Initiate Operation Wet T-shirt. Over.”

The stewards leaped out from their hiding places.

Within seconds, water roared from ten huge cannons I'd agreed to splurge on this week. The water slammed into the faces of the top Luthers.

“Illegal shift,” Pascal called out. “And another.”

Those able to resist the shift were still panicking as I'd once done. The climbing pack members lost their grip, toppling back to the red lake.

But the cannons had a major weakness, and Sascha would find it in short duration. Five more minutes could mean the difference though.

Some pack members on the tiers were engaged with stewards higher up. We could handle them while the cannons were still working.

“Big Red. Reindeer, direct close members of your team to aid west. Over.”

“*Reindeer. Roger that. Over.*”

One of the water cannons cut off.

Fucker!

The cannons were fed via pipes from the lake. Something Sascha figured out faster than was ideal. We'd painted the pipes the same colour as the iron ore, but that was all we could manage at short notice.

Another cannon stopped working. The wet T-shirt steward manning it raised his tranquiliser gun.

I checked the time.

Twenty minutes left.

"What's the score?" I had to know.

Pascal didn't stop her frantic scanning and tapping. "Unconfirmed score is sixty-five to eleven."

The pack would never reach the levels where most of the tribe shot from. Not enough of them to make a big difference.

Good.

Sascha could have something up his sleeve though.

My stomach churned as the last water cannon shut off.

I lifted my walkie. "Big Red. Wet T-shirt stewards. Retreat to higher ground. Over." One toppled unconscious to the ground as the order left my lips.

"Big Red again. Immediate cover for wet T-shirt stewards. Over." My shoulders eased as the Luthers turned their attention to dodging darts from above instead of chasing down my team.

Trouble, Booker snarled.

A pack member was toppling backward off the first level. A horrified steward stood before the falling woman, his tranquiliser gun raised.

Oh my god, she was unconscious.

"She's going into the water." I listened for shouts, but the pack was focused on climbing.

Shit!

I launched over the railing of the tower, hands windmilling as I free-fell.

You said we wouldn't get wet, Booker snapped.

Water closed over us, and I kicked upward, then wasted no time cutting through the water toward the cliffs.

The water was murky, but my eyes were unbeatable. I caught sight of dark skin ahead. Drawing in a huge breath of air, I submerged again and kicked downward.

This lake was fucking deep. My lungs strained as I gripped her arm.

I'd had my fucking fill of drowning. Utilising every inch of my supernatural strength, I propelled us to the surface.

We broke through, and I gasped for air.

The woman was an omega. Lisa's friend.

I held her nose and breathed twice into her mouth. I couldn't press on her chest out here. Treading water, I thumped her back *hard.*

The woman vomited red water. I rubbed her back until she was done.

She coughed a few times and settled into deep unconsciousness again. *Oh, yeah.* I pulled the dart from the woman's chest and towed her to the muddy beach.

Half in the water, I rested the omega on her side. She was breathing. Her pulse was steady.

She was okay. I sagged over her, panting hard.

Every time you say we won't get wet, we do.

My wolf was sulking. *She would have died.*

Don't care.

Unsurprising. Booker didn't feel the same protectiveness for the pack women and children.

I studied the fight on the surrounding levels.

Boom.

The final cannon.

My knees nearly gave way.

The two teams ceased fire and went their separate ways without a blink. Why was it so damn hard to do between times?

Pascal waved from the observation tower and held her thumb up. She must be certain of the win to do that.

I allowed relief to crash over me.

The weight crushing my chest didn't lighten—today was just about staying in the game.

For whatever reason Sascha was keeping his distance.

And that meant I had work to do.

13

The gardeners shrieked when Booker trotted into view. The stewards started early, and our run ran overtime today.

Taking over, I sat back on our haunches and lifted a paw, waving slightly.

One laughed, and the others relaxed.

Resuming our trot, I relinquished control to Booker again as we entered the manor.

Let's change. I have a meeting soon, I thought at her. *Wait. Where are you going?*

She beelined for the kitchen.

The cooks screamed, scrambling back.

Booker inhaled the scent of bacon and nudged a plate of it with our nose. One of the younger staff members inched forward and dangled a few slices near our mouth.

Don't bite off his fingers, I told her firmly.

She took the bacon offering gingerly and chomped it back. Activity in the kitchen resumed as the boy gradually fed us the entire plate full.

You about done? I asked.

That will suffice.

Gerry yelped as we loped down the hall. We trotted up the stairs and entered the bedroom door that I made sure to leave open before shifting.

After shifting, showering, and changing, I jogged to my office.

"Chantel just arrived," Tip-Toe Eleanor said from behind.

I jumped. *Jesus.*

Even with my ears, she was fucking quiet. "Please send her in."

Wade's mother entered soon after. My friend inherited his father's height and his mother's looks.

"Chantel. Thanks for coming."

She sat opposite me. "Wade said that you wanted to know more about the council. I'm happy to help however I can."

Truth.

"I appreciate that. When I took over this role the first time, I was learning the ropes. I have a handle on the day-to-day things now and I'd like to be more active on the council."

"Of course. That's your right. You hold the tenth seat on council."

My brows shot up. "Really?"

She cracked a grin that reminded me of her son. "Really. Due to the demands on your time here, we essentially run the council in your stead, but you're the mayor of Deception Valley."

What the hell? Seriously?

"I read the quarterly report. Everything is operating smoothly." I'd never met anyone outside of the pack who had a bad thing to say about the tribe. The council kept the public parts of this valley in great nick.

"As you probably saw, most of the gathered taxes go into road maintenance. The terrain doesn't make repairs easy or cheap."

I opened the report and studied the printed pictures of the council. Margaret Frey was on there, too, which was ideal. I'd met two of the other stewards. None of the locals rang a bell. "What are the council members like to work with?"

"The team fits well together. There hasn't been a new face there since the passing of Ted Harrington, a local who sat on the council for thirty years, so we've known each other a while."

That could prove to be a good or bad thing.

She hesitated. "It's your right to join the council, and your presence would be welcomed, I assure you. Is there a specific reason you wish to join?"

Yes. I'd like to help our enemy out.

I closed the report. "I believe we're limiting the reaches of our businesses. There are projects that could be introduced and developed to aid us in Grids, and the valley would prosper as a result too."

"Like?"

Might as well test out the reaction. "This valley's weakness and strength is our remoteness from other towns and cities. People pay more for the quality of our resources but exporting to surrounding areas takes up valuable human resources. Not only that, I'd guess our trucks ruin the roads far more readily than car traffic. In Grids, we're often restricted by what equipment can be delivered in a short timeframe. We need to stop relying on roads alone. I believe an airport would benefit the tribe greatly. In exports, with imports, and to bring more business to our region."

Her eyes rounded. "An airport?"

"Correct."

She blinked. "An airport helps us, but it would also help the Luthers. They could also bring in equipment and export goods."

"The tribe can't take the risk of funding this alone and I'm guessing the council won't want that either. We go in together. As a term of the final agreement, Deception Valley Exports would exclusively manage exports and imports via air. The public will have access via our company, but the pack will be forced to continue using roads and trucks for Valley Trade Services—or pay us for use of cargo space."

Honestly though, there would always be a market for offering land transportation at a lower cost. The pack could navigate the change. The tribe and pack would just fulfil different niches.

Chantel smiled. "It's ballsy."

"Luthers and tribe alike would have access to the passenger seats," I said in a casual tone, grateful she couldn't hear my heartbeat. "The public may suspect anything else."

I held my breath.

Chantel nodded. "There's no harm in that. The environmental impact would need to be assessed per the ideals of our tribe, but council decisions don't count toward Grids. The pack couldn't come after us. Terrie, one of the public council members, brings up an airport each year. Herc always shut it down."

Probably because he'd observed the wolf population decreasing and suspected they weren't just leaving. "When's the next council meeting?"

"Next Monday. If you're serious about this, you'll need to put forward a thorough proposal."

Crap. In what time?

"Knowing how busy you are, I'd like to offer the services of our tribe council members to take on the task."

I blew out a breath. "Honestly, I'd have no idea where to start, but are you sure that won't overload the five of you?"

"I have a feeling that the other Ni Tiaki council members will be as excited as I am, and we're old hands at proposals. As I said, Terrie submits an airport proposal each year, and I'm certain she'll happily work with us on it too."

I walked around the desk. "Thank you so much, Chantel. I'd still like to be as active in the proposal as possible. Perhaps we could all meet each afternoon at 2:00 p.m. to discuss details? I'd really like to present this next Monday."

She smiled warmly. "We'll see it done, Head Steward."

I watched her leave the office and returned to my seat.

If the airport came together, the pack would have a way to find their mates, a way to prevent their extinction if they stayed in the valley, *and* a way to leave if the tribe won and wouldn't agree to a truce. Assuming I could get my stewards to agree to a delay while the airport was constructed. Which wasn't certain.

It was a start.

Thursday mornings were relaxed. Our strategy teams were hard at work, and I'd listen to their initial ideas later.

I had a few hours to study.

I plugged in my laptop. While it woke up, I logged into the *Eastway Bank* app on my phone and transferred two hundred and fifty dollars of my first head steward pay into the account containing the last of Mum's debt.

Shouts erupted from outside, and I jumped up to peer out the window. The gardeners had congregated.

And all of them pointed in the same direction.

Oh my god.

Running, I burst from the manor seconds later and leaped down the front steps.

"Nothing to worry about," I hastily called to the stewards. "He's here to see me."

I bore down on the filthy pup. "You better not have come this far by yourself."

Panting, Axel flopped on his side, exposing his neck.

He's exhausted, Booker said.

I scooped up the pup. "Your mother will be out of her mind with worry."

He whined.

Yeah, I wasn't falling for that cuteness. He was in the dog box.

"Where's the nearest hose?" I asked Marty.

He led me to a tap beside the manor stairs. "Is that a Luther?"

"Yes. A very naughty one." Holding Axel by the scruff, I narrowed my eyes. "You're having a bath."

Oh, he *did* have some energy left.

"That won't help you," I chided as he tried to wriggle free.

The howling pup did manage to soak me from head to toe by the end. I wiped a damp sleeve over my face.

Marty returned with old towels. "Need these?"

"Thanks."

"I've never seen a Luther baby before."

Because there was only one.

Wrapping Axel in towels, I gathered him up and strode to the kitchen.

"Randi," I called to the first steward I saw. "Could you grab my phone off my office desk, please?"

Her eyes rounded. "Is that a tiny Luther?"

The tribe weren't immune to cute. Curious. "It is. I need to let his mother know where he is."

She hurried off, and I carted the quiet pup to the kitchen.

I patiently answered the same questions from the stewards there, then looked at Axel. "Tell me what happened."

He lowered his gaze, whining.

"I missed you, too, big pup, but you could have been hurt coming so far by yourself. There's a reason we stay with our parents for a while, and that's because they've lived longer and know more about staying safe."

The pup emitted a pathetic howl, and the kitchen staff *aww'd.*

Axel's tale wagged.

He's almost cute, Booker said begrudgingly.

I wasn't winning this conversation.

"Is he hungry?" Detta asked.

I glanced at the cook. "He's a growing Luther. The answer will always be yes, but he'll need to shift to eat at the table."

Axel wasted no time doing so.

I arranged the towels around him, then accepted my phone from Randi.

Detta set a muffin in front of Axel as I dialled Evelyn.

She answered immediately, "Andie. Is everything okay?"

There was a frantic undercurrent to her voice. No wonder. "Searching for someone?"

The line went silent. "Axel is there?"

"He is. Safe but tired."

I listened to her shout the news.

"Thank goodness," she breathed. "He's been gone hours."

Well, he'd had a long road to travel and only little legs to walk it.

"I grant the pack permission to collect him without penalty in Grids."

She hesitated. "And what about Axel's unsanctioned visit?"

Yes, that.

We currently held three penalty points against them. This could give us another point. "There won't be a penalty. I made a promise to the women and children, and that doesn't come with ties."

"On behalf of Sascha, thank you."

I pressed my lips together to stop myself from asking about him. "No problem."

"Sascha is okay. Tired and stressed, but he's putting food in his mouth."

Tears stung my eyes, and I blinked them away—too aware of the kitchen staff. "I'm glad to hear it."

"A few women have left to collect Axel. They shouldn't be long."

"No rush. He's enjoying being spoiled by pretty much everyone." I hung up.

News spread.

Stewards streamed in to gawk at the small boy steadily devouring an entire tray of muffins.

"Last one," I said when he took his sixth.

"Oh, go on. Let him have more," someone chided.

Hold on, I wasn't the bad person here.

Raising my head, I caught the scents of three Luthers outside. "Time to go."

"Phone," Axel said loudly.

Uh. "What?"

"Phone," he repeated.

Ah. "The saxophone?"

He nodded.

"Is that why you came?"

I inhaled his *yes*. Curiosity didn't kill cats. It killed baby werewolves.

"Playing the saxophone is a reward, Axel. What you did was dangerous, and so I can't show you the instrument this time."

Mutters broke out behind me.

Mothershitter. I really wasn't winning this discussion.

I held out a hand. "Your mother is outside. Let's go, big pup."

He blanched. "*No.*"

I held his gaze. "You were a big enough boy to come all the way here. That means you're a big enough boy to face the consequences. You can either walk outside on your own legs or we can walk on mine. What's it gonna be?"

He wavered between defiance and sheepishness. "My legs."

Ditching the towels, Axel walked butt-naked out of the manor.

"They won't be too hard on him, will they?" a steward whispered.

Jesus.

"Axel!" Jemma ran from the car to meet us.

She sank to her knees and wrapped him in her embrace. "I was so worried."

He started crying, and she stroked his hair.

Bailey joined me.

"Was everyone in a stir?" I asked.

"Worst one yet."

The omega woman I'd saved in Iron was with her. She stuck to Bailey like a barnacle and wouldn't meet my gaze.

I leaned forward. "How are you feeling?"

She spoke to the ground. "Better. Thanks to you."

"You shouldn't have been shot where there was a risk of you drowning. I extend the apologies of the steward who did so. He panicked in reaction to your presence."

Truth.

The woman nodded. "It happens."

I held out my hand. "I'm Andie."

She raised her chin for the first time and shook my hand. "Vivien."

Jemma approached with a calmer Axel. "*Thank you*, Andie. He's never left pack lands. I'm so sorry to put you in this position."

I peered at the tribe onlookers. "He was a hit, don't worry about it. If he vomits in the car though, it's because he devoured six muffins."

The Luthers turned disbelieving eyes to the stewards.

"Is everything okay with the pack women?" I asked.

Bailey gripped my shoulder. "We're doing fine. Do what you need to do."

My answering smile was grim. "I plan to."

The women left with the pup, and I turned to face at least fifty very curious stewards.

There went my study time.

14

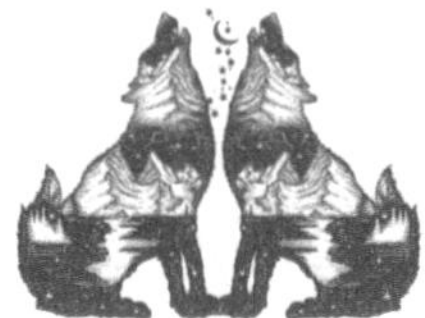

A fancy car rolled into view. I waved, both nervous and excited.

"That's a Rolls-Royce Phantom," Wade breathed.

The shiny black car?

I'd take his word for it.

Friday night and stewards were kicking back around the manor and grounds. No one was drinking, but I was happy to note morale was more positive than prior to our Iron win.

I had another grid to secure in four days, but tonight, I was determined to relax and have some fun.

With a vampire.

The car rolled to a stop, and I glimpsed the older man driving.

Wade fidgeted. "Whoa, let's not get on that guy's bad side."

Really? The man didn't look so bad to me.

The chauffeur opened the car door, and a long, golden leg appeared, followed by the rest of Basilia Le Spyre. Nude heels adorned her feet. The royal blue dress hugged her curves like a glove. She was around my height and completely, supernaturally gorgeous.

I inhaled Wade's anticipation. "Easy boy."

"I've never met a celebrity before."

Basilia raised her chin, topaz eyes glittering. *Yep,* she heard him.

The intensity of her eyes gave me the heebie-jeebies.

A petite woman with chestnut hair exited the vehicle. "*So* glad that drive's over."

I descended the stairs. "Welcome to Deception Valley."

Basilia's scent slapped me.

Enemy, Booker hissed.

Our fangs erupted.

"You fucking stink," I choked out, covering my mouth.

Basilia's face was scrunched. "Returned. You smell like a garbage place."

Her fangs were out too.

Tommy leaned in. "Rubbish dump?"

"A rubbish dump," Basilia amended.

I forced my fangs away.

We must naturally not like vampires, I told Booker. *Please remember she's a friend.*

I don't even want to eat her heart.

Never thought I'd hear the words.

I wiped my streaming eyes. "Is this normal for our kinds?"

"No idea." She held her nose.

Wade cleared his throat. "How about I grab something better to smell for each of you? It may help."

Basilia's blue eyes fixed on my friend, and his heart began to hammer.

Yeah, I felt some of it too. She was all predator.

"This is my best friend, Wade. He was born and raised in the valley."

Tommy extended her hand. "Wade, while these two are being strange, how about we go get that nice-smelling stuff you mentioned?"

They disappeared up the stairs.

"Will you stay with Basilia?" I asked the chauffeur. "If you're hungry, you're welcome to anything in the kitchen. Or a bed if you'd prefer to rest."

Basilia grinned. "She's not afraid of you, Fred."

He'd sure reacted fast with that knife when my fangs appeared though.

"Fred's going into town for a bit." She shot him a glance.

I smirked. "Right. Well, the best place to gather information is The Dens, the casino owned by Sascha Greyson. All of the staff are werewolves, but the patrons are human." I inhaled. "I suggest you change your clothes. You smell like Vissimo, and other Luthers may react as I did."

Fred bowed. "Thank you, Miss Thana."

Okay, maybe he was a little scary.

"Come on in," I said to Basilia.

We were both holding our noses now, and laughter bubbled up my throat at the ridiculousness of the situation.

Her eyes danced, then tilted her head. "There are a lot of humans here."

"You're used to less noise?"

She shrugged a shoulder. "Less noise, but around the same number. We have a lot of help and security at the mansion."

The mansion.

Oh to be a billionaire.

I guided her to the oldest sitting room.

She shifted her attention from the polished wood to the old books. "This place has been in the family a while."

"In the tribe, yes. The Thanas have lived in this manor for one hundred and fifty years, but we've always lived on this land."

"And where are the wolves?"

"On the opposite side of the valley. They call their territory pack lands, but the area is only on loan to them until the end of the game."

She focused on me, and I withheld a shiver at the laser intensity of her topaz eyes. "What game?"

Wade and Tommy returned.

"Roll this under your nose," he said.

I accepted the essential oil from him and obeyed. Orange scent filled my nose. I could barely smell Basilia through it. "That's better."

She sighed after doing the same with a second roller. "Much."

Wade took cocktail orders and got busy at the corner bar we'd stocked earlier.

Basilia sat with a grace that confirmed her otherness. "As I said. *What* game?"

"Holy shit." Tommy plonked down beside her friend.

I darted a look between them. "You have some history with supernatural games?"

"I told you," Wade called. "There was a game between two vampire clans, and one side recently won."

I vaguely recollected him saying that.

"*Our* side," Tommy jumped in. "Basilia owned them."

What I'd give to do the same. I smiled. "You're proud of her."

"Damn straight. You should have seen her. *Bam!* Do this. *Bam!* Do that. Be my minions. Except she freed the actual minions. Totally cool."

Wade passed Basilia a strawberry mojito. "Tequila for you, Tom?"

"With a lemon, please, Wadie boy."

They were on a nickname basis already.

I shook my head. "Right. The game. There's been a battle between the tribe and werewolves for over two centuries. The pack originally came here to find a new home after splitting from their old pack."

"Why did they split away?" Tommy slammed back a shot.

"Here, baby girl." Wade passed my gin cocktail.

I sipped and was rewarded by a burst of tart raspberry. *Mmm.* "Luthers have six different status of wolf. Five main ones. These statuses need to be balanced in a pack. The larger the pack, the harder it becomes. Half left with Sascha's father, Alexei."

"I've heard of him." Basilia sipped at her drink. "This isn't half bad. Want to work at my bar?"

"What bar?" Wade asked.

I smirked into my glass. He already knew and didn't want to come across as a fanboy.

"Forbidden." She crossed her legs. "The wolves ended up here, and there was drama with the tribe?"

"Essentially. The tribe discovered the newcomers transformed into wolves. Didn't take it well. The main issue is that the pack want the security of owning their territory, and the tribe doesn't recognise ownership of land at all. We're only guardians of the valley."

Basilia tilted her head. "Why don't the wolves leave then?"

It was a common question on the steward's lips, but I'd promised Sascha not to divulge the truth.

Wade took a seat next to me and gulped at his drink.

Whiskey. Ick. Maybe I could just lead Basilia around the truth. "What do you know of the other supernatural races around this valley and Bluff City?"

Her eyes narrowed. "There are others?"

"Demons and witches. You didn't know?"

"That's not common knowledge to our family," she said slowly. "I specifically asked Kyros once, and he only mentioned werewolves. He wasn't lying."

"Interesting," I murmured. "How is it possible you guys haven't encountered them?"

She frowned. "Exactly. What interaction have you had with their kinds?"

"Before arriving here, the pack battled against the demons to the north. The pack barely escaped them to get here. Since then, a witch coven has set up to the south of this valley."

Basilia stiffened. "Do you have any idea on their numbers?"

"The pack may know more. I'm told the demon kingdom is the largest in the world. Are you worried about them for some reason?"

"Just because we didn't know they were there."

Which was pretty odd. "Do you think they're hiding from you guys on purpose?"

She leaned back. "If they are, that's worrisome. This will interest King Julius greatly."

Wade choked on his whisky.

Yeah, I hadn't gotten around to telling him vampires had kings.

Something else occurred to me. "It may be a good idea for the pack and your people to keep in touch about the situation." The last thing I wanted was to be blindsided by other supernatural races with everything that was going on.

Or in the future.

"Agreed. Maybe we should work something out as a precaution." She finished her cocktail, and this time Tommy swiped up the empty, collecting mine on the way.

"Like an alliance?" That could open the door to negotiating an idea I'd had after our last phone call. Vampires could provide safe passage for the pack through Bluff City if the tribe won.

Basilia shrugged. "Tell me, you're advocating for the pack's safety, yet you're the head steward of the enemy side. What's your position in the game?"

Precarious.

"I want both sides to reach a truce. Sascha doesn't share the same view. He believes there will never be peace between tribe and pack. I need to win Grids to be in a position to negotiate for the pack while ensuring the wellbeing of the Ni Tiaki too."

"What exactly will you negotiate for the pack?"

Good question. "I'm focused on keeping the tribe in the game for now. When my younger sister discovered I'd become a Luther, she exiled me and weakened our position drastically."

Basilia arched a brow. "This wouldn't be the sister frequenting my club for the last ten days?"

I straightened. "You've seen her?"

"Some of my Vissimo employees work at the club. They noticed her last name and passed it on. Quite the bender she's having."

"Rhona's okay though?"

"I wasn't interested enough to notice after watching the camera footage. She's nothing like you."

Wade exhaled loudly. "*Thank* you."

I shot him a quelling look that bounced right off him. "She lost our father recently. Her mother a few years back. Me becoming a Luther was the final straw."

Basilia regarded me. "Then perhaps I judged her too quickly. I'm an orphan too."

"Make that three of us," I mumbled.

Tommy delivered our drinks.

Then Wade got more.

Then Tommy.

Both of them got steadily drunker. I couldn't feel any buzz, but the drinks tasted nice. Vampires must burn off alcohol fast, too, because the billionaire opposite me was just as composed as when she first arrived.

Our besties, rolling on the floor, erupted into loud laughter.

Basilia's lips crooked. She moved to sit in the armchair next to me. "An alliance between the clan and pack. The idea could hold merit."

"The two races could pose a serious threat to both of us." The more I thought of it, the more concerned I became about our neighbours.

"The problem being that there are less than one thousand werewolves in the pack, my mate tells me. We number upward of fifteen thousand. We'd bring far more to an alliance."

Not strictly true. "Your numbers are indisputable, yet your territory is far removed from the demons and witches. You only found out about them tonight, for example. We hold great value in our proximity."

"As scouts." She tapped her bottom lip.

"The differences in our powers could also prove beneficial. A Luther's senses are unmatched—as is our endurance. We're natural strategists. In wolf form, a pack can communicate over huge distances too."

The vampire pursed her lips.

I kept going. "The demons and witches are keeping their

existence a secret from your clan. Whether because of your sheer numbers or for more nefarious reasons, I'm unsure. But why not keep your own secret in case they do mean your people harm? An early alert from the pack could make all the difference, as could an extra thousand supernatural bodies who are designed for a siege. That's not to mention all the information we could gather as scouts."

The vampire tapped the rim of her glass. "I assume you're suggesting this alliance in preparation of the pack remaining in this valley beyond the game."

"The idea never entered my head before tonight. I'd just hate to win the game only to face another fight in the near future."

She hummed. "I'm not ready for another fight either. Ingenium was a shit show."

I set my cocktail on a side table. "Let's see where this goes then. If King Julius is interested in talking further, get in touch."

The vampire studied me. "Thank you for the information regardless."

"Happy to help. Anything to prevent more supernatural bullshit, right?"

Her focus didn't budge. "I'm not a fan of bullshit. If there's one thing I hate more, it's fucking games. When I get back to the city tomorrow, I'll take this to Julius on your behalf. While we wait on that, I want to know if there's anything I can do to help you on a more personal level."

My brows drew together. "Why would you go out of your way to do that?"

She took a deep breath. "I was once in a game that threatened to drive Kyros and I apart. I felt alone and powerless and afraid. If someone had been there to help me, things would have been easier to bear. Did you know that your heart misses a beat every time you say his name?"

"Sascha?" I asked.

Her lips curved as my heart skipped before resuming.

"I never noticed." My voice was soft.

"*Love* is the only game worth playing. So how can we win? Is it money you need?" She made a flippant gesture and a hint of her vampire stench reached my nostrils.

"Money? Thank you, but no." In the middle of rubbing my nose, I froze and lifted my gaze to hers. "Maybe there's another way you could help me though."

15

What was it about this day of the week that felt lonelier than usual?

Was it that I'd elected to spend the evening in my office while stewards laughed and let loose through the manor?

Whatever the reason, Saturday never felt lonely when he was around. After talking with Basilia most of the night about her immortal mating with Prince Kyros, I just wanted to skip the bullshit and be with Sascha.

I texted him. How many times was this now? Fifty?

I miss you so much.

Messaging a blocked number was the equivalent of writing a journal, but my soul ached with the need to see him.

Delivered.

I sucked in a breath. The message status hadn't changed since I left pack lands. He'd unblocked me.

Three dots appeared and my heart hammered. He'd read the message.

He was typing back.

Oh my god. Should I call?

"Wait for him to reply," I scolded myself.

Five minutes went by and the three dots disappeared.

A crushing weight filled my chest.

I typed again.

You need to see me too.
Please. Let's talk

The message showed a delivered status, but the three dots didn't appear.

He wasn't even going to give me the damn *dots*?

Nope.

No.

My desk chair skated along the ground as I stood.

Sascha *would* talk to me. We'd been through too much to fizzle out like this.

I was breaking into *The Dens*.

In style.

Running upstairs, I grabbed my second sexiest dress. The metallic mini didn't leave room for underwear. The cowl neck plunged to belly button levels. Thin straps criss-crossed my back in a lattice that would ignite the desire of those who caught sight of me.

I only needed to ignite one man.

Pairing the mini with black heels, I straightened my hair and swept on smoky shadow. Grabbing a clutch, I transferred the contents of my wallet and studied myself in the mirror.

"He will listen to you tonight." I swivelled to study my butt.

He'd listen, alright.

How are we getting in? Booker asked.

There's a staff entrance, but Sascha will sense me coming. Hairy will be on the lookout.

We need a diversion.

I covered my outfit with a long black coat that made no sense in summer and dodged around the outside of the manor to reach Ella F undetected. Leaving in this dress didn't give a great impression.

Diving into Ella F, I drove to town like a madwoman and parked at the petrol station again.

I couldn't get too close or he'd spook.

Scanning the busy street, I spotted a group of local teens near the riverside. They reeked faintly of alcohol.

Perfect.

I walked over. "Having a good night?"

They looked at me warily.

A girl in her late teens shrugged. "Yeah. What's it to you?"

"I need someone to cause a distraction so I can get into The Dens." Teens could smell a lie from a mile away. Best to be honest.

"Why do you need to sneak in?" a younger boy asked.

"There's a guy in there I want to see. He's the owner. He's angry at me and the bouncer won't let me in."

The girl's brow shot up. "What'd you do?"

I leaned against the railing. "He thinks I chose my family over him. He's hurt. But I only did it for him."

"Messed up," she answered.

Yep.

The boy exchanged long glances with the group. "Is there money in it?"

I looked at the empty bottle of wine near his feet. There was one between eight of them. They'd need more for it to have any effect, which they'd no doubt figured out.

I wasn't down with fuelling their efforts. "There would be money in it if I had your assurance you wouldn't ask someone to buy you booze with the cash."

Just like that I lost their interest.

"How much?" The first girl planted her hands on her hips. "I'm saving for a car."

Truth.

"I can swing twenty."

She smirked. "The people who run The Dens are scary. Make it fifty and you have a deal. I'll draw the bouncer away."

"How do I know you won't just take my money?"

Her jaw clenched. "I won't."

Truth.

Digging in my clutch, I extracted a fifty and passed it over, sincerely hoping Sascha wasn't already on high alert from feeling my presence in town. "Got a plan?"

"How do you think we got the bottle of wine?"

I didn't want to know.

Watching her cross the street, I started walking back to Ella F to throw Sascha off guard. I listened as the girl approached *The Dens*, slipping off my heels to hold them.

Shouts erupted, and when the girl took off up the hill, I sprinted toward the casino.

Hairy was in pursuit of her.

I grinned, boosting up the hill at—a very quick—human pace. Speeding past the line, I jumped the cordon to the gasps of those watching.

Success!

I donned my heels and strode into the bar.

Every pack member was watching me from their stations, but no one approached. In a bid to get farther from the exit, I weaved between the tables and dancing patrons to enter the casino.

What now?

Should I force my way into staff quarters? Sascha definitely knew I was here. I couldn't smell his reaction over the crowd, but he was in his office.

He could be watching me on the cameras right now.

Better give him a show.

Walking through the casino, I greeted the Luthers I passed.

"That's quite the dress, gorgeous lady," said an older gentleman with a moustache.

I'd never been attracted to older men. Well, that was ludicrous when I wanted a near-on one-century-old man for my own. But I'd never gone for the silver fox.

"Thank you, sir. Have a good evening." *Go away.*

"May I buy you a drink?" he asked.

I walked around the patron, but a hand latched around my wrist. Bliss flowed through my body, and my eyes fluttered closed, lips parting as the contact swept away my worries and replaced them with a surety that everything would be okay.

Sascha tugged me toward him, and I went.

I much preferred him in jeans—only jeans—but he was so fucking handsome in a suit. His Adam's apple bobbed as he took me in.

Our hearts pounded together. His desire danced with mine. Our scents merged so completely that I could barely tell one from the other.

"Sascha."

Now Basilia had pointed it out, I'd never miss the irregular skipping of my heart again.

"Andie." His voice was sharp. "What are you doing here?"

I rested a hand on his chest, half expecting him to deny me that touch. A small sigh escaped his lips as my palm contacted the space over his heart. "I—"

"If you're here to see me, then I can't help you."

"Why are you shutting me out?"

"What you did isn't enough?"

I refused to look away. "Not enough for this. There has to be a reason you're pushing me away."

"Maybe I've rediscovered my priorities."

His smirk hurt. Then again, it was designed to. I stepped so our bodies were flush and gripped either side of his face.

"No," I whispered upward. "I don't believe that." For the first time ever, I knew someone's feelings for me were bigger than the world.

He tensed under my touch, but joy emanated from him too.

My words elated him.

He didn't want me to believe that he didn't love me? How did that make sense?

I watched the ticking in his jaw, feeling the rapid flutter of his pulse under my palm. "If I'm wrong. You need to tell me. For good."

Sascha covered my hands with his. "I won't discuss the game with you, Andie. I'm sorry you put on that stunning dress for nothing, but perhaps it's better that you leave."

He didn't mean it.

He wanted me to stay more than anything.

"Is someone controlling you?" I asked under my breath.

Did his father have anything to do with this?

Sascha brushed his thumb over my cheekbone. "The only person with the power to control me is you, beautiful wolf."

"Then help me understand why you're acting this way. I'm confused." When I'd turned from Sascha, it was because of Herc's death. I'd been hurt, afraid, lost, and reeling.

There was no anger in Sascha though. Only grim determination.

Nothing about his reactions meshed with his actions.

He lowered his hands, drawing my hands away with them. "You need to leave."

I narrowed my gaze. He would speak to me before I left. "I'm a patron. I'm here to gamble."

Sascha's expression smoothed. "No, you're not."

"I am. I'd hoped to talk to you, but if I can't, then a game of..." I peered around. *Crap,* I only knew one game. "...roulette sounds perfect. Have a good evening."

Sidestepping him, I strode back to the exchange counter.

The delta there smiled and peered over my shoulder before quickly losing it.

"Hey, Cassie," I greeted her. "A hundred in chips. Any denomination."

Sascha leaned on the counter. "Just one hundred? Why not two?"

I beamed. "You're absolutely right. Why the hell not?"

My anger swelled in response to his.

Passing over two hundred, I swiped the casino chips into my clutch.

His mouth skimmed my ear. “Spending money that you can’t afford won’t change my answer, Andie.”

I shrugged a shoulder. “Of course not. I’m just here to see what the fun side of life looks like. It’s about time I decided to be irresponsible, don’t you think?”

“You don’t want to do this,” he growled. “You’re acting out because you’re angry at me.”

Angry? No. Well, not before I came here tonight.

I evaded his grip and entered the casino again.

“Can I join this table?” I asked Lisa at the roulette table.

Her gaze darted behind me. “Ah. Certainly?”

I took a seat on the end.

Crap. Now I was here, the thought of playing did make me uneasy—something I’d never felt as the table dealer. Laying down my money to gamble was opening a door I swore would always remain closed.

I shoved back slight nausea.

“Ten-dollar bets, thanks.” I passed over my chips.

Sascha vibrated at my back.

Lisa obeyed while casting furtive glances at her pack leader.

The two other occupants of the table didn’t react to the tension. How couldn’t they sense it? My spine was about to break from the effort of keeping it straight under Sascha’s fury.

Occupied with a werewolf at my back, who was so close that his heat seeped into my skin, I missed the next round.

“What do you want from me?” he spoke low and fast. “I’m trying not to involve you in this. You don’t *want* to be torn in two.”

That’s why he’d cut me out? “That didn’t matter to you two weeks ago. You just wanted me on your side. Why the change of heart?”

“Yes, I took it fucking badly when I realised you wouldn’t ever be happy on pack lands. I thought everything was finally working out for us, and I needed time to lick my wounds."

Lisa calculated payouts.

"You made an assumption," I told him quietly.

He stilled.

Lisa cleared the roulette table, and I selected three of my chips. My unease swelled, and I leaned forward.

A large hand took mine in an unshakeable grip.

Sascha spun me on the stool to face him. "*What* did I assume?"

My chest rose as I craned my neck to see him. "That I'd never be happy there. That pack lands could never be my home. You didn't stick around long enough to hear my real reason for returning to the tribe."

I tried to free my hand, but he didn't release it.

"Ma'am, are you okay?" one of the other players asked tentatively.

Couldn't blame him. Sascha's eyes were practically throwing fire.

I ignored the guy. "I need you to talk to me and not shut me out."

Sascha growled. "That comes with consequences that you've shown me you can't handle. What happens to us when I win the game? I smelled your reaction to my answer that day in the truck. You'll hate me for it."

So *that* was what made him shut down. The same realisation had driven me to put up walls too. "What if I won Grids, Sascha? What would you feel?"

His expression smoothed.

I had a strong suspicion it would end in the same result for us. Gently freeing myself, I faced the table again.

"Are you going to let this continue?" the other player said to Lisa.

Steeling myself, I reached forward to place my bet.

Sascha snarled and picked me up, throwing me over his shoulder.

I thumped his back. "I'm not leaving until you pull your thumb out of your ass, Sascha."

"She's done," he told Lisa. Calling to someone I couldn't see, he said, "Exchange her chips."

One of his hands covered my ass—ideal, because this was not the dress to be hauled around in like a sack of potatoes. People scattered out of the way as we passed.

I tried to boot Sascha in the gut. "Just try to throw me out. See how that works out for you."

His amusement spurred my wrath to unfounded heights.

When Grim opened the door to the staff quarters, I stopped battling.

Oh, he wasn't booting me out.

Sascha took us into his office and kicked the door shut. He sat me on the desk and crowded me. "What exactly would you do, little bird?"

Gripping the table edge, I glared upward.

"So angry," he murmured. "And it's all for me." He rested a hand at the base of my neck. "Do you know when you flush like this, the red goes down your neck?" His hand slid lower over my bare skin. "It covers your chest."

I sucked in a shallow breath.

Sascha lightly dragged his fingers between my breasts and continued down across my stomach revealed by the loose front of the dress. "Blood rushes to the surface wherever I touch."

It felt so good.

I let my head tip back as his fingers circled my skin. "We need to talk."

"Yes, beautiful wolf."

He latched onto my nipple through my dress and my eyes I'd never felt close flew open.

I jerked, but my violent movement was halted as Sascha clamped down on my hips. The heat of his mouth and tongue teased me through the material.

On the desk, I pressed my thighs together. "I can't think when you do that."

He released me, saying, "I know," before moving to the other breast.

Was he purposefully distracting me?

"I didn't mean to hurt you." I gasped as he circled with his tongue.

"I'm aware, little bird." His words curled around my painful heart.

"Then tell me why you're avoiding me."

Coldness stung when he released me.

Sascha met my gaze. "It occurred to me that you may have returned to the tribe to swing the game in the pack's favour. I fully expected to win Iron, and I didn't want you to have any hand in that."

He'd guessed why I left? "So you blocked me and made me feel that you hated me?"

"I didn't block your number." He gritted his teeth. "That was someone who believed they were acting in my best interest."

It took me a second. "Mandy."

His scent gave away the answer.

She would have had time to when I left pack lands and before Sascha returned. *Dammit.*

He continued. "I thought keeping you at a distance until Victratum ended would be easiest for you to handle in the future. You became so distant when the pack won Timber and Sandstone. You blamed yourself. I'd rather that you hated me."

I pushed him back and locked my trembling legs to stand. "Of all the crazy explanations!"

He watched me.

Fat tears leaked over my cheeks, dripping off my chin. "I want you."

"And I want you."

I brushed my straight hair back. "We can work together. That's how we get through this."

Sascha's eyes darkened. "You once asked if I'd be open to a different ending for the game. You were already thinking about negotiating some kind of truce."

"You guessed?"

He turned away. "Yes. And that will never happen."

My stomach plummeted.

A heavy silence sank its claws in.

"Have you really considered it?" My question rang in the office.

"I have over two centuries of data proving that a ceasefire between the Ni Tiaki and my pack will result in further bloodshed." He faced me again. "I can't do that to my pack. I *won't* do that to them. Most of us have lived through decades—and mostly centuries—of this foolish battle. We don't want to do it anymore. Why would I bargain for a peace that probably won't hold when we're in the strongest position we've ever had in the game? Just for my own happiness? You would never act that way yourself."

Heat crept over my jaw. "If the pack wins, over one thousand stewards are left without homes. If the tribe win, seven hundred and fifty Luthers face the same fate, if not death. There may be more risk in a truce, but if it works, *everyone* wins, including us."

"And if it fails, we're back to the start."

"Better to take a chance than to do nothing out of fear."

Sascha was in front of me in the next second. "Aren't you afraid? Are *you* terrified of tomorrow? Any damn second you could be stolen away." His ragged breath washed over me for a second before he spun and upended the desk and monitors.

I winced at the ear-splitting crash as everything smashed to the floor.

Sascha rested his hands against the wall, panting hard. With every harsh exhale, my chest tightened more.

"Sorry," he grunted.

Walking to him, I rested a hand on his back.

He slammed me against the wall so fast, I nearly lost my footing. I stared up into black eyes.

"Tell me what you feel," Greyson demanded.

This wasn't how things worked.

He was right. I was scared of tomorrow too. My grip on him was so fucking fragile and getting weaker every day.

My breath hitched. "I don't want to say these words while things are like this."

Black receded to show honey again.

"Please tell me, beautiful wolf," Sascha said low, his neck muscles taut. "I need something to hold to right now."

He didn't understand. "If I tell you and we end up not having a future, I—"

Sascha rested his forehead on mine. "Forget you're as afraid as I am. Pretend for a little while."

He caressed my neck with his free hand, and the power play undid the last of my restraint.

Fresh tears slipped from the corner of my eyes as our gazes locked. "I love you, Sascha. Is that what you want to hear?"

Joy filled him, but I shoved Sascha away to escape the cage of his arms. I paced in the office. Restless energy filled me. I pivoted sharply with each turn, trying to shake off the trapped feeling to no avail.

That was it.

There was no coming back.

"Little bird, come here."

"No," I spat.

Sascha hooked me around the waist and yanked me to him.

"Let go," I hissed.

He leaned forward and kissed my trembling bottom lip. "*Mate.* I'm honoured."

"It just means we're both fucked."

This man had no survival instincts. Of all the moments to grin, now wasn't the time.

"You love me, and I love you," he said. "What could be more powerful than that?"

So many things. "Unless you come to the table to negotiate a different outcome for the game, what happens will be more powerful. Whether I win outright, or you win outright, there's no victory for us. Don't you see?"

He shook his head. "I can understand your fear, but I don't agree."

And maybe he was right. But I couldn't take that risk. And Sascha wasn't willing to take a risk for peace.

I sighed. "I'm aware. So we'll both continue in the way we see fit, I suppose."

Sascha tilted my chin up and his lips met mine in a harsh kiss.

Why won't you fight for us? I silently asked as we pressed closer.

Sascha lifted me, and I hooked my legs around his hips.

His voice echoed in my mind. *I am, mate. Never forget it.*

I'd never heard his mind speak in this form. I clasped his face to mine, kissing him frantically. Warmth pooled between my thighs. *This feels so good.*

Good isn't a strong enough word for this feeling.

A lump rose in my throat. He was right. The word *unbearable* was more accurate. One day, these kisses may be bitter memories.

So I'd make the most of them.

Unhooking my legs, I didn't break from our kiss until my heeled feet touched the carpet again.

Walking to the middle of the room, I hooked a finger under one strap of my dress and slipped it over my shoulder. The material was tight around my ass, but half of my chest was now exposed. Without structural help, the second side pooled around my hips too.

Sascha's attention fixed on my breasts.

I moistened my lips. "There's a clock over our heads."

Our shared pain filled the air.

"One day, it stops ticking," I whispered. "I need you to touch me now."

My heartbreakingly handsome werewolf approached. "Do you know what I was thinking about when I carted you in here over my shoulder?"

I squealed as he threw me over his shoulder again. This time, he spun me so my face was against his chest.

Gripping my calves, he arranged my knees either side of his head. Murmuring wordless approval, Sascha held me in place with a large hand against my lower back as he peeled the tight skirt of my dress up to reveal bare skin.

This could not mean what I wanted it to mean.

Like he was devouring his favourite meal.

And with a hand on my ass, Sascha pressed his mouth against my core. I blasted a scream through our connection, clinging to his belt. My thighs clamped around his ears.

He stopped the ministrations of his tongue.

"More," I begged. *Please don't make me wait.*

His lips crooked against my sensitive flesh. That alone was enough to make me cry out.

"Not my style, little bird," he hummed.

Is that so?

I tore through his belt with my fangs and yanked the leather from the loops. Was extending my fangs near his erection a threat about what might happen if he didn't get on with the job?

Absolutely.

"Andie—" He choked against my core as I freed him and ran my hand up and down his smoothness.

I wanted him to experience what I felt when he touched me. *Can I put you in my mouth, Sascha?*

This mind connection was incredible. The dirty talking possibilities were endless.

His shallow breathes tickled me. I wiggled, but he pushed me onto his face once more, sucking *hard.*

The scream caught in my throat.

Wrap your lips around me. He growled.

With pleasure.

16

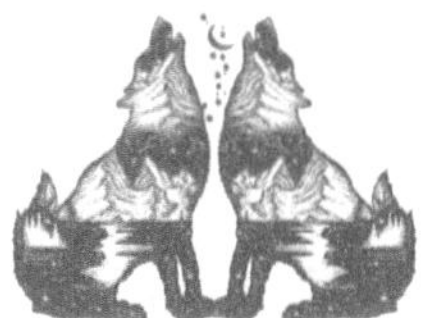

I sat in an antler throne opposite the Luther who'd given me the most earth-shattering orgasm of my life last night.

I liked to think Sascha received as good as he gave.

Was he thinking about it too?

Most of his team were smirking.

Yeah... Judging by the scent in the air, we both wanted a repeat.

"Your decision, Head Steward?" Sascha's voice held a dream-like quality.

Hairy snickered.

I caught an inquisitive glance from Wade. Okay, I stormed to *The Dens* to force a werewolf to compromise in a centuries-old supernatural battle and ended up doing something I could only describe as a vertical sixty-nine.

These things happened.

I cleared my throat. "We'll meet the pack in Timber on Wednesday."

As I expected, he said in my mind.

Did you expect to come apart in my mouth last night?

I grinned as he jerked on his throne.

Mind-speak was my new favourite thing.

Mandy wrinkled her nose, but Grim grinned widely.

"We'll see you then." I led my head team out of the pack house.

"You did something naughty," Wade sang under his breath.

Accurate.

"I have no idea what you're talking about," I murmured.

The head team filed into the van while Wade slid into the passenger seat of Ella F after casting me a suspicious look.

One guess what the subject would be on the drive back to the manor.

"Young wolf. A word."

I faced the fisherwolf as he rounded the pack house. "Alexei. I'm unsure what we have to say to each other."

Sascha appeared on the porch as I listened to the sounds of the van leaving.

"Father," he said. "No more."

"Your potential mate and I must come to an understanding," Alexei replied.

Consider me surprised that the guy's face could display love, but it was there for his son. If I squinted, he almost looked caring.

Sascha folded his arms. "*If* Andie consents."

A refusal lingered on my lips, but the fisherwolf's last comment spun in my mind. *Your potential mate and I must come to an understanding.*

There could be merit in that.

"You can have your word, old wolf." I held up five fingers to Wade inside the car.

I followed Alexei to our bench and sat. I missed this spot by the stream. It had a way of carrying my worries away.

He took the seat next to me. "My son is happier."

Would he like a play-by-play of why? Or...

Alexei sighed. "You told him how you feel."

"Is that a problem for you?"

"It's a problem for both of you."

I agreed. "It's bound to end in ruin, isn't it?"

Wrath rolled off the wolf beside me. "Is that funny to you?"

"It's the least funny thing in the world. Would you prefer I cry?"

Sascha's dad was strange. In some ways, he saw more than his son. In others, he was so blind.

The fisherwolf gazed at the stream. "I'd have preferred you left Deception Valley long ago, but that time has passed."

I glanced at the ancient Luther. "Your son has one chance to find his mate to become immortal and have children. Why would you get in the way of that? You appear to love Sascha, but you work against him. Do you hate the Ni Tiaki so much?"

The old wolf's blue eyes were so different to Sascha's. "I will always hate the races that cause this pack harm. Vampires. Demons. Witches. Humans most of all. Live through centuries of failed negotiations with a tribe who cover their greed with a supposed love of the land and then make your judgements. My son deserved better, and there is no way for him to find happiness now. Not without one of you making a compromise so severe that bitterness will poison your future. I choose a happier and shorter life for my son over a long and miserable one. Immortality isn't everything, young wolf."

At least someone saw just how dire things were for me and Sascha. His words were oddly comforting. And I'd give him one thing—hardly anyone in my life had ever spoken so honestly to me. What if Ragna had sat down like this?

Or Herc.

Or *me* with Rhona?

I could respect the effort he was making—if not the fact he'd rather Sascha die than be with me. "I haven't lived through two centuries of Victratum. I haven't even lived through one year of it. The benefit of that is I don't carry two centuries' worth of prejudice. I see your concerns and share some of them. I'm going to find a way to solve this for Sascha and me."

Alexei scoffed. "Like what?"

Wouldn't he like to know? I was done taking his bait. "Here's my proposal. When I fix everything, you agree to pack away the last few centuries and start afresh, no matter what it takes."

His eyes narrowed.

"Or is your hate for the Ni Tiaki stronger than your love for Sascha?"

He tensed.

I waited.

"And when you fail?" the old wolf asked. "What if you achieve nothing?"

Negative Nancy. "If I fail, you're welcome to continue interfering in our lives. You can see how much it bothers me."

This amused him. A really tiny bit.

Alexei hummed. "No, young wolf. Fail, and you must find a way to leave this valley for good. My son will be hurt by your absence, but anger and pain won't twist him."

Did he speak from personal experience?

He held out a hand, and after a beat, I shook it.

There were loopholes in what he asked. More to the point, I more than half agreed with him.

"In the near future, people may surprise you," I said to him.

Standing, I walked back to Ella F.

Sascha sat on the steps of the pack house, strung tight. "I'll never let you leave."

Direct. "It won't come to that."

"I know." He aimed the comment toward the stream.

Do I need to convince you about my feelings somehow? I thought at him, dragging my gaze over his muscular frame.

His focus returned to me. *Now that you mention it...*

The passenger door opened.

"Hi." Wade poked his head out. "Remember me? I'm right here, and this car doesn't have air conditioning, so keep the heat down."

I brushed my hair back. "Guess I better go."

Sascha walked down the steps.

I bunched my hands in his black tee as he cupped my jaw.

His grin widened as Wade slammed the door closed. We listened to his cursing through the window.

Sascha's lips touched mine and we melted into each other.

Kiss me harder, I silently ordered him.

He listened, and I moaned into his mouth.

Your claws are coming out, mate.

I broke away and sheathed the daggers peeking out from my knuckles. I lifted Sascha's shirt and stared guiltily at the eight trickles of blood. "Oops."

In reply, he tugged me in for another kiss.

The passenger door opened again. "Seriously! You're rocking the car. I'm too close for this shit, and *not* taking a contraceptive, I might add."

Wade slammed the door.

Sascha kissed my cheek. "Greyson is growing impatient for the next meet. He wants you to know."

The bite meet. "Should we arrange a time?"

Sascha arched a brow. "That's not really his style."

Dang it. Please not at the manor—though I'd be an idiot to put that challenge in his head. The wolf had an authority problem.

He can try his best to sneak up on me, Booker snarled.

Is this one for you? I asked her.

The capture meet and bite meet are done in four-legged form, yes.

I opened the car door. "Hey, Sascha? Heads-up that something is happening tomorrow that will interest the pack."

Sascha searched my face. "What is it?"

"Agree to work with me, and I may let you in on the details." I winked and slid into the car.

Wade glared at me. "We need to go to the health clinic."

"Why? What's wrong?"

"I think I'm pregnant."

This was the first time I'd visited Deception Valley Public Hall. Wooden trusses held up the roof of the large rectangular space. Double doors led to an industrial-size kitchen. Chairs faced the small stage where I currently sat with the other nine council members.

Margaret Frey used the table to stand up. "Good evening to you all. Before we distribute the meeting agenda, I'd like to welcome our tenth member to the table. Andie Thana recently inherited leadership of the Ni Tiaki, and she is bringing a new proposal to our attention today. Andie, may I introduce our public representatives—Gabriel, Wilson, Rose, and Terrie."

Terrie was the woman who'd brought up airport proposals in the past. Chantel had used a lot of the information from that, along with her help, when forming our own proposal.

I greeted each of the public members with a smile and caught their slightly awed greetings. The Thanas held a weird prestigious celebrity status in the valley.

Chantel confirmed the minutes of the previous meeting and the order of proceedings tonight before gesturing to me. "We have two proposals. The council will discuss these privately before opening the doors to the public. Andie. Over to you."

Nerves erupted in my stomach. *Here goes.*

This is already boring. Booker yawned.

I smiled. "It's a pleasure to formally meet the council. I understand this team has worked together for a long time, and I look forward to becoming part of that. First and foremost, I'm interested in the prosperity of this valley. Having moved to these parts from the big wide, I feel with absolute certainty that the beauty and resources of this land must be cared for and that we must provide for this wonderful community to the best of our ability. Today, I bring a proposal to the council for an airport in Deception Valley."

I handed a bound folder to each member.

"An airport." Wilson shot a look at Terrie, who beamed back.

The room filled with the scent of their eagerness and approval. I could feel some slight determination.

"An airport," I echoed. "Firstly, I'd like to thank the council members who helped me put this detailed proposal together on short notice. It was a great learning experience for me. Please turn to page one. I'd like to discuss the feasibility of this project."

Tracking their scents, I laid out the benefits of the airport for the valley's economy as I'd done for Chantel.

Don't forget the part about small businesses, Booker leaped in despite her earlier yawn.

I added that in. *Did I miss anything else?*

I'd stayed up most of the night, trying my best to memorise the information.

Not that I recall.

Two minds were better than one—if that's what we were.

Rose raised her hand. "What timeframe do you suggest, Andie?"

"Please turn to page six. A regional airport like ours needs surprisingly little to be operational." I inhaled their uncertainty when I announced the two-month window. "This may seem fast, but with myriad advantages for the valley and funding from the Ni Tiaki and Deception Valley Exports, the value for money for our council and the community is huge for little risk. I believe the sooner this airport is up and running, the better."

That helped Wilson warm to the speedy construction.

I moved through the communication, confidentiality, and probity rules—none of which I'd known anything about prior to three days ago.

Hell, I'd grown pretty good at swimming instead of sinking when thrown in the deep end.

I don't like swimming!

We're not going swimming, Booker.

That's what you always say.

"If you could turn to the final page, please. Here are three lists covering the legal, financial, and technical teams we would hire to form a binding offer between the tribe and this council. Adrian Gert, the site manager we heavily consulted when putting this proposal together, would be our choice for overseeing the building process." I rattled through some of the other names and took a deep breath. "Any questions?"

Rose raised her hand. "Who will fly the planes?"

"To begin, we may need to hire from the big wide. In the long term, the airport will provide a career opportunity for the young people in this valley. I'd love to hire locally as time goes on. Once a binding contract is established with the council, interested tribe members will be put through pilot training."

Wilson and Margaret smiled.

Gabriel flicked to the start of the bound folder. "This is a great proposal. The clear conflict of interest is that Deception Valley Exports would have a monopoly on cargo space. How will access to the public be assured? The reaction of Valley Trade Services needs to be considered."

Despite his congratulations, Gabriel was more on the fence than anyone. The timeframe really threw him. "Passenger access is absolutely guaranteed to everyone—local or not. The only restriction will be on seat numbers and flight frequency—like a normal airport. As you heard, during the next month, visitors to the valley and our local population will be polled to gauge demand so we're able to provide an adequate service out the gate. As for Valley Trade Services, they'll have the option to access air exports through our company. This deal will be exclusively negotiated and managed by Deception Valley Exports. However, I don't agree with the term monopoly. There will always be a market for land transportation. I envision that both companies will thrive through occupying different niches."

Gabriel considered that. "The land you propose for the airport will cost more to develop than the top site recommended by your experts. Is there a reason land from the timber mill can't be diverted for the airport? It will save the valley millions."

Yes, there was a huge reason.

One particular flat section in Timber ticked all the boxes but constructing the airport there would require the pack and tribe to renegotiate the parameters of the grid. Anything to do with the game businesses and battle grounds had to be negotiated with the pack. Sascha could simply say no.

Though it certainly wasn't in his interest to put up road barriers in this case.

"We'd prefer not to disrupt the running of the mill."

"I see. Whatever the agreed-upon site, will this land be granted by the tribe, or will there be a lease cost?"

I nodded. "The land can be placed in trust or leased depending on the council's preference. If placed in trust, then invested parties will be responsible for maintenance costs. If leased, the tribe will cover these costs. As long as the airport site takes aeronautical and air-transport requirements into account—as well as the environmental impact to the valley—our experts have agreed any of the suggested site options will suffice."

Dammit, the council seemed torn on that point.

"The timeframe," he remarked next. "Is there any reason to hurry through this?"

I met his gaze. "Is there any reason not to? Road repairs have almost concluded for the summer. To my knowledge, there's one other minor proposal on the agenda tonight. In all honesty, I wouldn't push so hard if not for seeing how much the valley will benefit from this. I feel an airport is long overdue."

I had to be prepared for every outcome, and I wanted to win Grids within two months. If the tribe couldn't be convinced to let the pack stay on, the airport would be their escape. If the airport wasn't finished in time, arranging safe passage through Bluff City with King Julius would hopefully provide another option. If the tribe *agreed* to let the pack stay, then the airport would allow Luthers to find their mates and act as a long-term route in and out of the valley.

And if none of that worked... I was fresh out of ideas.

Margaret Frey stood again. "Thank you, Andie. You've given us a lot to think about."

"Thank you for your time."

Phew. Now I just had to get through the public questioning.

Terrie worked through a sewage treatment proposal that appeared to be an update on a prior contract. No one seemed too shocked or interested.

Chantel leaned closer as Margaret wrapped up the second discussion. “We open to the public now.”

We rearranged our tables into a single row facing the empty chairs. There had to be at least two hundred seats. Thinking of the questions I just copped from the council, I braced myself, checking my hair and outfit in the reflection of the kitchen window.

Rose and Wilson opened the doors and four members of the public entered.

“That’s it?” I whispered to Terrie.

Her lips twitched. “Not many people turn out for sewage proposals.”

Fair enough. My proposal was submitted last minute and there wasn’t time to put it on the council’s website.

The four locals occupied one-fifth of the front row. I briefly outlined the airport proposal again and answered their questions within ten minutes. The locals seemed more shocked than anything. Poor things came here expecting good ol’ normal sewage.

Chantel had coached me in the next part.

I faced the nine people on the stage. “I move for the council to enter negotiations for a final binding contract to develop and build the first Deception Valley Regional Airport.”

Terrie leaped in. “I second the motion.”

To my surprise, we entered into a second round of debate for the public’s benefit.

This time, the council members only talked through Margaret in the middle of our row, and I mimicked their behaviour when I spoke.

A buzzer went off after thirty minutes, and I peered around until Margaret announced the conclusion of the debate.

What’s going on? Booker asked.

No fucking idea.

There was no hint of frailness in Margaret's voice as she said, "The Deception Valley Council will now vote on the motion."

I balled my hands under the table. The timeline would probably put people off. We just needed the majority.

Margaret stated, "Raise your hand if you support the opening of negotiations between the council, Ni Tiaki, and Deception Valley Exports toward a final, binding contract to develop and build the first Deception Valley Regional Airport."

Heart thumping, I raised my clammy-ass hand in the air.

Gabriel and Rose kept their hands down.

We had the majority.

I nearly sagged into a heap on the floor.

Yes!

You did it, Booker said, a smile in her voice.

We did it.

The meeting concluded.

"No hard feelings." Rose shook my hand. "I just prefer more information."

"Of course. We won't start anything without ticking the boxes we need to. I assure you of that."

Margaret winked at me. "Well done."

I took her hand. "Thank you for helping me."

"You gave my family a truth that has healed our aching hearts. There's very little this old woman wouldn't do for you. I did want to say that it's very unlikely the council can spend more money on your airport than is necessary. If you want my advice, you and the head team should pursue negotiations with the tribe for the site in Timber without delay. If the pack is adverse, then we'll need to come up with a more solid reason for choosing another site. But it will be a hard sell."

Right. "That's good to know," I said grimly.

"Miss Thana?" one of the locals asked when I left the stage.

"How can I help you?"

The younger man flushed and shook my extended hand. "I

work with The Valley Vine. I'd love to run an article on your airport if that's okay with you?"

We had a paper? "Sure."

Chantel rested a hand on my shoulder. "The Ni Tiaki and council will need to approve the article prior to printing, Otto."

He bobbed his head several times. "Of course. If I take a picture then, Miss Thana, and perhaps get a statement after?"

17

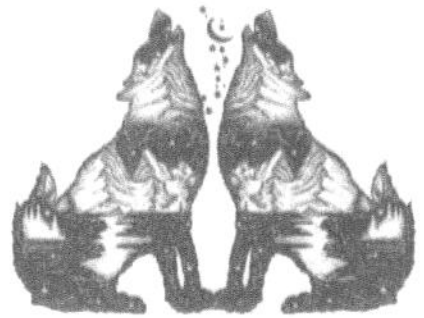

"Trixie." I placed my study notes and antique laptop into my bag. Half of my last assignment was completed to mediocre standard. "You wanted to see me."

The petite woman had endless energy that always inspired me to keep going. People like Nathan and Stanley were necessary to challenge my choices. Trixie did, too, but she and Roderick offered a positivity that balanced the other members. Valerie aside, Herc formed one solid head team.

She sat opposite me. "We've never lost possession of Sandstone. With Timber in pack control, too, I'm concerned that the numbers of unemployed Ni Tiaki relying on tribe funds will drain our reserves."

Crap. "What do the current numbers look like?"

She opened her folder and passed over a paper. "The figure at the top is the current fund balance. Currently, we're paying out $355,000 each week to match 100 percent of the stewards' previous earnings."

The tribe was rich, but that was a huge ongoing cost. "How long can we keep that up?"

"I spoke with Stanley. He expects that after three months, the depletion of our reserves will affect the strength of our position in Grids."

Management of finances was a big part of my ability to approve new strategies each week and also how much equipment we could replace.

I studied the second graph on the paper. "This is what happens if we win Timber tomorrow night?"

"Yes." She passed over a second paper. "Timber will help, but it doesn't bring in as much income as either Sandstone or Iron. Even if we win tomorrow, Stanley believes we should cut the wages of unemployed Sandstone stewards to 80 percent to give us the ability to continue as is in the game for a year."

Yikes. "If we don't win?"

"He recommends a 60 percent reduction in wages for workers in Timber and Sandstone."

Our community was more about contributing to the whole, so the tribe worked for low hourly rates as it was. Labourers earned around five hundred dollars a week. 60 percent took that figure down to three hundred. "Would their rent rate be reduced too?"

Each cabin came with a fifty dollar a week maintenance cost. That would take some stewards down to two hundred and fifty a week. Fine for a household with multiple workers and no children. Not so fine for everyone else.

"We could figure something out, I'm sure."

I nodded. "How soon after Timber will we need to move on this?"

"Sooner the better."

"Let's meet on Thursday morning at 11:00 a.m. to discuss our options. Ask Stanley to attend, too, please."

Trixie nodded and left.

I rubbed my temples

We could *not* afford to gamble with tribe money. With my childhood experiences alone, that path was a resounding no, but losing financial security would affect my plans for Clay and Water big time. I wanted to win quickly, but there was no guarantee of that.

My phone rang.

"Hey. Andie here."

"Mate."

His smooth voice trickled over me like heated water, and a shiver worked up my spine. "Sorry. Who's this?"

He growled.

My mouth spread in a grin. "Just a joke. Don't get your fur in a tangle. I meant to call you last night, but my brain was fried. There's something in the works—"

"Would that have anything to do with the picture of you in the paper with a proposal for a Deception Valley Airport?"

The Valley Vine didn't fuck around. "I wanted to talk to you before that released."

The silence mounted.

"Sascha?"

He took a breath. "Why did you do this?"

Really? The *airport* had clear benefits. "You know why I did this. The pack is trapped. With an airport, they can find their mates."

"So that's the only reason?" he asked carefully.

"What do you mean?"

"My pack are desperate for their mates, Andie. What do you think happens when the airport opens?"

My cheeks flushed. "I didn't do this to deplete the pack's numbers if that's what you're insinuating. I did it for the *opposite* reason."

Sascha sighed. "I needed to check."

"Did you now?"

"For myself, no."

"Are there others listening to this conversation?"

"Correct."

Closing my eyes, I mentally smashed the desk and furniture before answering, "Then you can tell them that I did it to save our wolves."

I straightened.

Booker sniffed in disdain. *Your wolves. Not mine.*

I just straight-up claimed the pack.

Squeaking, I hung up.

Sascha called a second time, but I screened him.

I've never said that before. I'd felt protective about the Luther women and children and wanted the tribe to be happy as a whole, but what I'd just said felt really, really significant.

I shook away the thought.

The more pertinent issue was how to not bankrupt the tribe.

You only have one grid and too many unemployed workers, Booker said.

Clever cookie.

Cookies can't be clever.

Wolves apparently don't speak English either, I countered.

She ignored me. *The pack have four grids though.*

Are you going somewhere with this...?

My wolf growled. *They usually only have three. More often, they only manage Clay and Water. A human that was less stupid than the others once told you the pack don't hire outsiders. So how are they coping with so much extra work?*

My mouth dried.

Using our mouth, she smirked. *Have a rare steak later, would you?*

Six hundred and fifty stewards were twiddling their thumbs, but the pack had to be working around the clock to ensure the smooth operation of four grids using the same number of staff they'd used in *two*.

They could probably use six hundred and fifty workers who knew werewolves existed and wouldn't cramp their Luther style.

I scrambled to grab my phone, then stopped.

Mothershitter. Stewards would take this idea about as well as discovering I had fangs.

But it was the perfect solution.

I groaned and pulled at my hair. "People shit me."

I hear you, sister.

Another Wade-ism? Lifting the handset, I dialled seven.

"Head Steward," Pascal answered.

"I'm calling an urgent head team meeting. There are a few things we need to discuss."

We hadn't held a video conference with the pack for a while, but Tuesday afternoons weren't the best time to meet face to face when strategies were being finalised, manoeuvres practiced, and equipment checked.

"Thank you for meeting at short notice," I said to the wolves on the screen.

Sascha stood in the middle of his lead wolves. Why did they always stand? On a side note, if Sascha ever decided to strip on camera for a day job, I'd subscribe.

He consulted the document before him. "We were very interested to receive your requests."

"That's an interesting way to paraphrase a contractual obligation to hear the other team if they wish to open negotiations."

Sascha lips curved. "We'll start with point one."

I gestured for him to proceed.

Total pissing contest.

This is like foreplay, I thought at him.

He didn't show any reaction on the screen.

Dang. Mind-speak had distance limits.

Sascha met my gaze. "You'd like to redefine the borders of Timber to allow for the construction of an airport. We don't see how this would benefit us, but the pack would need a copy of the tribe's contract with the council before considering anything."

He was such a bullshitter. Then again, I'd known he'd spin these negotiations to pack favour—it's not like the head team knew about the whole mating situation.

I jotted that down. "The tribe can provide the final contract for the pack prior to signing. We agree that no further amendments will be made after the fact."

All six of the wolves were scowling.

Wow... or had I missed the mark on the pack's reaction? I expected them to be overjoyed at this news. "The main points from the contract for your consideration are that Deception Valley Exports will have exclusivity on air transportation for imports and exports.

Grim stared down his nose at me. "Why would we ever agree to that?"

"You'll have the option to contract us for the movement of resources. However, keep in mind that we will move off the roads—completely, in time—leaving that niche to you. Our service will not be accessible to you for the importation of grid equipment, of course."

"*Of course*," Mandy muttered.

"What type of fees will be involved in the pack contracting space? I assume they'll be extortionate." Sascha crossed his arms.

Mmm, tight T-shirt. "Stanley, would you agree that fees can be negotiated in advance of signing the contract?"

The man on my left grunted. "Accounting for inflation, then yes, we can set the fees."

Sascha tilted his head. "The pack won't agree to anything other than fair fees. That is a make or break clause for us."

Sure it was.

Half of my team entered this meeting adamant the Luthers would never agree to an airport. I inhaled their shock and excitement at his words.

Wade spoke, "The pack would have complete access to passenger seats."

"And free travel," Sascha replied.

I laughed shortly. "The Ni Tiaki are paying for more than half of the airport, Mr Greyson, and even we won't travel for free."

He smirked. "Correct me if I'm wrong, Miss Thana. Your airport relies on this strip of land in Timber."

Maybe it was a good thing we weren't face to face. Because incoming lie. "Incorrect. While experts agreed that particular site is the best, there are other places outside of Grids that could be developed at a higher cost." I sighed. "Higher construction costs would unfortunately be passed onto our customers in the form of steeper fees. Business is business, you understand."

I doubted anyone without werewolf eyes noticed his lips twitch.

I continued. "*If* the pack wishes to press free travel, then the tribe would need to run numbers to see how many seats could be put aside each week for your travel. A restriction would be introduced where there would otherwise be no restriction."

Maybe that would help to reassure the pack that there wouldn't be a mass exodus to find mates.

Leroy shot me a look. "Timber is in our possession. The airport you're requesting to build will take 150 acres of our product away."

I didn't miss his use of the word *requesting.* Alpha brat. "The Ni Tiaki are willing to gift tribal land to the timber mill trust."

"A hundred and fifty acres of tribal land?" Sascha's focus sharpened.

Roderick cut in. "The wood contained in the gifted land will be of far greater value than what's currently being milled."

There's no way I'd gift virgin forest to the mill, but once upon a time Timber was bigger. The last time Victratum restarted, the parameters of the grid shrunk. The trees we intended to give back were now fifty years old, but not hundreds and thousands of years old like the rest.

"Pascal," I murmured. "Please send the land map through."

We waited as the six Luthers studied the boundaries.

Sascha glanced up. "That's a far lower number than 150."

"We believe it holds equivalent value. Plus, Timber won't be your problem after tomorrow when I win it. If you consider that parcel of land a loss, then it will be our loss, not yours."

The wolves scowled. Wade snorted.

Sascha regarded the map again. "While we can agree that the

trees on this land bring a small amount of increased value, the pack won't consider less than 135 acres."

A joke.

"We've offered 70. I'm willing to bring that up to 100 acres as a show of goodwill."

He considered me. "Let's split the difference. The pack will consider 117 acres in exchange for the taken land. You can keep the half an acre difference as a show of our good will."

So generous.

But all going well, Timber would be in my possession tomorrow. Did I back myself? Yes. "Agreed. I think we've covered the main—"

"There would need to be an exemption from Victratum's care of the land clause where this is concerned," Sascha's gaze bore into mine. "We wouldn't want to be considered at fault for milling older trees or for agreeing to relinquish land for the purposes of an airport."

Dammit. We needed more penalty points and that had been my best idea so far. "That goes without saying."

He arched a brow. "Even so. I insist."

When will you have sex with him? Booker asked.

Not the time, I mentally hissed back. Save me from werewolves with crushes.

The pack leader widened his stance. "I'll confer with my people and return with an answer on Sunday."

He better not fuck this up.

If you'd waited to show your butthole to him after this meeting, instead of the other night, we wouldn't be having this problem.

I ignored Booker's huffing laughter. "Moving onto point two then. You have jobs that require filling. We have people needing jobs. This move would be irregular, but so was the pack's *request* for grid announcements to be held face to face not so long ago. This exchange could benefit both of our people in more ways than financially."

The pack's scowls were gone.

They were all over the damn place today.

"The pack agrees to employ your stewards," Sascha announced.

"Just like that?"

My head team was surprised. Well, Wade was hungry. But everyone else was surprised.

"My wolves are working too hard. Due to our nature, hiring outsiders to work alongside us poses a big issue. This is a clear solution while Victratum continues, and one I planned to bring up on Sunday."

I recalled something else Trixie had raised in the past. "The reverse makes sense too. When the Ni Tiaki have four grids in our possession, we'll happily employ your pack to fill positions."

Sascha smirked. I smirked back.

"Our marshal is still new to her position." He glanced at Pascal. "If your marshal could mentor her through the process of drawing up a new agreement, we'd appreciate that."

"That's fine with me," Pascal answered.

Beside me, Stanley swore as Sascha's eyes flooded black.

Greyson stared out at me. "Soon, little bird."

The call cut off.

Right...

Nine sets of eyes riveted on me, the emotions of their owners ranging from curious to alarmed to amused—*Wade.*

Nathan broke the silence. "What was that about?"

"The next meet, I'd say." I stacked my papers. "His wolf is eager to keep going."

Wade finished his coffee. "Do you think he'll do it tomorrow in the grid?"

I pursed my lips. "Timber will likely be a close game. Attacking me in the grid will lose the pack points."

"It's an attack?" Trixie's eyes widened.

"A bite. I'm fairly sure that Sascha's wolf wants me in wolf form for it." *Hmm.* "I can't be sure, but I don't think he'll attempt something in Timber. After what happened with Herc though, I won't take any chances. I'll isolate from everyone else for the duration of the game."

Nathan cast me a strange look. "That will make you a target."

"They can only get one point from taking me down."

Pascal stood. "You're worth far more than one point to this tribe. The stewards rely on your excellent leadership."

Perhaps. We had a chain of command in place, just in case. Reindeer was always prepped to take over if I went down.

I checked the time. "Two hours before the gathering."

Sending stewards to work with the pack wouldn't be my choice alone. The tribe would either step up. Or they wouldn't.

But it had to be their choice.

"What do you think they'll decide?" Roderick asked.

A total of 64 percent had agreed to cater to my Luther needs if I returned as head steward.

I really hoped that 64 percent felt they'd made the right decision and were willing to try something new yet again.

18

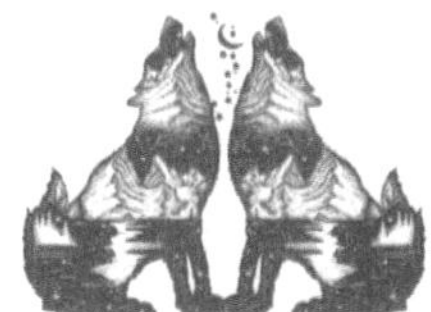

My stomach churned as the second cannon fired.

Are you going to shit yourself? I'd prefer to shift, if so.

Exhaling, I blinked a few times. *I'm okay. Probably.*

I listened to the pounding footsteps as Luthers entered the grid. The sound was only just audible over the frequency generators.

Booker took over our sense of smell, so I could focus on delivering orders. Tonight, we'd need to work hard.

They're climbing the trees, she reported.

Sascha would be a fool to alter his strategy. Even when Rhona knew about his plans to use the trees and countered, the pack won.

But he'd have new tricks up his sleeve too.

And so did we.

Timber had remained in our possession for 79 percent of Victratum to date and the grid bordered manor lands. My stewards knew this place.

They knew the tallest trees.

Where the most expansive views were.

And the best hiding places.

"*Reindeer. Luthers dispersing throughout grid. Over.*"

Good. The exact same strategy as a fortnight ago. Luthers were hardest to battle in a solid group—which was why Alexei mostly stuck to that during his stint as pack leader. Sascha was confident about their advantage.

Last time, the pack used nets to great effectiveness against us.

Snow's voice crackled in my ear. "*Group congregating J7. Twenty-seven.*"

Herc's first advice to me was to never say anything specific over the walkies. The pack always figured out our frequency and listened in.

The leader of the south team just told me that seventeen Luthers were in the trees in section K6.

I crouched in front of the map rolled out on the forest floor. There was a ground unit hiding in K7 awaiting orders. Seventeen Luthers fighting from the trees were too much for one unit.

There was a second unit in K10, and Snow was at one of our vantage trees in K8 with two members of her unit. They could help out too.

Rhona opted for a ground-only counter-attack last time, but I felt vantage points would help our ground teams immensely.

I clicked on my walkie. "Big Red. Wicked, initiate Operation Chuckles. J13." I spoke to the entire tribe next. "Big Red. J8 and J11, prepare to engage. Closest vantage, permission to engage also."

We needed the group of Luthers to move west so Snow and the second unit could help take the Luthers down.

Less than a minute later, the new West team leader replied, "*Wicked. Task completed. Over.*"

She'd just switched off a few frequency generators in K12 and fired a few times. Just for two or three seconds. We'd tested the result on my ears. The sudden sound mimicked a skirmish.

The fake skirmish should draw the Luthers in. "Come on."

"*Snow. J8. Moving fast. Over.*"

I readied my hand on the walkie.

"*Snow J9. Over.*"

I blurted. "Big Red. J8, J11, and closet vantage, engage. Over."

Squeezing my eyes shut, I strained to hear.

Nothing.

The group has halted, Booker inhaled.

Every steward had worked tirelessly to memorize a list of hiding spots in their section of the grid. There were *thousands* of hiding spots in total. The idea was to tease the Luthers to the ground so we could take them out safely. In addition, three stewards in each unit were on nets. If a Luther was shot in the trees, it was their job to catch the unconscious pack member as best they could.

The plan wasn't perfect, but I was at a loss of how else to prevent forfeiting points due to serious injury. That's what got Rhona last time.

"Snow. Group contained. Task complete. Over."

No one got away.

I smiled.

Wicked and Reindeer reported more clusters and I hurried to my map again, firing orders to the tribe. Numbers whirled in my head.

Listening to another report, I rattled off an order to the team in east. *Fuck me,* this code was a mind fuck.

A27 converted to B26, right? I hurtled more orders into the grid.

And the reports didn't stop.

Booker's updates were the only thing I could focus on other than the map.

Boom.

I jerked at the sound of the cannon. "It's over already?"

A glance at my watch confirmed an entire hour had passed.

Whoa. That was intense. My brain hurt.

Do you think it worked? my wolf asked.

I hope so. I really, really hoped so.

Gathering my map, I ran at Luther speed through the grid toward Pascal's usual position. *Guess Greyson isn't making a move for the bite meet tonight.*

He likes us uncertain, she replied.

He did. And was good at it.

I reached the north entrance and searched for Pascal's lily scent.

"Head Steward, how did we do?" a woman asked.

I squeezed her shoulder. "Unsure just yet."

Pascal had access to strategically placed cameras and heat sensor information so she and the other marshal could tally some of the score as the game rolled out. That meant I normally had some idea of where the tribe stood.

Ugh, so many things could affect the score tonight.

What if our plan wasn't enough?

The pack members we tranquilised at the start of the hour could have woken before the end—though we'd asked the stewards to monitor fallen Luthers.

Forcing bravado to the fore, I smiled and nodded at returning stewards.

Snow joined me and we fist-bumped.

"Good work out there," I told her.

"Back at ya. Got hectic, huh?"

"Coordinating units may be a two or three-person job."

She snorted.

I glanced around for Pascal again. "Anything else happen that I missed?"

"Not all of the pack went up into the trees. Greyson sent at least three larger forces on general sweeps."

Dang. "Many casualties?"

"More than we'd have liked," she replied grimly "Will the marshals take long?"

In this grid?

Always.

I cupped my hands around my mouth. "Stewards, you did amazing today. Let's head back to the manor to await the score."

The urge to shift and run to ease my nerves itched at me, but I didn't want to be alone to hear the result either.

With my stewards, I walked back to the manor in tense silence.

Tribe members soon packed the large lounge area that lead out to the patio and pool. Stewards who didn't even enter the grid had gathered too. Generally, we took a load off after grid night and had a few drinks and laughs.

Not tonight.

We spilled throughout the house and over the front lawn, barely making a peep.

"I swear Pascal is dragging this out on purpose," Wade said from the armchair next to mine.

I'd laugh, but... was she? "I thought this week would be easier to take than Iron."

Nathan sighed. "Some weeks, the game just means more."

Pascal entered, and I crossed the room to her at Luther speed.

I clutched her forearms. "Tell us."

Her lips curved. "Congratulations, Head Steward."

The room exploded in an uproar of shouts and cheering. Disregarding my ringing ears, I hugged Pascal tight.

She patted my back. "Well done. A convincing win."

"*How* convincing?"

"Twenty-five points convincing."

Wade and Cameron pulled me out onto the patio and a mic was shoved in my hands.

I breathed in the jubilation covering the manor grounds.

"Stewards," I said when they quietened enough to hear. "We did it!"

They jumped and hugged each other. This was enough to make a bad bitch cry—and I was a pretty soft-hearted bitch, really.

Swallowing the lump in my throat, I held the microphone to my lips. "I'm in awe of you once again." They'd executed such a complex plan to perfection.

My throat tightened. *Dammit.*

Wade ripped the mic away. "I don't know about you guys, but I wondered at least three times tonight whether our head steward was stopping for breath. I've never experienced another leader do that. Put your hands together, ladies and gents."

That about did it. I tried to be discreet about dabbing the corners of my eyes. Cameron ruined it by handing me a tissue.

I took the mic back after. "Two grids, and we're not stopping until we have all five. Enjoy tonight and—"

Stanley whispered in my ear and passed me two pieces of paper.

I studied the two slips. "One moment. I have the results of the poll we opened last night."

The crowd hushed.

I held up the two pieces of paper. "We polled the unemployed stewards separately from the rest of the tribe. The head team decided that as the affected group, their voice should hold particular weight in our decision." I read the result aloud, "Of the currently unemployed stewards, 83 percent voted in favour of working with the Luthers."

We were a tribe, but families had to look out for themselves within that. No surprises that the idea of taking a 20 to 40 percent pay cut hadn't appealed to most.

I held up the second piece of paper. "Of the tribe, 71 percent are in favour of working with the pack to fill grid positions, now and in the future."

This was *excellent* news.

Cameron once said that people found it hard to hate someone they knew.

I was banking on it. "Enough business for one night. Go forth and celebrate."

Tomorrow, we had work to do.

19

Greyson is cramping my style, Booker snapped. *A female wolf needs to run as though no one's watching.*

They did?

Sascha's wolf circled us from afar and had been for an hour. *He's trying to figure out how to bite us.*

Honestly, I would've just let him, but my wolf wasn't on the same page. Greyson had his work cut out for him.

He should give up. She growled. *Bad hunter. Puny strength.*

Booker leaped over a stream, careful not to get a single drop on our fur.

Greyson stopped, and she paused, too, until he resumed his steady pace.

Time spent in the passenger seat of a wolf body had taught me about a wolf's hunting habits. Booker rarely broke from her loping pace, instead opting to follow prey at a distance. If the prey let her get close enough, she'd break into a run to close the gap. Otherwise, she gave up the chase after exerting mild effort.

So far, she'd always let anything she caught go—thank fuck.

Do you think Greyson will only chase us if he gets closer? I asked her.

She leaped over a fallen tree. *Not if he uses our pack.*

What did you just say?

His pack.

That's not what she'd said. *You said our pack!* Booker accepted Wade, but that was about it. She tolerated Cameron, hated Rhona, thought Pascal *would do*, and otherwise preferred to think of others as cardiac muscle delicacies.

This was ground-breaking.

When did that happen? I asked.

Her horror seeped to me. *I don't know.*

I bit back on laughter. Claiming others would genuinely upset her. *It doesn't have to change anything. I won't tell the pack you like them. Or Sascha and Greyson unless you tell me it's okay.*

It comes with consequences.

Like?

Booker sighed. *Take a look. It's already happened.*

She sat back on our haunches.

I noticed the tiny pressure on my mind. Slight pressures.

Warm.

Six of them.

What are those? I asked. The pressure was tugging me gently, a piece of string I could follow to the other end.

She grumbled, *The pack.*

What? *You're joking me.*

Am I a comedian?

For the record, I'd watch a wolf comedian. *This happened just because you accepted the pack as yours?*

She snarled.

Were we still denying that? *So six of the pack are currently in four-legged form in addition to Sascha?* His presence still occupied the space under my ribs. *Is there anything else we can do?*

I can talk to any shifted pack member while in four-legged form. But I'm not talking to them. I don't care if you want me to.

You don't have to do anything that you don't want, I murmured. *Can I talk to them too?*

Just me.

Booker's view was clear, but the link to the pack intrigued me. We could check in on some of the women. Axel too. *Can they access our thoughts?*

That wasn't how it worked with Sascha, but I should check. Because... potential disaster if so.

Only what I tell them. Greyson can address all shifted pack members at once. His head team can deliver orders to those of their status. Currently, I could address all shifted females, but only as his mate could I speak to the entire pack at once.

There was an edge in her voice.

She was freaking out.

Can the pack feel us too?

If they take the trouble to look.

Then how about we shift back and keep this news to ourselves for a little longer?

Booker launched into one of her rare sprints and only slowed to trot through the manor grounds. She tilted her head to allow one of the gardeners to scratch her behind the ear.

"Hey, Andie," Roderick said around a mouthful of toast in the hall. "See you at eight."

I yipped in response.

Booker continued to the kitchen. The staff had set aside a plate of bacon and one of them left their station to hand feed us. Certain high-maintenance wolves refused to eat off the floor.

We shifted in our room. I checked my jeans and T-shirt combo in the mirror, and a strange contentedness filled me. For the first time since returning to tribal lands, things felt normal.

Things felt good.

The stewards in the manor were mostly accustomed to Booker's presence. With two grid wins—and one of them a turnover—in the bag, I'd once again proved my ability to do the job.

Knock, knock.

"Head Steward?"

The head gardener stood in the doorway of my room.

"Marty, can I help you?"

"There's... well, best come look."

I followed him outside.

Ah, fuck me.

A blue pickup truck was lodged halfway through a garden bed. *Sascha's* pickup truck.

Booker inhaled.

Essie the bacon sandwich thief.

I bit back a groan. "It's another young Luther. Please tell everyone there's no cause for alarm."

I crossed the lawn, eyeing the ripped-up grass where she'd lost control of the truck. Essie couldn't be more than fourteen, and she'd stolen and crashed the pack leader's vehicle.

I sighed.

She wasn't by the pickup. I tracked her to the trees behind the crash scene.

You taught her to escape to the trees, Booker said proudly.

That's when she was stealing food. Perhaps I'd encouraged this. *Oops.*

"Essie, it's okay. Come out." I listened to her sobs and sniffs.

The young teen left her hiding place and approached me barefoot, clutching her tear-streaked cheeks.

I looked her over. "Are you hurt?"

She gulped back another sob and shook her head.

"We better go inside then." Arm around her shoulders, I led her to the manor. The gardeners looked on, but I guess a teenage Luther crashing a truck was less exciting than a baby Luther waddling onto manor grounds.

I sat her down on a kitchen bench and perched beside her.

The staff quietened, glancing at us.

Essie wiped her face. "I was doing okay until the end."

My lips trembled. *Don't laugh.* Damn, she could smell it anyway. "You drove all the way from pack lands?"

She nodded. "Mr Greyson wasn't using his truck today. I heard him say so. And I wanted to talk to you about something. I thought I could get back in time."

"Are you hungry, dear?" Detta cut in.

The Luther's face brightened. The cook delivered a cinnamon scroll.

Why did I bother? "What did you want to talk with me about, Essie?"

"Everyone treats me like a baby, but I'm not the baby anymore—Axel is. I'm sick of people expecting me to always do the wrong thing. Why should I do the right thing when they don't think I can?"

Ah... I wasn't a parent. Not even close. How should I handle this one?

I brushed my hair back. "Have you told your parents you feel this way?"

"They don't listen."

"Maybe there's a way to make them listen?"

She narrowed her gaze. "Like what?"

"Well, when you normally talk to them, what do you do?"

"They yell at me and I yell back."

I pursed my lips. "What do you think when they yell at you?"

Essie cast me an exasperated look. "Okay, I get it. Talk about things when no one's yelling."

I exchanged an amused look with the smiling kitchen staff.

Once the teen had finished her scroll, I spoke again. "Essie, I understand you want people to treat you your age rather than someone of Axel's age. Try to remember that most of the pack are far older than you. Hundreds of years older. They love you, but they may have forgotten how they felt at your age. Speak calmly, and they'll be more inclined to listen."

The Luther sniffed. "Okay."

I squared my shoulders. "Earning people's respect requires treating people with respect. Today, you stole a truck and crashed it. I'm sure you realise there will be consequences."

She swallowed. "He's going to be angry at me."

"Probably. How would you feel if someone broke something of yours? Maybe there was another way to talk with me. What do you think?"

The teenager sighed. "Phone."

"That's right. You know that for next time, but now, it's time to face the music." I handed her my phone. "You need to call, uh, Mr Greyson, and then you'll need to contact Evelyn so she can let your parents know where you've been."

Blood drained from her face as she took the phone.

"You can take the call outside if you prefer," I offered.

Watching her leave, I nicked a scroll for myself and grinned with the cooks. Part of me had to applaud Essie's guts.

No way would I have nicked Alexei's car at her age.

I waited a few minutes before joining her.

She was crying, and after briefly listening to Sascha's deep voice on the other end, I left her to it.

The gardeners were trying to extract the pickup from a low hedge. Bending my knees, I lifted up one end of the truck and waited for them to scramble back before swinging the nose around and lowering it to the ground.

Essie passed me the phone. "Evelyn wants to speak with you."

I pressed the speaker to my ear. "Hey."

"Our apologies once again, Andie."

"It's no trouble. There is some damage to the garden though."

"We'll help to restore it," she said. "A couple of our male betas are on the way over with a tow truck. Do they have permission to enter tribal lands without penalty?"

My original offer extended to the women and children of the pack. But... the males were only coming because of a child of the pack. "Yes. That's okay."

Word spread yet again. Our Timber workers were already at the mill, but Sandstone stewards were waiting to begin employment with the Luthers next Monday. Soon, we had a crowd of them.

The teen gripped my hand when the tow truck arrived.

Hairy exited the vehicle with another werewolf I'd seen around.

"Essie." Hairy crouched down.

She leaped at him and wrapped her arms around his neck. He patted her back and held her as the other beta picked up Sascha's ride by himself and placed it on the tray.

Hairy glanced at me. "Thanks, Andie. This is becoming a habit."

Looked like it. "Not a problem. Essie?" I waited until she looked up. "You're always welcome to phone me if you need to talk. But I don't want to hear about you stealing cars again." *Stick to bacon sandwiches.*

"I won't," she whispered.

I like this one, Booker told me.

I blinked. She did? That was almost revolutionary.

"Is it okay to come back with a few workers to clean up the damage this evening?" Hairy asked.

"I'm sure our gardeners would appreciate that." After waving over Marty, I left the pair to discuss what would be needed.

The Luthers left soon after, and I faced the crowd of stewards, bracing myself for the inevitable questions.

Why are young Luthers coming here to see you?

The stewards couldn't start to think that my sentiments for the pack were influencing my choices. I could walk a blurred line, but I had to be very careful until both sides warmed up.

I checked the time.

Crap, I'd missed the meeting with the head team. Glancing at the manor, I caught them watching from the meeting room window.

Some days just didn't go the way I planned.

That's what I get for celebrating the normalcy of today, I said to Booker.

She ignored me.

Shocked gasps rang out from the gathered stewards. I frowned. What did I do?

They pointed over my shoulder.

You're kidding me? Who was it this time? Turning, I resigned myself to a morning of tiny dramas.

My feet froze to the ground as a silver Bentley drove into view.

Air lodged in my throat.

"It *is* her," someone exclaimed.

My mouth dried.

Rhona was back.

20

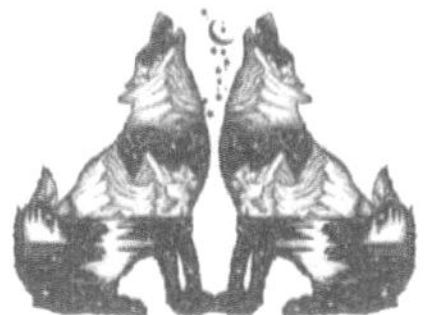

I stared at the ceiling of my room. The day had blurred by, and I could barely recall anything that happened.

"What's the plan?" Wade lay on the bed beside me.

About that. "Have you heard any more?"

"Not since ten seconds ago."

Rhona was staying with Foley in the cabin he usually shared with Billy. *Billy* had wisely elected to stay with Laura.

"I still can't believe she came back."

"That's what you said twenty seconds ago."

"Okay, but part of me really didn't think she'd find it within herself to return."

Rhona somehow found the courage to return, and that put me in danger of hoping for change between us. The thought could be disastrous. Rhona could just as easily be here to reclaim head stewardship.

My phone rang. "Hey, Pascal."

"Andie. A quick call to inform you that the head team visited Rhona ten minutes ago. We've made it clear a return to her position as head steward will not be possible."

They'd moved fast. "I appreciate you clearing that up."

That set the tone for Rhona's return, but what should I say to her? Should I wait for her to approach me or go to her myself?

I had to do better than last time.

That felt possible now all my secrets were out in the open.

"Rhona seems uncertain and not at all like the last time we saw her. Time will tell whether she has truly reflected on her behaviour."

My sister had proved innovative in the past. "I appreciate the update."

I hung up and thumped my head on the mattress. "I was literally walking through the halls today feeling great because things had settled down. This will stir the pot again."

Wade rolled toward me. "If you don't stir the pot, the food gets burned."

I scrunched my face. "Is there a deeper lesson in that?"

"I thought there might be, but it didn't work out."

I rolled my eyes. "Remind me to use a different analogy next time."

"In all seriousness, people are mad at her, baby girl. She kicked you out. We didn't have a say in the matter. Then, Rhona lost our grids. *Then*, she left us high and dry in our final hour. Between you being a Luther and Rhona being a selfish idiot, I'd say far more people are pissed at her."

She could still cause shit. "Last time, I tried to rise above her actions and that didn't work. But what if she wants a relationship with me at some point? Should that possibility change how I approach her?"

"I would have ditched her after the pro-violence rally, but I'm not you. Want some advice?"

"Please."

"You don't let many people in. When you do, you open *all* the way. But it's important to know your boundaries for people you love too. That way, you won't make a compromise you can't sustain. It may mean a bit of hurt now for less hurt down the road, you get me?"

I did.

"You should have your own talk show, my friend."

The sister doesn't deserve you, Booker snarled.

Maybe she didn't. *We need to go for a run.* The new moon was on Saturday, and today had proved an emotional test.

I nudged Wade. "Want to hang tonight? I'll be back in an hour. Maybe see what Cam's up to as well?"

Wade inspected his nails. "Sounds good. Only if I can pick your outfit, and I insist on doing your hair and make-up."

I frowned. "Really?"

"No, not really. Stop stereotyping me."

Laughing, I shoved him and left the room.

I'd shift in the trees tonight.

The elastic band under my ribs loosened as I reached the bottom floor. I stopped short.

Sascha was here?

Picking up speed, I exited the manor in time to see two pickups roll into view. Gardening supplies filled the back trays.

A shirtless Sascha, clad in dark jeans, exited the front vehicle. My libido was manageable when I prepared myself for his company, but when he sprung surprise visits on me like this...

I was so screwed.

There weren't words for how much I wanted him.

Forcing my legs to be stronger than a newborn deer's, I crossed toward the workers. Hairy was there again, with three others.

Then there was Sascha.

"Hey," I grunted.

Hairy grinned.

Ugh.

Sascha ambled toward me, shovel in hand. "Mate. We're here to clear up the mess."

"I guess you didn't want to get your shirt dirty." I winced as the words left my mouth.

His smile grew larger by the second. "My thoughts exactly."

Our lust tangled together until there was more than one grinning werewolf in the vicinity.

I dragged my feet back a few steps. "Right. I'll leave you to it."

"I begged Hairy to let me come. Why not stay and keep me company?"

"The new moon is making me antsy. And Rhona's back. I need to run."

Sascha tensed. "Rhona returned? When?"

"Not long after Essie crashed your truck. I haven't spoken with her yet, but I need to."

He glanced at the others. "I'll come for a run with you. We can talk it over."

Sascha managed hundreds of wolves and made so many different statuses work in harmony. "I'd like that, but Booker will be pissed if I let Greyson get too close. With the bite meet and all."

He couldn't bite me if he tried!

"She's making him work for it?" He leaned on the shovel.

I eyed the ripple effect across his muscles. "She called him a bad hunter with puny strength this morning."

Sascha laughed after a beat. "Greyson took that personally."

"Is he really called Greyson?"

"He wouldn't agree to be called anything prior to you naming him."

Really? "Booker refused a name at first. She said she didn't need one to reproduce."

The other men chuckled.

"Greyson refused one for nearly one hundred years for the same reason. You and Booker seem very close. I've wondered if that's a result of you shifting at a later age. Or maybe that you weren't born a Luther. There are slight differences between you and my wolves."

"Like what?"

"You appear to see colour. We don't—in either form."

Huh, true. I'd never thought about that. The only thing I'd noticed aside from the obvious powers was that my vertigo had disappeared. "Maybe me and Booker are smarter."

He regarded me, still leaning on the shovel.

My lumberjack fantasy had officially been replaced. Gardener Sascha for the win.

"Tell you what." I looked him up and down. "Give me a head start and I'll shift back to talk."

Not waiting for an answer, I turned on my heel and strode away, far too aware of his honey gaze on my back.

Once in the trees, I broke into a run to get past our cameras. Checking Sascha hadn't budged, I then stripped and shifted.

Immediately, tiny pressures filled Booker's mind. There were far more pack members in four-legged form this evening.

Ignore them, I told her. *Let's just run.*

We set off along Booker's favourite route around tribal lands. She liked to make sure other wolves knew not to fuck with her territory.

Translation: We urinated a lot.

Whatever. It made her happy.

When Sascha moved toward us, I took over and led us to the river where we shifted back.

Greyson won't bite me in this form, right? I asked her.

No, he'd be embarrassed to because you're weak.

You could have stopped halfway through that sentence.

Naked, I perched on a large and flat rock to dip my feet in the cool river despite Booker's hiss of displeasure.

I didn't look back at the sound of heavy pawprints.

A large head rested on top of mine briefly before Greyson licked my ear. Snorting, I batted him away.

Cracks and *pops* rose from behind.

Sascha's breath caught. "Do you have any idea how beautiful you look right now?"

"This is just payback for your shirtless gardener show." I hugged my knees to my chest as he sat on the rock beside me.

I looked at him. "Did you really beg Hairy to come fix the

garden?"

"I had to promise to be on my best behaviour. Does that bother you?"

What bothered me was that I felt like a blushing schoolgirl these days. "How did the gardening go?"

He caught some of my auburn hair, letting it flow over his large fingers. "No idea. I was just thinking about you naked the whole time."

I laughed. "I thought you came here to talk with me about Rhona."

"I take what I can get. You're blushing, mate."

I narrowed my gaze and he grinned.

"Tell me about Rhona."

"The head team have made it clear she can't return to head stewardship." I explained my doubts on how to best deal with her, and Sascha began to draw lazy circles over my back. My eyelids drifted closed.

"Your tribe is waiting to see what happens," he said when I stopped talking. "If they see Rhona come to you, sympathy will be with her. If you take initiative, the stewards will know that you aren't willing to let harder issues slide."

I'd mostly realised that. "I don't want to close a door with her that may still be cracked open."

"You can open the door in a way that lets her know exactly what you expect if she chooses to walk through."

"You're far more accepting of my analogies than Wade."

"Thank you, mate."

I jerked. "You need to stop that, or I'll fall asleep."

"That's what I was hoping for. We could stay out here all night."

My chest tightened. "I'd like that, but I have plans with friends."

He kissed behind my ear. "Cancel them."

I shivered. "Can't."

"Your nipples don't agree."

One glance confirmed they certainly did not.

"Goodnight." I touched my lips to his softly.

He flattened a hand against my upper back and forced me closer. I expected a harsh kiss, but he tensed before placing an equally soft kiss on my lips. "Goodnight, Andie."

I withdrew with every last bit of my self-restraint. The stewards had to see me return tonight if they'd seen Sascha leave to follow.

It felt so wrong to leave.

Worse each time.

I heaved a sigh. "I'll see you Sunday?"

"It feels too far away."

It really did.

I swallowed hard. "I'll need to run in two-legged form for a bit before I shift."

"Greyson said he won't try anything now."

"Okay, thanks, Greyson."

I ran into the trees and set off for manor grounds, sticking between the water and the cliff faces on my left.

Sascha was moving away. He'd crossed the river.

Far enough away?

Booker growled low. *Yes.*

Crouching, we shifted. Seconds later, Booker shook out our red fur and stretched. She paused as Sascha changed direction.

He was across the river but now moving toward us. Fast.

That seems... suspicious, I said.

Booker broke into a run, sprinting between the river and the cliff toward tribal lands. The manor was our safety.

We were faster than him.

This was a total set-up. We were trapped by the river on the right. Trapped by cliffs on the left. We couldn't go back the way we'd come because that took us farther from the manor, and Greyson had us beat on endurance over a long distance.

Our pants grew heavier as he drew alongside us on the other riverbank.

I'd never seen him run so hard. He didn't plan to lose.

See the narrow part of the river up ahead? I said to Booker. *He's going to cross there.*

He can try, she growled.

Greyson's snarls rang in our ears.

You need to jump over to his side of the river when he jumps to ours, I told her. *There's nowhere else to cross for a while.*

I'm not getting wet!

Of course she wasn't. *What's your plan then? Because his fangs are fucking sharp.*

I just need to beat him to the crossing and stay ahead.

That... wouldn't work. Ah, well. This meet had to happen. *Go for it.*

Booker doubled down, hurtling along the riverside toward the narrowest point like it was a finish line. I let her focus, listening intently to Greyson's thundering progress.

He leaped across the river and landed ahead of us.

Yelping, Booker tried to change direction but rolled across the forest floor. Bolting upright, she charged blindly, pulling up a moment later when we met with a cliff face.

Spinning, we tracked Greyson's padding approach toward us. The dark-brown wolf heaved to recover from his sprint.

He had us trapped.

Our tail was bolt upright. Our lips curled back in warning. A growl filled our throat.

Greyson's voice filled our head. *Give in to me, young one. You are a powerful female, but you are no match for me.*

I maybe had a few things to say about that.

Booker snapped her fangs. *I am a prize for a worthier male. You will sire weak pups.*

Ouch.

She went there.

Greyson snarled and closed the gap. Booker lunged in one direction. He cut us off, eyes focused on our every slight move.

She faked one way before darting the other.

We bounced off Greyson's body. She scrambled to establish distance again. He lunged and pinned us to the ground, lying bodily on top of us.

He rested his fangs on our left shoulder. *You're mine.*

Do that, and I'll kill you, she hissed.

Greyson bit down, and white coated our vision as fire shot through our minds. Instinct froze us as our yelp ricocheted off the cliffs around us.

Greyson maintained his cruel hold.

His growl vibrated against our wound.

The spears of agony pinning us in place began to shrink toward his fangs. Booker's yelp faded to a whimper.

You are mine, beautiful wolf. It was as though we'd become his sun.

He withdrew his fangs, and Booker yelped again but remained still as he replaced his fangs with his tongue, gently cleaning the injury.

We both relaxed, and Booker soon began to whine.

It's okay, Greyson told her. *I didn't want to hurt you, but it's done, and I won't ever hurt you again.*

She stopped crying, and when he'd finished, she stood on our shaking legs.

Greyson touched his nose to ours. *Mate, will you let me run with you at the new moon?*

Booker lowered her gaze.

Oh my god. She was totally crushing on him.

Girl really liked a good biter.

You can spend the new moon with me, she said shyly.

What was Sascha thinking right now? This had to be the cutest thing I'd ever witnessed. I felt like a proud parent.

Booker licked his snout and limped a distance away.

So...? I asked like the lame parent I didn't want to be.

He's an excellent hunter and a powerful wolf. He will sire strong pups.

Don't laugh. Don't laugh, I thought.

Be nice to have him along for the new moon, huh?

Guess so. We'll need to shift back for the next part.

Oh, yeah. No matter how many times this happened, I never got used to the heat business. By now, I wanted to experience bulk sex with Sascha, but without talking to him prior or knowing much about the heat, I couldn't do it tonight.

Taking over, I sat facing Greyson, who respectfully kept his distance.

I shifted and remained in my crouch.

"Yeow!" Fucking shoulder. I studied the torn skin that oozed blood. The bite was nowhere near what I'd envisioned, but it would definitely leave a mark.

Which was probably the point.

Wincing, I lifted my arms and nodded at Greyson to proceed.

Within seconds, Sascha crouched in his place.

Fire slammed into me a second later, and I shuddered against the booming urge to close the gap. It was harder to say the words when I wanted him—when I had to acknowledge the cold truth that we may not have this moment again.

I didn't want to treat him like crap, but nature didn't give a shit about my wants.

Sascha trembled where he still crouched. "Say it, Andie. Quickly now."

I squeezed my eyes shut. "*Doore koh e baka*."

The heat left me, and I supported my injured arm under the elbow as Sascha panted. Wobbling over to him, I sank to my knees and rested my head on his shoulder.

I didn't think he was worthless.

Sascha kissed my temple. "I know, little bird. How's that bite?"

With gentle fingers, he studied the wound.

I sat straighter. "Hey! You told me Greyson wouldn't try anything tonight."

"I possibly misled you on purpose."

My mouth bobbed.

He lifted a shoulder. "I want to have sex with you so badly that my blue balls are making me walk funny. I had to help Greyson out."

Laughing hurt my shoulder. "How's Greyson?"

"Very happy and proud."

We exchanged a smile.

"Booker?" he asked.

Don't tell him!

"She doesn't want me to tell you for some reason." I snickered.

Booker threw some of Wade's favourite insults at me, but something else had started to demand my attention.

I fidgeted.

Sascha quirked a brow. "Something the matter?"

"Not at all," I said sweetly.

His nostrils flared. "You feel some of the heat this time."

Did I ever.

I bit my lip and clamped my legs together, gasping, "Yes."

Sascha frowned. "Why this time and not after the last meet?"

"I don't currently care."

He blinked. "Right. Well, I best get going. Work at The Dens and all. See you Saturday evening for the new moon?"

A savage growl ripped from my lips, and the werewolf smirked.

He draped an arm over his knee. "You want me to stay? What are you going to do if I do?"

Playing it like that, was he? I opened my legs, reaching to show him.

Sascha gripped my hand. "Not on my watch, little bird. If you're feeling pleasure, it's because of me."

"That's what you think."

His smile dropped. "How often?"

I batted my lashes in response.

"I'll need to keep closer tabs on you, I see. Show me what you want from *me*, mate."

I pushed him flat with my good arm and ignored his predatory growl.

There were so many things I wanted to do that I didn't know where to start. Sascha Greyson's body was a buffet and I wanted to get my money's worth.

His erection stood to attention, and I took it in a firm grip.

"No sex." Every muscle in his neck was taut as he forced the words out.

I leaned forward and my hair fell around us in a deep red curtain. "Is that because I use sex as a weapon?"

I aligned my core along his erection and slid back and forward to show him what I thought about his little sex ban.

His eyes showed white for a moment.

I grabbed one of Sascha's fingers. Did I feel like that?

Hmm, not today.

"What's it gonna be?" he asked huskily.

He was totally, *totally* digging this.

I tapped my lips and stood.

"Need help?" Sascha challenged.

I placed a foot on either side of his head and lowered to my knees. His gaze flew directly up to meet mine.

Letting him glimpse my smirk, I lowered onto his face.

He wasn't daft.

I jolted at the sudden, intense pleasure as he lapped between my thighs.

My hips rocked against his mouth of their own accord.

Sascha groaned into me.

"Fuck," I whispered.

He had to be breathing, but I didn't know how.

I wanted to feel him too.

In a blur, I knelt the other way to view his body instead of the forest.

Snarling, Sascha reached an arm over my thighs and forced me back down to his waiting mouth and tongue.

It was so intense, and his grip didn't leave room for escape. My legs shook.

Someone should learn that revenge was sweet.

Extending my fangs, I dragged them along his lower abdomen. Sascha stopped moving.

That's right.

Taking his erection in hand, I took him in my mouth.

The clever man didn't budge an inch. I smiled around him. The length of my fangs only allowed me to shower attention on the very tip before they indented the skin around his base.

"Andie." Sascha's voice was strained.

He cautiously resumed his attention on me.

I slowly sheathed my fangs. Without warning, I took as much of him in my mouth as possible. Sascha shouted, half terror and *all* lust.

I listened to the pounding of his heart and bobbed a few times before extending my fangs again, letting him feel the indents.

I tried to move my hips again and snarled angrily when he didn't let me. Sascha sucked my clit into his mouth.

A silent scream consumed me. After a few beats, I continued my onslaught, extending and retracting my lethal teeth to terrorise him at intervals.

"Are your fangs sheathed?" he said urgently.

They were, but he didn't need to know that.

"*I don't care*." Sascha rolled us to the right, so he was on top, and ground into my face. I coughed, and he drew back.

I strained upward to chase him. I liked this game.

He spread my thighs wide.

I tensed, waiting for him to lick me again.

Oh, god. I could feel his breath.

When was he going to do it?

Tipping my head back, I prepared to return the favour and drive him to the point of insanity.

Sascha shoved all the way into my mouth again, closing the distance to my core at the same time. My scream was muffled.

He didn't stop.

We couldn't stop.

With him, I climbed.

And when we reached the top.

Together, we fell.

21

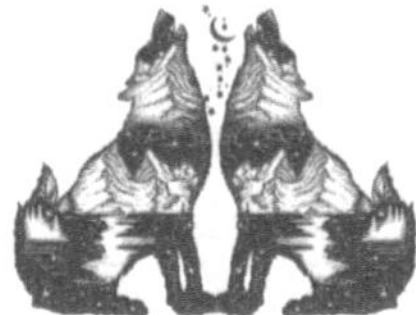

I held the phone to my ear with my shoulder. "Sorry. I really just—"

"Baby girl, I saw Sascha leave after you. I put two and two together."

I'd flaked on hanging with Wade and Cameron last night. By the time Sascha and I were done, it was nearly midnight.

That was the strongest partial heat yet—*boy*, was it ever.

"Let's rain check then. I'm heading out to see Rhona."

"Call if you need help hiding the body."

He hung up, and I strode out of the manor, stomach churning. Rhona didn't attend dawn training, but Foley was there.

I walked to his cabin, turning over his words.

He seemed to think that the Timber win changed Rhona's mind. The day before, she'd refused to return. The day after, she practically dragged him to the car.

I knocked on the cabin door. "Rhona, it's Andie."

A few seconds passed.

"I can smell you in there."

The door opened, and for the first time in over a month, I stared into emerald eyes so like my own.

Rhona stared at the ground.

Her arms weren't crossed. Her hip wasn't cocked.

I inhaled.

Jesus. Pascal was right. My younger sister was a fucking mess.

"Welcome home." I didn't make a move to hug her. "Would you like to talk outside?"

I perched on the top step, and she sat a few metres away with her back against the balustrade.

"Foley told me you decided to return after hearing the news about Timber." I tracked her scent. If I caught the smallest sign of decay, then the gloves had to come off. I could handle her disliking me—*not* working against me.

There was too much to lose.

Rhona didn't meet my gaze. "Yeah."

"This will always be your home. No one will take that away from you. But due to your past actions, there need to be clear conditions to your return."

She looked at me then. "So I'm not always welcome."

"You're welcome in the same way any steward who acts in the tribe's best interest is welcome. If you choose to act in a different way, that's a choice you make knowing the consequence. Put another way, only you can choose to leave this place by behaving selfishly."

Rhona returned her attention away to the cabin.

"I don't need an apology from you," I said softly. "I don't need to understand why you've done the things you have or even why you returned. Here's what I do need from you."

She tensed.

"You will immediately write an apology letter to the pack for your past violent actions in the grid. You will apologise to our tribe at a Tuesday night gathering for your past actions. That must happen within the next month. So you're aware, a condition of my return to head stewardship was that no extreme violence against the pack will be tolerated. Another was that there will be no derogatory comments made about my Luther nature. You're expected to abide by those also. The extreme mentality you inspired is dead, Rhona, and that's because the overwhelming majority of stewards want to win Grids more than they hate Luthers. That hasn't been the case with you recently, and while that worries me on a personal level, your attitude is dangerous for my stewards too. I'd like you to attend psychotherapy appointments. There are two psychologists in Deception Valley. One is a member of the public, and one is a member of the tribe. Both assure complete confidentiality—no one else will hear anything from your sessions, including me." I took a breath. "Otherwise, you're on grid probation and will not partake in the game until further notice. You're welcome to attend dawn trainings, of course."

She barely moved, though I could hear her shallow breaths.

"Any questions?" I asked.

"No."

I inhaled again.

No decay. Just a deep, *deep* shame.

That I could work with. Or someone else could. Too much had happened between us, and I wasn't the right person for Rhona anymore.

I nodded. "The tribe is upset about you leaving, but our stewards are loving and open-minded on most issues. Show them that you're sorry, and they'll believe you in time. The only way to earn back their respect is to respect them yourself."

It didn't escape me that I'd said the same thing to Essie recently. That's almost how I saw my sister sometimes—as a person who'd stopped feeling years ago and therefore stopped growing. Whether her mother's diagnosis or her mother's death had affected her, Rhona had a backlog of grief to process.

And I truly hoped she did.

I stood. "You're welcome to move back into the manor at any time."

When I'd walked out of earshot, I released a pent-up breath.

It was done.

Things might always be awkward as shit between us, but I'd opened the door and set my boundaries or whatever.

I entered the meeting room. "Morning. Where are we at with Sandstone preparations?"

Choosing Timber last week was a no-brainer, but we'd bounced between Clay and Sandstone for hours. There were long-term plans for Clay that we had to set up, but with our unemployment situation, going after a grid that we had a reasonable chance to turnover made financial sense.

However, if we *lost* in Sandstone, we'd regret not pressing on with our strategies in Clay.

Phew.

Roderick replied, "The new equipment hasn't arrived, but as soon as it's here, Gerry will begin manoeuvre drills with the stewards."

"The shipment was due yesterday?" I trawled through my folder to find the delivery confirmation.

"Correct. This is a company we haven't used before."

I pressed my lips together. "Nothing we can do about that. Let's focus on some of the other strategies our teams put together. One used the water cannons from Iron. Let's get the stewards trained in that operation in the interim."

We'd always used traps on the ground level in Sandstone but had no steward presence there. Yet we had the numbers to dedicate a force to the first level. More focus had to be on preventing and slowing the pack's climb.

"Stanley, Trixie, is everything prepared for Sandstone stewards to work for the pack on Monday?" I asked.

"The contract is signed," Stanley replied. "Some of the stewards are nervous, so we're holding a seminar on how to behave while they're there and what to do in a worst-case situation. They also need to understand the consequences of their actions to the tribe if tempers get the better of them."

Trixie added, "I'm working with Leroy and Mandy from the pack. They proposed that for the first week, our stewards can stick to work in one area. Next week, we can begin integrating with the pack to make the most of our different abilities."

"Great. Please report to me after the first workday and each Friday until Sandstone is back in our possession."

My mind drifted as the team started working through the most pressing items on our agenda.

Hours remained until meeting Sascha for the new moon.

I'd only gone through one. Booker did so great, but we were both nervous about Sascha and Greyson being around. It was a vulnerable time in some ways. I mean, we were a lethal predator for an entire night, but the new moon was the most out of control a Luther got.

"Is there anything else you'd like to discuss, Head Steward?" Nathan interrupted my daydream.

"There is." I studied the head team. "We have three penalty points. It's in our interest to gain two more."

Their faces smoothed.

Yep, this was shaky ground.

"You want to set something up?" Pascal confronted the elephant in the room like a champ.

"I won't condone underhand tactics. I do believe that we should actively try to catch a misstep from the pack. For instance, care of the land must be displayed at all times. The pack workers have been stretched over four grids and leaped at the chance to employ us. Why is that?"

One by one, the head team smiled.

My thought exactly. "I'd like a full investigation done in Timber to ensure best practices were maintained during the pack's possession. You mentioned a seminar for the Sandstone stewards, Stanley. Add another topic to the agenda, please. The workers are to assess what they can of the grid while working for the pack and report anything amiss. The pack manages Timber on and off, but they haven't possessed Sandstone in a long time. If there are hiccups, we'll use them to our advantage."

Trixie jotted notes down. "I'll set up a reporting chain."

"Thank you. If anyone has any last questions for the day, now's the time to ask," I said. "I'm unavailable until later tomorrow morning—it's the new moon."

"What happens at the new moon?" Roderick asked.

My team asked these questions casually, but I'd noticed that my answers became common knowledge to the tribe. They were promoting transparency, and I didn't see any harm in that. I was starting to think Sascha should reconsider Alexei's past example and be more transparent with Luther powers and their struggles. "Without sunlight, my wolf takes over from dusk until dawn. In the week prior to the new moon, I run more to give her what she needs. That prevents uncontrolled shifts and helps my mood. Once the new moon is over, I feel great."

His brows shot up. "Luthers always seem weakened and tired for several days after."

"What the pack shows you and actually experience are different things. They like to mislead the tribe on occasion."

I collected my paperwork. I had plenty of time to finish my last assignment before dusk. My study was enjoyable once, but I couldn't wait to get the extra task off my plate now.

Can you ask Wade to give us a bath? Booker said quietly.

Was that the equivalent of shaving your legs before a date? I had to be a cool wolf parent. *Sure. No problem. He may agree to brush us too.*

That would be agreeable.

She was going to kill me with cute. I pulled out my phone and texted Wade.

There were other messages there. From Basilia.

King Julius believes Luthers make better rugs than allies.
But he's willing to negotiate further.

That... was brutally honest. I hadn't even met this king guy and he gave me the heebie-jeebies.

I read her next message.

He sees particular value in your proximity.
That will be crucial to Vissimo involvement.
When is good for a video meeting?

Dang, that wasn't ideal. The pack may need to leave the valley, and if we entered an alliance and backtracked later, I had a feeling ol' Julius wouldn't react well.

I texted her back a time later next week.

I needed time to brainstorm.

Wade rang.

"What do you think?" I hoped he heard the amusement in my voice.

"There's nothing I'd love more than to wash and brush Booker."

I paused "Is this another stereotype trap?"

"What? A man can't enjoy making a woman wolf look her best? Less labels, please."

"Why does Booker get her hair done and not me?"

"I can work with what Booker has to offer. I only have so much skill, if you understand what I'm saying."

My shoulders shook with laughter. "You're a massive bitchhole!"

"The biggest, baby girl. See you soon?"

Apparently, I was spending my afternoon at a wolf beauty salon.

22

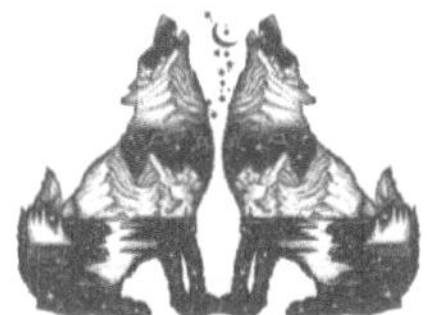

Seriously, if Sascha and Greyson didn't notice Booker's gleaming fur, she'd be so upset. She'd just preened through a public bath and grooming over the afternoon. Half of the tribe watched, and Booker loved every second.

Every second.

My wolf had vanity issues.

Bag thumping against my lower back, I ran from where I'd parked Ella F near Lake Thana to meet Sascha.

He was waiting.

"Sorry I'm late." I stopped to catch my breath.

Booker wanted to arrive late to give the impression this was a casual thing that she hadn't talked about non-stop since receiving the bite of her life.

Sascha wrapped his arms around me and touched his lips to mine. I looped my arms behind his neck, pressing closer.

"Mmm. Glad I'm here now." I relaxed into the happiness I always felt in his embrace.

Sascha stroked my hair. "I love you."

I opened my mouth. "*Shut up. It's my turn!*"

Whirling away, I covered my mouth. "Booker. Manners!"

Sascha's laughter boomed behind me, and I turned to find him wiping his eyes.

"That's even better than watching your face when you talk with her."

"My face changes?"

"Enough to guess the content of the conversation."

Huh. "I'm guessing that Booker would like me to shift now."

"Greyson's impatient to spend time with her too."

A loud, harsh purr left my mouth—all Booker—and Sascha started laughing again.

I groaned.

Back in the trees, I stripped off and stuffed everything in my bag before shifting.

On four legs, Booker trotted out to meet Greyson, who sat *very* upright waiting.

You are absolutely divine, beautiful wolf. He circled us. *Your coat shines like the sun. Your teeth are as sharp as your mind.*

I couldn't do this. Adorable overload would be my cause of death.

The sun dipped below the mountain ranges, and I felt the same volatile darkness from last month creep over my senses.

I look forward to eating hearts with you tonight, Booker said shyly.

Pick up line of the century.

It would be my honour, young one.

Touché.

Girl had him in the bag.

A wrinkle formed between my brows as I connected to my senses. *Stale air. Small space.*

Still dark?

Booker was fast asleep, and a shining happiness filled us.

Sascha was really close.

Sitting up, I studied his sprawling, naked form at the cave entrance.

Weak light streamed over him.

I approached but kept my distance at the sight of his extended claws and fangs. "Hey. Guarder of caves."

He jolted awake and rolled to look up at me. I'd never—not once—woken before Sascha Greyson. He was mussed up, and I had to control the urge to set him to rights.

"Are you going to stab me if I come closer?" I asked.

He blinked a few times and sheathed his claws and fangs in response.

I crouched. "Good sleep?"

His voice was husky from disuse. "A very good sleep."

"I'm hungry and there's food in my bag. Want to go back to the lake?"

As we descended from our elevated cave, I realised we weren't that far away from our starting spot.

We hiked toward the lake.

"Do you remember anything from last night? I just blacked out again."

"Little bits," he answered. "You may want to brush your teeth."

I blanched. "You're kidding?"

"Just... brush them. It's best not to know some things."

I swallowed hard, trying not to think of dangling rabbit guts.

He took my hand when we reached the narrow beach. "They had a great time."

"I'm glad. Booker was looking forward to it. She got herself all done up."

Sascha grinned, and my breath caught as the sun caught his honey eyes, making them appear nearly yellow.

So fucking handsome.

We found my bag and after dressing and brushing critter innards from my teeth, I split my food with Sascha.

Last time, I made the mistake of only bringing granola bags.

I gnawed on my fourth barbeque chicken drumstick, staring out at the glassy lake.

"You're deep in thought for a wolf after the new moon." He was lying on the forest floor and using one arm as a cushion—dressed in loose, grey trackpants too, which should be illegal on guys, full stop.

"I feel good," I murmured.

"I'm asking what's on your mind, mate."

Oh. "Grid stuff. Us stuff. Nothing different to the usual."

"I was wondering about Andie stuff yesterday."

"About her hot bod?"

His amusement curled around me. "That's a given. I found myself wondering why you experienced no heat after the kiss meet and the strongest heat yet after the bite meet."

Yeah, that had niggled at me. "Any ideas?"

"In the past, our mating gifts—and your partial heats—always seemed to come when you accepted my presence in your life more."

I'd first felt the elastic band sensation at the waterfall when Sascha told me about his dreams. "Fair point, but I'd accepted you more than ever at our kiss meet."

Sascha took a deep breath. "Maybe so, but you weren't happy on pack lands, Andie. We received the ability to mind-speak in this form as soon as you returned to the tribe. You were farther from me, and that made you more accepting of our situation."

His words filled the space between us.

Because he was absolutely right—and wrong at the same time.

"I wasn't happy on pack lands as things were," I eventually answered. "I felt closer to you but believed less in our future. That made me close up."

He gazed up at the brightening sky. "You weren't the only one. I was disappointed and it clouded my judgement. I closed up too."

Give me a guy with the ability to reason *any* day. I was deluded to believe alphas were my type. "When I went back to the manor, it felt like I was in a position to *claim* our future instead of watching everything unravel. I wasn't happier because we were farther apart. That felt—and will always feel—horrible."

Sascha closed his eyes. "Thank fuck for that. I miss you so much."

My throat tightened. "I miss you too."

"Will you ever be back?" Pain infused his words.

And my heart. "I believe there's no future for us unless a compromise can be reached between the pack and tribe. I can't leave my stewards in the lurch, and maybe doing the right thing by the pack was due to my feelings for you initially, but now, I care about them as well. We need to find a middle ground, Sascha."

He still disagreed.

"Your stance on working together is still the same?"

Sascha exhaled. "I'm not sure."

I'm not sure was better than *absolutely fucking not*. "What's holding you back?"

"A lot of my older wolves have lived through centuries of oppression. It's not just our history with your tribe. The pack we were once part of was ruled with violence and fear. Many of my wolves carry physical scars from the treatment they received at the hands of my father's brother. Then there were the vampires and demons. We've never owned something for ourselves. My people want a home they can rely on. They want to be safe."

That helped me to understand Alexei's anger. "I didn't know the old pack was that bad." I couldn't even fathom what it would take to scar a Luther.

"It was. Enough for half of them to flee toward the unknown with my father. My wolves have never had anything to call their own. That's why convincing them to give more won't be easy—maybe impossible."

"I wouldn't push this if I didn't believe it was best."

Sascha cocked a brow. "I know, mate, and since you just beat the pack in Timber, I guess I better start listening. You're smarter than me."

Stewards got a whole extra hour in the grid. That was the difference between us.

"Is that a maybe?" I held my breath.

"I need to test the waters and see if working with you is viable at all. Breaking their trust is something I can't do, and I won't give you hope before being sure of what I can offer."

That was something.

At *last*, it was something.

I could do this with his help. I knew it. "I'm asking a lot, I know, but I really am smarter than you. You should listen."

He rolled to his feet. "I only said that because I want to get in your pants."

"Uh-huh. Sure."

I squealed as he picked me up.

"When will we do the last meet?" I rested my cheek on his chest.

"Eager?" He walked us through the trees.

Eager was a freakin' understatement. If he was walking with a limp because of his blue balls, then I was using a damn cane. "Yes and no. Rushing into sex with you because of Grids and what may happen doesn't feel right. On the other hand, I do want to add another notch to my belt."

"That deserves a dunking." He walked into the water.

"Booker will seriously eat you alive. She hates water."

"So does Greyson." He winced as the water reached his hips. "Worst part."

I laughed.

He dropped me, and my shriek was lost as cold water closed over my head. I wind-milled my arms and emerged, hair over my face.

What the fuck, Booker screamed in my head.

Parting my soaking hair, I glared at Sascha. "You're in massive trouble."

"Am I? I seem just fine."

I launched myself at him.

23

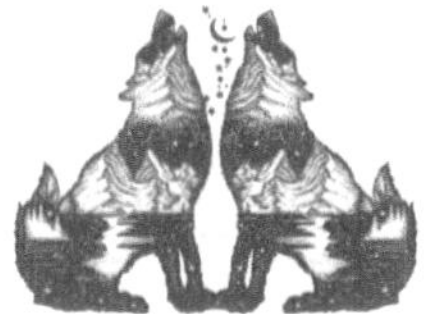

I read over Rhona's apology letter.

Short and sweet described it, but she'd done as asked. Apologising to the pack ruled by her father's killer was a difficult thing.

I handed the letter to Pascal. "Send it. The dent to her pride will soothe pack members who aren't convinced by her words."

"How did things go with her?" She scanned the letter to her tablet.

"She feels remorse. No ill-intent at this point."

Stanley joined us at the table, a mug of steaming coffee in hand. The end of day meeting was often more casual than the morning one. "Foley wants nothing more to do with her, from what I heard."

Foley had loved Rhona, and she'd led him astray big time. Good on him for choosing his happiness and standing up to her. I didn't think he'd have it in him.

"She attended dawn training this morning," I said as the others joined us. "In time, I hope she'll find a place here again."

Roderick set his tea down. "I'm not sure how you can be so forgiving."

"Do you have much family, Rod?"

"Four siblings and their children. Our parents are still living."

He also had a wife and three children of his own. "I have no family except Rhona. Having gone through what I have, I hold nothing but a sincere wish she'll find her way."

Grief connected my sister and I and speaking of her was always a reminder that there was pain I was ignoring to play this game. Ragna's actions were at the top of that list. I could only cast that issue aside for so long without consequences.

Trixie set down a document. "Here's the report from our Sandstone stewards."

My eyes widened as I thumbed through the three pages. "You're kidding me. All this? It's only been two days."

"Actually, that was after yesterday. There should be more today. They took the job very seriously, Head Steward. You'll notice there's picture and video content for all the reported lapses."

This was great.

I read aloud, "They were using an old horizontal shaft impact in one area instead of a cone crusher. What does that mean?"

Her face slackened.

Right. Me too.

I wasn't a Sandstone expert. "Anyone here know what this stuff is?"

Stanley took the document from me. "I can understand some. Most are minor issues."

"Will they get us two penalty points?"

"I'd wager not."

And I wasn't the wagering sort. We had to be sure before making our move. I didn't want to disrupt the new work dynamic between the pack and tribe otherwise.

I nodded. "Okay, let's ask the Sandstone workers to nominate ten experts to sit down with us on Friday morning. We need to know if there's enough to work with. On the plus side, if we turn over Sandstone tomorrow, our stewards can assess the entire grid."

Hmm. "We know very little about Clay and Water. If we turn those grids over, we'll need to hire pack members to cope with workload. Sascha won't hesitate to use the same tactic against us in that situation."

This employment agreement changed the game more than anticipated.

"We could form a Clay and Water initiative," Wade suggested.

"Good idea. I'd hate to lose a grid due to the best care clause."

Nathan tapped his pen on the table. "It may be worth hiring consultants from outside the area to guide us."

"I believe that cost would be warranted," Stanley interrupted.

I considered their ideas. "Let's roll with all of the above. Is there anything else to report?"

The head team turned as one to look at Roderick.

He grimaced. "The new equipment hasn't arrived."

I stilled. "That's days overdue."

"The company assures me it will be here tomorrow morning."

Wednesday. The day of the fucking game. "That's not ideal."

"No," he agreed, "Gerry is prepped to hold a last-minute practice tomorrow afternoon."

I dragged a hand over my face. This wasn't a simple manoeuvre. Without ample practice, there was a high chance the stewards wouldn't pull it off. "We've worked on the two back-up operations, right?"

"Yes. Those are ready to go."

But would they be enough to win? "There's nothing to do but hope the equipment arrives on time. Let's not use that company again."

"I considered telling them werewolves existed to hurry them along," he said.

The others chuckled.

In the wake, Wade said, "What are everyone's plans for the ball?"

The event was the weekend after next and my bestie was in full stress mode at this point. But he'd caused a stir already—I'd give him that.

"What are you wearing to it?" Trixie asked me.

"No idea." Tickets to the balls in my last years of high school were too expensive—especially with the outfit to consider on top. I'd never been to something like this.

"I'm sure some of your mother's things are around. She had beautiful style."

Which mother? "Savannah?"

"Yes."

I absorbed that. "That wouldn't sit right with Rhona. I'll figure something out."

"She was your mother too. A mother's dresses are heirlooms for their daughters."

Were they?

Wade leaned in. "Cam is already making your dress. And my suit."

She was? "Cam can do that?"

"You'll never hear her speaking about it, but yep. She's got serious talent."

The meeting ended, and I slowly walked to my office thinking over Trixie's words.

Savannah was a literal stranger to me. In another world, she could have been a mother I loved.

How crazy was it that I didn't feel like I had a claim to her things? Or even any feelings of *wanting* to see her stuff.

Stopping short of my desk, I peered to where my saxophone case leaned against the far bookcase. Would I feel any connection to Savannah in time?

Crossing the room, I worked the case clasps free and fitted the instrument together.

I studied the worn brass.

I'd played this for Axel not so long ago.

But he wasn't here now.

Did that mean I couldn't play?

Wetting my reed first, I fixed it in place, then drew my lips in around the mouthpiece and blew a middle C.

The note blared from the bell.

I swallowed hard as Ragna's voice rang in my ears.

Play me more, so I can remember.

Usually the note would resonate in my chest too.

I tried again with the same note, but if there was a connection there, I couldn't feel it.

Selecting one of my go-to favourites, I played the opening bars of "Feeling Good" by Nina Simone.

The sound didn't fill me with happiness. In fact, the idea of playing made me so very *un*happy.

Lump rising in my throat, I rested the instrument on top of the case.

I couldn't play it anymore.

My music was as inaccessible now as when I first heard Ragna wasn't my mother.

And I didn't see that changing.

How tense could someone get before they snapped into jigsaw pieces? "I swear the game gets worse each week."

Shouldn't it work the other way?

From the back seat, Cam squeezed my shoulder. "We've got this."

Stewards only got two hours to memorize the new operation this morning after the order finally arrived. If the operation didn't work, I wasn't sure we'd have enough to win Sandstone.

Losing Grids tonight would mean defending one of our grids next week before we could come back. Two more weeks without Sascha.

Love encompassed so many damn emotions, and misery was high on the list right now.

We parked, and I went to wait at my usual Sandstone spot while the others changed.

I inhaled and stiffened. "Rhona."

She stepped into view from behind a vehicle. "I'm not here to play. I came to ask if I can watch the game from the tower with you and Pascal."

Unexpected.

Nefarious?

"If you can convince me it's not for some secret plan to take over, then sure."

Rhona flinched slightly. "It's not, and I won't do anything to distract either of you."

I sniffed the air. "*Truth.*"

"You can smell truth and lie?"

That didn't alarm her. If anything, she smelled envious. "I can. It's nice. Simplifies things. Makes me less afraid."

Rhona withdrew again.

I studied her for a beat. "You're welcome to stand with us in the tower."

How could she make the right choice if she wasn't given the chance?

"Hey, Andie?"

I faced the incoming steward. After that, the tribe demanded my attention in a steady stream.

The cannon boomed seconds following my short pump-up speech.

Believe in your tribe, Booker said. *They've been in this position before.*

They were a well-oiled team.

Pascal was already in the observation tower when I arrived. She glanced behind me.

"Rhona's joining us to watch the game," I explained.

The marshal thought that was a mistake.

I wasn't totally sure Pascal was wrong.

A steady stream of reports flooded in.

"They've found most of our ground-level traps," I said to no one in particular. That wasn't something we'd encountered in Sandstone before, and that was one huge reason turnovers sucked.

It meant that half of our stewards had to work to restore our most effective traps and locate alterations made by the pack between times.

The other five hundred stewards would set up equipment for our new operations.

I watched as a cluster of stewards set up the water cannons. This time, we'd connect the pipes to water tanks on what remained of the middle tiers. The equipment wouldn't be as vulnerable to Luthers that way.

I'd radically altered our strategy in this grid, and it could blow up in my face.

Just below my spot, a smaller group led by Heather assembled the drones we'd never used in Clay.

I held the walkie up. "*Big Red. Into position. Over.*"

Would Sascha notice that not as many stewards were climbing today? From his entry point, with the curve of the quarry, he couldn't see this side of the grid. We'd made sure to set up the water tanks and drones out of view, but less rock-climbing stewards could alert him to something amiss.

"*Wicked. West in position. Over.*"

"Roger that," I answered.

Reports rang in from the other three team leaders.

We were as ready as could be.

I shook out my hands.

Pascal murmured, "Confidence, Andie. It's up to the grid gods now."

"If I knew there were grid gods, I would've left sacrifices."

Her lips curved.

Rhona was silent. Her scent was all over the place—determination, shame, and guilt.

What do you think? I asked Booker.

She's torturing herself or testing an idea.

That was my guess. Either that or she really did care how this went for the tribe.

Boom.

In Sandstone, the pack had always opted to enter slowly. That was before they had three weeks to dismantle our ground traps.

The Luthers *ran*.

They usually chose to start climbing once the first of them reached the middle of the quarry.

I readied my walkie to give the order.

... They weren't climbing.

I sniffed the air. *What's that?*

I'm not sure, Booker replied. *Don't move yet.*

A wolf was calculative to the extreme and this could make them hesitant. Sometimes, I had to override that natural inclination and make quick decisions, but this time, I agreed with Booker.

Releasing the walkie, I watched as the Luthers entered all the way across the surface level.

"Two points to traps," Pascal stated.

A blip on our usual figure.

I leaned forward. "They're doing something."

"That's what they did before shooting the climbing ropes to the top of the cliffs," Rhona said quietly.

Ah, yes. That made sense.

I nodded and clicked on the walkie. "Big Red. Prepare for Operation Paw Patrol. Over."

Out of sight of the Luthers' entry point, one hundred and fifty stewards hid on the lowest tier on the left side of the quarry, and the same number on the right.

Now, they sprinted along the first level to cover the entire length of the lowest step.

Only around fifteen metres of sheer sandstone cliff sat between them and the wolves—not enough for my liking.

A series of explosions echoed from the surface. Eight ropes embedded in the top cliffs.

Dammit.

I couldn't allow Luthers up to take out our bottom tier stewards yet. "Big Red. Prepare for Operation Superwoman. Over."

The cliff stewards moved in response to my order. Our lag time up there was a big disadvantage.

I checked on the positions of my team below. "Big Red. Initiate Operation Paw Patrol. Over."

Luthers were climbing the ropes.

I lifted the walkie again. "Big Red. Initiate Operation Superwoman. Over."

Pairs of cliff stewards worked with smaller versions of two-man saws to cut the pack's reinforced ropes.

That was the cue for most of the remaining stewards to open fire. The pack took shield cover in response to Sascha's howl.

Ten minutes in.

This was as good a chance as any.

I paced along the railing. "Big Red. Prepare Operation Hamster Wheel. Over."

A small number of the paw patrol stewards ceased fire to flip large metal grills into place.

The tribe had kept this strategy on the back burner for years and we'd had the grills in storage ready to use. The gratings were a Luther-sized version of a cat-proof fence. Giant rollers covered the bars.

As the guinea pig, I could say that with certainty, the grills were an absolute bitch to climb over.

The only way was to rip the entire grating from the cliff face via the outer framing—or via sheer luck.

Lowering each grill into a forty-five-degree angle required three stewards. I winced as one grate dislodged from its bolts and crashed to the surface.

But the others all jutted out from the lowest tier as intended.

Stewards scrambled to cover the gap created by the missing grill as Luthers congregated there.

Crap. "Big Red to Reindeer. Cover needed at Operation Hamster Wheel defence. Over."

"*Reindeer. I see it. Roger that. Over.*"

Reindeer redirected two units high on the wall to focus fire there.

The pack shot more ropes at the cliffs.

Six more.

My Operation Superwoman stewards hurried toward the insertion points to saw through.

Hmm. We wouldn't hold the lowest tier forever. It was a fine line between waiting too long and giving up the ground too early. I pursed my lips. "Big Red. Operation Paw Patrol, initiate phase two. Over."

In a subtle wave, the stewards below changed their positioning —specifically, they covered the grill framings.

The aim was to shoot any Luthers who realised they could rip the grills away. We'd doused them in wolfsbane to help.

More ropes exploded to sink into the top cliffs.

We weren't harassing the pack enough.

Thirty minutes remained.

Give the order for the other operations, Booker said. *We can always fall back on our usual strategy. And we have the last manoeuvre as back up.*

If a wolf was urging me to move, then I should definitely listen. "Big Red. Prepare Operation Hairdryer. Over."

Seriously. Who came up with these names?

Some of the paw patrol stewards retreated from firing at the grills and pushed our water cannons into place.

It would take several minutes to get them in position.

"*Snow. Incoming drones! Over.*"

I cursed. Shielding on the cliffs was awkward. It wasn't something we could do in seconds. "Big Red. All stewards shield *immediately*. Over."

A pack drone shot into the air at the same moment at least four grills were ripped from the fixings.

Fuck.

"Big Red. Prepare Operation Mosquito. Over."

My mosquito stewards, covered in protective gear, ran across what remained of the middle tier on either side of the quarry.

I waited until the last pack drone had ascended above their spot. "Big Red. Initiate Operation Mosquito. Over."

Our drones shot out and descended on the pack.

For a while, there was near complete silence as both sets of drones spun in rapid circles, launching tranquiliser darts.

I grimaced as cliff stewards who hadn't managed to get their shields in place went limp.

Our drones were navigated back to the middle tier as the pack drones slowed and descended.

Crunch time. "Big Red. Prepare Operation Batman and initiate Operation Hairdryer. Over."

Some paw patrol stewards manned the water cannons while the others continued to fire. The pack had ripped off most of the grills —*dammit.*

I needed to call the lowest stewards to safety soon, but those on the cliffs could help them with cover fire for now.

"*Reindeer. More drones incoming! Over.*"

"You cunning fucker," I muttered. "Big Red. Hold your shield position! Over." I bit my lip, thinking fast. "Big Red. Initiate Operation Mosquito a second time. Over."

Our drones weren't loaded with more darts, but the Luthers didn't know that. I just needed them to hesitate and not gain height while my cliff stewards were forced to shield.

I gritted my teeth as a fresh onslaught of darts showered the cliffs.

Everyone but my Operation Batman stewards were mostly covered.

Darts embedded in some legs and arms that the shields couldn't quite protect.

"Three Operation Batman stewards," Pascal murmured.

I swore again.

The pack drones lowered, and ours returned to the middle tier. The pack had shielded, but our bluff wouldn't work again.

Despite the water blasting out from our cannons, Luthers were reaching the first levels.

"Big Red. Wicked, Snow, send replacements for Operation Batman. Two west. One south. Over."

Paw patrol stewards needed to get out of there. If Sascha planned a third aerial attack, we were screwed.

There wasn't time to hesitate. "Big Red. Stewards, resume firing positions. Cover bottom tier. Over."

I hoped that order didn't bite me on the ass.

"Reindeer. Task complete. Over."

"Wicked. Task complete. Over."

Our hastily practiced operation was fully manned again. *Here goes.* "Big Red. Initiate Operation Batman. Over."

Ropes burst from the top cliffs to the opposite side.

"Come on." I exhaled slowly.

The Batman stewards clipped themselves to the ropes and wasted no time soaring across the quarry.

Face down, they opened fire on the Luthers below.

Yes!

"Big Red. Paw Patrol, shields on and climb. Over."

If they could reach the middle tier, we'd be okay.

Those on the water cannons would probably be shot, but they continued working as Batman stewards soared over the quarry, and paw patrol stewards ascended the sandstone walls.

One Batman steward was hanging limp in the middle of a wire, rendering the entire wire useless.

But they were nailing it.

This game is carnage, Booker said in awe.

Yep. I'd never experienced a grid match this intense.

"Something's wrong over there." Rhona pointed.

Tribe members were scrambling to reach an unconscious steward. I gasped as her anchor dislodged and she dropped to the next safety point.

Muted screams rocketed toward me from those looking on.

I blurted into my walkie, "Reindeer. Take over head steward controls. Over." Jumping onto the railing, I launched at the cliffs to my left and extended my claws part way.

Puncturing the sandstone, I worked fast toward the middle of the quarry where the unconscious woman hung.

I could feel Sascha closing in as well.

Panting hard, I reached the steward and took her weight over my shoulder. *Oh fuck.* Our claws were not made for this load.

She's clipped to the rope, Booker reminded me.

"Hand her over." Sascha was breathing hard too.

He was stronger.

Hissing at the pain in my claws, I nodded. He transferred her to his shoulder, and I unhooked her from the ropes.

Grunting, Sascha descended to the middle tier. I caught my breath, clinging to the wall.

"Fancy meeting you here."

Pain exploded across my cheek, and I saw white. I clung on and blinked at Mandy for an instant before her fist replaced my view of her smirk.

She connected with my jaw again.

My claws slid free of the sandstone.

I cried out.

How high are we? Spin around, Booker shouted.

Air rushed past as I struggled to face the ground.

But I already knew we were too high up to come out unscathed.

A huge body collided with mine and the air rushed from my lungs. Sascha wrapped around me, cradling me tight.

We rocketed toward the ground.

And hit.

My head cracked against Sascha's chest.

His arms slid from my back. Pain reverberated through my body where I lay atop of him.

Clutching my head, I rolled off, trying to see past the black cracks in my vision.

"Sascha?" I slurred, crawling back to him. *Booker?*

I'm here, she said groggily. *There's blood.*

I called out to Greyson and didn't receive a reply.

Forcing my way through the throbbing pain, I focused on Sascha again. Blood seeped out from under his head.

I checked his pulse. *Slow.*

Too slow.

"Sascha," I shouted.

My heart pounded as I heaved him sideways to check his head. The split nearly made me vomit.

"*No.*" Black closed in on my mind. "Sascha! Wake up."

Evelyn pushed through the midst of the fighting Luthers.

She dropped beside me, feeling for his pulse. She inspected his wound, and I watched on in desperation as she checked his eyes and felt his pulse again.

"His heartbeat is strengthening." She sat back and sighed.

"He'll be okay?" My voice cracked.

"Yes."

I covered my face. She wrapped me in her arms, and I cried against her shoulder.

"The idiot c-caught me," I explained.

"Yes, dear. I saw. Very stupid of him."

Chaos was all around us, and I just didn't care. I sniffed hard and pulled away.

"Is Sascha alright?" Mandy asked in a tiny voice from behind us.

Evelyn growled, all menacing mother.

Red blanketed my vision as I turned to Mandy. Fangs bursting from my gums, I launched at her and tackled her to the ground.

Drawing my fist back, I slammed it into the delta's face twice.

And then once more for fucking luck.

Her head lolled, and my brief satisfaction ended as I felt a sharp pinch in my back.

Spinning in a drunken circle, I met Grim's gaze.

"You shot me," I accused.

The gamma shrugged. "No hard feelings."

"Bastard."

He smiled, and I slanted to the ground.

24

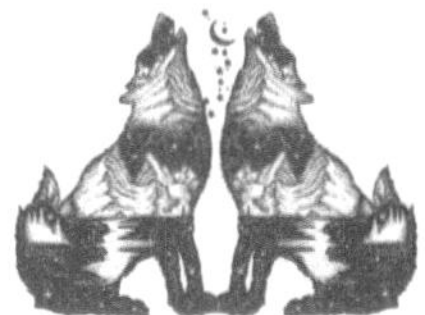

I clutched my head and rolled. “Mothershitter.”

“I’ve always wondered what that means. Then again, what does bitchhole mean? These are questions that only the consumption of red wine can answer.”

Forcing an eyelid open, I found Wade sitting on a chair beside my bed.

“Ouch,” I told him.

“Your forehead copped a pretty decent injury. No joke, you looked like a white-trash unicorn for a whole hour.”

Booker?

She didn’t answer, but as panic threatened to close in, I recalled Grim darting me. Tranquiliser affected our wolves more than us.

“I fell?” It had to be sometime in the middle of the night because no one in the manor made a sound.

“Sascha caught you. I can’t believe he isn’t dead.”

My heart stalled and horror saturated my very soul. “Tell me he’s alive, Wade.”

“I got Evelyn’s number. She’s texting hourly updates. He opened his eyes for a bit. She said he’ll fully recover.”

My heart resumed beating, and I dragged in a harsh breath.

Some of the horror remained though.

I'd felt panic when Herc aimed his gun at Sascha, but I'd never *truly* understood just how his death would break me until now.

My very being screamed against that existence.

I touched my face, wincing at the deep pain in the centre of my forehead. "I can't remember what happened after we hit the ground."

Wade kicked his legs up onto the bed and crossed them at the ankle. "Let me give you a play-by-play."

"A genuine one, please."

"This may sound Wade-esque, but it's accurate." He cleared his throat. "Mandy punched you twice in the face, throwing you from the top cliffs. No one's sure what compelled her to do it—the move would have always lost the pack points. But moving on. Sascha dropped the unconscious steward he saved like she was burning sack of shit and launched after you like he was Wolverine. Our steward fell a few metres to the middle tier and is bruised but otherwise fine. Sascha hit the ground with you in his arms. You wept like a child on his mother's shoulder after screaming his name. Every steward saw Sascha take the brunt of the hit for you... They also saw your distraught reaction when you believed him dead."

I groaned.

"The upside is that the tribe also saw you beat the Christmas spirit out of Mandy—they think you're a total badass."

"What's everyone saying about me and Sascha?"

"Uh, well, they saw how you truly feel about Sascha Greyson. It's... some are shocked. I'm not sure it's in a *bad* way—but I guess we'll soon find out. Until now, you haven't once let feelings you have for him affect your effort in the grid, so that's a definite bonus."

I'd planned to lose to the pack if Sascha agreed to a truce, but the tribe didn't need to know that.

Jesus. The next few days would be hell dealing with the fallout, and Rhona would have seen everything too.

I sighed. "Are you sure Sascha is okay?"

"Positive, baby girl. He's going to get better. Plus, he managed to make the tribe super uncomfortable by risking his life to protect you."

"How? My head hurts too much to think."

"He put your life above the game. He provided unshakeable proof that he's more than the savage beast. That will probably shock the Luther-haters more than your feelings for him."

Huh. Hoped so.

I rested back on my pillows. "You've been here all night?"

"You betcha. Cam was, too, but I told her to get some sleep an hour ago. The stewards are all asking about you."

"Thank you for being here." I sucked in a harsh breath. *Oh my god.* "Did we win Sandstone?"

"Five minutes. It took you five minutes to ask."

"Tell me."

"There was one point between us and the pack. We won."

"*One point*," I repeated in a daze.

Wade grinned. "You turned over another grid, baby girl."

I closed my eyes.

We won. We had three grids.

Yet I could only think about Sascha. About how much I wanted to be beside him. "Can you call Evelyn, please?"

"I want a better reaction to our win first."

I stared at him.

"For now, you get a pass," he rushed to say.

He dialled and put the call on speaker.

"Wade, hello," Evelyn answered immediately.

I braced myself against the lingering horror. "How is he?"

"Andie. Sascha woke and is asking for you. Would you like to speak to him?"

"Please." I listened to murmuring voices.

"Mate," Sascha answered.

Wade fanned his face.

A lump rose in my throat. "You're alright."

"You hit your head. How do you feel?"

This wasn't becoming about me when he'd nearly died. "I'm fine. Has your head healed?"

"Grim shot you," he growled. "I was worried what it might have done with your head injury."

"Sascha. *Are you okay?*"

"It will take a day or two to get back on my feet," he admitted.

Anger surged. "Why did you do that? I could have landed better. You had to absorb the shock from two bodies." My voice broke. "How is your back not broken?"

"Don't be upset, beautiful wolf. My back has healed now."

My eyes rounded. "It *was* broken?"

"I heal fast," he said hastily. "Thank you for being worried about me though."

A tear slipped from my eye.

"She's crying," Wade said.

Fucker.

Sascha sighed. "I'd much rather see you to know you're safe."

"Maybe I could visit you tomorrow? With pack permission."

"Permission granted."

Another tear joined the first. Sascha never sounded tired, but near-death had done it. "I'll see you tomorrow then. Sleep and rest."

He murmured a disjointed goodbye, and I ended the call.

Wade's eyes were wide. "Baby girl, you are *so* far gone,"

My bottom lip trembled. "I know."

Sascha nearly dying made the consequences of Grids real in a way nothing else had. *This* was what stood to happen unless I won.

Sascha could die.

I could lose him forever.

Wade leaned over and wrapped his arms around me. "You don't need to be afraid."

But I did.

I really did.

🐾🐾

The office door was slammed against the bookshelf.

I glanced up, phone held to my ear. "Let's suspend work in Sandstone today. The focus is on cleaning up darts and compiling a thorough inspection of the pack's management." I listened to Trixie's reply. "Alright. See you this afternoon."

I hung up. "Wade. Can I help you?"

He squared his shoulders. "You certainly can."

Striding forward, Wade tossed a thick folder on my desk. He leaned forward on his hands to peer into my eyes.

What the hell?

"I'd like to take you back to 1846," he said grimly.

I inhaled my friend's determination. "If you need to."

"We can both agree it's imperative."

Can we? "The floor is yours."

"Since its birth, the Annual Deception Valley Ball has formed the cornerstone of relations between the public and the Ni Tiaki. The event fostered friendships and business networks between our people. In an isolated town, the ball was anticipated as *the* event of the year. Women would spend the year creating their outfits as shown in some old pictures I pulled from records—"

"Where are you going with this?"

He spoke over me. "The ball of today is a sad, weak replica of what once was. Our tribe has allowed this tradition to fall into woeful despair, and I strongly believe it is our solemn duty, *now more than ever*, to resurrect this event to its full power."

Wade opened the folder and I eyed the thickness of the contents.

He began again. "Luthers, tribe, and—"

"I have a call that I can't miss in five minutes."

Wade glared at me. "This is important."

A lot of preparation had gone into his presentation. "I'm not saying it isn't. I'm saying that you need to get to your point. You know I'll listen."

He maintained his glare for another beat before sighing heavily. "Fine. Prior to the last fifty years, the Deception Valley Ball always meant a week off Grids. I want this tradition reinstated. The ball was once vital to relationships between tribe and public, but in my humble opinion, it can be used to the same effect between the pack and Ni Tiaki now."

Humble wasn't a word I'd apply to Wade.

Ever.

I leaned back. A week off Grids for the ball...

We had three grids in our possession and the two hardest battlefields remained. The odds of winning Clay or Water were far lower than those we'd already turned over.

A week off Grids for the ball would mean an extra week to prepare for those grids.

A week off could affect my steward's winning momentum though, and that wasn't something to disregard. Morale held great importance.

Then again, improving relationships between Luthers and stewards felt like an insurmountable task, and one that *had* to be achieved to form a lasting truce.

Every little effort could help.

Wade hadn't breathed in thirty seconds. He really did believe in this ball. My friend was smart about people.

I nodded. "I'll back you on this. I can see the benefits. It's up to you to convince the head team. Put together an official request for the pack after. If Sascha says no, my hands are tied."

He smirked. "He'll agree."

That comment should probably worry me.

Controlling Wade would be like controlling a flood, and I needed to be in the conference room three minutes ago. "Go get 'em, tiger. Let me know how you get on."

Grabbing a thin folder—my life was 100 percent folders these days—I rushed from the office.

In the conference room, I switched on the large screen and

connected my device to the laptop. I only had time to take a steadying breath before a phone symbol appeared.

I shook out my hands. This call was important.

It wasn't every day I spoke to a vampire king.

Drawing my shoulders back, I answered the call. "This is Andie Thana."

A huge space came into view. Smooth stone registered before the two thrones drew my eye—because they were thrones. The number of bodies came next. Upwards of ten vampires.

The biggest of the two thrones was occupied by the largest man I'd ever seen. A heavy crown sat atop his head. The woman sitting on the smaller throne to his right was clad in an elegant tiara and nipple tassels.

So there was that.

She was fucking *gorgeous.* I mean, all of them were, but she was next level.

I swept my gaze over the others, finding Basilia two spaces from the king's throne. A male who rivalled the king for size stood between her and the left side of the throne—Kyros?

There were four females of varying breath-taking appearance present, and the rest were equally breath-taking males.

Was this the royal vampire family of Bluff City?

They perused me as intensely as I did them.

I tilted my chin.

Topaz eyes gleaming, Basilia stepped forward. "Andie, it's nice to see you again."

"And you. Greetings, King Julius, and to what I assume is your family."

The king did nothing to acknowledge my comment.

Interesting.

"Allow me to introduce everyone," Basilia said. "You know about Kyros, of course. This is our clan leader, King Julius. Beside him is Queen Titania." She ran through the names of the others, but I focused on the names of those with crowns.

That seemed like a good idea.

"You are alone," the king spoke at last. "Is this not a serious negotiation?"

The intimidation game? Perhaps. His question did hold merit. The entire royal family had assembled to hear me out.

I bowed slightly. "I mean no disrespect, your majesty. Has Basilia apprised you of the current situation in Deception Valley between pack and tribe?"

He dipped his head. "I am informed."

"Navigating this alliance alongside the pack must be done with care. There are old prejudices and emotion is always high. When I take a potential deal to Sascha Greyson, then I'd prefer the parameters of any alliance to be partially formed."

"You expect Clan Sundulus to enter into negotiations at all when success is so unsure?" he boomed.

This fucker was moderately scary—I was glad this meeting was a video call.

"I have no expectations," I answered. "Only a desire to see less bloodshed over a meaningless game."

He sat back in his throne. "Indeed. And yet did not these same werewolves attack us unprovoked not long ago?"

Not long ago? How old was this guy?

"I'm sure it came across that way to your clan. Would you like to hear what I know on the matter?"

His eyes narrowed.

He didn't like being questioned.

I waited.

"Proceed," the king said.

Yes, sir. "The pack here was originally part of a larger pack whose leader ruled with extreme fear and violence. It takes a lot to scar a werewolf, King Julius, but many of the wolves here carry such wounds from their time under his rule. Alexei, brother to the leader, convinced half of the pack to join him in a quest to find safer territory where they may live in peace. They landed on your shores, and their presence was taken as an attack. Ten thousand battered and worn Luthers arrived in Bluff City, and thousands less made it out alive. When they did escape Vissimo, they ran into demons. Of the ten thousand wolves that left in hopes of a better life, only 15 percent of them made it to Deception Valley."

"You attempt to persuade me with tales of woe and despair," he sneered.

"I give you facts and leave you to interpret them how you will. I can see why the sight of ten thousand werewolves inspired the response it did."

Kyros cut in. "Only seven-hundred and fifty Luthers remain. Why?"

I'd agonised over this since Basilia's visit, but it was time to break a promise I made to Sascha. The only promise he'd ever asked of me.

More and more I'd started to believe that general knowledge of this secret would change how the tribe and others perceived the pack.

I met Kyros's green gaze. "Witches, Demons, and Vissimo surround the pack on all sides. They're trapped and can't leave to find their mates. Luthers have one mate in their lifetime. Without that mate, they can't have children and nature does not grant them immortality. The lifespan then is around four hundred and fifty years. The pack has slowly been dying off."

The blonde sister gasped.

In fact, most of the royals appeared faintly disturbed.

"The wolves need access through our lands as part of an alliance then?" King Julius's eyes glittered.

Clever bastard.

But I couldn't give him that much power in the negotiations.

"I'm currently building an airport so small numbers of the pack can leave to find their mates. Safe passage through your territory would be appreciated as part of a deal, but not necessary."

The king studied me. "Where is our assurance that the werewolves will uphold their end of the bargain if they can leave at any time via your airport or if we grant them safe passage through our territory? From my understanding, if your tribe wins this game, then the pack may be exiled from the valley too."

"Where is our assurance that your clan will uphold their end of the bargain either?" I replied. "If Luthers give their word, they won't break it. Small numbers of them would be absent at any given time in pursuit of their partner, but we can cap the amount to ensure enough scouts are available at any given time." I took a breath. "I realise this alliance depends on the outcome of Victratum, the mercy of my tribe, and the willingness of my pack to enter into a deal. I'm not unaware of how uncertain that makes a potential partnership. So to avoid a situation where the pack can't uphold their side of the deal, I recommend we only finalise a deal once I've won the game."

A handsome vampire with dark features grinned. "You seem certain of the win, but that's quite a gamble."

I smiled without humour as I met his eyes. "I never gamble, Prince."

The vampires fell quiet at my words.

I focused on the king again. "There are those in the pack who fought and won against demons. They hold first-hand knowledge about combat with that race. They've had some experience with witches also. The downside is that both the demons and witches are aware of pack presence here. On previous scouting missions, they've responded with violence."

"Your tribe," Kyros said, "it's in their interest to play a part too. As humans, they could move about largely undetected."

I stared at the crown prince.

Oh my god. It *was* in their interest.

I'd been so focused on the pack's safety that I hadn't considered—

"Would your tribe also agree to such an alliance, do you suppose?" The queen's voice was as beautiful as her face.

"Potentially," I drew out.

Very possibly.

The tribe would need to remain in the valley. The threat of demons and witches would remain.

Fuck. This could be exactly what I'd been looking for.

"Is something the matter?" Basilia asked.

I forced a smile her way, recalling my current company. "King Julius, in alliance with Clan Sundulus, the tribe and pack would monitor the activity of demons and witches bordering our lands. We would also, in combination with your clan, endeavour to compile information on the weaknesses and strengths of both species in preparation to defend against future attack. This information would be freely shared. All parties would come to each other's aid against either race and coexist peacefully for the duration of the alliance. I hold none of the prejudice of my race against yours. I believe this partnership is in both of our interests. Particularly, the size of the demon kingdom is worrisome for us all."

The king's expression didn't alter. "If the wolves remain in your valley, then an alliance may be reached between all. I will not include safe passage through my city as part of our arrangement to make it easy for the pack to abandon our deal. That is not in the best interest of my clan."

Dammit. "Then I ask instead that you consider safe passage in separation to any alliance, King Julius. As said, if my tribe doesn't show mercy, the pack could have no choice but to leave in haste. Leaving in a large group would give them an advantage wherever they end up next. You could save a great many lives, including the lives of what few children the pack currently has. This would not be a business deal, but an act of mercy."

"I am not in the business of mercy, werewolf," he answered coldly.

"Once you were in the business of a game though, and maybe once you hoped for clemency for your loved ones. This would be a mercy the pack would never forget."

He narrowed his gaze.

I bowed again. "If the royals of Clan Sundulus wish to pursue an alliance between our peoples, I'll happily involve key members of the pack and tribe."

Basilia's eyes were gleaming again. "You've given us a lot to think about."

I'd never felt more serious in my life. "Likewise. Thank you for your time."

I knew how to win the game.

I knew how to end this war for good.

25

I miss you, I thought at Sascha.

He'd mostly healed by now, but I could still feel a slight fatigue leftover from my head injury, so he had to feel like crap.

Mate?

I sat up in bed. *You can hear me?*

Whoa, not just that. I'd felt his curiosity too.

Sascha. What's going on?

He was contemplative. *An after-effect of the bite meet perhaps. I haven't tried to speak to you at a distance since then.*

Neither had I.

I can feel your shock, he said.

I can feel your emotions too. Crazy.

From here, our mating gifts intertwine more.

He'd told me that a while ago. *Does the emotion thing only work when we open the phone call?*

That's how you think of this? Amusement.

Kind of. My human mind had to put wolfy things into normal lines sometimes. *How are you feeling?*

Good, mate.

That was a lie. Ha, this new gift was awesome.

A little tired. Nothing to worry about.

I wish you were with me.

I wish the same.

I toyed with the bedspread. *Any luck talking to the pack about a truce?*

Not much, he said grimly. *Those I've approached mostly believe as my father does.*

Dammit. *What will it take for them to listen?*

Hearing actual proposals for a truce.

That involved revealing a whole heap of stuff I wasn't sure they could handle though. *Where do you stand, Sascha?*

You can't be happy doing less than your best for the tribe. I feel the same for the pack. I want to work with you. The moment there's something viable, I'll do so without hesitation.

After Kyros's casual comment, I did have something to work with.

Wade burst into my room with Cameron in tow.

"What's going on?" I eyed the garment bag.

"Dress fitting." She held it up, cheeks tinged pink.

Look, I've got to go. Ball dress fitting.

I agreed to Wade's week off.

You did? That wasn't in the pack's best interest.

The communication cut off.

I shot Wade a look. "How did you convince Sascha to agree to a week off the game?"

"He listened to my presentation. Unlike some people."

"Sure he did. How did you do it?"

Wade snickered. "I tried to play nice. Said you were tired and could really use a mate who understood your needs."

I snorted. "You have zero boundaries."

"Yeah, well, he didn't go for it. Seemed amused. Luckily, I'd compiled a list of Sascha's ex-lovers. I said you'd receive the list. And let me tell you, he's one hundred. There were a..."

He trailed off at my expression.

"But," Wade blurted, "far fewer than there could have been?"

I threw off the blankets. "Right."

"*Good one, idiot*," Cam muttered.

"No, I knew he must've had other partners. Wolves do that." I frowned. "He's just never mentioned it, and I never wanted to know."

Jealousy was new for me.

Whoa, did I feel it now.

"Do you want to see the list?" Wade cleared his throat.

Cameron rolled her eyes. "Ignorance is bliss with these things. Such a guy."

Yeah, the last thing I wanted was for my view of some pack females to be influenced by Sascha's past.

Wade coloured. "One had a red tinge to her hair, if that helps? Much more a strawberry blonde than your auburn. Very *sexy* auburn."

Cam whacked his arm. "Shut up already." She faced me, shaking her head. "We need you to try this on."

I forced my mind from the ugliness churning in my stomach. "Wade said you made this. I never knew."

She shrugged. "Just a hobby."

Wade made a sound of derision. "Hobby, my ass. Andie, you will look like an untouchable Thana. And Sascha will only have eyes for you in this, believe me."

He better. Because I was feeling extremely fangy. "You really didn't have to do this, Cam. Thank you."

"I *wanted* to," she pressed. "You have enough on your plate."

Wade glanced sheepishly at me when I padded to the garment bag.

"It's okay," I said. "But I don't want to see the list, okay? Get rid of it."

"Deal, baby girl. Now, get naked. We've got a job to do."

I obeyed and shrugged into the pale gold ensemble. My jaw dropped. "You made this?"

"I know, right?" Wade mumbled.

Bright red, Cameron pinned and tucked lose sections. The gold went well against my skin and brought out lighter undertones in my hair I didn't know existed.

They helped me out of the dress after.

I grabbed a pair of jeans and tank top and dressed.

"I've cancelled all your meetings next Friday," Wade announced.

"You *what?*"

He raised both hands. "Before you get in a tizz, we have a whole extra week until Grids. You can take one day off now and then, Andie. Your hair will thank you for it. Seriously, when was the last time you had it cut?"

I thought about it. "By someone else?"

"Yes. By someone in a salon."

Never. "You're going to cut my hair?"

"A professional will, yes. After our steam room and massage appointment. You *will* look better for this ball if it's the last thing I do."

Cameron sighed. "What he means to say is that we've arranged a pamper day. The head team are fine with it. Everyone is looking forward to some time off."

I hadn't considered my team in this. "They are?"

She nodded.

My friends were usually right. The entire head team deserved a day to unwind and recharge. "I'll be there. Right now, I'm expected elsewhere."

Grabbing a jacket and slipping into knee-high boots, I then speed-walked to the meeting room. *Sorry, Booker. We'll run later, I promise.*

Maybe Greyson could come?

I switched channels. *Sascha, Booker wants to know if Greyson can come for a run later.*

His reply was immediate. *He'd love to.*

My cheeks warmed, courtesy of Booker's glee. *She's looking forward to it.*

I cut off the chat and stepped into the conference room.

The tables were drawn together. Trixie and Stanley were in attendance, along with five representatives from Sandstone.

I greeted everyone, then took my seat. “We’ve had a few days to assess Sandstone. What are the findings?”

Trixie set a report in front of me.

It was ten pages *at least*.

“I’m not going to pretend I have a speck of the knowledge each of you do,” I addressed the nervous workers. “We need to know what each point means, and the impacts of each point. So you’re aware of what we intend to do, currently the tribe holds three penalty points. We need two more. Whatever we take to the pack needs to be failsafe.”

The row of workers nodded.

A woman in the middle cleared her throat, “There’s one major lapse, Head Steward. The rest certainly add up, but one in particular had significant environmental impacts.”

Perfect.

“Show me,” I said.

She thumbed through her copy. “Page four. Fifth point down. The area where we dump our extraction waste products was assessed. During this, it was found that waste products had been dumped in the wrong area, near a small waterway. The fluoride levels there were tested and found in excess of 1 mg per litre, which is in direct violation of our practices.”

From my council stint, I knew that the population of Deception Valley relied on our clean waterways. “That’s a hazardous level?”

“Some data maintains negative effects in young children. We monitor waterways around the waste disposal area closely.”

“Are we able to prove that the loads were dropped in the wrong area by the pack and not us?”

Trixie replied, “Yes, Head Steward. Photo and video footage is a routine part of grid turnovers. We take footage on the Wednesday evening prior to a match, and also upon resuming management of a grid. We have before and after pictures, and the pack will have their own.”

We had an ace. “Excellent. In your expert opinions, what is the combined environmental impact of the rest of these points?”

The woman spoke again. “There’s a level of environmental impact that the pack and tribe agree—in strict terms—can’t be avoided with the extraction of natural resources. Each of the mentioned points, long-term, would have created a mild negative effect on the quarry itself and the surrounding area. *Combined,* there’s current data to support our opinion that the long-term environmental effect of these lapses would have been significant.”

“Thank you.” I glanced at Stanley and Trixie. “The pack will argue that no long-term effect was displayed even if we can prove it with external studies. What do we have against that?”

“Care for the land must be displayed at all times. The contract is clear,” Stanley answered. “It doesn’t matter whether they had the grid for a week or a year. It’s their duty to heed the guidelines constantly.”

Trixie faced the row of stewards. “Is the data you’ve based your opinions on absolute? Are there studies proving the opposite in existence?”

Ah, good point.

A man at the far end raised his hand. “New data does arise, but policies and procedures for each grid are updated annually. These were agreed upon by our tribe and the Luthers.”

My lips curved. “So the pack have already agreed that the data used to form the policies is the most accurate and valid information.”

Some of the Sandstone stewards smiled back.

“Exactly,” the man said.

Perfect.

I skimmed over their other points, but they largely meant nothing to me. “I can’t do these points justice. Stanley, do we need special permission to bring stewards into official meetings?”

“Just advanced notice. We’ve done so before in past negotiations.”

"How much advanced notice? I don't want to give Sascha time to prepare."

"Five minutes would do it," Trixie supplied. "I can clear protocol with Pascal though."

"Please do." I glanced up at the quiet Sandstone stewards. "Before we go through the rest, I need to make it clear that this information must be kept to yourself until it's revealed to the tribe. No one outside of this room, barring the rest of my head team, can know. This could very well be what we need to turn over a fourth grid. Do you understand?"

They nodded.

"When will you make your move, Head Steward?" the first woman asked.

The only thing about now *having* an idea on how to form a lasting truce was I felt grossly unprepared for the end.

Possessing four grids felt too close to the potentially disastrous consequences. I naturally wanted to resist and delay, but that wasn't best for my stewards. "I'll make my move after the Deception Valley Ball."

26

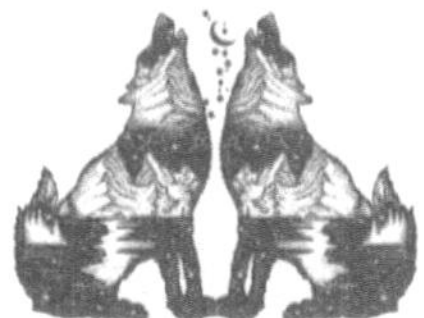

I re-read the message to double-check my eyes weren't cold-hearted liars.

King Julius liked you.

"Like fuck he did," I told my office.

My office agreed.

I read Basilia's other messages.

Not many can speak to him without pissing their bike shorts.
He's given me a draft contract for your consideration.

I really hadn't known what to think after video chatting the vampire royals. In the wake, it seemed like I didn't have enough to offer.

I texted back.

Thank you. This is good news.

Her reply was instant.

Check your email.

I opened the mail app and found an unread message. "Pretty sure I never gave her my email address."

Guess billionaires have access to spy shit.

Opening the huge attachment, I skimmed through the first few pages of the draft contract. This was weighted in favour of the Vissimo. Business wasn't always business, but it was this time.

I typed a second text.

That other thing we discussed.
I have dates.

Three dots appeared, and my heart thumped.

Her message appeared.

Send the details and it's done.

I exhaled. *Booker, I'm not ready for this.*

We've done all we can do alone. It's time to involve others.

That's what had me so terrified.

No one else wanted what I did. Sascha came close. Wade and Cameron close behind him, but everyone else wanted to outright win. Others wouldn't see my plans the same way I did. They could react badly. *Really* badly.

Yet, the only way forward was to take this step.

Courage, Andie. Start with Sascha, Booker said. *Go from there.*

She was right.

Steeling myself, I dialled his number.

The phone rang once.

"You're using the actual phone?" he answered.

This method felt more formal than telepathy. "I'm ready to tell you everything. Just you and me."

He was silent. "How big is this?"

"It could be what we need. The pack, the tribe, and us."

"When and where, mate?"

I licked my lips. "Somewhere private. How about the place Herc's will was read? Can you leave now?"

"Give me twenty."

This was happening.

Sascha wanted to help me, but there was so much he had to consider. Hell, I *got* where he was coming from. There was every chance he couldn't support me in this.

If so... this probably wouldn't work.

I listened to his footsteps and the deep thrum of his pickup engine. "Sascha?"

"Mate."

"Just... you'll need an open mind for this."

His tone was dry. "I'd gathered."

I hung up and grabbed my keys.

Sliding into Ella F, I took the road to Lake Thana, driving two-thirds of the way alongside it before locating the hilltop road. If not for Booker's daily runs, the hidden corners of Deception Valley would still be a mystery to me, but this particular spot was burned in my memory. Once, I drove up this road as Andie Booker and came down as Andie Thana.

Sascha wasn't there yet.

Turning up the collar of my jacket against the wind, I approached the rock where Herc's will was read.

Pascal's words rang in my head. "*Will you protect the stewards of Ni Tiaki with your final breath, Andie Thana?*"

"*I will.*"

"*Will you lead us in Victratum to the best of your ability?*"

I whispered, "I will."

The rumbling of Sascha's pickup reached my ears. He parked, and I listened to his footsteps.

"You're nervous," he said at my back.

Understatement.

I turned, hair whipping around my shoulders. "Hey."

Sascha darted a look over my face. "Tell me then."

I shoved my hands in my jacket pockets.

Where to start? "The problem with peace in the past is that we didn't have a cause to unify us. Until recently, all I could think of is that we both share a love of this land. But that's also been the source of our discontent, and that's why attempts at peace have always failed. I've found something that could hold us together—long-term."

"I'm listening."

I winced. "This is the part you need to be open about."

He could smell my dread, so he didn't laugh.

Sascha stepped forward and tilted my chin up. "You know what I need to consider. Within those bounds, I'll do what I can."

My plan required him to act outside of those bounds. "Days after learning I was Herc's daughter, I placed a call to our importer list to introduce myself. One was a vampire and she asked about the werewolves in Deception Valley."

Sascha's expression hardened. "You want to work with vampires."

"In a later exchange, she was surprised to learn that the largest demon kingdom in the world bordered part of Bluff City, and that witches bordered them on the other side. They had no idea either supernatural race was in the vicinity—something both of us found unusual and suspicious."

This intrigued Sascha, but the hardness remained.

I ploughed on. "I entered negotiations with the royal Vissimo family of Bluff City. My initial goal was to barter safe passage for the pack through their territory."

"The airport." He interrupted.

"Will take months. I needed a more immediate solution."

Sascha focused on me, hope rising from him. "Their answer?"

I laid a hand on his chest. "The negotiations quickly changed to something bigger—to the proposal of an alliance between pack, Vissimo, and tribe. Not only were the vampires unaware of the demons and witches, but they're too far away to monitor the situation if either of these races look to expand their territory in the future. Obviously, this should be a concern for us too. In an alliance, our proximity to the demons and witches holds great value to the Bluff City Vissimo. The pack has first-hand knowledge of demons and witches, and is capable of aiding the vampires, and vice versa, in any battle. And as humans, the tribe have the ability to scout and gather intel undetected—and are also training to fight."

"The tribe and pack would constantly put themselves in harm's way to monitor and gather intel. There seem to be few perks for us and a lot for the vampires."

"Either way, whoever remains in this valley must educate themselves about our neighbours. Why not do so with fifteen thousand vampires at our back? Combined, the tribe and pack number less than two thousand. We'd greatly benefit from a powerful friend."

That struck him the most out of anything I'd said.

I might be getting somewhere. "What if the pack won today, only to face the largest demon kingdom in the *world* in fifty years? Our supernatural neighbours pose a serious threat that we need to prepare for, and Grids has given our people the perfect training to fight that battle. That aside, this threat is the only way I've thought of to convince the tribe and pack to a truce. I'm not saying peace will be easy, but with a cause to unite us, time and determination can do the rest."

Sascha hummed.

I tracked his rapidly changing scents.

His expression wasn't reassuring. "The vampires slaughtered thousands of my wolves, Andie. Those who made it to the valley and still live haven't forgotten it. For them, the horror is fresh. What you're asking with the vampire alliance is likely too much."

"The pack wants a place to call their own. They just need to hate vampires less than they want that. Why do you think the tribe has a Luther for a head steward? Some things are stronger than fear and loathing."

"You've proposed a way for the pack and tribe to hold a truce. You haven't offered the pack a home."

"The tribe doesn't own land, Sascha. What you're asking is something they would never give themselves."

"What about a middle ground?"

I studied him. "Like what?"

"Just under one hundred years ago, the tribe placed their land in trust to protect it from outsiders laying claim. The tribe could place land in trust for the pack. We wouldn't own the land, but it would be legally binding. This could be an acceptable level of security for my wolves."

If the tribe won, why would they place land in trust for the pack? Where was the incentive?

I had to think on it. "*If* I could convince the tribe to do that, would the pack enter an alliance with the tribe and vampires?"

"A home is what they want above all else. They'll be more inclined to listen."

I'd take that answer for now. "I'd like to continue negotiations with King Julius, and I'd like you present. I'm happy to send through his draft contract today. It's heavily in favour of the vampires, but I expected no less. He seems mostly reasonable... under the ancient Vissimo king vibe."

Stepping closer, I hugged his middle. His arms wrapped around me.

We swayed together for a time.

"I need your help," I whispered.

"I know, little bird."

To win, we couldn't do what had always been done. We had to push our people down the safest path.

Werewolves hated vampires? Okay, fine. Vampires were willing to put their beef with the Luthers aside to benefit their clan.

The pack wanted a home? Great. Where else would they go? They could leave the valley only to meet freakin' gargoyles or some shit in another area. They *knew* this territory. And now they had a way to find their mates.

"I can't promise the pack will come to the table without a land solution from the tribe, but I'll read over this king's contract." Sascha paused. "I'll also attend further negotiations."

My shoulders sagged. "Thank you."

"I want to give you a yes, so we're clear."

"It just feels hopeless sometimes. I want everyone to be safe."

He kissed my temple. "Everyone will be safe. Shut your eyes, mate. I'll paint a picture for you."

I smiled against his chest. "What kind of picture?"

"The kind where there's no game and we wake up together each day."

Tears stung my eyes, but I obeyed. "I'm listening."

Nine shocked faces looked at me.

"You want to what now?" Nathan asked.

I'd decided to broach the subject with my head team before I lost my nerve.

"We're surrounded by supernatural species," I repeated with false calm. "When we win Grids, under the current terms of Victratum, the pack must leave the valley within twenty-four hours. My mounting concern is that their exit would leave us open to invasion from demons, witches, or vampires looking to expand their territory."

That's what I might do if I heard a juicy patch of unclaimed land was free.

Pascal's brows were nearly in her hairline. "What exactly do you suggest?"

"The obvious solution is a new agreement between pack and tribe. Luthers have abilities we don't, and stewards have abilities they don't. Our fight needs to be against those who could attack this land in the future. We should combine forces."

Stanley frowned. "That's well and good, but past truces have always failed."

"That's because we've always fought over this land. Every death on either side has been due to that dispute or Victratum. Two and a half centuries have proven we can inhabit the same space."

"So..." Trixie trailed off.

Maybe this was a lot for a Thursday morning.

"The largest demon kingdom in the world wraps around half of this valley," I told them. "There are likely tens of thousands of them. The vampires occupying Bluff City number upwards of fifteen thousand."

Stanley spoke again, "Even if an alliance were possible, how are one thousand stewards and less than a thousand werewolves going to hold back so many? What if the demons, witches, and vampires are working together already?"

"I'm glad you asked. I happened to meet a vampire a while back."

His jaw dropped.

I lifted a shoulder. "We had a lot in common. She was turned into a Vissimo, and we both went through sudden introductions to the supernatural world via mating processes. I didn't know it at the time, but that woman is the mate of the crown prince of the Bluff City vampire clan. Through her, I was able to reach their leader, King Julius, to discuss the possibility of an alliance."

"Vampires," Nathan echoed.

I suppose this really was a lot for a Thursday.

Maybe any day.

I nodded. "They were interested and highly concerned to discover demon and witches were in the area. In return for the tribe and pack monitoring these races, they'd be willing to come to our aid if ever needed. As said, there are over fifteen thousand in their clan."

"You want an alliance between the pack, tribe, *and* vampires?" Wade asked in the wake.

Was it a good sign that vampires worried them more than werewolves?

"As Stanley noted, our current numbers are a weakness. We need an ally."

He blew out a breath. "Right."

I looked at the head team. "As a leader, I see two sides who are wasting their time trying to beat each other, when in reality, we've lived with each other for hundreds of years. I fear the inability to see beyond our past will see us all dead."

"The pack would be happy to remain on borrowed land if we form an alliance?" Pascal asked.

She'd seen what I hadn't.

"I approached Sascha Greyson yesterday to apprise him of the situation. More than anything, his pack want a home. He believes the only way to convince his people to an alliance is to reach a land compromise that offers them some legal security."

Nathan shook his head. "That's what this game has been over the entire time."

"Incorrect. The game has been over the right for the pack to *own* land. Sascha Greyson has proposed that land is placed in trust."

"Outrageous," Stanley boomed.

Was it? "That's what the tribe did for themselves."

"Because it's our land."

"We don't own the land, Stanley. We're merely its guardians. Or have you forgotten?"

His face changed colour.

"We don't need to agree to a trust, but we will need to brainstorm other proposals if not. *If* we make this decision to protect our steward's futures via an alliance."

Pascal frowned. "I've just never understood why the pack don't leave. There have to be other territories around."

Time to draw back the curtain for them too. "There are a few things everyone in this room should know. I was specifically asked not to reveal these to the tribe, but I'm breaking my promise because this information will change our tribe's general outlook on the pack. Since Luthers came here, their population has halved.

That's because this valley is surrounded by other supernatural races, and the pack can't leave without a fight. The inability to leave means most of them can't find their one mate. Without their mate, Luthers can't have children and their life expectancy is finite."

"What happens if they lose Grids?" Roderick whispered.

"Exactly. They'd need to fight their way out. Many would die. Maybe all of them. The Luthers have never abandoned this valley because they can't."

I scented the dawning comprehension in the meeting room. They were as surprised by the news as I'd been.

I hoped I'd made the right choice by telling them. It was news the entire tribe should know, but I had to come clean with Sascha before that.

"Is that why you pushed the airport?" Trixie eventually asked.

"The airport benefits stewards, the pack, and the valley. However, I won't deny that the pack's situation weighs heavy on my mind. There are children in the pack, and I won't be responsible for sending them and over seven hundred and fifty pack members to their slaughter. In fact, if that ever becomes the decision of the tribe, I'll no longer be a part of this community."

Nathan glanced up. "Some may feel you're working for both sides."

"I took an oath that I would give my last breath to see this tribe succeed, and I won't forget that oath. My actions on the tribe's behalf prove my loyalty." I held his gaze. "The *pack* took me in when this tribe threw me out. I care for many of them now. That, as well as knowledge of these foreign threats, has changed my definition of what success looks like for all. I believe compromise is the only safe way forward for tribe and pack."

He nodded and—to my surprise—almost smelled accepting.

I held up the thick contract before me. "We have a lot to discuss in coming days. A land proposal. An alliance. A different ending for our stewards. As a starting point, here's the draft contract from King Julius. It needs a lot of work, and I'll need your help to do it. On Monday, I meet with him for further talks. Pascal, Wade, and

Stanley, I'd like you to sit in on that meeting. Sascha Greyson will join us also."

The three of them nodded.

"If any of this goes ahead, it will be a lot for the tribe to take in, Andie."

Roderick's point was valid.

Wade took the Vissimo contract and thumbed through it. "I guess what Ro is asking is *how* do we explain this to the stewards?"

Good question. Not everyone in this room was on board with me. The next couple of days would show whether they came around or not. One thing was certain—I couldn't unload everything on the stewards at once. Yet time was a massive issue. "Both sides love this land and want to protect it. Neither side wants to face uncertainty in the future once the game ends. We know each other far better than we know demons or witches. Those are the points to hammer home. As for timing... we need to figure that out."

Pascal took the contract from Wade. "This could take months to finalise."

"I've seen what the pack and tribe can achieve separately. Imagine what we could do together?"

She regarded me with a peculiar expression.

"Yes?" I arched a brow.

"Just thinking that I was right. You are the leader that we needed."

"I'm glad you think so." I straightened. "I need your honest opinions and reactions over the next few days. *All* of them—every negative thing you can think of. If this works, it's because we did our part to troubleshoot, so don't hold back."

"We surely have some time to think this over?" Stanley said uneasily.

"On Sunday, I plan to turn over a grid with penalty points. Next Wednesday, I plan to win Victratum. We have six days to figure out a truce between pack and tribe, an alliance with the Bluff City vampires, and the tribe must be brought up to speed in that time also."

Trixie's heart thundered. "We've won Clay three times in one hundred and fifty years. We've *never* turned over Water."

My life since accidentally discovering werewolves had revealed one clue after another. Since living on pack lands, I'd started piecing them together.

The plan wasn't perfect, but if there was ever a chance to win one of the two remaining grids, this was it.

"You know," I said conversationally, "the Victratum contract specifically states that mercenaries can't be hired to fight for either side. It says nothing about freely offered supernatural aid that doesn't involve them engaging in fighting at all." I grinned. "Interesting, don't you think?"

27

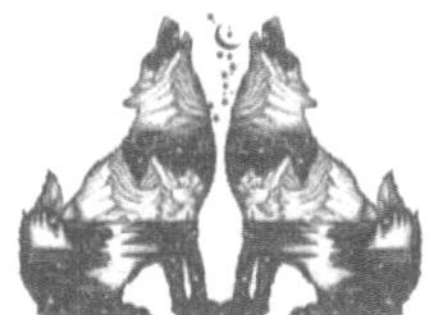

Who needed sleep anyway?

Not me.

I rubbed my temples. "Alright, tribe gathering on Sunday morning and Tuesday night." It was the best we could do with so little time.

"I can't believe this is really happening," Trixie said.

Yep.

This morning, the majority of the head team voted that the possible threat from demons and witches warranted a change in our approach to the end result of Grids. It was a small but significant win.

Wade patted Trixie's back. "Makes you realise how shocked our ancestors must have been all those years ago when they discovered werewolves for the first time."

And they'd lived with Luthers for decades before discovering the truth.

I gathered my papers. "We have a plan to roll out information to the stewards. Let's meet again tonight to discuss a land proposal."

Wade raised his hand. "I have final Deception Valley Ball stuff to do after our pamper day. Can I be exempt?"

The pamper day and ball were the last things on my mind. "Of course. Is everyone else available?" I counted the nods. "Great. I know we'd arranged to have this day off, so thank you. Let's meet at 6:00 p.m. after dinner."

After the meeting, Wade walked down the hall with me. "You're still good for ten?"

"Sure. I need to put some things in order for the day first. Meet you outside in... forty-five?"

"Done. This is just what you need. Trust me."

I forced a smile. "I look forward to it."

Hurrying to my office, I started pouring over our plans anew.

Am I missing anything, girl?

Booker usually slept after our extra early morning run. I received a grunt in reply.

"Have you got a minute?"

Rhona stood in the open doorway.

"... I have a few minutes."

She entered as if unsure whether the bookshelves would topple down on her head. "You're going out with Wade and Cam for the day, I heard."

Was she planning a coup? "I am. How can I help you?"

Rhona lingered by the chair opposite my desk until I gestured for her to sit. There was a whole heap of shit between us, but I hated seeing her so uncertain.

She scratched her cheek and jerked a thumb at my saxophone. "Do you get much of a chance to play? I've only heard you the once."

"Out at Foley's cabin?"

"I've moved out. I'm in the cabin you had for a bit, actually, but I was at the river at the time. Heard you underwater and all."

Right. "I don't play often, no."

Rhona opened her mouth and closed it. She opened it again. "I wanted to congratulate you on the Sandstone turnover. You understand head stewardship in a way I didn't and never will."

To be fair, she only had a few weeks in the seat.

"I'm not sure *never* is the right word." I leaned back. "That wasn't the best time for you to try the ropes."

"Dad was right to change his will," she whispered. "I let his choice get under my skin. I convinced myself the tribe needed me, but really, I became so obsessed with proving he made the wrong decision. My actions were selfish, and in the end, all I did was prove he made the *right* choice. It took nearly losing Grids to make me see the truth, then when I realised what I'd done, I ran instead of owning up to my mistakes."

Whoa.

Fucking *whoa.*

I never, *ever* expected to hear those words.

What should I say? "You returned to take responsibility in the end. That means something. And you found the strength to tell me all this today. That means something too."

Rhona looked at her clasped hands.

My turn. "I played a large part in making you feel alone and helpless, and I'm so sorry for that. I lied to you for selfish reasons, and because I couldn't find the courage to face you. We both ran away, Rhona. Just in different ways."

"I did horrible things to you." Her voice broke.

"You were pushing me away. I knew that. I'd done it myself in the past." If there was one thing a relationship with Logan taught me, it was that.

"How can you ever forgive me?"

This was the moment I'd hoped for and never expected to get. Rhona could do the same horrible things to me in the future. Except when it came to my sister, I'd been a fool so many times, it didn't make sense to be smart now. "You're forgiven."

Tears spilled from her emerald eyes. "*Why*?"

"You tell me."

She choked on the words. "Because you love me?"

"Yes. I do. I can't easily *forget* what happened, but with time and effort from both of us, we can rebuild trust."

Rhona wiped her face. "I want to do that. I don't know how."

"For a start, how about you join me in the observation tower next Wednesday? I valued your input during Sandstone."

"I'd like that." She paused. "I saw you screaming when Greyson hit the ground."

I watched her closely. "I thought he was dead."

"You love him."

"I do."

She took a thin breath. "I was remembering what you said a while back about him dying if you were killed. You said his death would break you, right?"

I shuddered at the thought. "It would."

"It sounded like it when you were screaming," she said quietly. "I've been speaking to the tribe psychologist about Dad. Obviously, what he did was fucked up. I'm trying to wrap my head around it all, and it sometimes makes me think about what Ragna did to you."

"I'm not sure how to process that," I admitted. "It's this massive roadblock in my head. Kind of scared to crack it open."

"I heard Murphy was a werewolf. Do you think Ragna was mated to him?"

"She was."

"Then that explains how shitty she was growing up, right?"

I lifted a shoulder. "I'm not sure it excuses it. The gambling, perhaps. But she never had the guts to tell me I wasn't her daughter."

Rhona grimaced. "Your scream when Greyson hit the ground just made me think; what if Ragna was screaming like that inside after Murphy's death? What if she was screaming until her last breath? Dad had no excuse for what he did other than hatred, and I wish so badly there was something to justify his lies. But you know your mum wasn't in her right mind. I don't know if that makes a difference to you, but it would for me."

People wanted to know why I was so forgiving of Rhona.

This was why.

No one could speak to me the way she could.

"It wasn't the gambling or finding out she had a secret family in Deception Valley." My voice wavered. "It was finding out I wasn't hers. I could take everything else but that."

"Being a mother isn't about sharing blood, it's about the bond they share with a child. She was your mum."

I stilled. "You think so?"

"You never cared about Dad's part in the lie—or my mum's. You only cared about Ragna's because you loved—and *still* love—her so much. Let me ask you something. Your mother fought through years of cancer when death would have finally freed her from grieving Murphy. Why did she do that?"

My eyes blurred. I swallowed several times before my voice worked. "She loved me?"

"More than the escape of death, Andie. Judging from that scream I heard, managing what she did was no small feat."

It really wasn't. I'd tasted that consuming horror for a few seconds.

"If you have any profound revelations about Herc, you're welcome to share them."

I wiped my eyes, laughing slightly. "Not yet, but I'll keep that in mind."

She stood. "I just wanted to let you know that I came back to fix what I did and make amends. I thought I'd struggle most with you being a Luther, but you're not all that different."

"You were raised to hate werewolves. It takes a lot to undo that way of thinking. Recognising there's a problem must be the first step."

"Yeah." Rhona sighed. "You should know from the get-go that I probably won't forgive Sascha Greyson for what he did. Every time I look at him, Dad's death comes rushing back."

If someone killed Ragna, I wasn't sure I could forgive them either. "Whatever you decide with Sascha is between you and him. As long as you can respect my feelings are different to yours, then our relationship can be a separate thing."

Wade burst into the office. “Bitchhole, you better—” He stopped short, looking between us. “Aw, shit.”

I grabbed my jacket and bag. “Are we late?”

“Uh, we will be if we don’t leave now.”

Rhona walked around Wade to the door. “Have a good time.”

I’d have a far better time now.

Things felt right again.

Not completely, but more than before.

I rushed past my saxophone but wrenched to a halt as Rhona’s first words echoed in my mind.

Oh my god.

“Rhona?” I called.

She glanced back. “Yeah?”

“Are you free around four this afternoon? I want to test something out and could use your help.”

28

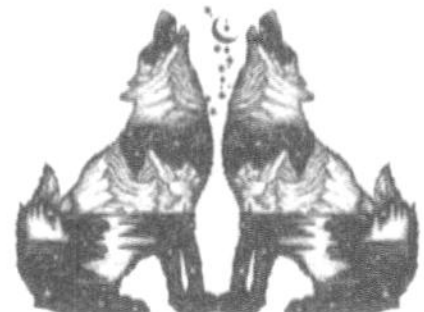

I frowned.

"*Please* stop thinking about head steward stuff for five seconds." Wade hissed. "You know what, make that all night. You don't have any meetings until tomorrow. Switch. It. Off."

This was his big night. "Sorry. I will. You're right. I'm really excited to see what you've pulled together."

Wade had kept the ball preparations hush-hush. Aside from the colour of my dress and his matching outfit, I knew nothing.

I should be worried.

He kissed my cheek, and Cam, curling my hair, shooed him away.

"I've got to run final checks." Wade smoothed the front of his shiny gold suit. "I'll meet you two there. Text me when you're outside, so I can make a proper entrance."

I tucked away my grin. "We will. This is going to be great, Wade, seriously. I know how much effort you've put in."

He flashed me a nervous smile before sweeping out the door.

I met Cam's gaze in the mirror. "I feel the population of Deception Valley is about to be enlightened."

She clipped a pin in place. "I'd say so."

Studying my appearance in the mirror, she then pinned a wispy piece of hair away. "There." She took a photo of the back and showed me the picture. "Tell me how good I am."

"How the hell did you do that?" The thick, loose braids circled my head like a tiara. I couldn't see where one braid began and the other ended. The rest of my hair flowed down my back in soft waves.

"Skill," she replied. "Are you good to do your make-up?"

"Sure. Can I help you in any way?"

She licked her lips. "You can get one of the drinks from my bag. And one for you."

I vacated the mirror spot and riffled through her bag. "I'll join you, but alcohol really doesn't work on me anymore."

"I'll live for us both."

Stealing a corner of the mirror, I brushed on foundation as Cam started on her hair. I never put much thought into my make-up, but this felt like a big occasion, so I paid careful attention. Wade would absolutely kick me out of the ball if I made him look bad.

Contemplating the assortment of eye shadows, I decided on a light brown for my crease and blended a dusty pink over most of my lid. I dabbed a shimmering gold at the inside corner.

I'd already put on liquid eye-liner—because women who could do that after their eye shadow were elite. I swept on mascara and stood back.

Thank you, YouTube tutorials.

"That's perfect," Cam murmured, already applying her lipstick. "Sascha will get a massive boner."

"That's what I'm going for."

"Actually though. Are you?"

"I'd be offended if he didn't get a semi."

She chuckled and proceeded to put on false lashes like a pro. "Have you guys sealed the deal?"

"Many deals. Sex? No."

Cameron's jaw dropped. "I thought for sure you'd tapped that months ago."

I walked to the wardrobe and freed my dress from the hanger. "Tell me about it. Sex is the last mating meet though. It means a lot to Sascha. And me too."

Cam checked her appearance and left the mirror to help me slip into the pale gold dress.

"Does the thought make you nervous?" she asked.

Hmm. "I've always enjoyed sex, but this feels a lot more like we'll make love. I don't know what to expect."

I was nervous.

And felt silly for feeling that way too.

She drew up my zipper, and I arranged my boobs for optimal cleavage. The dress had a low square neckline with straps the thickness of my thumb. That's where the simplicity ended. At the waist, the dress flared out in thick, dramatic pleats that would keep everyone half a metre from me on all sides unless they dared to crumple Cam's creation.

"It fits like a glove," I ran my hands over the pale, sparkling gold. "Thank you."

"You look so beautiful."

I glanced over my shoulder. "And that makes you want to cry?"

She sniffed. "I've seen what you've fought through, Andie. For us. Others may not say it, but *thank you* so fucking much. Wade's right. Tonight, forget about everything and just have a good time."

I squeezed her hand. "I'll do that, Cam. I promise."

Tonight, I'd just be Andie.

Cam's strappy, plum-coloured dress was harder for us to get in place. When we'd managed that, time was short.

Shoving into our heels, we booked it to Ella F.

"This is not the ideal car for ball dresses," Cam muttered as she helped to shove my dress inside the vehicle.

Laughing, we set off.

I could feel my excitement building now I'd promised to let loose.

Sascha would be there. What would he think when he saw me?

I stole a few peeks into the rear-view mirror to check my appearance.

"Hey," Cam said when we reached the outskirts of town. "I wanted to say about the sex thing. You shouldn't worry, but if you have any questions about sex with Luthers, let me know."

I had no idea when the last meet would happen, but I wouldn't mind a few pointers. "I'll take you up on that."

A steward playing valet for the night waved us forward. I directed Ella F to a parking spot right by the front doors of the hall.

Cam dug out her phone and texted Wade.

Sascha was inside. I could feel him.

Jesus. My palms were sweating. I looked in the mirror again.

"How will we get out?" I asked Cam.

Wade found us snorting and chuckling a minute later.

"Finally," he snapped. "You're seven minutes late."

We shut up.

Wade shucked me from the car like an oyster from its shell.

"How are things in there?" I asked.

"Perfect," he snapped again.

Yikes.

"Let me see you." I grabbed his arms and looked over his face. Smoothing a strand of his blond hair back, I straightened an imaginary crease from his suit jacket. "This is your night. You're going to enjoy it. Take a deep breath with me."

He did so, then rolled his shoulders a few times. "Sorry. I'm better now."

"Of course you are. You're taking the hottest gal in town to the ball."

"You have two less testicles than what's ideal for my current preference."

"Can't help you with that, I'm afraid."

"Sascha could."

"Hands off." I was already struggling to get a certain strawberry blond off my jealous mind. There were a few female Luthers it could be. Was the woman inside and standing too close to Sascha?

My gums ached at the thought.

"My lady." Wade held out his hand to me, shooting a look at Cam. "You have to walk in by yourself. You don't match us."

Her lips twitched. "Fucker."

When she'd entered the noisy hall, Wade exhaled.

This ball meant more to my friend than just an important Deception Valley tradition. Some people in that room had likely made his life hell at some point. "This is why you cultivated a strong friendship with the head steward, remember? Show everyone you don't give a fuck what they think."

He held my hand tight. "I used you to get here, and now I'm going to enjoy it."

"That's right... baby boy."

"Baby girl, you did not just make my night by calling me baby boy."

Cringing slightly at the thought of listening wolves, I managed to keep a straight face. "Baby girl did."

"Baby boy is happy."

"Good, because that was a one-off."

"Fair enough."

Holding hands, we walked to the entrance.

The pulsing music cut off, and I blanched. *What the fuckery?*

Pascal lingered inside the doors, and at the sight of us, she lifted a mic to her lips. "Announcing Mayor Andie Charise Thana, beloved Chieftess of the Ni Tiaki tribe..."

I could leave the mayor part of that behind, but the chieftess title was badass.

"... with her esteemed date, Wade Nathaniel Begathry."

My esteemed date had clammy-ass hands.

Or was that me?

I let Wade take the first step.

"I forgot to say," he said as we moved into the hall. "You look alright."

My sarcastic response died as I saw the hall interior.

Gold and white covered every surface in the old building.

Twinkling lights filled huge balloons. The room felt like an enchanted fairy kingdom.

"*Wade*," I hushed. "It's gorgeous."

We walked down the long, sparkling rug. Crowds lined it either side.

Sascha was behind them to the right and, annoyingly, out of sight.

"We need to sit on our thrones," Wade whispered.

I peered ahead and moaned. Two thrones. *For fuck's sake*. Leroy and Hairy would have a field day with this. "You're unbelievable."

He ignored me, waving to the crowd like they were avid fans.

We climbed the three stairs, and I sat on the largest throne, cheeks burning. Wade took the—only slightly—smaller throne beside me.

The population of Deception Valley stared up at us, and I stared back.

My friend sighed happily. "Look at our minions, baby girl. Breathe it all in."

"You have an unhealthy relationship with power."

Pascal passed the mic to Wade.

He rose. "Welcome to the Annual Deception Valley Ball. Tonight, I ask that you kick back, relax, dance, drink, and get to know your neighbours. It's going to be a great night! But first, I'd like to speak more about the vision beside me."

I nearly burst out laughing. He was such a lying bastard.

"As you know, the Ni Tiaki were greatly saddened by the recent passing of Hercules Thana. His eldest daughter took on the huge role Mr Thana filled for decades, and ladies and gentlemen, she has done an exceptional job. I, for one, am so very proud of her."

The crowd applauded, and Wade reached out a hand to me.

I took it, smiling at him.

"This woman is the future of our valley," he continued. "In her short time at the head of our table, Andie Thana has proven she has what it takes. Now, a few words from the woman herself."

Ugh.

Grey eyes twinkling, he shoved the mic into my hands.

If I stood in this dress, I'd fall down the stairs. *Sitting it is.* "Thank you for gathering for this momentous occasion. In a town like ours, good relationships between neighbours is paramount. We rely on each other far more than those in the big wide. The Deception Valley Ball is a historic reminder of the seriousness of fostering and strengthening bonds with one another. I hope everyone leaves this ball having met someone they didn't know yesterday. I look forward to meeting more of you tonight and in the future."

The crowd politely applauded. I gestured to Wade. "Lastly, tonight wouldn't have been possible without the man beside me. Please put your hands together for Wade Begathry, a person who has quickly become someone I can't do without, and a person who is as kind as he is intelligent. Wade, you've done such a spectacular job. Thank you on behalf of our town."

The crowd roared with approval.

Wade loved every second of it.

I handed the mic back to Pascal and scanned the room for the one person I wanted to see.

"Mayor Thana," Terrie greeted from the bottom of the stairs.

With less of the audience's attention on me, I risked standing and gladly left the throne behind. "Terrie, how are you?"

Conversation with her led to conversations with the other council members, Wilson, Gabriel, and Rose. Sascha hadn't moved from across the room, but I seemed to be moving farther away.

Escaping another conversation, I'd managed one step toward Sascha when Walter Nash swooped in to speak with me at length about the airport.

When I excused myself from *him*, I was introduced to the oldest member of our population, and then the youngest.

Finally, I followed the tugging under my ribs.

"Head Steward?"

Seriously?

I smiled at the older woman. "I've seen you around the manor, but I can't recall your name."

She pressed her lips together. "My name is Judy. Up until a month ago, I was the organiser of this ball."

Yikes. She didn't smell happy about it either. "Wade told me you agreed to hand over the task to him. Thank you for that. It means a lot to him."

"He said that you'd decided to revamp the ball and put him in charge."

Wade, you mothershitter. "I see." Subject change time. "What do you think of the result?"

She wrinkled her nose, but I inhaled her begrudging respect and a slight embarrassment.

"I'm very grateful for the years of work you put into this event," I said. "From all reports, you've pulled off the ball for a long time. I did intend Wade to work alongside you, so please let me know if you'd like to rejoin the team for future events. It would be a great shame to lose someone with your experience."

Judy forced a smile—though slightly less offended than before. "I'll let you know."

"Great. Is there anything—"

Rhona touched my arm. "Hey, got a minute?"

I grimaced at Judy. "Please excuse me."

When we were a few metres away, I grabbed her arm. "Thank you."

"Looked like you needed saving. Celeb life, huh?"

"Want to switch like old times?" I joked.

I stilled, wondering if she'd take that the wrong way, but Rhona arched a brow. "I've spent years cultivating this scowl to keep them at bay. Not a chance."

"Worth a shot. How awesome did Wade do with the hall?"

I hadn't seen my friend again since our speeches, but he'd be preening for his admirers all night.

"Yeah, he's in his element tonight." Rhona jerked her head. "Cam looks like she's in hers too."

On my conversational journey, I'd noted the stewards hadn't left the one side of the hall, and the pack hadn't left the other. Cam was over on the Luther side dancing with her wolf lady.

Oh, shit. She totally let the cat out of the bag. "That's her girlfriend, Emily."

"She's dating a Luther?" Rhona blurted.

"A pack member, yes. For a while now. They're very happy together."

I inhaled her conflicted scent.

I'd expected solid revulsion.

"I see." Rhona took a breath. "Look, I came to tell you that I'm going to head back home. Dad and I always came to these things together. It's a bit much."

I nodded. "Of course. I can understand that."

Rhona wrapped her arms around me.

Frozen, I didn't immediately respond. She'd *never* hugged me first—not even when we got on well. I lifted my arms and hugged her back.

Her cheek rested against mine. "I'm glad to be back."

We untangled from each other, and she released a pent-up breath.

"See you later," she said.

Rhona just hugged me for comfort. *I'm not imagining that, right?* I asked Booker.

The sister can get fucked.

Right. *I'm going to find Sascha before I'm waylaid again.*

This entire night is ridiculous.

Booker was having a blast.

Waving at Grim and Lisa, I weaved between the Luthers and spoke briefly to Evelyn, Jemma, and Kara.

The elastic band under my ribs tightened, and I glanced into the far back corner.

My eyes met his. The world funnelled.

He'd left the suit jacket behind. Shirt sleeves rolled up, top buttons open, and black shoes gleaming. I took in the man leaning against the wall in the shadows, and the confines of my chest were too tight to contain everything I felt.

Sascha.

Greyson.

Mine.

He made no move to come to me, and I hovered. Did he want me to approach or keep my distance? We'd never been in public together.

Blood poured into my face as the moment extended.

Sascha was apparently stuck to the floor. Maybe he didn't want to give the wrong impression or something?

Turning, I halted when he jerked.

Beautiful wolf, come here, he blurted in my mind.

Peering back, I arched a brow. *Why don't you come here?*

Uh...

I strode toward him. *Are you still hurt?*

Not quite.

"What is it? What happened?" I asked when I stood before him.

Leaning on the wall beside him, Leroy snorted.

Was something funny?

I folded my arms. "You look nice."

"You look nice," Sascha repeated.

Leroy snickered, and I glanced between them as a faint red tinged Sascha's face. Were they laughing at me?

I brushed my wavy hair back, and Sascha choked on a breath.

Okay. "I'm not sure what's going on. I'll leave you guys to it."

Was it the presence of the stewards? He wasn't like this when I visited pack lands to check on him.

That was not how I hoped he'd react when he saw me.

Lowering my gaze, I hurried back through the Luthers toward the stewards' side.

"You look wonderful, Andie." Roderick approached with his wife.

I forced my shoulders to relax. "Thanks. Wade and Cam had everything to do with it."

"They have great taste."

I absently chatted with Roderick and his wife, unable to tear my internal focus from Sascha. When he started moving across the hall toward me, my heartbeat tripled.

"Andie?" Roderick said.

I shook my head. "Sorry, could you repeat that?"

He opened his mouth but closed it as a warm body stopped directly behind me.

"Andie?" Sascha said.

I glanced over my shoulder. "Yeah?"

The werewolf cleared his throat. "I wondered if you'd like to dance. With me."

Roderick's surprise gave way to amusement. His wife darted a look between me and Sascha.

"Oh. Sure."

Taking his offered hand, I let Sascha lead me onto the dance floor where couples were swaying for a slower number. Thank fuck, because I was not a dancer.

Swaying, I could do.

Grossly aware of the scrutiny on us, I didn't relax into him as my body screamed at me to do. Sascha held my hand in a loose grip and slid his free arm around my waist.

"You look better than nice," he said seriously.

... Thanks?

"Have other women ever remarked that you have a way with words?"

He winced. "What I mean is that you look beautiful."

I peered at him. "Wait, are you nervous?"

Sascha flushed.

Flushed.

My jaw dropped. "You are!"

He sighed as soft chuckles rose from the Luther corner. "I couldn't think what to say to you when you came in. Well, I'd planned what to say, but then you came over, and I forgot the words."

Bemusement radiated from him.

I tried to contain my grin, but it escaped.

That put a different spin on earlier. "I was too nervous to notice you were nervous if that helps."

"I'll be one hundred in a few years, and you're in your twenties, so not really."

I laughed as he spun me.

"What were you going to tell me?" I asked.

Now who's vain? Booker said smugly.

He cleared his throat. "That you're the most beautiful thing I've ever seen. Woman, that is. Not thing."

My shoulders shook. "Relax, Sascha. I don't bite. And thank you. You look very handsome tonight." *Every night. All the time.*

Sascha brought his mouth to my ear. "Would you look at that?"

Turning my head to follow his line of vision, my attention snagged on Stanley and the *pack member* he was leading to the dancefloor. The other couples were human and human or Luther and Luther.

"Shit," I whispered.

Every member of the head team was doing the same. Some of their spouses too.

No way.

Cam was already with her girlfriend. Wade, watching proceedings, hurried to Jemma and bowed with a flourish.

"You didn't plan that?" Sascha held me tighter.

"That's all on them."

My eyes widened further as Hairy, Leroy, and Lisa crossed the room to the steward side. I held my breath as they approached Detta, the head cook, Jessi, the tree-hugger, and Marty, the gardener.

The tribes' shock swept outward, clashing against the Luthers' shock in the middle of the hall.

Shock wasn't the only emotion.

Disgust.

Fear.

Suspicion.

But all three of the stewards said yes to dancing with a member of Sascha's most trusted wolves.

"You didn't plan that either?" I whispered.

Nope, his voice rang in my mind.

What does it mean?

His brows lifted. *Change? For better or worse.*

Yeah, the scent in the hall was uncomfortable and conflicted to say the least. *You told your team about the alliance then?*

Sascha nodded. *I wanted to test their reaction first.*

I'd done the same with my head team. *How did it go?*

Mixed, to say the least.

I blew out a breath. "Right." *Same with my head team, but over the last two days, they've come around to the idea and voted to support alliance negotiations and the possibility of a land proposal.*

His focus snapped to me anew. *Really? A land proposal?*

I'm convincing. I winked. *In all honesty, they spent five hours last night trying to think up every possible way to give the pack security without a land trust, but so far, they're yet to find it.*

Because there is none, he said grimly. *Believe me.*

I did.

I jerked my head at Hairy and Detta as they twirled by. *Seems like you got through to them.*

I'm more surprised than anyone.

Why should you be? Our pack respects you, Sascha. They know when hierarchy is needed and when it's not. Look at them now.

We studied the Luthers.

Alpha stood by delta. Beta by gamma. Omega with alpha. Every possible combination. After experiencing how strongly Booker and Greyson clung to their sigma status—and how confronting it was for them to alter their views—I only had the utmost respect for the enormity of Sascha's daily task.

He didn't just play Grids each day. He managed a delta's need to prove themselves.

The headstrong will of an alpha.

The disinterest of a gamma and timidness of an omega.

Betas were the most stable presence, perhaps, but that made them extra indecisive—a quality wolves possessed in droves as it was.

Then there was Greyson to manage too.

Sascha pulled me closer again, and I let him.

He lowered his head. "You know—"

Alarm sirens wailed overhead, and I clapped my hands over my ears, crying out at the pain ripping through my head.

Danger, Booker snarled.

She was moving us before I'd processed that she'd taken over. She placed our back to the nearest wall. The sound cut off, and—chest heaving—I searched for the source of the sound.

It was an alarm, I explained to her, quickly double checking my fangs and claws were away.

Too loud, she growled.

I know, but everything is okay.

She'd only taken over like that once—when we'd taken an unexpected trip over the waterfalls.

My mind cleared of her fear, and I pushed off the wall.

Where's Sascha?

I found him across the hall in a similar position to mine.

What the hell just happened?

More importantly, did anyone just shift?

Locating the other Luthers, I stared at their groupings.

And blinked.

Deltas stood with deltas. Alphas with alphas. Omegas with Omegas. Every status had abandoned their prior place to stand with their own status.

Being sigmas, Sascha and I had done the opposite.

Oh my god.

I caught a few flashes of fang amidst the groups, but it seemed the older Luthers had naturally assumed an outside position, shielding the younger werewolves in the middle, out of sight.

Wade stormed into the kitchen and reprimanded two teens

who'd snuck a cigarette and decided to smoke it inside. Sascha and I walked to each other.

"Do you think anyone noticed us?" I asked under my breath.

He frowned. "No. The humans panicked too. I can't smell anything amiss. As long as no one's phones were out, we should be good."

In this day and age, that was a big *if*. Then again, ball attire wasn't really friendly for the size of modern cell phones either.

The music resumed and so did our swaying dance.

My heartbeat eventually settled.

I wanted to ask, Sascha thought at me. H*ave you given any thought to the sex meet?*

Was he just casually bringing that up?

My heart decided to pound again. *Not really. I was waiting for you to bring it up. You're the responsible one.*

Responsible. He was amused. *Nothing about what I want to do to you is responsible.*

His arousal surged, and mine followed like a moth to a flame.

His gaze burned into mine. *What do you think about tonight?*

I tilted my chin. *Why tonight?*

Because things are changing. Fast. I can feel the itch. I don't know what time we have left, and I don't want to lose this moment with you.

He wanted to have sex because of the game.

Sascha searched my gaze. *That disappoints you.*

I don't want to have sex because we're afraid of tomorrow.

He lifted a hand to my cheek. *Aren't you afraid of tomorrow, little bird?*

He meant that figuratively, but his words were accurate to an unsettling degree. Tomorrow, everything would change.

I dropped my attention to his chest.

Sascha stopped moving. *What is it?*

I couldn't tell him about our plan with the penalty points, but I'd wanted to find the right time to come clean about breaking my promise. So far, I'd told vampire royals and my head team.

They were specks on telling the tribe tomorrow morning.

There's something you should know, I started.

His scent took on a guarded edge.

I broke a promise to you. And tomorrow, I plan to break that promise to the full extent. I inhaled his confusion. *There are secrets the pack keeps that I believe should be general knowledge. It may help others understand your struggles.*

Understanding dawned. *You've told the tribe that we're trapped here. That we're dying off.*

Not the whole tribe yet, I rushed to say. *You underestimate the open-mindedness of my stewards. It might—*

"It might?" he said aloud. Silent again, he added, "*Telling them we're entirely at their mercy might do what exactly?*

Help them understand, Sascha. That's where this truce has to start.

Who knows? he demanded. *Wade? You have no idea what you've done, Andie.*

The head team. And... the Vissimo royals.

Sascha staggered back a step. *You told a vampire clan numbering over fifteen thousand that we, a tiny population of wolves, are backed into a damn corner?*

No one liked to feel trapped. Wolves least of all.

I didn't present it as a weakness. I made sure to—

You broke your solemn word to me. His jaw clenched. *I've asked very little of you, Andie, but I made it clear that when you gave a promise, I expected you to keep it. You betrayed the one thing I asked you not to.*

Sascha walked around me.

I hurried in his wake.

The stewards need to understand why the pack never left, I shot at him.

His strides weren't hindered by a mountain of material, and he'd reached the parking lot by the time I exited the hall.

Sascha. Please come back.

The werewolf turned under the light of the moon.

You knew my limit, Andie, he said grimly. *That was harming my pack.*

No, I thought at him emphatically. *That's not why I did this at all. It was the opposite.* Halfway down the stairs, I ignored the attention on our silent exchange.

I'll be sure to tell them that. I'm sure it will fix everything.

I clutched my cheeks. *Where are you going?*

Sascha started the engine. *Away, Andie. Away.*

29

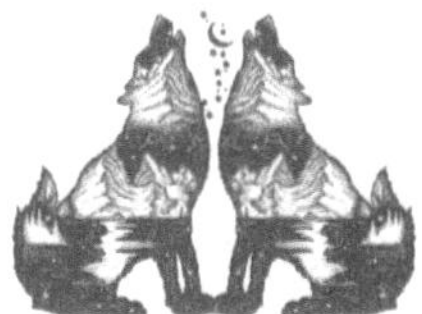

"Nervous?" Wade rasped.

He looked like roadkill. Someone overindulged last night.

"Not really." After the bitter ending of the ball, I just felt cold and empty. I'd underestimated how much Sascha's consistent support *filled* me. Even in his absence, a layer of comfort usually surrounded me.

Not anymore.

The thought of losing Sascha made me feel sick. I'd *never* seen him so furious—not at me anyway. And I was about to divulge the truth to a whole lot more people.

Would he ever forgive me? Maybe I should have informed Sascha *before* I spilled the beans to the vampires and head team. Or maybe agonising over this was foolish when he'd probably have reacted the same way.

If I wasn't so certain this was the way forward, I'd abandon the plan.

"No nerves?" Wade pressed. "Nothing at all?"

I didn't fear the tribe. I believed in them.

There's a reason males and females in a pack are separate entities,

Booker said. *Different people look at the same problem with different eyes. You've chosen correctly.*

What would I do without her? I really didn't know at this point. *I love you.*

You're the most tolerable human I know.

My mood lightened a smidgen. "Thanks."

"No problem. I think everyone had a great night," Wade replied.

I'd spoken aloud but rolled with it. "You did the best job. I *did* happen to speak with Judy."

Wade cleared his throat. "Oh, yeah? What'd she say?"

"You dropped me in it!"

"Okay, but I really wanted to organise the ball."

I scowled at him.

"Sorry. That wasn't cool." He pressed a quick kiss on my cheek.

I softened. "You should be sorrier for making me sit on a throne."

"That will never happen."

Knock, knock.

Pascal popped her head in. "It's time, Andie."

"Everything is set up?"

"Everything."

I truly trusted this woman. "Thanks, Pascal. You've done so much."

"A speck on your efforts, Head Steward."

The smell of her grief had strengthened in the last few days. With all this talk of truce and change, I wouldn't blame her for thinking back to her mating call with Daniil and what could have been.

Leaving the manor, I walked through the midst of our stewards. They babbled and chatted happily, unaware of what would be unleashed upon them.

If I was successful today, my stewards would lay in bed tonight and tense at the sound of every creak and groan of their cabins.

I climbed the stairs and stood before the mic. "Stewards. We gather on our tribal lands as we and our ancestors have done for centuries—as devoted guardians of this land and all those within it. Before I start, does anyone dispute our ongoing duty to this valley?"

Everyone here—even my biggest critics—felt a connection to this place deep in their soul.

"Tonight, my words will shock you. They will make you fear for your life and future and those of your loved ones... those of the people surrounding you. The secrets I share are revealed with one purpose in mind. To keep this tribe alive for generations to come."

They weren't smiling anymore.

Yeah, this wasn't a normal gathering.

"Upon becoming a Luther, the pack leader divulged the following information to me for my own safety. I was sworn to silence. But against his wishes, I have decided to break that promise because without breaking it, I see only bloodshed and pain."

I let them absorb my words, noting Nathan behind the camera recording my every word. There was too much information to unload in one sitting. Stewards would have access to the recording to watch however many times they wished.

They stared up at me, anxious, wary, suspicious, and already fearful. I seized the determination building in my chest.

I was doing this for a reason.

For them.

For the pack.

For Sascha and myself.

"At some point, every steward has asked themselves the same question. *Why don't the pack just leave?* The tribe was here first. The werewolves could go anywhere. I used to ask myself the same question too. Before I explain, there are three things you need to know. A Luther has one mate in their lifetime. Without that mate, they can't have children. And without their mate, they are mortal."

The screens Nathan used to run through tribe strategy flickered on around the lawn and stage.

I freed the mic and stood to one side just like in the business presentations I'd had to record for my degree. "Keep those three things in mind, please."

I nodded at Trixie who was in charge of the slides.

On the screens, a map of the valley and surrounding areas appeared. The land north and east of the valley lit up red.

"Does anyone know what this region is?" The boundaries didn't obey any human map.

No one called out an answer.

"That," I told them, "as I recently discovered, is the approximate territory of the largest demon kingdom in the world. They occupy our entire northern border and the east also. Does anyone here know anything about demons?"

No one budged.

Fear had taken the forefront though confusion had ramped up too.

The slide changed to add a blue section to our south. "*This* is the territory of a witch coven that covers us to the south."

A third section lit up green.

"Most stewards know about the vampires in Bluff City," I said. "Their clan totals more than fifteen thousand."

I returned to the microphone stand. "As you see, this valley is surrounded on every side by other supernatural races. Why is that pertinent? Since the Luthers arrived here, their numbers have halved. Perhaps you believed some had left the valley. Perhaps you asked yourself why the others didn't do the same." I gestured at the map behind me. "They're trapped. It's impossible for the pack to leave without risking what few numbers they still have fighting their way out. To give you an idea of that risk, ten thousand Luthers arrived on the shores of Bluff City long ago, but after a battle with vampires and then with demons, only fifteen *hundred* made it to Deception Valley. Because the pack are trapped, most of them will never find their mates. Remember, they cannot have children without their one mate. And they are mortal without their mate too. To put it plainly, the pack isn't leaving. They're dying."

I gave them a moment to absorb that.

Shock. Fear. Confusion.

I paced the length of the stage. "Why is this of concern to *us* though? Well, while the Luthers have occupied this valley, other supernaturals haven't claimed this area for their own. We haven't had to contend with demons, witches, or vampires. But here's my question to you, stewards. What happens if we win Victratum and the Luthers leave? Who and what will come next? Fifteen thousand vampires? Thousands of demons, and likely *tens* of thousands of them? Witches? When will they strike?" I took a breath. "Will we win the game after hundreds of years, just to face battle after battle for this land in the future?"

Fear.

Good.

I let the silence swell. "Between this moment and Tuesday night, I want you to think about that one question... What happens if the Luthers leave?"

The screen behind me shut off and murmurs broke out.

I softened my voice. "We're in the unique position of knowing what may lay ahead. Don't let that lure you into a false sense of security. On Tuesday night, we will decide on a solution that will determine whether this tribe has a future."

I let them chat, listening in on their comments.

This can't be true.

Why didn't the wolves tell us?

I don't believe it.

She's a Luther now. She just wants them to stay.

"Now to the second announcement," I called through the mic.

They gradually quietened.

I scanned their midst, noting the number of pale and stricken faces. "We utilised the week off Victratum to prepare for both Clay and Water, though we announced Clay to the pack. Thank you for the extra practice you've put in. I know it will serve us well in the near future. *Tomorrow*, we host five hundred guests on manor lands. These guests will help us in the game next week. They'll likely stay until Thursday morning. I expect every steward here to treat those guests with the utmost respect and hospitality while they're with us."

I wanted my stewards to work with the Vissimo before revealing what they were.

It could make my job on Tuesday night a lot easier.

"Over the next three days, we'll practice as we've never practiced before." My expression hardened. "I've seen what this tribe has done. I've been amazed time and again by how seamlessly last-minute operations are carried out in the grid. This week, this tribe needs to do better than ever before. By Tuesday night, you'll understand why."

I gestured to Rhona a few rows back from the front. "Over the last two days, Rhona and I put together a special recording. This will be distributed by Nathan after the gathering. Please make time to listen to the recording today *on manor lands only*. Preferably with headphones on. This evening, Gerry will call a special training to run through a new manoeuvre. Lastly, Monday through Wednesday, the workday will end at midday to allow ample time to run through our operations."

The stewards didn't know what was happening, but they'd registered something serious was afoot.

I smiled. "Any questions? Nothing too big to announce today, as you've heard."

That earned me a few laughs.

Their nervous reaction trailed off as Rhona waved to me from the bottom of the stairs.

She climbed and crossed to me.

I switched off the mic. "What's wrong?"

Her hands shook. "I'd like to speak to the tribe if that's okay?"

Uh... to say what? I'd just released a series of bombs on them. They couldn't take much more.

"I need you on board today." I wanted to trust her, but this was just too important.

She nodded. "I'm not here to make trouble."

Her scent confirmed that. At least, it confirmed that *Rhona* didn't believe her words would cause trouble.

We'd turned a corner on Friday. "Please be careful not to overload them."

Switching the mic back on, I passed it to her and left the stage.

I wedged between Wade and Pascal to watch.

Rhona had never looked tinier as she stood facing the people that she'd left high and dry.

My sister spoke, "When I came back, Andie told me one condition of my return was to apologise to the tribe for what I did. She thought you deserved an explanation."

Crap. Where was she going with this?

Rhona's throat worked. "I don't deserve an opportunity to stand before you and explain what happened or why I did all those things. But Andie gave it to me anyway despite how I treated her. So I'll take this chance. I'd like to start behaving the way a real steward should."

"Oh my god," Wade hushed. "What did you do to her?"

Me?

This was all Rhona.

This was my sister.

"Here's how it started," she whispered.

30

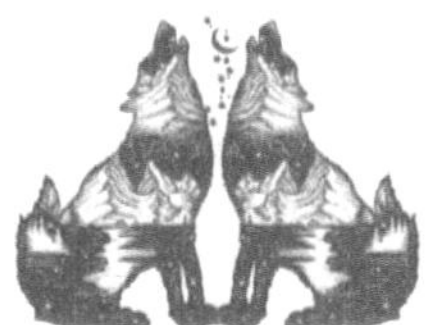

I peered down the table at my head team and the two nominated Sandstone experts. Twenty minutes ago, the pack received our summons. Legally, we had to be transparent on the reason for a negotiation.

Sascha hadn't spoken to me since last night, and now he'd learned that I planned to seize a grid via penalty points.

Something I was doing for him.

Life was fucking twisted.

"We go into this bartering for five penalty points," I said. "The contract clearly states that any lapse in care of land clause will result in loss of a grid. The minimum we'll accept is two penalty points, which will allow us to turn over another grid anyway."

The mood in the room was tense.

"Roderick, please put the call through." I'd requested that this call occur over video. Sascha could have denied the request, but it hadn't been in his best interest to. Previously, Luthers had so many advantages over stewards during negotiations.

Now I possessed the same edge.

Sascha couldn't lie without me picking it up.

I watched the phone symbol on the screen.

Three rings.

Seven rings.

The pack answered on the eighth. Not their worst record by a long shot.

"Greetings to the pack, and thank you for responding to our summons."

"Head Steward," Sascha said coldly. "Greetings to the head team also."

At times, his team had acted the part of disliking me. This time, I had a feeling nothing about their expressions was faked. Leroy's face made Mandy appear almost calm and forgiving.

Sascha had told his wolves what I did.

Strength, Andie, Booker said.

I tilted my chin. "When my stewards turned over Sandstone, they noted an extraordinary number of lapses in the care of land clause during the pack's occupation of the grid. Pascal, please send through the list to Mr Greyson."

The silence as she did so and the wolves perused the thirteen-page document was horrible.

"Some of this was before the turnover," Sascha noted.

"Excuse me?"

"Three pages of these reports are dated prior to the turnover of Sandstone while your stewards worked for us." Dark encroached on his glinting honey eyes.

I allowed some of Booker to shine back at him. Greyson could bite me. Well, he had. But he could do it again. "The care of land clause is always in effect. It's the duty of pack and tribe to ensure this clause is enforced at all times. Do you dispute that?"

"No," he answered. "It's nothing I didn't expect from you."

I tried to absorb the jab without showing any hurt.

"Then let's move on," I continued. "Per the terms of Victratum, a lapse in care of the land results in five penalty points to the opposing team."

Leroy and Hairy were off to one side, conferring with wolves I assumed had the most sandstone knowledge in the pack.

Hairy whispered in Sascha's ear.

"The issues you've raised are minor at best," he said. "The care of land clause requires proof that environmental harm has occurred."

We'd only sent through the minor issues. I'd decided to lure him in and test the ground before revealing my real ace. "I'm disappointed at your apparent disregard and disrespect for this land, Mr Greyson."

I'd once witnessed Herc talking to Sascha like this.

Never did I think I'd be able to negotiate this way.

He opened his mouth, but I interrupted. "Policies and procedures are formed for each grid with the agreement of both pack and tribe. When creating these best practices, *both* sides acknowledge the research studies referenced are the most current and accurate available. The data used to generate our latest sandstone procedures proves the long-term effect of all the reported care of land lapses on that list. The pack did not act in accordance with those policies and therefore, as agreed between both sides, the pack has negatively impacted this land."

There was no way to refute that, other than that pack actions were short term.

Sascha didn't reply, listening to Hairy again.

"I'd like to introduce two of our sandstone experts, Isabelle and Dominic," I said. "They will briefly outline the environmental impact of each item on the list you possess."

"You don't have enough here, Head Steward," Sascha said lazily. "You're grasping at thin air."

I narrowed my gaze but didn't respond.

The two stewards stood and bowed in my direction.

"Head Steward," Isabelle murmured before facing the Luthers. She was nervous, but I had to applaud her composure. "I'd like to direct everyone's attention to transgression one."

Transgression, huh. I may have to borrow that word.

There were over one hundred minor lapses.

I settled back and allowed those who knew far more than me about sandstone take the reins. Sascha's *expert* battled back at intervals, but it became clear our stewards were far more knowledgeable on the subject.

I took the opportunity to survey the pack members and Sascha for any sign of their reaction.

Dominic finished outlining the last lapse. He bowed my way again and sat.

"Thank you both for explaining the seriousness of these impacts on our beloved valley." I looked at Sascha. "The penalty for a lapse in this clause is clear. Five penalty points. However, in acknowledgement of the pack's lack of experience in this grid, we're willing to extend goodwill and accept a penalty of three points instead."

"There's no proof of environmental impact." Sascha returned. "And so there's no case here. However, as we have the utmost respect for this valley, in *goodwill*, we're willing to accept a penalty of one point."

Yes!

I didn't celebrate aloud or otherwise move. "You profess to care for our surroundings, and yet offer so little."

Our teams volleyed arguments back and forward for a time.

I tapped a finger on the table. "Tell me, Mr Greyson. If you'd spent several months in possession of Sandstone and the environment suffered for it, what penalty would you be prepared to pay then?"

"We'll never know, Miss Thana."

Dammit. He didn't fall into my word trap.

"The contract is clear on this matter. Any lapse in best practices results in the loss of five points. But for the listed issues, the Ni Tiaki, very generously, accepts one penalty point from the pack."

Sascha released a breath. A tiny breath that everyone else missed.

He spoke, "I'm glad we could reach a—"

"I'd like to present one more lapse in the care of land clause," I said pleasantly. "Pascal?"

Our marshal sent through our ace.

The pack members read over it. Their so-called expert blanched and cast Leroy a wide-eyed look.

Yep.

I had him. "As you'll see, in comparison to the last issues, this is far bigger. A waterway was compromised. Not only do we have dated photographs, we have videos of all the testing carried out at the waterway. There's proven environmental impact. I'm sure you're as shocked and devastated by this news as we are. Would you like to hear from our experts on this issue?"

Sascha listened briefly to his sandstone Luther. They had to be muting their microphone because I couldn't hear the conversation.

When their conversation wrapped up, Sascha faced me, never grimmer.

"We are indeed shocked and devastated too. As you previously mentioned, our lack of experience is our excuse."

Clever wolf. But he couldn't get out of this unscathed.

He forced the words out. "What penalty does the tribe propose?"

I read the betrayal in his expression.

Sascha may hate me now, but if this worked—*if*—then we were one step closer to our ending. Assuming he still found me worthy after everything I'd done. Fear churned in my stomach at the thought of his rejection.

"This is a clear violation of the care of land clause," I stated in a clear voice. "The rules are clear. We have the right to five penalty points."

I let that sink in.

"But," I stressed, "the tribe is grateful for the opportunity you gave us with employment in Sandstone. We acknowledge that possessing a grid you haven't possessed in a long time is bound to carry a learning curve. We're willing to be generous once again."

"Indeed," Sascha growled.

"In addition to the already agreed-upon penalty of one point, we will accept a further one-point penalty for this specific issue to bring the total to two points."

I knew what he was feeling.

It's what I experienced when Rhona lost Sandstone.

The ground was crumbling under his feet as he contemplated his people without a home—or dying around him. As he considered what might become of us in time with this lingering like poison.

And like Sascha back on pack lands, I wanted to do everything possible to make him feel better.

I wanted us to be happy for more than a few minutes strung together. So I didn't waver.

A leaden beat passed.

"The pack accepts the total penalty of two points," he said quietly.

His words were a kiss on the mouth and a punch in the stomach.

Jubilation filled the room, emanating from my stewards, but I'd never felt closer to tears.

Sascha's jaw clenched. "The Ni Tiaki hold five penalty points. One of our grids is yours. Which will it be?"

No sane Head Steward would choose Clay with our horrendous track record in Water.

"The Ni Tiaki claim Clay." My voice rang through the space.

Lisa blinked three times.

Yeah, I'd decided on the insane path.

For several reasons, one of them being that last Sunday, we announced Clay as the next grid.

The pack would only have three days to prepare for Water. No time to order equipment. Very little time to brainstorm and train. Whereas we'd already had ten days practicing for the grid.

The gloves were off.

Sascha inclined his head. "We'll prepare for the turnover of the grid on Thursday morning as per usual procedure. Congratulations on four grids, Head Steward."

I didn't want his congratulations.

I wanted *him*.

Sascha ended the call.

31

I stood at the manor entrance with my head team as Basilia Le Spyre made her second entrance.

She was in a white car this time and driving.

"Who's the guy?" Wade asked.

Crown Prince Kyros was crammed into the passenger seat and looking faintly harassed. As Basilia ripped down the wheel and fish-tailed into a parking spot, it wasn't hard to guess why.

"Her mate, Prince Kyros." I walked down the steps as a few SUVs drove onto manor lands too.

Our guests had started to arrive. Many more would follow, but they'd stagger their entry into Deception Valley over thirty minutes so werewolves in town didn't notice the stream of traffic.

The SUVs were filled with employees of Basilia's who'd once served Clan Sundulus to pay off debt, or so I understood the matter.

I'd come prepared with orange-scented oil this time. Having already dabbed it under my nose, I offered to the vampire princess as she exited the car.

"I'm sorted." She held up a small bottle.

"How was the journey?"

"It's much more entertaining to drive. So many tight bends. It flew by. Right, Ky?"

Prince Kyros shut the passenger door. "Yes, my beauty."

My lips twitched at his stricken expression. "I'm glad."

I faced the neatly parked black vehicles, certain my guests would hear every word. "Welcome to Ni Tiaki lands. Thank you for agreeing to help us win this game and for coming so far. There's a possibility that a Luther guest will arrive in an hour. Please stay in your vehicles and follow my head team to parking spaces around the back. You will be shown to refreshments and your accommodation. I ask that you stay hidden until negotiations conclude as Luthers have very good ears and very good noses."

Trixie and Nathan would make sure those yet to arrive received the same instructions.

"A possibility he'll come?" Menace filled Kyros's voice. "We came here to negotiate seriously."

I got the feeling this vampire kept his power tucked away. Even now, though, my body wanted to react to his menacing threat. My head team reeked of adrenaline.

"There was a misunderstanding with Mr Greyson," I answered. "The negotiations can still move forward."

"You reek." His green eyes blazed.

I smiled. "Ditto. Want some oil?"

"He refused to weaken his sense of smell." Basilia sighed.

The head team watched on in silence as I led the vampires into the manor. They knew the true nature of our guests, but it was obvious their reaction was greater than mine.

When Basilia and Tommy visited alone, Wade's reaction wasn't this strong.

Actually, he smelled far less stressed than the others. He must cope better for some reason.

After refreshments, we gathered in the conference room.

"Is this house for sale?" Basilia glanced around.

She considered this a house? How big was her damn mansion? "The tribe don't acknowledge ownership of land. This valley is in trust. I couldn't sell it if I tried. If I did try, the tribe would place me in a freezing river and whip me with reeds."

The billionaire hummed. "That's a no?"

I exchanged an amused look with Wade. "It's a no."

"Thought I'd check. Shall we begin then? It doesn't seem Mr Greyson is coming."

The door burst open, and my heart leaped into my throat as Sascha strode into the room.

He froze. His fangs exploded as he whirled to face Kyros and Basilia. A terrible growl ripped from his throat

Yeah, I hadn't told him Vissimo would actually be here. Consider it a little test before Water.

"Sascha, these are representatives of King Julius. May I introduce Crown Prince Kyros Atagio and his mate, Princess Basilia Le Spyre."

Sascha stalked to stand in front of me, extending his claws.

Kyros was having a battle of his own. His green eyes flared. His fangs were visible—sharp but far smaller than ours.

"They *stink*," Sascha snarled.

"Yes," I said reasonably. "Horrible, isn't it? We smell quite bad to them as well."

The hairs at the back of my neck rose at the combined threat of Sascha and Kyros's ripping growls.

This wasn't a great start.

"Would you like some orange-scented essential oil to help?"

"No," Sascha snapped, now edging us both back to the wall.

I caught Basilia's eye under his arm. She grinned from behind Kyros.

The vampire stepped around her mate. "If you'd both prefer to suffer, then at least control yourselves so we can begin."

Following her lead, I escaped Sascha's body cage. "Maybe you'd both like to step out for a few minutes to compose yourselves?"

Pascal, Stanley, and Wade were slammed against the farthest wall. I listened to their thundering pulses, taking the seat opposite Basilia.

Wade was the first to join us at the table. Pascal was next—Stanley close on her tail.

Copies of the second draft contract sat in a neat pile. I took one off the top. "Has King Julius had time to go over our revision of the contract?"

She nodded. "He has and gave his permission to Kyros and me to work on a final contract."

Sascha walked to stand behind me.

"Move," he said to Wade.

Wade quickly made space between us, and Sascha slotted in his chair.

Thank you for coming, I thought at him.

He glared. *It wasn't for you.*

Ouch. *Regardless, thank you.*

It had to kill him to be so protective right now when he wanted to rage at me instead.

Sascha cut off our line of communication. He rested a, now crumpled, copy of the revised contract on the table. I'd sent it to him in the hopes he'd still come today.

"My pack has reviewed the second draft contract. Though better, it still leaves many areas open to a concerning degree." Sascha turned the page. "Clause 2b, for instance. It's heavily weighted in the clan's favour."

I turned the first page, hope twinging low in my stomach.

He was here and actively participating.

It could mean everything.

Or nothing at all.

"Well and good, werewolf, but we offer the tribe and pack far more than they offer us in return," Kyros fired back.

"There is a *possibility* we may require your services. In fifty years. Or one thousand. Conversely, there's a *certainty* that Ni Tiaki and pack will put themselves in regular danger for your clan. For fifty years. For a thousand. Always. Our contribution will be tangible and trackable. *We* will offer the only advances in knowledge on the other supernatural races." Sascha leaned back, resting an arm over the back of my chair. "All your clan needs to do is sit there and look pretty. Shouldn't be a problem for you."

He did pretty well until the parting jab.

A growl filled Kyros's chest, shaking the table.

Basilia faced him, and I watched their expressions alter.

Oh my god. They could mind-speak too?

I inhaled Sascha's surprise.

"There's merit in what you say," Basilia said. "How about instead of wasting hours deciding who has the most to offer, we just agree that we bring equal value to an alliance?"

Sascha glanced at me.

It's the best we'll get.

He didn't answer my silent comment. He addressed the vampires again. "To 4a next. The suggested parameters of pack and Ni Tiaki responsibilities are too strenuous. Our involvement must take into account that tribe and pack alike will still have day jobs and require personal time with family and for themselves."

"That's for pack and tribe to negotiate," Kyros said. "I came here under the impression you'd be more prepared for this discussion."

"We take this alliance seriously, Prince Kyros," I replied. "There's a long-held grudge between us. Our people need time to come around to the idea of burying the hatchet. In addition, Sascha's Luthers have long memories, and they lost thousands to your clan. They're exceptionally loyal to those they lost, and this makes it hard for them to consider an agreement with Vissimo, let alone one with the tribe."

Instead of retorting, the prince nodded.

He liked to use some of his father's tricks and was far more subtle about rolling them out.

"Would an official apology from our clan help with the matter?" Basilia tilted her head.

Kyros shot her a look.

"Perhaps not," she murmured to his silent remark. "But your father is reasonable."

Sascha was unsettled.

Did he come here today ready to view vampires in the same way stewards viewed Luthers?

"That would go a long way with the older members of our community, yes," he said gruffly. "They value humility."

"The tribe is happy to negotiate the parameters of clause 4 with the pack and present you with our proposal." I met Sascha's hard gaze.

Sascha pressed his lips together. "The pack will attend."

He hadn't forgiven me by a long shot, but he'd do the right thing.

I'd take it.

I didn't dare relax in my chair as Sascha flipped two pages ahead. There were fifty in the document.

Negotiations between werewolves, vampires, and humans had begun.

This could blow up in my face.

But in all honesty, I was used to the feeling.

I listened to the sounds of the gathered stewards. Their happy babble was a thing of the past.

"*There's no way out of this.*"

"*We don't have enough numbers.*"

"*This whole time the werewolves were protecting us from demons.*"

My brows lifted. I wouldn't go that far, but if the tribe believed that, I wouldn't correct them.

Other than that, they were appropriately afraid of what was to come.

Good.

Now, the stewards just had to come to the right solution.

And it *had* to come from them.

I unplugged my headphones and exited the Water app screen. Tucking my phone in my pocket, I grabbed my saxophone from the chair and placed it back in the case.

With no other excuse to delay, I left the manor.

The tribe quietened at my passing, and I didn't drag out the moment needlessly by stopping to chat as I usually did.

My head team stood at the front, each holding a microphone.

They'd worked around the clock since last Thursday. Stanley looked ready to drop.

"Thank you all for getting us to this moment," I said for their ears only. "It's up to our stewards now."

Wade's nod was as terse as the others.

They dispersed through the crowd.

I caught Rhona's curious gaze from the second row but turned away to climb the stage stairs. Freeing the microphone, I looked at the tribe and inhaled their uncertainty, confusion, and fear.

"There has never been a moment so important in our tribe's history," I addressed them. "On Sunday, I asked that you consider what happens if we win and the Luthers leave the valley. Tonight, we will make a decision for our children and children's children."

The stewards weren't stupid. They'd guessed where my question was leading.

But they didn't have all the facts just yet.

"First, I wanted to ask how the training with our guests went yesterday and this afternoon."

There was a general murmur of approval. Some excitement.

They still had no idea our guests were vampires. I'd watched them practice with the Vissimo at interval. Though my stewards' heartbeats increased and their scent changed slightly in reaction to the supernaturals' presence, for the most part they felt nothing more than curiosity. Basilia had seemed to think so many Vissimo would cause panic in them, but I wondered if regular exposure to other supernaturals had given this tribe a certain resilience over the centuries. Strangely, those who didn't react as strongly felt the most wariness about our guests, but they were few.

I nodded. "I'm glad to hear it. If Gerry spoke, he'd shout your praise. Thank you for your effort."

That earned a few laughs, but the mood quickly sank back to trepidation.

"There has been a development in Grids that myself and the head team decided not to impart with you all until now. We wanted the focus to be on memorising the influx of new strategies. On Sunday, there was a meeting with the pack. Two of our sandstone experts attended also. The meeting was called to settle concerns our sandstone stewards had picked up on while working for the pack."

Their spying job was no secret within the tribe, but only a handful of our sandstone stewards knew what had happened with the reports.

My hands shook slightly—not with apprehension. With *anticipation.* "As a result of that meeting, a grid was turned over—"

There was a collective breath-hold.

"—to us." I finished. "We are now in possession of Clay, bringing us up to a total of four grids."

The tribe *exploded.* I grinned as they shouted and screamed, watching on as they hugged each other.

We'd possessed four grids three times since the game's origins.

I waited as the stewards celebrated, breathing in their relief and excitement.

I waited as their happy calls quietened.

... As their happiness morphed to determination and realisation.

Yes.

Tomorrow could be the end, and where would we be then? Five grids rich, and on the cusp of something more frightening than anything we'd faced?

Their nervousness swelled.

I returned the microphone to my lips. "Tomorrow, we could win Victratum. This game could be over. One week ago, that would have been a cause for celebration. Now, we know better."

This gathering had to be different from anything I'd done before.

I perched on the edge of the stage. "Please take a seat on the grass. If you're near a steward unable to do so, please help them to a chair at the back."

Five minutes later, the tribe was more comfortably situated. This felt far more like the more informal gatherings during the new moon.

"On Sunday, you learned many new things," I said. "What are your thoughts about what you heard? Raise your hand, and a head team member will be along with a microphone. Please don't hold anything back. We must come to a decision on this tonight for obvious reasons, and I don't believe this should be my decision alone—or that of the head team. Please be aware that the decision made will be final."

A steward stood, Wade just behind him.

"Drake," I greeted. "What are your thoughts?"

He swallowed. "It seems hopeless, Head Steward. If the Luthers leave, then other supernaturals might come, but even if we work with the pack, we'll number less than two thousand. You said there are *tens* of thousands of the other races. Aren't we better to just win Grids and see what happens in the future? Plus, if the other races attack, they could kill the remaining Luthers. Why would the pack stay and put themselves in danger when there's an airport being built and they can go?"

There were more than a few nods.

"Our numbers are a problem," I answered. "Can anyone see a solution to this?"

No one raised their hand.

I continued, "We'll come back to that. For now, pretend that numbers aren't an issue. Let's move on to the other part of Drake's comment. Why would the werewolves stay when they'd be in danger? To that, I pose a question to you all. Why wouldn't *we* just leave? We aren't trapped. We could escape and never need to worry about other supernatural threats. Don't forget that most of the pack have lived in Deception Valley for over two hundred and sixty years. Their lifespans are far greater than ours. Think of the connection you feel to this land after ten, thirty, or seventy years. The pack consider this valley their home, and that's why they'll protect it. Just as we will. But to stay, the pack would need to feel they *can* call this valley their home. That's a certainty."

Another steward stood. Trixie crossed to her.

"Jessi."

"Head Steward." She tugged at her hemp tunic. "I guess in any partnership, both sides need to feel they have a reason to work together, but to call this home, the pack would want what they've always wanted, wouldn't they? That goes against everything Ni Tiaki value and I'm worried that would cheapen the sacrifices our ancestors made to fight for our home. I want a solution, but it seems impossible."

"Thank you, Jessi." I pursed my lips. "I believe there are two parts to a solution. One, this tribe firmly believes the land should be protected. Care of the land has been a clause in Victratum since day one. The pack have always, until their recent lapse due to inexperience, displayed the utmost consideration for this valley. Those who have visited pack lands have witnessed the care Luthers take with their territory. On this point, the tribe and pack are of the same mind, but continued care of the land could be a condition of any proposal we make to the pack."

"And what would our proposal be?" she asked.

"Which brings me to the second part of a solution. Ownership of the valley has and always will be against our tribe's code. The pack has made a proposal already with our code in mind," I announced. "But I want to ask you to come up with solutions before presenting that."

The tribe stared up at me.

Yeah, that was pretty much the head team's reaction.

Stanley held the microphone out to Margaret Frey.

"They won't remain as guests, and we won't let them own the land," she said. "So there's only one solution. We do for them what we did for ourselves one hundred years ago. We gift them land in trust."

Her words created a stir.

I wasn't sure I'd ever loved the woman more.

She sat, and the stewards whispered to each other.

"What do others think?" I prompted.

"What if the pack took advantage of the trust somehow?" a steward named Jeffery asked.

They were getting there. "Perhaps adding a safety clause to the contract as well as a care of land clause would be a good idea."

The stewards began to debate with each other. I chimed in at intervals to keep the discussion focused.

After twenty minutes, I drew their conversation to a halt. "On behalf of the pack, Sascha Greyson has presented a similar proposal to what you've discussed. He believes that if his people are offered land in trust, then they will be open to an alliance with us against the outward threats we face. We would work in tandem to collect information on the surrounding supernatural threats and to work on our operations and defences in readiness of any future attack. The tribe has strengths the pack doesn't, and the opposite is also true. Our chances of success are far higher if we work side by side. That doesn't mean we need to do anything against our Ni Tiaki code. *No one* owns lands in this valley, and that will continue. We can return to the pack with a counter proposal and include any safety clauses we like, but I'm in agreement with Margaret Frey. This is the only way I can see that we can put the land feud to rest and protect this tribe's future."

"We're still only two thousand against *tens* of thousands," Eleanor spoke into Nathan's mic.

I dipped my head. "At one point, I'm sure our ancestors wondered how they'd ever hold their own against werewolves. But... I agree with you. We don't stand a chance with our current numbers."

Shock. Fear.

Bitter disappointment.

"Over the last few weeks, I've been in talks with the vampires of

Bluff City," I told them. "As you heard on Sunday, they number more than fifteen thousand."

I absorbed the wave of their horrified reaction, listening as they breathed the word *vampire* with horror.

In the first lull, I jumped in again. "We're in need of friends right now. Not only does an alliance between pack, tribe, and the Vissimo clan offer greater security, but it prevents any potential alliance between demon, witch, and vampire against us at a later date."

Pascal handed her mic to Tessie.

"*Vampires*," the council woman repeated. "Who drink human blood?"

There was a loud outcry at her statement.

"The idea of a vampire is terrifying." I studied them closely. Were they aware of the difference of this reaction to their reaction over Luthers? On some level, the tribe knew werewolves weren't a threat. "More than that, the *unknown* is terrifying."

Some stewards were standing now, unable to stay seated.

I let the outcry die down. "On Monday, five hundred guests entered tribal lands. You've trained with these guests over the last two days." I paused. "Did you ever wonder what they were? Because I can tell you, they're not human."

Silence.

"Our guests are vampires."

My stewards had been quiet in the past, but this took the prize.

I forged on. "At the beginning, I asked how your training with them had gone. You were approving and even excited. My apologies for the subterfuge, but I wanted to show you something important." I gripped the microphone tight. "I smell your fear now you know the truth—and it's a natural response. Fear warns us to proceed with caution in new territory. Fear helps us to fully consider our options before making big decisions. To be *ruled* by fear of the unknown is another thing. If we don't regulate our reaction, then with time that natural response festers to something darker. Fear can become avoidance. Avoidance to wilful ignorance. Combined, that becomes an angry disregard that rots to blind hatred. Yet at the root of all that remains one thing. *Fear*. Those who hate have allowed that emotion to rule them. What's more, they've convinced themselves they don't feel fear at all—that their hate is warranted and just. And that makes them small. Tiny."

Some people here were tiny.

For a time, I was on my way to becoming one of them.

But they were a minority before my return to head stewardship and they became less each day.

Hate could be reversed.

If there was one thing I blamed some of my Thana ancestors for, it was their encouragement of bad will between *Ni Tiaki* and pack.

I refused to be that leader.

I got up and returned the mic to the stand. "The stewards in this tribe are *not* tiny people, but there's real danger in allowing our fear to regulate the crucial decision we must make. It's *normal* for so much change to feel unsettling and scary. The game could end tomorrow. We could enter a partnership with the pack and face a fight against outside threats. We could align with a vampire race we haven't had many dealings with. With all that to consider, you wouldn't be alone in wishing to avoid all of it, but I urge you to check that emotion in its tracks. This tribe and this head team have your back. I will not allow harm to befall any being in this valley—tribe, pack, or members of the public. And that is why I present the following plan to you now."

The head team joined me up on stage as discussed.

"A series of polls will be sent out immediately after this gathering. You will determine if we approach the pack with a counterproposal or if they will be exiled from the valley. You will decide what clauses are added to a partnership contract between us. *You* will choose whether the tribe pursues negotiations with the vampire clan to form an alliance against outside threats. I stand by what I said earlier. This is not my decision, but the entire tribe's.

The future of the Ni Tiaki is in your hands. I only ask that you decide truly and without fear in your hearts. Because this is it."

I'd done everything I could.

And it didn't feel like enough.

Nowhere *near* enough.

"Pascal," I murmured. "Please do the honours."

Tablet in hand, the marshal sent out the polls.

Fuck.

It was done.

The fate of Deception Valley was in my steward's hands.

I swallowed back my own fear. "Stewards, we have one grid to turn over. What I've told you is unsettling to the extreme, I know, but as ever, we must focus on the task at hand. In light of that, the results of this poll won't be announced until after the game tomorrow night."

Pascal leaned closer. "Sent."

"Please return home and vote without delay," I said to them gravely. "Get what sleep you can. Tomorrow, we end Victratum for good."

32

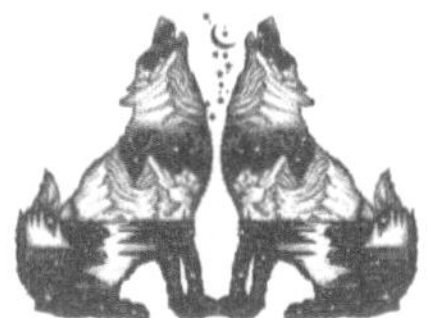

The stewards are voting on entering land negotiations with the pack, I thought to Sascha. *And the alliance with vampires.*

No response.

He'd barely looked at me on his exit from the meeting with Kyros and Basilia. Sure, he'd come to the table and agreed to at least *pursue* the alliance, but...

Sascha had always supported me.

To think we'd come so far to fall down at the last hurdle threatened to undo my determination to see things through.

Without him, life was an empty thing.

I love you, I thought at him.

As he'd done since Sunday, Sascha closed the bond as soon as I opened it. With anyone else, I would have moved on.

With him, so much was now impossible. I couldn't pretend the anguish away.

I've felt what you're feeling now, Sascha. Our pack is going to be okay. I promise you.

Nothing. A lump rose in my throat.

My phone rang, and the leaping of my heart was entirely pathetic.

"*Mandy*?" What the hell?

I answered. "Hello?"

"Andie. I need permission to enter the manor without penalty in Grids."

Hmm. Mandy wasn't my biggest fan in recent times. She was also a pack female.

I leaned back in my office seat. "Permission granted. Any illegal action taken while on manor lands will be enforced, however."

She hung up.

I caught the purr of a car motor. The vehicle stopped outside the manor, and soft footsteps crunched on the gravel before sounding in the hall.

Mandy entered the office, a stack of boxes in her arms.

"What can I do for you?" I asked.

She set the stack down on the coffee table. "I've changed my mind."

I didn't answer.

The delta crossed her arms. "You want Sascha."

"Took you a while to catch on."

"Took you a while to admit it."

"And still, I'm unsure why it's any of your business."

Mandy shrugged a shoulder. "I'm a delta."

"And you crave recognition, right?" My reply was soft.

She coloured.

There was a tinge of defiance in her scent.

"Correct me if I'm wrong," I watched her closely. "Sascha's top wolves are chosen because they've essentially mastered the shortcoming of their status."

Mandy tensed. "What are you saying?"

"By deciding that you knew better than Sascha or me, you disrupted the harmony of the pack. That's unacceptable in any pack Luther, more so in one meant to be a role model. What did you hope to achieve, Mandy? And was that worth our entire community?"

She sighed and sat. "I fucked up, okay."

"I'm glad you're aware of that."

The delta stared at her hands. "Sascha put me on probation after I punched you in the grid. I've never seen him so angry." She raised her gaze to mine. "Or you."

I'd never hurt someone the way I hurt Mandy that night. "You nearly killed him."

She nodded. "I let my ambition to see him happy become something else. I realised that as soon as you fell. But when you hit me, I realised something else... You love him."

Honestly, it was none of her business either way, but she could smell my agreement.

Her eyes glittered. "I watched you at the ball. It confirmed my suspicion."

"I'm so happy for you," I said drily.

"You deserve him."

"And you're missing the point. It was never your job to decide whether we deserved or loved each other. By involving yourself, you disrespected the person you profess to care about. You disrespected me too."

"I know. That's why I figured I'd interfere one last time—since I'd already made a mess of things." Mandy jerked a thumb at the boxes. "There are twenty-seven other boxes like it in my trailer."

I glanced at them. "And they are?"

"All the research ever done on you. Every fear, wish, and hope."

"The boxes from his wardrobe? I thought that was just capture-meet stuff."

"Male Luthers keep records from the moment they meet their mate until the end of the call."

I frowned. "You just took them without his permission?"

"They belong to you." She shrugged a shoulder. "Last night, Sascha told the pack that he severed communication with you after hearing you'd divulged pack secrets. I can guess how that may be affecting you."

Ouch. He did?

I got that breaking my promise reflected poorly on him as

leader. He was the one to tell me after all. Trust with the pack was everything.

But ouch.

"Read the contents of the boxes," Mandy said. "They're the male Luther version of a love letter, and it's common practice for pack females to keep the capture meet notes always. Bringing it here is my way of saying sorry."

"For hitting me or blocking my number on Sascha's phone?"

The delta winked. "Both. I'd hate for him to fuck things up after all this time by being a damn moron. When did ignoring a woman ever work out for a man? Seriously."

I'd say never. "He has a right to be angry. But I didn't tell the tribe to hurt the pack."

She waved a hand. "Most of the pack see what you're trying to do, and most of us are old enough to understand simple rules can't exist in a complicated game."

I'd never thought of it that way. "You still shouldn't have brought the boxes here."

The delta smirked. "But you're glad I did. How soon after I leave will you start reading?"

The stewards and Vissimo were currently practicing. I'd watched on for the first hour to see how the tribe reacted now they were aware of our guests' supernatural natures.

I'd join them in three hours to go over my part.

Until then, I'd planned to agonise over the game tonight.

I cocked a brow. "Fair point."

"Am I forgiven?"

"As long as you leave. I've got some reading to do."

After helping her with the remaining boxes, I listened for the sounds of her leaving before removing the lid of the box labelled *One*.

Inside were stacks of thick folders. I extracted the top folder and retreated to the only free sofa chair.

The first page was dated less than two weeks after Ragna's death.

I met her tonight.
My mate. At last.
She's human.
I pushed her in a hole before I realised what was happening. Her anger stole my breath.
Stewards came upon us, so I trapped her in the hole, hoping to return after the game, but the tribe found her.
She was really scared.
... I might have fucked that up.
My dreams are filled with the smell of vanilla, oranges, liquorice, and pumpkin spice. The woman in them still doesn't have a face or a name.
I can't rest until I know who she is.

The scribbled note was followed by pictures of me leaving the manor and entering the riverside apartment.

My jaw dropped.

He followed me after that night, I said to Booker.

Stop being surprised by obvious things.

Remind me to stop waking my wolf from naps. She didn't cope well.

I worked through the next documents.

One was the car registration for Ella F—he'd known my origin was Queens Way before we'd met the second time.

While he didn't break into my car until the second day—I'd slept in it the first night—he *did* watch me bathe in the river.

I can't wait to feel her skin against mine.

I shook my head. "You fucking creep."

But now, it wasn't creepy at all. Mandy was right. These notes were akin to a love letter.

These boxes were a collection of all Sascha's thoughts about me.

My heart squeezed to painful levels.

She's the niece of Hercules Thana and has no idea about supernaturals.
What am I going to do?
He'll turn her against me. He's already closing in.
I don't want this life for her, but I can't find it in myself to make her leave.
Fly away from this while you can, little bird.

I still remembered how strange his behaviour was back then. Whenever I'd mentioned leaving, he'd interrogate me, then let me go. He'd always seemed to barely hold himself back.

But Sascha had always given me a choice.

The first archive box contained everything up until I'd first realised Sascha wasn't entirely human. I read a page ripped from a business diary next.

Andie made me come in my pants like a teen.
Afterward, she looked horrified. She lied about being with her ex-boyfriend to escape my company.
I didn't mean for things to move so fast.
For some reason, she's scared of what she feels around me.
Soon, I'll need to explain what's going on. It's not fair to keep up this charade. But what if the truth is too much?
Every day I wake up expecting her to be gone.

There was a smaller note from a memo pad right at the bottom of the box.

If there's one thing I'll always be grateful to Hercules Thana for, it's convincing Andie to remain in the valley.
My mate isn't on my side. She's afraid of what I am.
But she's here.
I can still look at her.
Smell her.
Hear her heart.
She's here.

I dashed away tears and picked up a voice recorder wedged down the side. There were several small tapes scattered in the box too. Grabbing one, I inserted it and pushed Play. My saxophone rendition of "Feeling Good" by Nina Simone rang out.

I set the recording on the coffee table to play.

The second box showed the start of Sascha and Greyson's detailed capture meet research.

Everything. Photos. Food wrappers. Clothing and trinkets.

And one repeated question.

Why does my mate hate casinos?

Logan inadvertently answered that question when he visited from Queen's Way and spilled the beans about Ragna's gambling past and the debt I'd inherited.

I checked my watch.

Ugh. In three hours, I only worked through three of the thirty plus boxes. I just wanted to sit here and read through the rest.

Right now, I didn't have that kind of time.

But Mandy had fulfilled her purpose in dropping the boxes off.

The strength and depth of Sascha's love for me was unshakeable. *Undying.*

After reading through some of the boxes, surety of our bond filled me once again.

He was being torn between the pack and me right now, just as I'd been torn between the tribe and him. He couldn't break trust with his people.

Unlike my stewards, the pack could smell a lie.

So I wouldn't keep tugging on one of his arms—we'd made that mistake before. When the war was over, he'd come for me.

Because Sascha Greyson was mine.

The world couldn't keep us apart.

It just wasn't powerful enough.

33

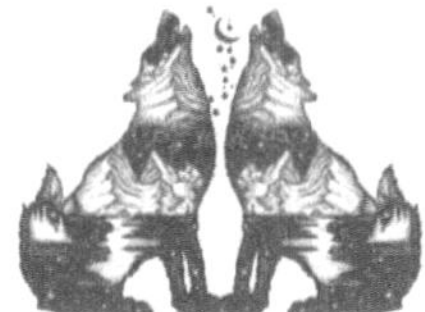

"Pull over. I'm going to vomit," I forced out between clamped lips.

Wade shot me a glance from the driver's seat. "You've said that four times already. You can't vomit today. It's bad luck."

Oh… then I just wouldn't?

Cam sighed from the back. "Can you guys believe this may be the last time we drive to a grid?"

The thought distracted me from the bile threatening to surface. The concept *was* strange, and I'd only experienced a matter of months of Grids. These guys had to feel all kinds of unsettled.

I mean, yes, a weekly battle against werewolves would end.

But also the cornerstone of steward routine.

"What will you guys do if we win?" I asked.

Wade lifted a shoulder. "See what happens. Always thought I'd leave, but with the demons and witches, I don't know if that will sit right."

Losing Wade on a daily basis would be horrible, but the world didn't revolve around me. "If you want to leave for a while, there are stewards to fill in. Come back when you can. Not too long though or I'll hunt you down."

He smiled my way. "Thanks, baby girl."

Cam said, "This thing with Emily is serious. I want to see where it leads. What about you, Andie?"

"Bulk sex with Sascha Greyson," Wade sang.

I mean, ideally. "My future really depends on what the stewards and pack decide. If the stewards and pack come to a truce, Sascha and I will be together."

Wade frowned. "What if the pack leaves?"

Yeah, I still had no idea. That's why I felt so damn nauseous about the possibility of the game ending tonight. "There are demons and witches to consider. I'm meant to abandon the stewards to that?"

"You can't be happy without Sascha though," he pressed.

That was a certainty. But regrets were a real thing, and they liked to follow me through life. I had to make the choices I could live with to reach the man I wanted. And it was the same for him.

Too damn loyal for our own good.

I blew out a breath. "It's not an issue unless we win."

Oh my god.

We were fighting for the fifth and final grid.

"Pull over. I'm going to vomit," I groaned.

"No can do, baby girl. Suck it up."

I glared at him. "If we win and you stay, I'm not letting you organise next year's ball."

Wade jerked the car wheel left and right. Ignoring my shouts, he parked in my head steward spot. Pretty sure that was the only reason he always offered to drive.

Stewards milled around, some already in their thin wetsuits.

I squared my shoulders, then unclipped my belt.

Wade nudged me, winking. "There's our head steward. Go get 'em."

Yeah, at this point, I wanted the game to end as much as I didn't. "Thanks."

They left to change, and I grabbed my saxophone case and backpack from the boot before finding a spot inside the tree line that left me visible to stewards but invisible to peeping pack members on the opposite shore.

Pascal joined me. "How do you feel?"

I pulled a face at her. "Confident and ready to go."

She laughed quietly. "As long as the tribe believes it, then feel however you want."

Truth. "I was speaking with Wade and Cam about what they'd do if Grids ends. What will you do?"

She looked up from her tablet. "If I were younger, maybe the idea of the game ending would excite me. As it is, I fear losing something that has always pulled me through hard times. I'm unsure."

Pascal didn't mate Daniil, but they'd seen each other at least once a week to carry out marshal duties. Even apart, they'd shared companionship.

"Do you see yourself anywhere else?" I inhaled her immediate denial.

"I see myself throwing everything into protecting the tribe against demons and witches. For those of us who dread the game ending, the new focus will bring comfort."

Fighting demons and witches brought her *comfort*. I wasn't sure the tribe realised how resilient they were sometimes.

"Head Steward?"

I turned to Heather. "Hey."

"How does this go on the oxygen display again? Ha!"

Pascal nearly dropped her tablet at the woman's nervous, barking laugh.

I crouched by the steward's oxygen tank and studied the full reading. "Got the sticker? It goes directly over top."

Heather peeled off the back, and I held the tank as she placed the sticker. Now, it appeared as though her tank was nearly out of oxygen.

Sascha was the master at using such tactics against us. He put his wolves in the trees so we couldn't shoot them without risking points. He sent them into water without tanks, so we had to divert huge numbers to ensure pack members didn't drown.

It was beyond time we used a similar strategy against him.

Without killing my stewards.

Everyone would go in with a fake tank. They were under instructions to show any attacking Luthers the dial.

It wouldn't stop the pack shooting us, but the trick would put them at the same disadvantage. Until they figured it out. Hopefully the guise would hold for half the game.

Heather lugged her tank away.

I opened my saxophone case.

"That was an ingenious addition to our strategy," Pascal murmured.

How did she look at me *and* the tablet? That's what I wanted to know.

"The saxophone? Thanks, but Rhona gave me the idea."

I assembled the instrument and held it by the bell.

Ready to play? Booker said.

Guess so. Are you ready to do your part? We'd both be forced out of our comfort zones in the next two hours.

I'd play the saxophone to deliver orders to the swimming Ni Tiaki tonight—something that would solve our massive communication problems in this grid.

After the talk with Rhona, picking up my sax felt easier. Because she was right.

I was only so angry at Ragna because I'd loved her so much.

Yes, an explanation would have helped me understand the gambling and low moods and her inability to care for me. Yet by keeping secrets, she'd attempted to protect me from a brother she strongly suspected of killing the love of her life.

Could I be sure that my actions would be any different in that situation?

She'd done her best while carrying the horrible burden after Murphy's death. And when cancer appeared to take her away, she'd fought it. For *me*.

I'd been the second love of her life.

Playing to potentially end the game that drove Ragna and Murphy from their home felt... *right*.

In another world, she'd be beside me now, clad in a wetsuit and placing a fake sticker on her tank. She would have supported me through everything in the last few months. Grey-streaked auburn hair flowing free. Emerald eyes filled with mischief and dreams.

I could respect what she'd gone through to live for me.

I could grieve what she'd lost that made our lives so hard sometimes.

... I could still call Ragna my mother.

Tonight, I'd play my saxophone for her, as I'd always done. My mother would be with her tribe again.

I closed the case and placed the instrument in a black cloth bag that would keep Sascha in the dark until my part was revealed.

"Andie?" Roderick called to me. "It's time for a few words."

Didn't people say that at funerals?

The stewards had gathered between the two columns of parked cars. I couldn't locate a rock, so I jumped to grab a low-hanging branch and swung myself up Luther-style.

Maybe I shouldn't have chosen this spot. Were the leaves shaking as hard as my insides?

"Stewards," I pitched my voice higher, "we stand on Lake Thana about to claim our fifth and final grid." I surveyed their silent mass. "Please link hands and close your eyes."

Immediately, some of their nervousness ebbed.

"The stewards around you are your heartbeat. Listen to their breath. Feel their warmth and the soft wind on your face. Know that our ancestors surround us, cheering us on and willing this game to be over. Don't think about tomorrow. Don't think about yesterday. Take this moment to think about what you need to do the moment you step into the grid."

I took the chance to do the same and felt Booker preparing herself too.

"Open your eyes," I called. "Stay linked."

They did so, and their new calm echoed mine.

"Not long ago, we were four grids down. I asked you to remember that sickening, fearful feeling that your life would be uprooted. That you'd soon leave everything you knew behind to face uncertainty. The pack feels that way tonight with the added knowledge that an attempt to leave this valley will probably kill them all. Coming here will feel like walking to their death. So when this game ends, I want you to put yourself in their shoes. I ask that you be respectful of their position."

I let that sink in.

I raised my fist. "Stewards, Victratum ends tonight."

"*Victratum ends tonight.*"

"Victratum ends tonight," I shouted from my tree branch.

They roared their response. "*Victratum ends tonight!*"

Boom.

Ever a well-oiled team, the stewards surged forward, streaming under my tree perch towards the lake.

At the back of the group, Rhona paused beneath my spot. She'd enter the grid as part of Reindeer's unit tonight.

I nodded at her. Rhona nodded back and ran after the north team.

"Ready?" Pascal asked from below. She held up my saxophone and backpack.

No. "A girl guide is always prepared."

I jumped down and took the instrument from her before walking with her to our boat.

Pascal directed us around to the concealed end of the lake that was off limits to the public. Not far from here, the pack managed a hydro power plant that supplied energy to the town. I'd never actually seen it.

Kind of ironic that wolves controlled the Water grid when they hated getting wet.

When Pascal killed the engine, I secured our boat to the ladder, then climbed to the top of the observation tower, taking care not to bang my saxophone.

I didn't waste time.

For a while now, it had felt like a clock was ticking above my head.

I had a strong feeling there weren't many seconds left.

Pulling out my phone, I studied my cues a final time as reports from team leaders sounded through my walkie.

"*Frequency generators up.*"

"*Cameras in position.*"

I'd needed some visibility under the surface.

"*Bases in position.*"

"*Skis loaded.*"

Ten minutes left.

I drummed my fingers on the rails. "Come on."

"*Wicked. Set up complete. Over.*"

Perfect. She was in charge of two parts of our main operations.

Five minutes.

"*Reindeer. Set up complete. Over.*"

With two minutes remaining, her report was echoed by my other team leaders.

That was close, Booker growled.

They had a lot to set up. Ready, girl?

Let's fuck some shit up.

My wolf was big on the swears. If she had her way, I'd be inked up with a permed mullet by now.

I changed the frequency on my walkie and brought it close to my lips. "Big Red. In position? Over."

The reply from the designated head vampire—a woman called Laurel that Basilia had highly recommended—crackled through. "Affirmative. Awaiting your order. Over."

Boom.

My heart pounded at the inside of my ribs to escape.

Peering to the opposite side by the cliffs, I watched the Luthers slip from the trees into the water. The stewards on the nearest cliffs opened fire, but as per usual, the pack largely ignored them.

"Two points to us," Pascal said.

Better than nothing. That could be the difference if this grid was like our Sandstone win.

When the last of the pack was in the water, I lifted my walkie. "Big Red. Bats, prepare Operation Circus. Over."

I left my cliff stewards to set up and drew my tablet out of my backpack. "I finally feel important," I murmured, earning a soft laugh from Pascal.

On the underwater cameras, I watched my stewards holding up their oxygen tank dials to approaching Luthers. I hissed a *yes* as the pack abandoned their nets and swam any unconscious stewards to the surface.

Of course, I could partially shift and listen in on Sascha's orders, but the pack would sense Booker's presence too.

She was an ace I couldn't reveal yet.

I drew out my saxophone.

There were diving masks that used the ultrasound technology to communicate, but Luthers had no trouble picking up the signal. I could also communicate with my stewards through walkie technology, but being underwater, they couldn't reply.

Under the surface, they communicated with hand signals—much as divers did. But we'd always, *always* been caught off guard in this grid because my stewards couldn't see what the Luthers were doing.

From here, I could.

First, I connected the new microphone to the bell of my sax, and then turned on the portable speakers that three stewards lugged up for me.

I peered over the railing of the observation tower and double-checked the situation on the cameras again.

The pack were converging on my south stewards.

Standing, I took a breath.

This is for you, Mum.

I blew two short notes. They blasted through the speaker. My stewards had spent the last four days memorising this code system.

Go south.

Jet ski and boat engines revved. The east and west teams closed in on the south to provide back up.

Crouching over the tablet, I watched the swimming Luthers spin to face the incoming threat.

There was another benefit to the pack strategy Sascha used in Water. While the wolves were busy in the south, they weren't watching anywhere else.

I raised my saxophone again. Three sharp notes and one long.

North. Medic.

They'd administer a tranquiliser antidote to any fallen stewards they could reach.

"We came out on top of that," Pascal announced.

Sascha would split the pack up.

My south, east, and west stewards packed unconscious Luthers into the boats and jet ski trays. We'd take them to pontoons dotted around the lake—heavily guarded pontoons.

The pack split into two groups as seamlessly as a school of fish.

I placed the mouthpiece against my bottom lip.

West and east.

One sharp note. I waited a beat and then blasted four.

North and south would both supply backup.

The majority of our jet skis and boats had just reached the pontoons to unload knocked-out pack members, but the rest raced to help too.

I winced as a Luther grabbed hold of a jet ski and shoved the steward driving into the water.

The jet ski immediately stopped—we weren't stupid, the pack couldn't operate the machines—but the Luthers could still seize them to eliminate our speed.

The pack split in three.

The smallest force hunted our jet skis, and my stomach twisted as more and more were rendered useless.

Only twenty-five minutes had passed.

I needed ten more minutes, but we were dropping like flies.

Shit. We had to have numbers for the finale.

I paced along the railing, blasting notes to guide my tribe.

"We've lost 64 percent fewer points than is usual for us in Water at this point," Pascal told me.

"Estimate?"

"Three hundred and eighty-four."

Fuck. There was no *way* we'd taken that many points from the pack.

We need to change our approach, I said to Booker.

She received my proposed strategy in a stream of thought. *Agreed.*

Thirty minutes to go.

We had to take the risk or losing was a definite.

I blew three long notes. *Prepare for Operation Fang.*

A series of thuds from behind made me whirl.

Pascal stood at the top of the ladder with her tranquiliser gun aimed downward.

"Nothing to worry about," she said easily.

Crossing to join her, I stared down at Leroy and Grim sprawled unconscious in our tiny boat.

Ha! Booker said gleefully.

I shot my marshal a look. "Thanks."

She'd already resumed tapping on her tablet. Multi-tasking queen.

Next. "Big Red. Prepare. Over."

Laurel replied, "Roger that."

Vampires, *check.*

I switched the frequency. "Big Red. Bats, initiate Operation Circus on my mark. Over."

"*Roger that.*"

Nets, *check.*

An orange flag popped out of the water to the south.

Then the west.

East.

The north flag didn't rise. I checked the cameras and cursed. The pack had combined once more to hit my stewards there.

We had to move ahead without north for now.

I clicked back to the vampires. "Big Red. Initiate Operation Fangs. Luthers gathered at North side. Focus numbers there. Over."

The thing about Vissimo?

They were fucking fast, faster than a Luther. Waiting out of sight and earshot, then sprinting to join was nothing for them—especially with our frequency generators to help out.

Even I couldn't hear them approaching to surround as much of the lake's perimeter as possible.

Abandoning my walkie, I let three short and three long notes loose through my sax. *Initiate Operation Fangs.*

The water churned and chopped as my stewards swam for the lake shore.

By now the pack had to know my sax didn't mean anything good.

I could feel their suspense.

I needed their panic.

Booker?

I won't let you down, Andie.

You never could. My wolf wanted this boring game over as much as I did.

"Pascal, please turn off the frequency generators."

A second lapsed. "Done, Head Steward."

Fear.

It was immediate.

I smelt the cloying scent rise from the pack as the sound of a stampede rose in a wave from the forest.

Now, Booker.

My fangs and claws burst forth as Booker partially shifted on our behalf.

Vampires burst from the trees, racing between the near rows of stewards into the water.

The pack split from engaging my north stewards. A beat passed before Reindeer finally raised her orange flag.

More fear.

But Sascha would control the pack in seconds.

Booker seized hold of the seven hundred and fifty small pinpricks dotting our mind, and her shout boomed in my mind.

Separate! She snarled at the pack. *Protect. Survive. Retreat. Fight. Get back.*

She kept up her tirade, and I could feel the drain on our vital energy.

I yanked on the connection between me and Sascha to further distract him.

Total bitch move.

I managed three before he wrenched back.

Okay, that wasn't so comfortable.

We continued our battle as Booker continued booming her orders. I would've expected Greyson to seize control by now. He held more power over the pack by far than Booker.

Vampires shot through the water toward the Luthers like missiles.

Strategic missiles.

They darted close to the pack, never making contact.

They had one job.

To cause panic.

If not for the orange-scented oil under my nose, the smell of so many Vissimo would overwhelm Booker completely. We could smell the vampires underwater too—something I'd tested on Monday before Basilia and Kyros left.

I balled my hands as five distinct groups of Luthers began to form. *Yes!* Tearing my eyes from the surface, I crouched to check the cameras.

Where were the betas?

People were harder to recognise underwater. Hairy swam by a camera, his fangs descended.

Got you.

Booker still shouted her silent orders, and I left her to it, standing on wobbling legs at the barrier again.

I clicked on my walkie. "Big Red. Bats, seal off north quadrant."

The betas were the real danger in what came next. Too damn level-headed for their own good.

With Greyson struggling to settle the pack, betas would be the backup.

My hands shook from fatigue.

My legs folded, but I lifted my saxophone to sound a series of signals. Important signals.

Gammas. West.

Alphas. South.

Omegas. South-west.

Deltas. East.

That done, I started playing the most chaotic song I knew —"Yakety Sax" by Boots Randolph.

A Luther's senses were their strength—also their weakness.

The speaker faced away from me, but even Booker struggled to maintain her concentration through this song, though we'd practiced several times.

"Yakety Sax" was also the final order.

My stewards entered the water again and opened fire on pack members fleeing the vampires.

It was fucking cruel, really. The last time they'd seen Vissimo, they lost thousands of their brethren.

I slid along the ground and rolled to watch over the edge of the observation tower.

"Bats. Task complete. Over."

The betas were secure. Part of my north team maintained their fire on the status while the vampires worked to extract unconscious Luthers and deposit them at our pontoons.

The other statuses would soon stabilise, but luckily for us, each status had a weakness. Something I'd managed to figure out.

Gammas tended toward laziness and disinterest, so the stewards there opened a path to the lake shore and waited in the tree line by frequency generators.

The gammas took the bait.

They dropped to the sand.

Omegas were easily rattled, but I wasn't sure how their stubbornness to obey orders would come into play. One in three of my stewards were armed with strobes.

The water around the omegas flickered and flashed. The strobes would further rattle them even if they refused to give up the fight.

I squinted South to the alphas.

For apparently being the strongest status in the pack, alphas were the easiest to manage.

We'd given them three choices. The shore. A pontoon. And staying put. Most of the alphas had surfaced, and I could see them arguing from here as each vied for control over the others.

Too many chefs spoiled the broth.

Too many alphas fucked everything up.

Deltas.

Dammit, I couldn't move.

"Pascal. What's happening east?"

"Luthers are scattering. Most are scaling the cliffs."

I smiled. We hadn't been sure exactly where each status would end up, but the cliffs were perfect for the deltas. Ambition and glory were their weakness. Alphas may seek to control others before making a move, but deltas wouldn't bother. They were a collection of one-man armies.

None of them would work together, and so they'd all get in each other's way.

I closed my eyes, listening to Booker's weakening orders to the pack.

This was the last thing she'd wanted to do.

But she did it for us.

For Sascha and Greyson.

"Pascal?" I murmured.

She crouched by my side.

As black closed in, I spoke my last order. "Whatever time is left. Administer antidotes to fallen stewards. Give the order."

Pascal smoothed my hair back. "Roger that, Head Steward."

34

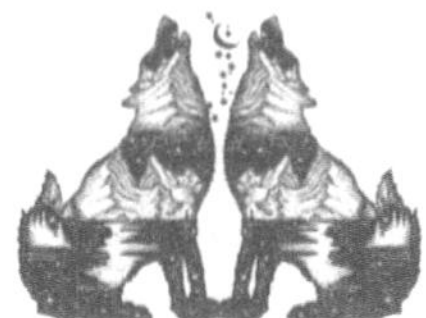

Strong arms held me.

A growl that would be menacing to anyone else brought me comfort.

I opened my eyes.

"Sascha?" Unbearably tired, I smiled at him.

He squeezed me tight. "Andie."

The healing I always felt at his touch was ramped on high.

I frowned. *Really* high.

His arms slid away, and I rolled off as he toppled sideways to the sand.

I scrambled to his side. "Sascha?"

His heartbeat was slow. Breath laboured.

"What's happening to him?" I shouted.

Stewards and Luthers surrounded us. I didn't care.

Evelyn stepped forward. "You weren't in the best shape, dear. He healed you. He'll be okay soon."

As she said it, his heartbeat stopped dropping and began to strengthen.

My lower lip trembled. Forgetting our audience, I rested my head on his chest and held him close.

Don't you dare try to heal us in return, Greyson scolded.

Okay, Booker and I replied meekly.

Sascha's arms came around me, and covered in sand, we held each other.

We can intentionally heal each other now? Before, we'd touched and waited for the bond to do its thing. What I'd felt just now... Sascha had *pushed* the healing into me or something.

Our bond twists together, remember? he said wearily. *But our ability to heal is finite. As is your power to command the pack as you did.*

I'd known that. Booker was in control. She'd promised not to push any further than a depletion we could recover from in a day. I'd risked Sascha's life in the past by accident and wasn't about to do it again.

Of course, he'd chosen to nearly kill himself to heal me anyway.

Please don't ever do that again, I told him.

If the situation were reversed, little bird?

If I'd known we could do this, then I would have poured nearly everything I had into him in Sandstone. *Fair point.*

The murmurs around us surged as the whine of a boat engine reached my ears.

The marshals, Sascha said in response to my confusion.

Oh my god. The game.

Greyson snorted, and I felt Sascha's affection.

Something you want to share? I pulled back.

His lips twitched. *Greyson enjoyed refusing to control the pack in the grid. Very much.*

I bet he did. *And how did you feel about that?*

Well, let's see. I enjoyed that my wolf refused to control the pack in the grid. Very much. Luckily the pack understands that allowances must be made for sigmas...

My mouth bobbed. *You planned to let Greyson help me all along.*

I didn't discuss it with him in advance of the grid, he thought at me, *but I trust my wolf completely.*

That was a whopping *yes. For the record, your fake cold shoulders don't work anymore. I knew you were on my side.*

His joy brushed against me like a cool breeze on a summer's day. *I'm glad to hear it, mate. It only took months of blasting you with charm while dangling sex in front of you to build that trust.*

I'd laugh. But that was an accurate summary of events.

Sascha, I'm sorry about breaking my promise. Truly.

You made the right choice even if I didn't like it at the time.

Seriously. How the hell did I *ever* think alphas were for me? Emotionally stable men for the win.

I crouched to help him stand.

Sascha wrapped his arm around my shoulders as the marshals clambered onto the pier and walked towards us.

This is it, huh? His voice entered my mind again.

If the tribe win, then yeah. Guess it is.

Either way, Andie, if the game doesn't end after your little vampire ruse, then the pack and tribe will sit down and work out a truce.

My eyes widened. *You mean it?*

"Yes," he said aloud. "This game has gone on long enough." Sascha peered back over his shoulder.

I glimpsed a stern-faced Alexei in the front row next to Evelyn.

Pascal and Hana, the Luther marshal, approached.

Sascha dropped his arm from my shoulders, and I took his hand, gripping it tight.

"Head Steward," Pascal said. "Pack Leader."

Jesus, was she trying to kill me?

"By sixty points, victory goes to the Ni Tiaki," she announced.

I covered my mouth and sank to my knees in the sand.

It was over.

The news was passed back through the tribe. Maybe that should have been my job, but I couldn't move.

I listened as stewards began to cry. Great, gulping sobs of relief from years of battle in Grids. I hadn't needed to remind them to be respectful to the pack. Cheering was the last thing on their minds.

Standing, I hugged Pascal in response to her mounting fear.

"You'll be okay, my friend," I whispered.

The older woman nodded, tears slipping over her cheeks. Passing over her tablet, she joined the rest of the tribe.

I faced Sascha.

He sank to his knees.

"*Please* don't do that. It's a stupid clause." My cheeks burned. "Stand up."

"My pack concedes the win of Victratum to the Ni Tiaki. Per the terms of the game contract, Deception Valley now belongs to you."

I'd say only the Luthers could hear his words.

"I accept. Get up."

It would have killed Greyson to bend a knee. Then again, he really only cared about one thing. Him and Booker both.

Sascha's expression was sombre.

Mine too.

Ending the game was a major hurdle to overcome, but the war wasn't over yet.

Dread mounting in my stomach, I turned Pascal's tablet on and logged into our tribe system.

"What are you doing?" Sascha said.

I exhaled. "The poll results are on here." No one had seen them yet. Only I had access.

"Your attention, please," I called.

Luthers and stewards gradually fell quiet.

A wet-faced Wade approached and handed me the microphone from my sax. He set the portable speaker next to me.

I lifted the mic. *Here goes.* "Last night, every member of the Ni Tiaki tribe participated in a set of polls. These polls outlined decisions they needed to make for our future and the future of those in this valley. I have the results here now."

Fuck.

It was seriously horrible that even after going through Victratum, everything hinged on the contents of this file. I'd be so glad to never hold another poll in my life.

"Courage, mate," Sascha said quietly.

I tapped on the file. "The tribe were asked if they wished to approach the pack with a land proposal in the interest of entering a truce or if they wished the pack to be exiled from Deception Valley per the rules of Victratum." I swallowed. "The tribe voted in favour of approaching the pack with a proposal in hopes of a truce."

Most Luthers were shocked. Their scents changed rapidly. Relief. Disbelief. Hope. Fear.

I spoke again, "The tribe were asked if they wished to pursue further negotiations with Clan Sundulus, the Vissimo of Bluff City, to form an alliance against outside threats. They voted in favour of continuing negotiations."

Locking my legs, I scrolled through the results of the third poll. The tribe had also voted on which clauses they wanted included in any truce with the pack.

A care of the land clause.

An exit clause if the pack ever turned on the Ni Tiaki.

A non-violence clause that would result in land penalties for both sides. The last thing I'd wanted was for a truce to dissolve the second a Luther hit a steward or vice versa. Instead, both sides would lose land as a consequence. It was something both sides held dear, and considering the tribe had far more land, the clause had reassured many.

In time, they'd learn my wolves wouldn't hurt them though.

Opening a new email, I attached the poll results and sent them to every member of the tribe. Over 85 percent unified for the biggest decisions. The closest results were those for the truce clauses.

I looked up at Sascha.

There was one last thing to do before I could fall into his arms. And I planned to do that as soon as possible.

I walked to stand before the pack and lowered the mic. "I'd like to formally invite your pack leader and his top wolves to meet with me and my head team tomorrow morning to discuss an ongoing truce. Victratum is over for good. Moving forward, the Ni Tiaki believe in partnership with the pack. They realise that this cannot happen without giving you a secure home. They're willing to do this. Are you willing to speak with us?"

The pack members exchanged glances.

Alexei's gaze bore into the side of my face.

Sascha strode past to stand with his pack. He inhaled and smiled before returning to my side to take the microphone. "The pack will meet with the Ni Tiaki to discuss a truce. We can both agree we have larger concerns to focus on together. And as a gesture of goodwill, I would like to gift the tribe with everything the pack has gathered on demons and witches over the last two centuries."

My mouth bobbed. They *what*?

My stewards gasped and broke into whispers.

"We were preparing to fight our way out," Sascha explained. "What we've found is concerning. We hope it will jumpstart any future plans and make us more valuable in a potential alliance with Vissimo. To be clear, whatever the pack's decision on a truce or alliance, we will gladly leave all our gathered information with the tribe. We trust the land in your hands and don't wish to see it overrun by other powers—supernatural or human."

That *really* hit my stewards hard. The pack hadn't erupted into violence at the closing of the game. They weren't angry or sullen or vicious.

They'd accepted the result and had offered us something extremely valuable without any ties.

I could smell that while his pack were considering a truce with us, an alliance with vampires was still a solid no for many. My grid stunt likely didn't help. The smell of the vampires hung thick around the lake though they'd vacated as discussed to return to manor lands.

"The Ni Tiaki extends its heartfelt thanks to the pack," I said in awe.

He bowed slightly.

I wanted to take all of this as a sign that things would work out.

But I just couldn't believe the game was over. Not until it was really done.

"Pack. Return to our territory." Sascha stepped forward and closed my numb fingers around the mic.

Turning, he stalked after his wolves and disappeared into the trees.

"Stewards," I said hoarsely. "Let's head back to the manor."

After Booker's work in the grid, I was still shaky. Wade and Cam took control and led me to the Jeep.

We didn't speak much on the way back.

A few stewards may celebrate because we beat the pack.

The majority would just celebrate because Victratum was over.

The game was over.

Wade drove the Jeep through the gates I'd once entered as Andie Booker, and I felt a shift within me.

"What is it?" he asked.

My hand was in his. I smiled tremulously. "Change."

My friend squeezed my fingers tight. "Good."

Stewards streamed into the manor and grounds—everyone of all ages in attendance. The youngest had no idea werewolves existed. They *did* know that their parents and loved ones fought against the people on the south side most Wednesdays.

They knew that was over.

One day they'd know the truth, but they wouldn't ever play Victratum themselves.

The stewards' shock slowly melted to pure relief and happiness. Their elation seeped under my skin, and for a time, I milled in their midst to receive their hugs and congratulations and gratitude.

I listened to their fears upon seeing me unresponsive after the game.

I reassured them about what was to come and encouraged them to enjoy tonight.

But half of my heart was on the south side and it pulled at me.

Wade dragged me to a dark corner of the patio. "Leave."

My brows shot up. "Why?"

"It's midnight."

I gasped. "Ella F has turned back to a pumpkin again."

He rolled his eyes. "Funny."

I thought so.

"You've spent enough time with the tribe. Leave. Go to Sascha."

My pulse thumped in my ears. "Why?"

"To play him the saxophone naked. I don't care." Wade rolled his eyes. "You've done the head steward thing. Our fanged guests are gone. Go do who you really want to do."

"What will you tell the tribe?" I brushed my hair back.

"Nothing. You're going to get in Ella F. And unapologetically drive to your wolfman. Got it?"

They'd know where I was going.

And actually, I was okay with that.

I hugged my friend tight. "I love you."

"I love you, too, baby girl. You should shower first though. Just saying."

I sniffed. The guy had a point.

I weaved between tribe members on the patio and eventually reached the hall. Walking to the stairs, I paused by the office. The door, which I'd absolutely locked, sat ajar. Light streamed out.

I pushed the door open to reveal Rhona.

"These boxes are filled with notes about you." Rhona didn't apologise for snooping.

She must feel better.

I walked into the office. "They contain everything Sascha has ever thought about me. Well, most of it. I assume that he'll keep records until the end of the mating call."

Rhona lowered the piece of paper in her hand. "It's like a love letter."

"These are the most vulnerable words he'll ever write," I replied. "Anyone who reads them will see into his mind. And they'll learn everything about me too."

Rhona glanced up.

I inhaled the way her cut grass and vanilla scent tangled

together and intensified with the strength of her yearning. For both of those things.

The innermost thoughts of her father's killer.

An in-depth and true knowledge of her sister.

This could be another mistake.

By now, I trusted my gut.

"Read them all," I offered. "Just lock the door after, please."

Her eyes rounded. "You *want* me to read them?"

"Real trust starts somewhere." Closing the gap, I took her in my arms.

Rhona hugged me back.

I breathed her in.

"Are you sniffing me?" she accused.

"You smell like cut grass and vanilla." Luther pups usually took on their mother's scent, but I was willing to bet that Rhona inherited the vanilla from Herc—possibly after Savannah's death.

For myself, I chose to believe I got vanilla from my mother. And maybe the orange scent from Murphy.

"You just stink," Rhona eventually said.

"I've been informed." My question was *how* I stunk so bad. I'd played saxophone and passed out. But whatever. "I'm off for a shower. Take your time with the boxes. I'll be with Sascha tonight."

Rhona stilled, but took a breath and slowly relaxed. "I hope you have a good time."

Those words required equal vulnerability to those she'd soon read in the boxes.

"Thank you." I closed the office door after me.

And smiled.

35

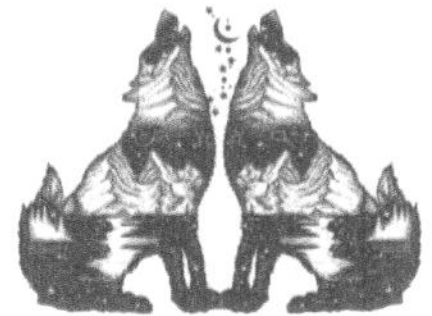

I rolled down my window. "Hey, Grim."

Poor guy got knocked out earlier and *still* landed gate duty.

He glared. "Andie."

"I hope the tranquiliser isn't hitting your wolf too hard."

"I hate being darted."

I smirked. "Ditto. Now we're even. I'm here to see Sascha."

Grim waved an arm, and I smelled his begrudging respect.

It's possible that I'd have some egos to soothe. No one wanted their faults and weaknesses exposed. Luthers were no different, especially when they worked so hard to overcome the vice of their status to make things work in a pack.

Hopefully Mandy would help out with the deltas because out of everyone, they'd hold the strongest grudges.

"Thanks." I drove on.

I'd showered, then stood in front of my mirror and changed ten times.

Shorts and a T-shirt were the casual result of that angst.

Super seductive choice, Andie.

Alas, the fear of appearing overly keen won over the sexy dress, the sexy jeans, and the sexy crop top.

I parked outside Sascha's bungalow and got out of Ella F.

He stood in the open doorway. "I hoped you'd come."

Nothing could have kept me away. If Wade hadn't given me marching orders, I would have snuck away an hour later.

Stepping into his embrace, I inhaled our scent. Pine, musk, river water, and sweat played with vanilla, oranges, liquorice, and pumpkin spice.

I sighed. *Will everything be okay, Sascha?*

Yes, mate. I'll do everything in my power to see it done.

They were words I'd waited a lifetime to hear—or so it felt. Rising on tiptoe, I brushed my lips against his.

We both shuddered with what it promised.

I played with the wet ends of his brown hair. He'd just showered too. Was that in response to me driving over?

My silent laughter swept outward.

Sascha trailed his nose along mine. "What's funny?"

So many things.

Nothing at all.

I looked into honey eyes I loved. "Sascha. Will you take me to bed?"

He froze on the spot. Turned to stone.

"You need to promise me an unforgettable night though," I whispered in his ear, uncaring that any wolf who was awake could hear my words. "This guy's been holding out on me, so it's been a while."

"Oh yeah? Why did he do that?" Sascha unfroze and slid his hand to the bottom of my shorts.

Clearly, he didn't object to the outfit.

I ground into him. "He said he wanted it to be special. I think he was luring me in."

"Sounds like he was using it as a weapon."

"Mmm. Should I be angry at him for that, do you think?" I pressed kisses up his jawline.

He groaned and turned his head to speak against my open and ready mouth. "No, you should admire his..."

I ground into him again.

"Have sex with him," Sascha blurted.

A slow grin spread across my lips. "Gladly."

Taking my hand, Sascha led me away from his bungalow.

I glanced back. This seemed counter-productive. "Where are we going?"

"There's a place for this thing."

He deposited me in his pickup truck.

Sascha burned rubber leaving pack lands and drove us farther east. We wound up to the place we'd once come to for our failed date.

He turned down a dirt road, and the pickup screeched to a stop.

A wood cabin. "What is this?"

"A place for couples going through the mating call."

I shimmied out Sascha's side of the truck, and he swung me into his arms.

Sascha stopped and gazed downward. "Andie, I don't want to deny the heat tonight. What do you want?"

He was only asking that question *after* bringing me to the mating cabin. I withheld my laughter. "Guess you'll find out."

Sascha paled.

He held me close and managed to open the door.

I eyed the inside of the cabin.

It smelled clean, but I had to know. "How many couples have used this?"

"No one. We're the first mating since it was built."

My brothel germ concerns melted away. "Nice to have somewhere private."

He grinned. "This was built in sympathy for the pack actually. Mating couples in the heat aren't very considerate and have endless endurance—so I'm told."

Oh. Right.

Sascha sat me on the bed.

My eyes narrowed. "This has been freshly laundered."

He scanned my face. "I'd thought something might happen after the ball. I wanted to be ready."

The thought of making love in dusty sheets didn't appeal. "You may proceed."

He yanked on my legs and I flopped back, laughing.

I propped myself up on my elbows. "Sascha?"

"Mate."

My stomach swooped. "I've never been with a Luther before."

His nostrils flared. "I sincerely hope not, little bird."

"If I do something wrong, will you tell me?" *Ugh,* embarrassing. I flopped back again and covered my face.

Gentle hands forced my hands away.

"Beautiful wolf," Sascha said. "I've never been with someone raised as human. Will you tell me if I do anything wrong too?"

The words were only meant for my comfort, but I accepted them at face value.

My cheeks warmed. "Yes."

Sascha leaned in to kiss me, and it was like stepping into a warm bath. We melded together, slipping further into each other than humanly possible. Our thoughts merged into a single, steady stream of consciousness.

Our scents were indistinguishable.

Our hearts thudded in unison.

The bond *burned* between us.

I paused for breath. "I love you so much."

"And I you."

His neck muscles were taut, and I smelled his restraint, but he didn't hurry.

I lifted up as Sascha worked my T-shirt up and unclipped my bra. Growling, he bowed his head to my chest and worked there until my claws started to extend.

He left me squirming to remove his clothes, then returned to unbutton my shorts and slide them down.

Skimming his palms up my thighs, he sighed. "So fucking beautiful." In my mind he added, *You can't be real.*

I'm here and I'm not leaving ever again. I knew it the second Wade drove through the manor gates after the game.

Sascha had waited for me.

I'd waited for him.

And now was our time to be.

Sascha whispered a sweet kiss on my lips. He spread my thighs and settled between them. I wriggled at his breath on my sensitive skin.

He kissed both of my inner thighs, and I clutched at the blankets.

Sascha sucked my clit into his mouth.

My body began to shake.

Sometimes, he tortured me with cruel slowness. Neither of us could do that tonight. His mouth worked furiously. His tongue circled and laved and circled again.

A soft cry left my lips, and instead of tensing, my body went entirely limp.

It knew what was coming.

I had nothing against the fire licking my body. "Sascha."

At least I tried to say his name.

My eyelids fluttered and my body trembled violently under his touch. Sascha inserted a finger inside me and moved his hand at Luther speed.

It shouldn't be possible to feel more.

My mind couldn't fathom more.

I arched off the bed, screaming as I shattered into a million pieces.

He didn't relent. The pieces of me continued to shatter.

Break.

Savage snarls ripped from him as I gasped and writhed, shrieking as pleasure turned to pain. And *still*, I wanted it.

More.

Always more.

I tried to shove him on his back, but Sascha didn't budge. His eyes were wild. He gripped my ankles, and I yanked free to kick him in the chest.

Rolling off the bed, I placed my back to the nearest wall and grinned at Sascha. "That all you got?"

Shoulders heaving, he lifted the bed and threw it out of the way.

My grin faded.

Blurring forward, he slammed his hands either side of my head.

"Not nearly," he breathed.

I reached for his erection.

Sascha spun me to face the wall, shoving me against it. His hand delved between my legs.

"So wet for me," he purred. "Do you like this, beautiful wolf?"

I'd never been so fucking turned on in my life, but I snarled at him, pushing my ass out to arch my lower back.

Sascha released me, and I nearly slipped free of his hold before he slammed me back in place.

Cheek against the wall, I moaned, "Please."

Gripping the back of my neck with one hand, he guided his tip to my entrance.

Oh, fuck. Yes!

"You're *mine.*" His voice boomed in my ears and in my head.

Sascha battered at my mental defences, and I automatically threw everything I had back at him.

He hovered outside my body as we both attempted to seize control of the inner battle. Giving up wasn't an option for either of us.

We broke.

At the same time, we surrendered to each other completely.

I widened my stance, and Sascha pushed all the way inside me.

Legs shaking again, I rested my forehead on the wall. *Oh my god.*

Sascha released my neck and stroked my back, unmoving within me. Leaning forward, he kissed my shoulder over Greyson's bite mark before drawing out.

We both shook.

"Andie?" he panted.

"I want it all. No more waiting."

Sascha growled and shoved inside again. My scream was lost in his roared shout as he settled into a rapid, brutal pace.

I shoved back onto him, keeping pace like my life depended on it. His fingers found my clit, and I lost the tiny remaining grip on my senses as he pressed and circled, never breaking in his ruthless rhythm.

It was coming again.

Sascha swore as I started to tighten around him.

He clamped his arm over my hips and pulled my body flush against his. My head rested back on his shoulder.

"You feel so fucking good." He brushed his cheek against mine.

Me? How about him?

My body tightened until Sascha was forced to slow his pace. The firm strokes undid me.

Oh!

A single growled word ripped from my throat. "*Mate.*"

He squeezed my clit—as though I'd needed any extra help—and white light exploded behind my eyes. In my mind. Through my body.

I was carried away to the place only Sascha could take me.

To the place only he could find me.

His roar was distant in my ears, but the feel of our body—of *him* within me—was never stronger.

We floated for an age.

But in minutes or hours or days, I became aware of my panting breaths.

... Our movement had stopped.

There was something hard under my cheek. The floor?

We were on the floor.

When?

"Sascha." My voice cracked. "Are you alive?"

His chuckle sent delicious aftershocks through me—considering we were still attached and all.

"I don't think so, mate."

"Neither am I. What do we do?"

"Just stay here?"

He was spooned around me. Sounded good.

"Did I hurt you, Andie?" he asked. "Things got rough. Something came over me."

I inhaled his concern. "Me too. Was that a kinky wolf thing?" I'd wanted him to hunt me and prove his strength. Hot didn't begin to describe it.

Sex with Sascha Greyson got two thumbs up.

"I suppose so. No one told me that would happen though, or I would've said something."

"I know. I enjoyed myself. Don't worry."

He released a pent-up breath.

"So," I said. "Not to ruin the mood. Just checking I can't get pregnant." I'd meant to ask prior.

Oops.

"We aren't mated." He kissed up the back of my neck. "You can't get pregnant yet. Even if we mate, Luthers don't reproduce quickly—though quicker than other supernatural races."

"Is that why you don't have brothers and sisters?"

"My mother nearly died giving birth to me," he said. "My father refuses to put her at risk again."

That explained a lot.

"Hey, Sascha?" I shivered with each kiss he gave me.

"Mate."

"What happens next?"

"As soon as we separate, the heat will consume us both."

"And you really like the idea of that," I murmured.

His lips curved against my shoulder blade. "How can you tell?"

Sascha was ready for round two.

"A gut feeling," I said demurely.

"Do you want to accept the heat?"

I'd torture him some more. "How long does it last?"

"Hours or days. In cases where the heat is denied, heats err on the longer side."

There'd been a whole heap of denial in recent months.

No joke.

Twisting slightly, I delivered him with a soft, lazy kiss.

Smiling at the dreamy haze in his gorgeous eyes, I slid off him at last.

Painful desire struck me with the force of a waterfall. I just managed to rest a palm on his chest as his eyes flooded black. I knew mine were the same.

"Do your worst, mate," I whispered.

The red flames consumed us.

36

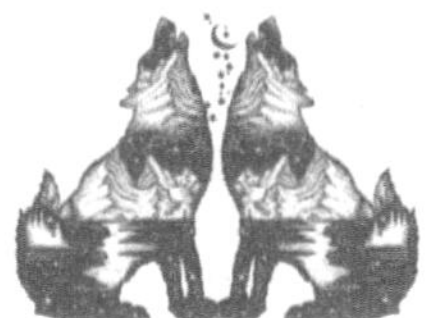

I stretched on the bed, Sascha's scent surrounding me.

The sound of a trickling stream reached my ears. My lips curved.

Our bungalow.

Mate? Sascha spoke in my mind.

A woman goes through the heat for a guy and wakes alone?

A woman goes through the heat and sleeps for an entire day after.

I bolted upright, staring down. Sascha's black T-shirt covered me. *A whole day?*

Fuck. What day was it now?

My phone was plugged in on the bedside table.

I gasped. *It's Monday!*

Sascha walked into the room.

"Five days." I pressed a hand to my cheek. "The truce."

I stood and wobbled in a circle, trying to locate clothing. Any clothing would be great. Showing up in this T-shirt... not so much.

"Mate."

"Everyone will think we've forgotten."

He grabbed my shoulders. "Andie. I woke yesterday. The pack alerted the tribe to the delay. Everything is fine."

I sagged against him. "Are you sure?"

"As sure as I am that you need food and water."

My stomach rumbled in reply. "I feel incredible."

A warm understanding filled me unlike anything I'd experienced. I felt Sascha's presence inside my body—all of him. I'd gained a radar of his exact wellbeing. And it didn't feel new either. This development was vaguely familiar. It must have come on after the sex meet and really settled in during the heat.

He gripped my chin and delivered a soul-affirming kiss. "So do I. Thank you for that gift."

I hummed. "Back at ya."

He kissed me again. "Food and drink. You haven't had anything in five days."

Sascha led me to his wicker furniture and pushed a glass of water into my hands.

I gulped back the cool liquid, and he filled the glass again.

After two more, I slowed. "Maybe I was thirsty."

"So was I. When I woke in what remained of the cabin—"

"What remained," I repeated.

"—I drove us back here and nearly collapsed outside the pack house. Something my wolves found extremely amusing."

Four days of sex would do that to a person.

"Will we remember everything in time?" Already, pieces were coming back to me. I recalled our twin sighs and hot gasps. His hands roaming my body. Him bearing down on me as I sprinted through the trees.

There was a waterfall involved at some point.

Oh... we definitely bit each other.

I sucked in a breath, assaulted by a montage of him slamming into me over and over again. He'd only ever stopped to heal me before we'd entered another round. For hours and *days*. *God,* it had felt like nothing would ever rid me of that lust. And that incredible warmth that connected us now tinged every memory of the heat I'd regained so far.

Wow.

His eyes gleamed. "It took me a few hours to get all the details back, but yes."

I pursed my lips. *Dammit,* he already knew.

A heat with you defied all of my expectations, he thought at me.

My chest loosened.

I grabbed a fistful of *Corrie's Chocolate Chip Chocos*.

Sascha stroked my hair. "I arranged a meeting with the head team while you slept. We agreed nothing would be signed until you woke, but everyone was agreeable to opening negotiations. I wanted you to wake to a different future."

I met his honey gaze. "Thank you. You didn't have to do that."

"You did so much of this yourself. I wanted to."

"It's nice to skip the tedious part for a change," I admitted.

He slid a document from underneath the food tray. "Here's what we've figured out so far. Let me know your thoughts. I think it's pretty near perfect. Currently, our pack and your tribe are in agreement about the contents."

There was an *actual* truce contract before me right now.

So many times, I never thought we'd get here.

"I'll leave you to look it over," he said. "Would you like me to call a meeting tomorrow morning?"

"Tonight, please."

"Done, beautiful. One more thing. Wade said to check your phone when you woke, or he'd smash your saxophone. I snuck into the manor and stole it just in case he was serious."

I followed the tilt of his head to find my sax resting atop my black case.

Sascha left the bungalow.

Booker?

Yo.

That was a new one. She was a slang sponge. *How are you?*

I'd like you to stop talking and eat more. More water too.

My heart squeezed at the deep contentment under her response.

Returning to the bedside table, I grabbed my phone.

Ten messages from Wade.

Bet you're having sex.
But seriously, where are you? The meeting's about to start.
Daaaamn, we could erupt into war, but you stopped to have SEX? Who even are you? So proud, baby girl.
Two days... $10 says you can't walk after.
Three days. I'm open-minded, but shit, Andie.
What's Sascha wearing? Suspenders and an axe, plz.
FOUR DAYS. Stop having sex for five damn seconds!
Lol. Just occurred to me that the pack literally could have buried you and I just calmly accepted the ol' sex marathon cover story.
... Omg, are you actually dead?
Either way, R.I.P Andie's vagina.

Laughing, I called him.

"Is this the ghost of Andie Thana?" Wade answered.

"This is the living version of Andie. How are things?"

"*How are things?*" he screeched. "Five days. What the hell happened?"

As he asked, I was rammed with a memory of me and Sascha tearing apart the cabin in a far more dangerous version of the dominance game we'd touched upon in the sex meet.

Neither of us had backed down for most of that day. But when we did...

I clamped my thighs together as a burst of heat surged through me.

"A lot, and I mean a *lot*, of great sex," I said weakly.

Wade exhaled. "Thank god. You'll be so much easier to tolerate now. You were so tense all the time."

"Tell me about it. Don't feel tense now."

"Bet Sascha's muscles were tense though."

I grinned. "How has the tribe been?"

"You chose the best time to embark on a sex quest. Everyone was hungover the first day. Most were hungover the second day. With the game over, stewards have just enjoyed normal life without the practices and meetings. They do want an answer though. Limbo isn't nice for anyone."

I flipped back the first page of the treaty. "Just reading over it now. Anything of particular interest?"

"The head team are happy with it. We didn't want to take the proposal to the tribe without you there, but the contract includes all the voted clauses, some extras that we borrowed from the Victratum contract, and also a few bits and bobs from the draft contract with the vampires. Oh, Basilia got in touch. I told her you were having sex. She said *enjoy*."

Of course she did.

"Have the Vissimo sent back another revision?" I asked.

"Yep. That will take more work to finalise though."

The vampires were into closing every potential loophole for sure.

"Sascha's scheduling a meeting for tonight. Hopefully, we can hammer things out and finalise this thing."

"I can't wait." Wade's voice gained a sly edge. "You may be interested to know that *Sascha* was very impartial in the negotiations. It was almost as if he was representing both of you. That's why we were able to get this done so quickly."

A slow smile spread across my face.

"My conclusion," he said. "Is that you have magical lady parts. My only critique is that if you'd had sex with him three months ago, this could have ended a lot sooner."

"Goodbye, Wade."

"Next time, put out for the team!"

I hung up and traced the lingering smile on my lips before picking up the peace contract between pack and tribe.

37

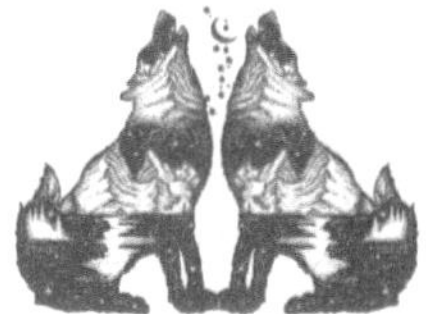

On my gold stage, I played the last verse of "You Make My Dreams" by Daryl Hall and John Oates on my saxophone, swaying to the upbeat rhythm.

Patrons from the big wide filled *The Dens*—even more so than my first encounters with the place.

Rounding off with two shrill staccato notes, I swept a small bow and prepared for my next song.

An arm circled my waist and I was plucked off the stage.

Sascha deposited me in front of him. "You're done for the night, beautiful wolf."

His gaze roamed over my curve-hugging gold dress. I'd dressed to match the stage again—sue me.

"Like what you see?" I held my sax aside to loop an arm around his neck and press against him.

"Always and increasingly."

His bemused tone reflected my thoughts on the subject. If there was a limit to this bond thing, we hadn't found it. One day, I'd just combust and rise from the ashes as a sex toy instead of a phoenix.

"You're done for the night," he repeated. "Mum said you need to get enough sleep before tomorrow."

A nearly one-century-old werewolf was conveying his mother's orders. Adorable.

"Guess I should listen then." I peeked up through my lashes.

He regarded me seriously. "I want to show you something."

I inhaled his nervous anticipation. "Okay."

He grabbed my case while I collected my water and phone. I greeted the incoming deejay before following Sascha through the bar toward the casino.

"This way," he said.

"You're very bossy tonight," I noted.

"I'm not usually bossy though."

Do you think something is up, girl?

Booker hummed. *He's sweating.*

He was. "Everything alright?"

Sascha forced a grin.

We weaved between the last tables and entered the exchange area where patrons happily cashed in chips—some of them not so happily.

We stopped in front of a large board with a velvet curtain over the top.

Sascha lifted my saxophone over my head and rested it atop the case out of the way of any drunk patrons

He took both my hands. "Andie. Tomorrow is our mating ceremony. We've come a long way to get here. I wanted to take this chance to say that if you choose me, you'll be assured of a supportive and caring partner with a proven track record in the bedroom."

Oh my god. Was he pitching himself to me? "Sascha, there's no need—"

"If the privacy thing is an issue, I'll build a cabin elsewhere for us. Any concerns, then I want to hear them. You know I'll work with you on this."

Lack of privacy wasn't an issue.

"Where has this come from?" I asked weakly.

We'd both been tense in the last week with the upcoming mating ceremony and signing.

Sascha yanked the velvet curtain away.

I stared at the board.

CLOSING
Patrons, please be advised that *The Dens* Casino will soon close.
The bar area will remain open.
Exciting new ventures await.
Sincerely,
The Pack

He was closing the casino?

Sounds of dismay echoed at my back as patrons caught sight of the sign.

"Why?" I whispered.

Sascha stood ramrod straight. "We only opened it to fund our efforts in the game. You don't like casinos, and I don't want you involved in something you don't agree with. This is my mating gift to you."

Crap, are we supposed to get Sascha and Greyson a gift?

We are a fucking gift, Booker retorted.

"Sascha." I read the sign again. "Thank you. You didn't have to do this. Won't the pack miss the money?"

"We have plenty saved from the casino, and we'll still run the businesses for Clay."

Clay was included in the pack's trust land.

He gestured to the back room. "We'll convert that area into something different. Maybe a club or function area. Plus, there are several tourism options I'd like to pursue. Outdoor work is perfect for the pack, and Deception Valley is filled with opportunity—particularly with the airport up and running."

Local businesses had already profited from the airport opening. The airport was also the reason for the two-and-a-half-month delay in our mating ceremony. Apparently, the mating of a pack leader was a big deal. Though our wolves hadn't possessed the means to visit the outside world, they'd managed to track down other Luthers online who were now attending tomorrow.

Two members of our pack had already found their mates too.

I ran my hands up Sascha's arms. He was so tense. "Really. Thank you. You know you have nothing to worry about tomorrow, right?"

His smile was far more of a grimace. "Yes."

That was a no.

I stretched upward to kiss him. "I love you."

"Love you. Mum says you need to get rest." Sascha dragged me back through the bar and shoved my sax and case into my arms. "Go rest."

He marched off and Mandy joined me.

"You saw that too?" I murmured.

"You know how human brides are called bridezillas? It's the opposite for wolves."

No kidding?

"Seriously," she whispered. "Don't set him off."

Sascha stopped at the staff door and glared back at us.

Jesus. "Better go. You're still helping me to get ready tomorrow?"

She walked with me to the door. "I'll sit there while Wade and Cam fuss, yes."

I grinned and strode out of *The Dens*.

"Hear the news, gorgeous?" Hairy called.

"Sure did. How's the pack about the casino closing?"

"Like anyone was going to argue with him in this mood."

Sounded like Sascha had shown me his most relaxed face over the last week.

Hairy winked. "We are actually okay with it. Gotta keep our new top female happy."

If someone told me a year ago that I'd become *top female* by age twenty-one and be okay with it, I would've punched them in the throat.

Laughter bubbled up my throat. "Thanks, Hairy. See ya tomorrow?"

"Wouldn't miss it for my mate."

Lie.

I walked around the back of *The Dens* to Ella F.

Someone gripped my wrist, and I lifted my closed fist, spinning on the spot.

Wade wrinkled his nose. "If you bruise up my face before my big day, I'll be pissed."

"I couldn't smell you over the garbage." I lowered my arm.

He glanced around. "What garbage?"

Oh. I smiled at the shadows. "Nice to see you, if not smell you."

Basilia Le Spyre slipped from them. "I could take offence to that. But ditto."

She tossed me her oil, and I dabbed some under my nose.

Lavender.

"Come on." Wade looped his arms through ours. "Party at the manor. Women and extra cool men only. Tommy and Cam are waiting in the Jeep. We're going to successfully get you drunk."

"Did you clear this with Sascha?" I glanced in the direction of *The Dens.*

"You're joking, right? Guy's stressed to snapping point. This is a secret hen's party."

"Okay, but I'm not *really* getting married."

Wade opened the back door of the Jeep and Basilia faced me.

"You're mating with a werewolf forever. *Immortal* forever," she said. "This is 100 percent marriage."

Nerves erupted in my gut. *Fuck.*

It was.

Wade jammed a gaudy veil on my head. "You look better. Let's go. After our last failed drunk attempt, I've written out a new method."

He'd made it his mission in life to get me inebriated since Victratum ended and the truce was signed. So far, he'd failed.

When he succeeded, I had a strong feeling my friend would leave the valley for a time.

"Bring it on." I lifted my head. "Maybe quick. Sascha's coming."

Wade shoved me in the vehicle and leaped onto the driver's seat.

We burned rubber leaving *The Dens.*

I glanced back and saw Sascha staring after us. "Busted."

I won't be out late, I thought at him.

Good. Because Mum said you need rest.

Matezilla Sascha was too cute. *Promise, I will. See you tomorrow, handsome.*

I'd planned to stay at the manor tonight anyway.

Maybe this was far more like a wedding day than I'd imagined.

Tommy leaned forward. "Wade says you're pretty much living on pack lands now but you're still leading the tribe. Is that strange?"

"It feels right to be involved with all parts of the valley." Spending more time on pack lands was a natural result of wanting to spend every moment with Sascha. With things gradually defrosting between tribe and werewolves, the stewards had taken my overnight and weekend absences really well. Of course, it wasn't ideal long-term, but I had a plan for that.

Cam peered over her shoulder. "Mayor. Chieftess, and—what are you in the pack again?"

Dammit. "Top female."

The Jeep exploded with loud laughter.

"Goals." Basilia grinned.

"A modern female's dream," I answered. "Is the entire royal family here with you?"

"They'll fly in tomorrow morning. Kyros is at the manor, but Wade said he has to stay in his room tonight."

The vampire princess clearly found this hilarious.

Only my best friend would tell a vampire crown-prince what to do.

We drove through the manor gates, and my eyes rounded at the giant marquee covering the manicured front lawn. "You've gone all out."

Wade's voice trembled. "Only the best for my girl."

Cam eyed him. "Are you crying?"

He exited the vehicle and slammed the door.

"Definitely crying," she said.

Outside, pack women mingled with female stewards. Pascal was speaking with Evelyn. Mandy with Trixie. Rhona stood apart but had a smile on her face.

It was early days, but I knew—I *knew*—we could do this.

Tommy and Cam slipped out and sandwiched Wade.

But Basilia remained behind. She studied me for a beat. "Congratulations, Andie. You did it."

"It finally feels right."

The billionaire shot me a gleaming look. "Bet winning felt good too."

Well… couldn't deny it. I frowned. "Hey, could I ask you something serious?"

She shrugged. "Sure."

"How easily do vampires get drunk?"

"Stay still," a bleary-eyed Wade snapped at me.

We were in my manor bedroom, which was mostly empty now I'd moved in with Sascha. *Really* moved in, too—I'd put my clothes in the wardrobe and drawers and everything.

Tommy lay in the foetal position on the floor. Cam had her sunglasses on inside as she finished my hair and make-up—Wade directed her unnecessarily. On the window seat, Basilia filed her nails.

Mandy was flopped on the bed, playing on her phone.

The humans in the room made the mistake of trying to keep up with the supernaturals last night. Neither Basilia or I achieved drunkenness for more than a few minutes, but it was amazing how quickly dummies could be arranged in erotic scenes with a really fast vampire helping out.

As my wolf, Booker wasn't affected by alcohol, but she hadn't seen fit to stop me.

Rhona entered the room. "Nearly ready? People have left for the meeting hill."

"She's ready when she's ready," Wade hissed.

My sister scowled. "Not my fault you overindulged last night. Don't treat others like shit."

Vampires and werewolves wouldn't take Wade on, but my sister would.

He grumbled an apology.

Dabbing my lip gloss on, Cam straightened. "There. Radiant bride."

"I'm not getting married," I said mutely.

Rhona helped me up, and I faced the mirror. Cam had put my hair up today. Wavy tendrils softened and framed my face. It looked natural but took her two hours to achieve.

Wade had insisted my make-up stay minimal—a simple smoky eye and peach lip with a peach hue on my cheeks.

Tommy crawled to the wardrobe. "Dress."

With Wade and Cam's help, I slipped it on overhead.

The boho dress was white. Full-length sleeves, a low-cut back, and scoop neckline flowed into a simple long gown. The lace pattern gave the appearance of most of my skin showing through the dress, but a nude slip was stitched beneath.

"It's so beautiful, Cam," I said again. "Thank you. Please open up a shop here. Your things are to die for."

Basilia lifted her focus from her nails and made a small sound of surprise. "That's impressive. Let me know if you want help with start-up costs for that shop."

Cam paused in twitching my dress into place. "Really?"

"If your manufacturing process is ethical and environmentally friendly—which I assume with Ni Tiaki values, it is—then I'm interested."

My friend's mouth bobbed.

A knock sounded at the open doorway. Kyros opened the door. "Ready, my beauty? Our family landed. We should arrive at the ceremony ahead of them."

King Julius was coming to my wolf wedding today.

It made sense to tie a happy event to the signing of the alliance between pack, tribe, and clan. I hoped this alliance would pave the way to healing for the pack—and Vissimo too.

Tommy and Basilia left with Kyros. Mandy joined them to navigate them to the correct place.

Cam slipped silver foot chains over my feet, clasping them around my ankles. Wade slipped thin bangles up my forearms, and —blinking suspiciously fast—set a sunflower crown upon my head.

Leaning forward, I kissed his cheek. "Thank you for my party last night, Wade. And for everything."

He dashed away a tear. "I'm okay."

I squeezed his hands. "You're okay."

He's not okay, Booker noted.

Nope.

"Ready to go?" Rhona tossed her keys and caught them again.

"One more thing." I grabbed my phone off the dresser and opened my *Eastway Bank* app.

Seven hundred and thirty-two dollars of Mum's debt remained.

Wade and Cam peered over my shoulders.

I had fifteen hundred in my personal account.

"You're paying it all off?" Cam asked as I typed in the full amount.

Sure fucking was. Closing my eyes briefly, I took a deep breath, then clicked Confirm Transfer.

Thank You. Payment Confirmed.

My friends sandwiched me in a hug, and I grinned.

"Congrats," Rhona called.

I smiled at her.

"This time stay out of debt," Wade said.

Well, I still had student loans, but they were interest-free for now. Honestly, it would just be nice to pay off *my* debt for a change, instead of Mum's.

Walking to Sascha today with less financial burden felt right too.

Lighter than I could remember feeling since Mum's death, I climbed into Rhona's silver Bentley. She arranged me in the car and closed the door.

All three of them were silent on the drive to Lake Thana.

Of course, they chose *now* to stop talking.

Oh, fuck. I was totally, *totally* getting wolf married. I breathed thinly and did my best not to wipe my sweaty-ass palms on Cam's beautiful creation.

This was ridiculous. Why was I nervous?

Sascha wanted me.

I wanted him.

But he had acted strangely this past week. That didn't mean anything, right?

Greyson hasn't really spoken to me during the last few morning runs, Booker admitted.

Crap. We were both nervous as hell.

Rhona drove up the hill road, and I looked over Lake Thana, which extended to my left. Clean up in the lake took *weeks* after the last battle there.

Since the land fell in tribe territory, they'd taken over management of the Water businesses. But we'd employed most of the pack—they were far more experienced than us in that department. The other wolves had spread between Sandstone, Timber, and Iron.

However, in the last month, the head team and I had put together a long-term plan to decrease production across the board. Exclusivity wasn't a bad thing, but not caring for the environment was unacceptable. In my opinion, during Herc and my grandfather's stint as head steward, the tribe had become too greedy in what they took from the land.

We didn't need to keep that up.

Rhona parked behind the crowd.

The *huge* crowd.

"Fuck me," I whispered. How many guest wolves were here? There were over two thousand in attendance. Someone had set up freakin' *bleachers* for those at the back.

Wade and Cam left the car, but I gripped Rhona's arm when she went to do the same.

"Walk down there with me," I blurted.

"I thought this wasn't a wedding," she said drily.

"I lied to myself."

She smirked, then frowned, giving me a second to understand exactly what I just asked of her. Please walk me down the aisle to your father's murderer.

Rhona pursed her lips. "It would be my honour as your sister."

I sniffed.

"Don't cry."

Yes, ma'am.

Wade hauled me out, and Cam arranged my dress around my bare feet.

"White is for virgins," I remarked. "This is false advertising."

Chuckles from the supernatural in the audience told me they hadn't missed the comment.

Oops.

Wade and Cam went on ahead, and soon, a slow drumbeat started—something pack gammas contributed to most ceremonies apparently.

Rhona held out her hand, and I took it.

Sascha was waiting.

My legs dragged me toward him, and I focused on my breath and ignoring the crowd as I approached.

Grass tickled my bare feet, and I welcomed the soft autumn breeze cooling my warm face.

The crowd murmured in appreciation when they saw me,

which Wade would absolutely brag about later. My friend stood at the inside of the front row, balling his damn eyes out.

I paused to give him a one-armed hug. "I love you."

He babbled a wordless reply, and I kissed his cheek, sharing an amused glance with Pascal and Cam over his shoulder.

Stop kissing other men and come here, beautiful wolf.

I continued with Rhona and my gaze locked with Sascha's at last.

Gorgeous, *gorgeous* honey eyes.

Their effect on me only grew each day. I swallowed hard as Rhona halted us in front of him.

Sascha tore his focus from me to look at her.

Her dislike was plain.

His regret was equally plain.

"If you hurt her," Rhona spoke, "then I'll slit your throat and take the land penalty on the chin without regret."

Yikes.

"If you love and care for her," she added, "then in time, maybe we'll be a family."

Sascha nodded. "I consider myself warned. I've seen you in combat."

Rhona passed my hand into his, and the tension drained from us. The world disappeared as I stepped into his embrace and sighed.

"I missed you."

Sascha buried his face in my updo, inhaling. "You get more beautiful each day."

Both of us jumped as someone cleared their throat.

"If you don't mind." Alexei's face was carved from stone.

Whatever he thought about me though, he was here for his son.

"Proceed," Sascha told him.

His father cocked a brow at the order but raised a microphone to his lips for the benefit of the tribe. "Thank you for coming together today to witness the decision of my son, Sascha Alarick Greyson and his potential mate, Andie Charise Booker Thana."

Getting rid of the name Booker didn't feel right when my wolf had claimed that as her name.

Alexei recited a brief history of the mating process for the benefit of the gathered Vissimo and stewards.

"Do all concerned parties agree to voice their decision now?" Alexei glanced between us.

I looked at Sascha. *What?*

Follow me. He smiled. "I, Sascha, agree."

His fangs and claws slid free, eliciting an interested hum from our vampire guests. As black flooded his eyes, gravel filled his voice. "I, Greyson, agree."

Your turn, little bird.

"I, Andie, agree."

I allowed my fangs and claws to burst free. A lesser amount of gravel roughened my voice, but the tone certainly wasn't human. "*I can't wait to sink my fangs into you.*"

Heat flooded my face. *Booker!*

Greyson replied seriously. "*Can I sink my fangs into you too?*"

"*I hope so. I like to be hand-fed crispy bacon in the morning too.*"

"*I'll see it done.*"

"*Then I, Booker, agree.*"

I pressed a hand to my burning cheek as my fangs and claws retracted.

Sascha joined the audience in laughter, pulling me in for a swift kiss.

Alexei raised a hand for silence. "A mate is for eternity. From this moment forward, should you both choose, your lives, bloodlines, body, mind, and spirit will be one. But what you possess must be respected daily, never taken for granted, and held in utmost regard. No one and no *thing* can come between you." His attention fixed on me. "That is what it means to be mated."

Didn't I know it.

"Face each other now."

Sascha growled slightly at the order but did as bade.

My chest tightened as I faced the werewolf that I loved more than was humanly possible.

"Sascha, Pack Leader of The Deception Valley pack. My son. Do you find this female wolf worthy to be your mate through life? To trust and cherish and protect?"

"She is more than worthy," he said simply.

Tears sparked in my eyes.

Alexei tilted his head to me. "Andie, Head Steward of the Ni Tiaki, Mayor of Deception Valley, and top female of the pack, do you find this male wolf worthy to be your mate through life? To trust and cherish and protect?"

My throat closed. I nodded, taking both of Sascha's hands. "There's no one worthier."

Greyson was back. "*Mate*."

Booker slid into the front seat again. "*Mine*."

Since the mating call began, a tension had resided in me—in *us*. I'd gotten so used to the subtle angst. But now it drained away. The deepest parts of my mind and heart relaxed.

Sascha tilted my chin up. "Too late to leave now."

I threw myself at him and fixed my lips to his. The cheers of the crowd melted away, and heat swept through my body as our bond urged us closer and higher. Sascha groaned into my mouth as I swept my tongue alongside his.

He inched up the hem of my dress as I started on his shirt buttons.

"Son. Daughter. Perhaps another time?"

We both blinked at Evelyn.

Sascha let go of my dress "Of course, Mother."

I released his shirt. *Oops*.

He took my hand, and we walked back down the aisle together.

At the back, I spotted Basilia and Kyros standing with the other vampire royals. A few more Vissimo who I hadn't seen before had joined. My eyes dragged over their row until I found the king and queen.

King Julius waved at me, practically beaming.

... Uh, okay?

Basilia glared down the row at him.

Sascha lifted me into the tray of his blue pickup. Leroy winked back at me from the driver's seat. Tonight, everyone would party on pack lands. I couldn't wait for the tribe to see the wolf territory—most of them for the first time.

My mate sat on the hay bales in the tray and cradled me on his lap.

Leroy led the convoy back along Lake Thana.

I peered ahead at the bridge connecting the north and south sides of the valley. Members of the public lined it.

They tossed flower petals over us.

I laughed. "Did you plan this?"

"I believe the council put out the word. Most think we got married because you probably got pregnant at the Deception Valley Ball."

Oh my god. I suppose we'd only known each other half a year. *Hilarious.*

Leroy drove us under the red oaks lining the south side of the valley.

I looped my arms around Sascha's neck and rested my forehead against his. *I love you, mate.*

Happiness filled him. *Thank you for fighting for us.*

Didn't seem fair to leave you with all the work.

The fields on pack lands were harvested last week, and the marquee from last night had been set up here. Tables and seats dotted the tent space. The sun was high and bright, and the pack had scattered benches and cushions around.

"You've never seen Luthers celebrate." Sascha lifted me off the tray.

"Should I be worried?"

"Mildly."

Cars piled in, and deltas directed them to parking spots.

We walked into the marquee, and King Julius and Queen Titania joined us soon after with Kyros and Basilia.

Pack leaders came and went, congratulating me and Sascha on our mating. Most seemed bemused by the presence of so many humans and more baffled by the attendance of Vissimo. This situation must be unique in the supernatural world.

Pascal approached, and I hugged her.

"You look stunning." She squeezed me tight.

"Thank you. How are the tribe doing?"

"Well. Fifty stewards are delegated to monitoring the tribe in case some partake of too much alcohol and do something idiotic. Most stewards are curious to see pack territory."

Curiosity was good.

Alexei approached with Evelyn.

He slid a look at his son before staring at King Julius.

The vampire king didn't react.

"The pack received your formal apology," Alexei said stiffly.

"I'm glad," the king replied.

"I led this pack when we lost thousands to your clan, but as much blame rests with me as it does with you. In the interest of not wasting thousands of more lives, I'll put the past where it belongs." He shot a look at me. "A cunning wolf dragged a promise out of me that I never expected I'd need to uphold."

He'd agreed to start afresh if I managed to pull this stunt off.

If he wanted to use me as an excuse, then that was fine by me, but that wasn't why Alexei was burying the past.

"She is a cunning wolf," King Julius replied. "The most enterprising and intelligent woman I've met of her age."

Basilia narrowed her eyes. Kyros seemed to be struggling not to laugh.

"Shall we get the formalities over with so the celebration can begin?" I gestured to the table behind us.

Two members from each party were required to sign.

I grabbed Basilia as she moved to take the seat beside King Julius. "Am I missing something?"

She huffed. "Julius's amusing himself at my expense. Let's just say he wasn't so accepting of me."

A glance at the king confirmed he was certainly enjoying her irritation.

"How about you help out with mine then? We can just swap." I jerked my head at where Alexei sat next to my mate.

King Julius lost his smirk.

It relocated on Basilia's lips. "Deal."

I took my place between Sascha and Pascal at the table.

The alliance contract was fucking huge, but I didn't mind that so much. Misunderstanding posed the greatest risk to a venture like this—something the vampires probably understood.

The Vissimo signed first.

Luthers signed second—Alexei clenching his jaw as he did so.

Pascal and I exchanged a smile.

I signed above the *Head Steward* title and slid it onward to the older woman. I listened to her swallow and smelled her grief intensify.

"So others don't need to hide," I said softly to her.

Tears were in her eyes. "This would have made Daniil so happy."

She signed.

Gesturing to Wade for the microphone, I accepted Sascha's hand to rise.

"Stewards of the Ni Tiaki. Luthers of the Deception Valley pack. Vissimo of Clan Sundulus. Our alliance is sealed and complete. May we always prosper together in peace and against those who seek to disrupt the harmony and safety of our lives." I waited for the quiet applause to subside.

Like me, I was sure the thoughts of many had already turned to our next task. I hoped our efforts would always remain a prevention and nothing more. We'd faced enough adversity—the pack especially—to last another few lifetimes.

"Welcome to our guests from around the world. It is my and Sascha's honour to welcome you to this valley and our pack territory. We look forward to knowing you better in time."

I glanced to where most of the tribe had convened—the women

had mingled together far more than the men, no doubt because of Wade's hen party last night.

"Before we commence celebrations, there's one last thing I'd like to announce."

Sascha squeezed my calf.

Calm floated through me. "While I will always remain with the Ni Tiaki in spirit and as an active contributor to our community, my time as head steward has drawn to a close."

An alarmed outcry rose from my tribe.

"As you know, I found myself the heir of this mantle unexpectedly, but ruling is never something I aspired to. I hope to remain on with the tribe in whatever capacity the next head steward agrees to." I paused. "As to *who* our next head steward will be, I believe that decision should belong to the tribe as a whole. Nominations for the role open tonight and will close in a week, after which a vote will be held. To be clear, you can nominate *any* steward for the job. I will remain on for one month to ensure the smooth transfer of all tasks to our new leader."

The tribe was shocked, but their immediate alarm had subsided somewhat with my assurances I'd still be around.

I belonged with the *Ni Tiaki*. They had a claim on my heart and always would.

But my soul belonged with my mate.

The rest of my heart was split between the pack and this land.

Though it was traditionally a head steward mantel, I would remain mayor of Deception Valley to ensure public power was better balanced between the pack and tribe—alongside officially becoming top female in the pack and working with the next head steward to set a tone for the future of our peoples.

I smiled. "I'd like to take this moment to nominate Pascal Anders for the role of head steward."

I inhaled the stewards' reactions.

Approval.

Good.

Pascal was an ideal choice for many reasons, and a discussion with Rhona had confirmed her adverse to leading again.

"That's all," I said, winking. "Now, go have some fun."

Pascal gaped at me when I sat again.

I glanced at her. "I hope you were serious when you said you wanted something to focus on."

"I was, but—"

"You should have been head steward a long time ago, in my opinion," I said quietly. If not for the tradition of passing leadership down through the Thana family, she would have been.

Sascha grabbed me as the band started playing.

We hit the dance floor and mingled with others until the light began to fade.

"Hey." I jerked my head. "Who's that with Wade?"

Sascha looked over my head. "A Vissimo called Gina. We spoke briefly."

She and Wade were hitting it off. Big time. Both of their hands were drifting. *Yikes.*

I noticed we were dancing closer to the edges of the marquee.

"Are we going somewhere?" I grinned.

"Yes."

Ducking beneath a lantern, Sascha tugged me after him. We ran through the field. He stopped and swung me into his arms.

"I had this idea when I first saw you today," he said casually.

"Oh yeah?"

"Yeah. It involved you in a bed of hay. Naked except for that sunflower crown and those sexy chains on your feet."

I pursed my lips. "Sounds itchy."

"Good point." He removed his shirt.

"Now you're talking."

He had a destination in mind, and soon we came across stacks of hay. Sascha spread his shirt out and extended a hand up to me. "Mate?"

I accepted his help to kneel on the shirt in front of him.

Our lips touched and breathing became the second priority.

Drawing away, he slipped a paper from his back pocket. "I have something to show you. It arrived this morning. This is just a photocopy. I didn't want to crease the actual document."

I studied his peculiar expression, taking the paper.

CERTIFICATE OF GRADUATION
This certifies that
ANDIE CHARISE BOOKER
has fulfilled course requirements in study of a bachelor's degree in
BUSINESS AND COMMUNICATIONS

It was signed and dated by the registrar and chancellor of the college.

I stared at it.

"You passed with a merit overall," Sascha added. "Your transcript is waiting with the certificate."

"I expected to barely pass," I croaked. Half of me had expected to fail. "Guess my grades over the first three years saved me."

"Congratulations. You did it." He kissed my nose.

My throat tightened.

I *did.* This was something all of my own—something I'd earned despite the hard times and uncertainty.

I beamed at the piece of paper.

"Dad's framing your real certificate as a mating gift."

"He is?" *Wow,* that was thoughtful.

Sascha hummed and captured my lips in another tender kiss.

He slid the sleeves of the white dress off my shoulders. The dress pooled at my waist, and he sucked in a harsh breath.

"How long is immortality again?" he whispered.

"Forever," I replied.

"*Thank fuck.*"

I placed a hand in the centre of Sascha's chest and listened to the synchronised beating of our hearts. "You have me out here all alone at this haystack. Did you have any other ideas when you saw me today?"

Honey eyes full of promise bore into mine.

This would be my life every single day.

My mate guided me flat and smirked at me over the top of my bunched dress. "Just a few, beautiful wolf. Should I start at the top of the list?"

Yes, please.

The End.

COMING IN 2021

FAE ADVENTURE ROMANCE...

Grab Your Copy Today!

BOOKS BY KELLY ST. CLARE

Supernatural Battle

Vampire Towers (Paranormal urban romance)

Blood Trial

Vampire Debt

Death Game

Werewolf Dens (Paranormal urban romance)

Shifter Wars

Moon Claimed

Wolf Roulette

Court of Honey and Ice (Fae adventure romance)

with Shannon Mayer

A Court of Honey and Ash

The Darkest Drae (Dragon shifter romance)

with Raye Wagner

Blood Oath

Shadow Wings

Black Crown

The Tainted Accords (Royal fantasy romance):

Fantasy of Frost

Fantasy of Flight

Fantasy of Fire

Fantasy of Freedom

The Tri-World Exchange

(The Tainted Accords Novellas):

Sin

Olandon

Rhone

Shard

The Tri-World Exchange Set

Pirates of Felicity (Pirate fantasy romance):

Immortal Plunder

Stolen Princess

Pillars of Six

Dynami's Wrath

Veritas

Eternal Gambit

Mortal Trinity

Last Battle for Earth (Dystopian romance):

Earth's Warrior

Rebel's Crusade

Traitor's Mandate

www.ingramcontent.com/pod-product-compliance
Lightning Source LLC
Chambersburg PA
CBHW020932310726
48980CB00007B/737/J